T0323894

LILY

LM DEWALT

central
avenue
publishing
2012

Dedicated to my best friend, my chef, my personal assistant, my moral support, my husband. This book would not have been possible without your constant support and your belief in me and in Lily.

LILY

⤲ ONE ⤳

Baboom, baboom, baboom.

Over and over it played like an annoying song you wish would end.

If being a vampire was as romantic, exciting and perfect as movies made it out to be, I would be happy. But I am not. I refer to myself as a person out of pure habit. I am far from a person. To be considered a person you have to be human. I am not. You have to eat food. I do not. You have to sleep. I do not. You have to have a beating heart. I do not.

"Enough of this self pity!" I said as I walked away from the window toward my dresser. "This is your life. Deal with it!" I realized as I opened the top drawer I had said this aloud. What did it matter? There was no one to hear me. If I did not speak aloud to myself, I may forget how to use my voice. That would be strange.

It was time to get dressed and go out. Anything to sate this burning thirst. Besides, I couldn't stand the sounds coming through the thin walls. They made my mouth water.

Looking in the bathroom mirror, I decided to wear my hair down. It was a good place to hide from staring eyes. So what if I look like a mad-woman hiding behind a veil of hair? That was my business. My brown eyes looked almost black, showing my hunger. I needed to do something about that, fast.

On my way out the door, I grabbed my black leather jacket off the back of a chair. I'm not sure if I wore it out of habit or for the sake of appearance since I never felt cold. I was a good actress, doing things because they were expected, but I usually didn't bother because it wasn't always worth the effort, pretending to be human. Don't get me wrong, I was human once. But when I spent most of my time alone, what difference did it make?

As I went down the stairs to the front door, I couldn't help but notice the mailboxes. The names of the tenants were neatly taped to the bottom of each box. There were four: Clara Warren, the old lady across the hall; me; Samantha and Paul Worthington; and Jack Collins. The other tenants were here long before me and would be here long after – as always. I could imagine people thinking of me and referring to me as "the lady that left."

Just as I grabbed the doorknob to step into the brisk night air, the door was yanked open and Jack walked in with his dog. The dog shook himself before he realized I was standing there. As usual, he let out a growl from the back of his throat. The fur on the back of his neck stood straight up. Jack tightened his grip on the leash and looked at me with embarrassment. The dog continued to growl and sniff. I stood motionless.

"I am so sorry. I don't know what's wrong with him. Silly dog! He usually likes everybody." Jack looked back and forth between the dog and my feet as he spoke.

"That's okay. He doesn't mean any harm. He's just being protective." Keeping my eyes on the dog, I tried not making any sudden movements.

"Let's go, silly dog. Leave the nice lady alone." He squeezed past me and around the side of the banister. He rushed down the hall but glanced back with an apologetic look. I turned the knob and left the building as fast as I could manage while appearing as if all were normal. If I moved too slowly, he might take it as an invitation to talk to me and that's something I didn't want right now. I didn't want to know anything personal about the people in the building. I didn't want to hear their thoughts. Besides, quenching my thirst was more important.

Walking down the street with no particular destination in mind, I looked at the houses nestled along perfect yards or hidden behind picket fences and imagined what it would be like to live in one. What would it be like to have a husband, children and a job? What would it be like to have dinner with a family at a table with fresh linen and place mats instead of in some dark alley? I let those visions run through my mind as my feet carried me around the corner and in the direction of Joe's Place. The local corner bar would be full of possibilities tonight, despite the frigid temperature.

I reached the door just as someone was leaving and she held it open for me. Avoiding her eyes, I thanked her as I passed. I felt her tense and knew she sensed something about me. That is how most humans react to my presence. They keep their distance but they never really know why. It is an internal defense mechanism they are equipped with, even though their minds are too closed to notice.

Looking around the smoke-filled room, I noticed a handful of tables open and chose one in the back corner. The table wobbled, though there was a matchbook under one of the legs. The ashtray was filled with butts and there was a crumpled napkin next to it. Oh well. Not the classiest of places but it was best being concealed behind a cloud of smoke. Besides, if I was going to feed tonight, this was the best place, besides the police station, to get the kind of meal I desired.

"What can I get you?" The waitress, a petite blond with blue eyes and a pony tail grabbed the ashtray and the used napkin as she looked at me. Her eyes filled with questions her lips refused to ask. Lucky for me that she dismissed her thoughts as crazy. I did not want what was on her mind tonight. That would be a distraction and while most days it is what I enjoy to pass the hours, tonight, I needed something different.

"A glass of white wine, please." I kept my eyes on the table.

"Would you like a menu?"

"No, thank you. Just a glass of white wine," I repeated as if she would have forgotten in the past two seconds. Sometimes I think I underestimate the human mind's potential.

"Sure thing." She carried the trash away.

In my years of hanging around dark, smoky bars, I discovered white wine is the easiest thing to pretend to drink. I could dump it into a plant or under the table before anyone noticed there was a puddle. It was also a scent I rather enjoyed. Hard liquor had an overpowering, medicinal scent that was distracting to my overdeveloped sense of smell. Beer reminded me of the day after a frat party with its stale aroma. White wine had a mild, flowery scent.

She set the glass and clean ashtray in front of me and turned to walk back to the bar. She appeared to have no desire to spend an extra second by my side. It was apparent by the look on her face that she had no idea why she couldn't be affable toward me. But she wasn't rude.

Sitting with my fingers around the glass, I let my mind start to open and search the thoughts in the room. It was something I learned to control over the years, listening when I wanted and turning it off when I didn't. The only time I had no control over it was when I went long periods of time without feeding. People's thoughts flooded my mind then and there was nothing I could do to stop it, except feed. It wasn't just thoughts I could hear. It was also whispered conversations. Sometimes it was hard to distinguish what was thought and what was spoken without seeing lips moving. Not that I needed to be too close. My eyes could pick up the smallest movements from great distances.

The couple at the end of the bar was telling the bartender, who happened to be Joe himself, about the new vampire movie they just saw. The man said it was too farfetched. The woman said she loved it and thinks vampires are sexy and she wished they were real. She would love to have their power, their looks, and their sex appeal. Of course, movies make vampires out to be very sexual beings with superhuman qualities. As the man spoke to the bartender about other horror movies, the woman's thoughts were about her desires. I wished I had an excuse to talk to her about it. It's not like I could walk up to her and say, "Excuse me, I was just eavesdropping on your thoughts and I think you couldn't be more wrong!" She would think I was insane. All I could do was laugh.

Looking around the room, I concentrated my energy on other thoughts. As I looked at the seated figures, it was hard to ignore the deafening sounds of their beating hearts and the blood rushing through their veins. My mouth watered and my throat was on fire. At first, I noticed nothing out of the ordinary. Nothing interesting. Nothing condemning anyone to the inevitable death that awaited.

"Can I get you something else?" I jumped, startled as the waitress stood next to me eying the untouched glass of wine. I was concentrating on everyone else in the room and did not hear her coming.

"No. It's fine, thank you. I guess I'm just not that thirsty," I said without looking at her. I stared at my glass so she couldn't see the panic on my face. Damn! I had been distracted and not tuning in on the whole picture. That could be dangerous. It wasn't often someone was able to sneak up on me.

"Well, if you change your mind, let me know. I'm Lori." Now she had a name.

"I will," I replied, picking up the glass to show her I was about to take a sip and put an end to her worry. Of course, I would not.

"I can take the ashtray away…guess you don't smoke. You're one of the few I ever see here who doesn't. Everyone else…Oh my God!" She stopped talking and focused her wide eyes toward the entrance. My curiosity piqued. A hulking figure had just entered. At first glance, I pegged him as a truck driver. Many truck drivers stopped here on their way through Washington, probably headed to Alaska. He had the typical beer belly. His graying hair was stuffed under a dirty baseball cap and his beard looked unkempt.

"Something wrong?" I asked Lori without taking my eyes off the man. Her right hand was on the wobbly table for support.

"Oh my God! Oh my God! That's my ex! How did he find me? I gotta go. I'll tell Joe I'm sick. I gotta go." The color drained from her face as she backed away.

My eyes returned to the man, who was taking a seat at the bar. I wanted – no, needed – to get in his head as soon as possible. I shut out everything else in the room for the time being and focused. After listening for a couple minutes, I knew. I wanted him.

I looked around the room for Lori and noticed Joe pointing to some tables while another waitress looked on. She was safe. She would always be safe.

I wanted the man at the bar to come to me. It was easier that way. I felt less guilt if it was their choice. I thought about him sitting with me, laughing, my hand on his knee under the table, leaving the bar together, inviting him into my mind. He turned and scanned the room. One woman sat alone but was reading a menu. Then, his eyes reached my face. He turned away, for a second. After a deep breath, he turned his gaze back to me and stopped. I smiled. He picked up his glass without looking away and all two hundred plus pounds of him walked toward me without hesitation. I had my catch of the day. It was too easy.

As I shoved his barely breathing body away from me in the cab of his truck, I thought of Lori. She would probably try to run again. After all, he had shown up here, in Olympia, Washington. She didn't know that it was only a coincidence that he was here. He did not know she worked at Joe's Place. That was just a coincidence. He stopped driving because he was hungry and wanted a beer. It just so happened, I was hungry too.

I looked at his limp, lifeless body with both satisfaction and disgust. Disgust because women could love someone as vile as him, because someone like him could manage to get away with something like that. And Lori did love him in her own way. She was afraid of him but she loved him. I looked at the wounds on his neck. I would love to leave them there as a mark of triumph, like a signature on a work of art, but that would cause chaos. Imagine the news headlines. *VAMPIRES IN OLYMPIA*. No way!

Time to cover up my trail. Making sure he was no longer breathing, I bit the tip of my tongue until I tasted blood. I grabbed his cold neck and rubbed the blood from my mouth over the tiny wounds. In seconds the wounds closed as if they had not been there at all. He looked like he was asleep. If I hadn't killed him myself, I would have thought he was. Even if they performed an autopsy all they would find was that he was missing blood. With no possible explanation as to how the blood exited his body, they would have no choice but to presume he died of "natural causes." Too bad. And at such a young age. "What a waste," I said aloud as I climbed out of the cab, my appetite and conscience fully satisfied.

Humans held a certain fascination for me. The criminal type, like this Frank Carver, uncaring, selfish and ignorant, I had no use for. This animal had begged for his life. Should I really have listened to his mind when he remembered how he killed Lori's unborn child after shoving her down the stairs yet again? God he was delicious!

As he'd taken his last breath, I looked at him and smiled. "This is for Lori," I'd whispered. His eyes grew wide with fear then rolled back in his head. I had avenged her and she didn't even know my name.

ᑭᑭ TWO ᑭᑭ

While channel surfing, I realized how bored I was. Maybe it was time to move on. New place to live, new address, new faces, new thoughts, new criminals. But it didn't matter how it was disguised – it was still the same, lonely, boring life. Not life. That stopped in 1938. Existence is the right word. I could bring up a list on my computer of the cloudiest cities in the country, maybe even the world, close my eyes and point to one. Without doing research on the police activity and crime rates, it would be like a challenge.

Challenge wasn't something I had much of, at least not anymore. It was a challenge in the beginning, when I became what I am doomed to be for all eternity. The only difference being that I was not alone then, at least not for a while, a short period of time in which I knew love…or so I thought. I shook that thought from my mind as soon as it popped up, shaking my head as if the memories would fall out. Now wasn't the time to think about *him*.

Maybe I should start writing again. When I was a child, I loved scary stories. Stories about vampires were the most intriguing. They sounded magical. I read anything I could find on the subject, from fiction like Bram Stoker's *Dracula* to tales of legends and myths in the newspapers or magazines. I even tried to write my own stories until my grades suffered and my parents put an end to it.

Through my teenage years, I spent most of my time at home. As an only child, it was my responsibility to take care of the house and cook the meals while my parents worked in their store. Once the housework was done and my school subjects taken care of, I went to my room, locked the door, and wrote. I made up all sorts of worlds where vampires lived happily ever after. Since I was not supposed to be writing, I hid the stories under a floorboard by my bed.

My fantasies were always the same. A handsome, beautiful vampire came through my window at night. He walked to the side of my bed to tell me he had been watching me for a long time, loving me from a distance, and could not stay away any longer. It had to be now, on this night, that I became his and joined him for all eternity. Then he would get down on his knees and put his arms around me. He would look into my eyes and brush his lips against mine before moving on to my neck. We would fly out the window together, with me in his arms, and live happily ever after.

In my dreams, I never imagined the details between his lips touching my neck and us living happily ever after. I never thought about the "after" either. Maybe if I had, I would not be where I am today. Had I contemplated what it meant to be a vampire, I would not have become one. Not that I had a choice in the matter. It was what it was and there was nothing romantic or magical about it.

I heard my parents talking through their closed bedroom door one night. "It's not normal for a girl her age to be home all the time," my mother said.

"It's not normal for a girl her age to have no suitors either. And have you noticed she doesn't have any close friends?" My father replied.

"I don't know, John. She is a little shy but she seems happy enough. What ever happened to that girl, Elizabeth?" My mother said in a hushed voice. "She doesn't even mention her anymore. It's as if she never existed."

What happened to Elizabeth? Good question. Elizabeth, the one girl at school I had something in common with, grew bored of me.

"What do you think of the new boy? I think he's kinda cute!" Elizabeth admitted, excited, one afternoon as we walked home together.

"I think he's alright. I wouldn't bite him though," I replied, kicking stones as I walked.

"What in the world is that supposed to mean?" She stopped to glare at me. That was the first time I saw anger in her eyes.

"I mean…if I were a vampire, I wouldn't make him one. What else?" I replied shrugging my shoulders.

"Is that all you ever think about? Vampires? There's more to life than vampires! Yeah, it was fun to make up stories but this is the real world, Lily. Vampires are NOT real!" She started walking again, no, stomping was more like it, and I had to run to catch up. "What's the difference? He was staring at you anyway. They all stare at you. Not that you even care!"

"I didn't notice. Are you still coming over?" I asked looking down so she couldn't see my face was burning red.

"I just remembered…I have to do some ironing for my mother. I'll see you tomorrow," she said as she waved over her head and walked in the opposite direction.

That was the last time Elizabeth and I said anything to each other besides the polite small-talk required when you spend all day together in school. We had nothing in common anymore. She had boys and I had my made-up world. Don't get me wrong, I could have had boys. Boys looked at me though it was always someone else who pointed that out. I was a pretty girl. I was what one could call *petite*. Boys looked at me but never approached. I knew deep down there wasn't something wrong with me. I figured they could sense I had no interest in them. It didn't matter. I had my writing. I had my dreams of becoming a vampire, maybe even a writer, which ever came first.

When I turned eighteen, my parents started setting me up on dates with young men they thought suitable. I conceded to dating these young men, not wanting to refuse anything of my parents, but it never amounted to anything. Most were once and done. A couple of them asked me out on a second date but gave up when they realized I had no interest. Not that I ever *tried* to be rude. I listened to their chatter and bragging. When they tried to ask me questions about myself, I started talking about my writing. That's when they got that look in their eyes. That look that said they wanted to run as fast as possible from the crazy girl with the wild imagination. That's as far as any of them ever got; a second and last date.

I jumped as the remote hit the floor. I was so absorbed in my thoughts; again, I did not hear someone walking up to my door until the soft knock startled me. Who could it be? No one ever knocked on my door. I sat very still and listened. Maybe if I ignore it they will go away. No chance. I heard three louder knocks.

I slid the door open a crack to get a look at the intruder. Clara, small and frail, stood there with a look of pain on her face.

"Yes?" I said looking at the floor. In the two years I had lived here she never said anything other than "hello" when we passed in the hall.

"You're Lily, right?" she asked in her sweet grandmotherly voice.

"Yes. Are you okay?" I looked at the floor and her feet. Her pink slippers looked much too big for her. They also looked very old. Avoiding people's eyes made you notice a lot of footwear.

"I'm okay, honey. Just a little sore from my arthritis, don't know if I can make it down the steps. I was wondering if you would be a dear and get my mail. I'm expecting a letter from my grandson. He's in Iraq. I'm worried about him, my Tommy, such a sweet boy." She tried to get a look at my face. My hair hung in front of it. The last thing I wanted to do was scare her. Not that it was too obvious, at least not indoors under artificial lights. My skin would look a little too pale maybe but normal enough.

"Sure, just let me put on shoes. I'll be right over for the key," I said, assuming the key was in her apartment since she held nothing but a cane.

"Okay dear. Take your time." She backed away from my door giving me the opportunity to close it.

I found the mailbox with her name and put the key in the lock. I retrieved the many catalogs and envelopes stuffed in it. It must have been a while since she last came down to empty it. She should have someone to help her. I was locking the box when I heard the jingle of keys down the hall. Great. That must be Jack. I wanted to get away, before he had a chance to talk to me, but of course, the key jammed. My strength didn't seem to matter. If I yanked, chances were I would rip the whole row of boxes out of the wall. That would be worse. This required technique, not strength.

"Let me give you a hand with that. Happens to me all the time," Jack said as his hand lunged for the key. He didn't give me a chance to move my hand before he reached it. As soon as his warm skin touched mine, I jumped and staggered backward. Did he feel it? What do I do now?

I looked up in time to see him rub the tips of his fingers. I was behind him so he couldn't see my face. He shook his head. *Nah. I must have touched the metal…not possible…that cold…must've been the metal.* I didn't want to hear his thoughts. I didn't want to know. Where he'd been and what he'd done was his business.

"See…if you just jiggle the key a little like this," he maneuvered it from side to side as he pulled, "it should come out."

"Thanks," I whispered as he dropped the key into my hand. He must think I am such a timid freak. I didn't want to know what he thought. Never mind that. It was safer for him that way.

"Hey, Lily. We've lived here a long time and I realize I don't know you. I'm sorry about that. I get into my own little world." Now he looked at the floor. I realized I stopped breathing when he said this. Not that I needed to breathe as often but it was something my body did automatically. I was afraid of what was coming next.

"How about if you come over for dinner tomorrow night? I've been told I make a pretty mean lasagna...unless you don't like Italian." He peeked up at me with his face still aimed at the floor, his cheeks taking on an appetizing pink.

"Uh...your dog doesn't like me. Remember?"

"Oh yeah. I don't know what's wrong with him. Maybe we could go out instead," he suggested, still hopeful. Maybe I could steer him in a different direction and he would forget all about it.

"What's his name, anyway?" I asked still avoiding his eyes.

"His name...uh...you're going to think it's strange but his name *is* Silly Dog."

"That's really his name? How did he end up with that?" I asked trying to steer the conversation to some other place but also a little curious.

"When I brought him home from the pound he was so excited in the car. I put him in the back seat but he was determined to sit up front. He kept trying. I kept stopping him. Then, I heard breathing by my ear and when I looked behind me, his head was stuck between the headrest and the seat. He was panting with his tongue hanging out. It was so funny! I had to pull over and – just like the key – jiggle his head out. The first thing I called him was Silly Dog and it's been Silly Dog ever since." His eyes found me just as I looked up at him. He looked like a normal guy asking a normal girl out on a date. No fear on his face.

"That is pretty funny," I said and looked down at his feet. No shoes, just very clean white socks.

"So how about it?" he asked still trying to look at my face. I thought a moment. Nothing. I couldn't come up with a single reason as to why I couldn't have dinner with him. I couldn't tell him I didn't eat or that I had to work because even though I didn't, I would have to answer questions about where and when. Nothing to tell him except...

"Uh...okay I guess," I whispered through a lump in my throat. That was probably not the excited answer he was expecting but he should be happy it wasn't a NO. Why wasn't it a no? Why couldn't I get my lips to form that simple little word? If he had any idea what I was he would be happy if I said no.

"I'll pick you up at seven," he said with a proud laugh. Was he proud I had said yes or proud that he made a joke?

"Okay. I'll see you then." I said as I started up the steps. I didn't give him a chance to say anything else. I don't know what else he could've said that would have made it worse. It was bad enough.

I knocked on Clara's door and it swung open. She sat at her dining room table and waved me in without looking up. "Anything from overseas?" she asked.

"I think so. Maybe this one." I handed her the pile with the small envelope on top, the one with all the colorful stamps. It was small but very thick. It had the words *DO NOT BEND* underlined at the bottom.

"Ooh. There must be pictures. He's such a looker that boy. Let me show you. He'll be home soon. He's about your age." She fumbled to open the envelope but her bent fingers wouldn't allow it.

"Here, let me help you," I said as I took the envelope from her hands, careful not to touch her. I opened it and handed it back. I didn't want to look at the photos, didn't want to know anything personal about her, so I muttered some excuse about having something in the oven and turned to leave.

"Another time then. Here's something for your trouble. You are very kind. It's hard to find people like you now a days." She held a baggie of chocolate chip cookies for me.

"Oh you didn't have to but thank you." I took the bag.

As soon as I was secure in my own apartment, I set the baggie on the coffee table and sat back and stared at it. What had I done? I had tried to keep these people at a distance and all of a sudden – wham – two in one day. How could I be so careless? There was no logical reason for me to answer the door except my own boredom and curiosity. First, the old lady who thinks I'm nice and then the guy downstairs who is probably smiling because he has a date tomorrow night.

About tomorrow night: what am I going to do? How can I get out of this? Maybe if I tell him I came down with something. No. That would just delay things. He would want a rain check. I was used to having food in front of me and pretending to eat, had even swallowed some once and nothing happened. I did it because a date insisted I taste a piece of his steak. No better steak had ever existed and I just had to taste it. I put it in my mouth, chewed, and swallowed. Nothing happened except that it got stuck in my throat. I had to go to the ladies' room to pull it out. That wasn't much of a dilemma. I could put on my usual charade in front of Jack. That wasn't the problem. The problem was that it couldn't have any kind of happy ending.

Besides the fact that I was better off alone and didn't want to be intimate with the people who lived around me and the fact that I never entertained the thought of him as anything other than a neighbor was the fact that he was human. He was human and I was not. Vampires and humans do not mix…ever.

I can't believe she said yes. What an idiot I am. Why did I wait so long? What was I afraid of? His thoughts flooded my mind before I had a chance to react. I was too busy thinking similar thoughts. Why did I say yes? What do I do now? Even if there was the slightest possibility that I had any romantic interest in Jack, which I did not, this could never amount to anything. I could never touch him. I could never kiss him. He would notice how cold my skin was. He would feel my cold breath. And even if we managed to get past all that with no major dilemma, we could never do what regular human couples do. That was out of the question.

I lay on the sofa and pushed buttons on the remote control without looking at the television screen. No matter how much I tried, I couldn't stop thinking about all the "what ifs." What if he wanted to go for a picnic in the park on a beautiful sunny day? A rarity in this city but it did happen. That sounds like a typical outing for a new couple. I choose the places I live because of their lack of sunny days. The sun does not kill a vampire, contrary to popular belief. It does, however, make us freaks, straight from some low-budget horror flick. When the sunlight hits our already pale skin, it reflects the light and makes us seem whiter than white. It's also not comfortable on our eyes. People worry then because they think we're ill. I have gone out in the sunlight when I could not avoid it. It's possible due to the miracle of cosmetics and foundation purchased in darker shades. Turtlenecks and long pants come in handy too. Then I just need to worry about my face and hands.

It was useless, thinking like this. It didn't matter how much I rationalized any possible scenarios. There was no way that anything could ever happen with Jack. I owed him that. I wish he knew he should take Silly Dog's warnings. It was quite clear the dog was protecting him, to me at least.

I knew what I needed to do and what I had to do tomorrow evening. I had to perform.

SOMETIME IN THE early afternoon, after spending countless hours playing a video game, I decided I had enough of trying to keep my mind clear.

I had to figure out a way to get out of the commitment I'd made without hurting his feelings. I grabbed my jacket and threw it over my shoulder as I walked out the door. A walk would do me good.

There was a park a few blocks away where I often sat on a bench with a cup of coffee and watched people. I didn't drink the coffee; it was just one of my props. Another thing I enjoyed was pretending to read the newspaper. People seemed to stay away if they saw you had a purpose. At the park, I did what I would not do in any place I ever resided. I listened to thoughts. It didn't feel like I was intruding because these people were strangers and I expected to never see them again. So I gave myself permission to do it as much as I liked in a public place. After all, most of my meals came to me that way.

I purchased a latte that day, just for something different. The cup felt like bath water as soon as I wrapped my icy fingers around it. As I walked out the door of the shop, I noticed the people passing me on the street were wearing jackets. Okay. It was cold today...too cold for most humans to be walking around town in short sleeves. I set my cup down on a window ledge and slipped my arms into the jacket, picked up my cup, and put my left hand in my pocket. I felt paper. What could it be? I let possibilities run through my mind. It was small, a little thicker than a regular piece of paper...hmmm. After playing with it for a few moments, I gave up and pulled it out. A movie stub, one I had forgotten to place in my box of memories. Now that the mystery was solved, I wondered how pathetic it was that I played these games.

I found a bench that was not covered by old, wet newspapers. I stretched my legs out and looked around but saw no one. It wasn't quite late enough for anyone to be on the way home from work. I took the lid off the coffee and sniffed. Coffee had an inviting aroma. I watched the steam making its way out of the cup and into the air. It was entertaining to see how long it was until I couldn't see it anymore. It didn't matter how good the coffee smelled, it still wasn't an appetizing smell, just inviting. It invited conversation and friendship. Blood had an appetizing smell. That was a smell that made my mouth water and my dead heart feel like it might start beating again.

I sat in the same spot for half an hour, staring at the trees and watching two squirrels chase each other, before the first human appeared. I heard her heartbeat before I saw her. She was almost running because she had a dog walking her. She struggled to keep up with the dog's eager pace, hanging on to the leash. I could just imagine what would happen if the dog caught sight of the squirrels. The poor woman would be dragged across the muddy ground. I couldn't help but laugh at the image that created in my mind. As they got closer, I heard her. *There she is again. Sitting by herself… too cold to be sitting still like that…never moves.* Just then, I remembered humans expected some type of movement at regular intervals so I picked up my cup and brought it to my lips. I breathed in the aroma and set it back on the bench. This woman had seen me before but I did not remember her. I might have remembered the dog though.

"*STOP. SIT.* What is your problem?" The dog tried to lunge in my direction. It was up on its hind legs pulling at the leash. Its hackles raised and it was whining, trying to get to me. I could not own a dog. They knew something was different about me, knew something was wrong.

I should say something…did she notice? I can't. She scares me. I'll just walk away. She didn't notice…she's always in her own head or something. She managed to get control of her dog and head in the opposite direction.

Wow. That was fun. Maybe I could amuse myself that way more often, walk into a pet store and enjoy the show – or better yet, the zoo! I was thinking of all sorts of funny scenarios involving animals when I looked down at my watch. It was close. In less than two hours he would be knocking at my door and I had come up with no excuses. Too late for the zoo now.

∽ THREE ∽

I stepped out of the shower and wrapped myself in a towel. I walked to the mirror and, as I wiped the fog off, noticed my hand was shaking. What was wrong with me? Could I be nervous? If I was acting like this, I could just imagine how he felt. It would be amusing to listen to his nervousness but that wouldn't be fair. Instead, I thought about myself and how I was feeling. I had no idea why I felt this way. I had no romantic interest in him so, therefore, no need to impress him. The sole reason I could figure was that I was so out of practice with dating – not that this was a date.

It had been a long time since I had any type of deep or meaningful conversation with anyone, human or vampire. All those human things, like indulging in gooey desserts, crying over sad movies, listening to juicy gossip, didn't matter anymore. How could they matter to someone else? I couldn't imagine the questions he would ask. He had seen me coming and going from this building for the past two years, always alone. The last person to enter this apartment was the man that connected my cable and Internet. I had never invited anyone up nor had anyone ever asked to come in. I have standards that I pride myself in, despite what I am: neat, quick, and most of all, unobtrusive. I was just nervous about answering questions I didn't have answers to.

After drying and arranging my hair, I went to my dresser and looked through my clothing. He never said where we were going so I wasn't sure what to wear. I chose a pair of black corduroys and a black sweater, casual rather than dressy. I looked in the mirror and thought about my image and what others would see. Too gloomy. How typical of the living dead to wear all black! I took the sweater off. I looked through everything again and put the sweater back on. I went to my jewelry box, pulled out a necklace, and put it around my neck, closing the clasp. I walked back to the mirror. I heard it hit the floor before I realized it had fallen off. When I bent to pick it up I saw a piece of paper under the chair. It was the movie stub I had planned to put in my memory box. It must have fallen out of my jacket when I threw it over the back of the chair as I came in.

I reached my arm under the sofa. Adjusting my fingers around the box, I pulled. I took the lid off without paying too much attention to it. I just wanted to place the stub inside and slide the box back underneath. When I reached in to put the stub on the side where all the other stubs were, I realized they were not there. Oh no! Wrong box. I pulled out the box that contained memories I did not want to see or ever think about again. It hurt too much, still, after so many years. This box full of memories was all I had left of *him*. I slammed the lid back on it with such force that the plastic pieces scattered. I didn't care. I gave it a shove back under the sofa and, in my anger threw the movie stub into the trash can.

Why was I so stupid? Why did I hang on to something that caused pain? He was gone. He would forever be gone. I needed to get the thought of him out of my head. I had wasted too much time on him and he wasn't worth it. I had other things to worry about right now, so I went back to concentrating on those.

I wasn't going to worry about the color I was wearing. If he happened to ask me what my favorite color was I could always say, "Isn't it obvious?" I looked in the mirror one more time, happy that a vampire casting no reflection was only myth, and arranged a few locks of hair that were hanging in front of my forehead and decided I was as ready as I was going to be.

I wanted to hear his approach. I did not like being taken by surprise and that had been happening too much lately. I was not concentrating enough on my surroundings. I was too busy letting my boredom take over and allowing my mind to take flight. I looked at the clock and noted I still had ten minutes before he was due but I heard something, a key turning a lock, soft footsteps on the stairs, a rapid heartbeat accompanied by quick intakes of breath. He was trying to calm himself down. What did that mean? He didn't want to talk to me just out of pure loneliness? He wanted what I could not and would not be able to give him? I was afraid of that.

"Hi. I know I'm early. I hope that's okay." He smiled as I pulled the door open.

"Yeah. It's fine. Just let me grab my jacket…oh, and my purse. Be right out," I said as I shut the door and returned with a jacket and an empty purse. I wasn't in the habit of carrying a purse but I kept one around for "special" occasions.

"That was quick," he said with a smile and moved aside to let me go down the stairs first. I must remember not to move at my regular speed.

"Small place," I replied, looking at the steps as I walked, as if I was afraid I would trip and fall. I'd break the stairs before I did any damage to myself.

"So…what's your favorite food?" he asked rushing past me to open the door. So, there were still gentlemen in this world.

"Oh, I don't know. I eat just about anything. Any place you pick is fine."

"I just wanted to make sure you weren't a vegetarian."

I couldn't help but laugh aloud. "I am *definitely* not that," I replied looking up at his face for the first time tonight. He was smiling and for some reason it helped me relax. His heartbeat seemed to have calmed down a bit too. "Like I said…I eat just about anything."

"Good. I have a place in mind. It's new so I haven't been there yet but a couple of guys at work say it's good. It's not far. My car's just across the street."

I never noticed what he drove. The times I had sat at the window and seen him come in from work I never watched him get out of a car. Now he led me to a big, boxy vehicle. I remember they were called station wagons back then but this was a bit different, higher. I never paid much attention to cars. I just drove one whenever I wanted to get far away. The rest of the time I walked or ran. It was faster that way. I wasn't able to fly…unlike some vampires.

He opened my door and waited to close it for me before he walked around to the driver's side. I could see the smile flash across his face as he passed in front of the car. I shook my head, ashamed of what I was doing but yet somehow relieved that I was. I realized it was not good for me to spend so much time alone. Maybe a friend wasn't such a bad idea. He started the engine as soon as he sat down and then glanced over at me before he put the car into drive. *I don't want to be rude…I can't take chances though. Maybe I better…no…it's her choice.* I was hearing his thoughts without trying and it frustrated me but at that moment, I realized I hadn't put on the seatbelt. I forgot he didn't know I wouldn't be killed in a car accident.

The buckle snapped into place with a loud click and I saw relief on his face. Only then did he pull away from the curb. His hand reached up to the visor and he pulled out a CD, without looking at it, and slid it into the player. Soft music started playing and he kept the volume down to a reasonable background noise. Not what I had expected: classical music. I looked straight ahead as he drove. I couldn't think of anything to say so I waited for him to start talking but he looked more confused than anything. His heartbeat was so loud I couldn't quite hear the music. I had to say something. This was maddening.

"Are you okay?" That was better than nothing.

"Oh, yeah…sorry. Just thinking. Not used to having someone in the car with me," *especially not someone that looks like you do.* He looked straight ahead again, his grip tightening on the steering wheel.

"That's okay. I know what you mean," I said and then forced myself to turn my face and smile at him…just a little smile to lighten the mood. That seemed to work. The muscles in his hands relaxed.

"So, what do you do?"

"Nothing right now. I'm kinda between jobs." I bit my lip as I said this. Hopefully he won't push the subject. I hadn't fabricated any stories for my lack of employment. No one had ever bothered to ask. People didn't question me about anything personal. Most of my relationships had been superficial. I couldn't tell anyone that I was still living off of someone else's guilt money. Nor could I tell them I attained some of my *income* from the criminals I hunted. I considered it payment for keeping the streets clean.

"I think I would go nuts if I didn't work. What would I do with myself? I don't know how you handle it. We're here. No traffic tonight."

He slid the car in between a Jeep and a pick-up truck. He had his door open before he turned off the engine. I reached for the door handle and then stopped myself, remembering he liked to do it. He was a gentleman. I sat back and waited. How slow humans are.

He held the door open for me at the restaurant and even went as far as waiting for me to be seated before he took his seat. That was impressive. You don't see manners like that anymore. The waitress came over before we had a chance to worry about speaking to each other.

"What can I get you to drink?" she asked. She didn't as much as glance at either of us. This was someone who did not like her job. I had no idea what to order. I bit my lip and looked at Jack. He was waiting for me to order first, of course, but saw that I didn't know and ordered himself an iced tea.

"I'll have the same, please." The waitress' eyes flashed toward me like all of a sudden there was a second person that came out of nowhere. *What is wrong with her? Something weird...high voice...what's wrong with her eyes? Iced tea...I think...he said...the same...yeah.* Great! Jack sits there like everything is normal. But the waitress...she notices.

She walked away and I tuned her out. I looked at the menu. I should order the cheapest thing possible, so he didn't waste money. Most of it was going in my empty purse, anyway, as soon as he looked away or excused himself to do a human thing like use the bathroom. It might offend him though. He might think I was assuming he couldn't afford better. What a complex thing dating is. No wonder I didn't miss it. Okay. Maybe just this once I could listen to his mind.

I still can't believe she said yes. I can't believe she's sitting here...with me... wow! She's so beautiful. Why isn't she married? Sure should be snatched up by now...I would have...

Okay. That wasn't one bit helpful. That's what I get for cheating. I realized that the whole time he was thinking he wasn't looking at me. He still had his nose buried in the menu. Not at all what I wanted to hear.

"I hear they have excellent pizza here. Not the greasy pizza joint kind but more gourmet. Do you want to share one?" He put the menu down and looked at me hopefully.

"That sounds good. Anything but anchovies..." I closed my menu and set it down. Not that I had any idea what anchovies tasted like. I never tasted them when I was human but it sounded like the right thing to say. Like they do in movies. Did *anyone* like anchovies? Doubtful. How was I going to get pieces of pizza into my purse? I hadn't thought that through.

He ordered a margherita pizza and two salads. The waitress asked what kind of dressing we would like on them, still looking just at me. *I wonder what kind of drugs she's on...with her eyes like that...hmm.* I knew oil and vinegar had been my favorite so I asked for that. That one was easy but the waitress was getting on my nerves. Maybe my eyes looked this wild because I was hungry and I would eat her any minute! That was a fun thought. I imagined myself lunging at her, my hair flying wildly. In her haste to get away, she stumbled, almost dropping the menus. I was glad she had seen that fun little image. That should teach her a lesson for sticking her nose where it didn't belong. I hadn't realized I'd laughed aloud until Jack interrupted my thoughts.

"What's so funny?" he asked still looking at the waitress as she pushed her way in through the kitchen door.

"Didn't you see her almost fall? I know. That was mean of me...to laugh like that." I couldn't help it. After all, I had caused her to panic but he didn't know.

"I didn't notice," he said and took a sip of his drink. *I was too busy admiring you. You are breathtaking when you smile...your eyes light up... wish I could do that to you...maybe one day...* "So how long have you lived alone?"

"A few years. I didn't think I would like it at first but now...I love it." I could remember the way it felt to have *his* hands on me, cold yet demanding, like he owned every inch of my body. He did it so seldom that I craved it always. Could I ever feel like that again? The memory faded when Jack cleared his throat.

"So...you're not in some sort of long-distance relationship, are you?" he asked. He was very direct. I must give him credit for that. No skirting around the issue.

"Not at all. I don't do well in relationships." I placed my hands on the table and started playing with my napkin. I didn't have to lie about that either. My mortal relationships had been brief. My immortal relationships had been just plain complicated. I grew bored with people. The only one I ever had true feelings for grew bored of me. No warning at all. Not an inkling. Not a clue.

"Well, I happen to find you fascinating. Did you know you are very mysterious?" he said as he started playing with his napkin. Humans had little habits like that when they were feeling insecure. I learned to mimic those actions, only this time, I was the one to start it. It was like riding a bike, I suppose. Once you start interacting with humans, no matter how long it's been, all those little quirks come back. Being around other vampires was much easier. Being around humans, that was a challenge. I liked challenge.

"Never thought of myself that way. Just shy, I think. I was always quiet." Another bit of truth. Talking to him was easy. I didn't even hesitate before I spoke...until...

"I'm curious...did you ever think about me?" Now he was playing with his spoon. Like I thought: very direct.

I cleared a throat that didn't need clearing. No idea what to say. Should I try honesty? What did people do in a situation like this? Think...think...

"I've wondered why you live alone." That should do it. Nothing to read into that. Answer a question with a question.

"I got divorced about two and a half years ago. Never bothered after that…dating that is. I was too pissed and I knew I might take my anger out on some unsuspecting woman."

The waitress came with our pizza. She set it down with shaky hands and put a plate in front of each of us. She didn't bother to look at me this time. She didn't even bother to think. As soon as she confirmed that we didn't need anything else, she ran away. Jack put a slice on my plate before serving himself.

"This looks good. I hope you're hungry. It's pretty big." He picked up his fork and knife and started working on his slice. That was a relief. Cut pieces of pizza were easier to hide in a purse than a full slice. The sauce would be messy enough without trying to fold up and stuff a whole slice in. I followed suit. He noticed I didn't pick up my utensils until after he had.

"Too hot to pick it up." He seemed to be trying to make me feel more relaxed. I appreciated that. I would be a lady and take just one slice. I knew a lady didn't like to let her date see her eat. I was glad for that silly rule, it was good for me.

So divorced? What did one say to that?

"I'm sorry to hear about your divorce."

"Are you kidding?! It's the best thing I ever did. Best gift I could've given myself."

"Really?"

"I got married way too young, just out of high school. It was a mistake." He looked sad.

"Why did you do it then?" I asked. It was too late to take it back. That was too forward of me but he didn't seem to mind.

"I guess I figured that was the best I could do. A self-esteem problem I think. Anyway, we grew apart and realized we had nothing in common. We were married and she was dating…other men. That wasn't working for me." He smiled as he remembered why he wasn't sad about this. "I look at it as a trial run. You ever been married?"

That was a hilarious thought. For better or for worse, in sickness and in health, 'til death do you part? Please! "No."

"I'm sure it's not because no one asked. I can't imagine that."

"Honestly…no one ever did. I am only nineteen though." Did he think I was older?

"You seem more mature than nineteen to me." He took a bite, taking his time to chew.

"I've always been that way. I was born old…I think." Funny. If he only knew how old I really was. Yeah, Jack, I'm a young looking ninety. It's all that *Oil of Olay*.

As soon as he excused himself to use the men's room, I put a handful of pizza in my purse. No one was looking. I scanned the room and started picking up thoughts.

I hope she doesn't want dessert…can't wait to get her home…

Is this stuff supposed to be food? Not worth the price…

Wish I didn't have to work tonight…

If I eat anymore I'll explode for sure…

Jack came back to the table and smiled. I couldn't help but smile back. It was easy to do. I was feeling more and more relaxed with him. *Wonder if I should ask now…may be pushing my luck…worth a shot…*

Listening to the rest of the room to distract myself was okay. Listening to Jack, a big no-no, so I waited for him to work up the courage to ask me whatever it was he wanted to ask. I couldn't imagine what would cause so much hesitation.

"I was thinking since it's still early…maybe we could…" He took a gulp of his tea. "Go see a movie…that is…unless you have to get up early or something."

That was all it was. I sighed with relief and said, "Sure. That sounds good." I said yes without thinking about it. How could I have done that? A dark movie theater with a mortal man was a bad idea. Men had expectations in the dark. Something as simple and innocent as holding hands couldn't happen with me. As soon as he felt my icy skin, he would be repulsed, if not terrified. What did I do now? Not panic…that's what. I had done well so far…

"Are you ready to go? That new vampire movie is playing at the mall. It's supposed to be excellent, if you like vampires."

"Sure. Vampires are good." I grabbed my purse as the waitress put the change back on the table. Again, she avoided my eyes. How fitting that he would take me to a vampire movie. Little did he know he would be sitting right next to one. A real, honest-to-goodness vampire. I was curious to see what this movie would be like anyway. It was worth the risk just to get a good laugh.

It had started to rain while we were inside and everything was wet. In the lights of the parking lot, everything sparkled. It was kind of surreal… just like this whole evening was turning out to be. I kept the pace with him though it was hard. Humans were so slow. One of the lights in the parking lot was making a deafening humming noise. I couldn't wait to get inside the car where the windows could keep the sound out. The only sound I had to listen to then was his beating heart. I would take that over the buzzing anytime.

We rode in silence for a while. It was a comfortable silence. He looked at me and smiled once in a while. I was curious to know what he was thinking but did not intrude. It was a quality most immortals possessed and few of us learned to control. The choice on whether or not to be intrusive was purely personal.

When we got to the mall, he drove around the lot for a few minutes looking for a parking spot. There were none available near the theater and it had started to rain again.

"I'll drop you off at the door and then park. It looks crowded so if you don't mind…here…take this…could you get the tickets?" He handed me money and pulled up to the curb.

"I don't mind walking," I told him. I was honest about not minding the rain. It felt good on my skin. It was a sensation I could best relate to a warm human touch.

"What about your hair? You'll be cold if it's wet."

"Honestly. I don't care about that." And I truly didn't. As far as being cold…well…

"You're the boss." He pulled the car into a spot around the back of the theater. It wasn't as well lit as the front.

I decided to take my purse into the theater with me so I could excuse myself to the ladies' room and empty the contents into the garbage can. It would be colder when we left and he might turn on the heat. Heat might warm the pizza and he might smell it. He may wonder where that came from considering we hadn't brought a doggie bag. Silly Dog wasn't allowed pizza and Jack said he was bad at eating leftovers so when he offered the rest to me, I lied and told him the same.

We were lucky enough that the movie was showing in two theaters. Most of the people in line were kids…teenagers.

Look at the old people…

I want to sit all the way in the back…don't like the front…wonder if Jane is here…

If I get a large popcorn I'll look like a pig…but I'm so hungry…I should've eaten today…

Nothing interesting. I listened while he purchased our tickets. He ordered a soda at the snack bar and asked me if I wanted anything. I said I was still full.

"From one slice of pizza? At least a soda." He looked at me like a child begging.

"Sure. Diet Coke." We grabbed straws and a couple of napkins and found our way to theater number 12. How many theaters were in this place?

"Where do you like to sit? I usually take the back." He scanned the back row as he said this so I nodded. Wow it was loud in here. It was like a whirring of thoughts…so many I couldn't make out a sentence. I had to shut that off.

"Thanks for doing this with me. I don't mind coming here alone. It's not like you can have a conversation in a movie but I hate the pitiful looks I get." He took his jacket off and stuffed it in the seat next to him. He held his hands out for mine so I slid it off and handed it to him.

"I go to the movies by myself a lot. I like the theater in town. I like the feel of the old place," I said. I liked the memories the old theater brought back, memories of happier times, of times when that theater was the new *in* thing to do.

"That is a nice one. I go there once in a while. Wouldn't it be funny if we were both there at the same time?"

"It's very possible. We'll never know." I placed my soda in the cupholder on the arm of the seat between us. I liked having that barrier. He looked at it but didn't say anything. Just then, the theater went dark and lights flickered on the screen. The previews were starting. I slid down in my seat and got comfortable. I was anxious for this movie to start. As much as I had loved writing about vampires when I was a child, I loved seeing movies about them too, though books were always better. In the books you could envision the characters and the scenery how your mind wanted. In the movies, they were right in your face, the way the movie company wanted you to see them.

The movie started after three previews and the whole theater was hushed. Thank God! I was having a hard time turning it all off. It would have been hard to concentrate with all the *wondering how everyone will look* going on in the room.

It was a dark, gloomy, sunless place in the movie. Just like this one. The characters were beautiful, as is typical of vampires. It is, after all, how we attract our prey. I could get into this. The female lead was likable but a bit standoffish, pissed at the world. Very amusing. Hmm…Reminds me of someone.

A rustling sound and a pounding heartbeat caught my attention. Jack was breathing so fast I thought he was going to hyperventilate. His right hand moved toward mine, in spite of the large soda sitting between us. The tip of his fingers touched my skin and there it was…he jumped, pulling his hand away as if he had been bitten by a venomous spider. His eyes grew wide.

"See. I told you you'd get cold. Here, take my jacket." I knew this would happen. He was scared. He was trying to rationalize what his mind had to be suggesting at the moment, that there was something wrong. Something very wrong.

"Thank you. I must have had my hand on the cup too long. I guess I am a little cold." I allowed him to wrap his jacket around me. I had no choice but to listen now. I had to know what I was dealing with.

It could've been that. I didn't see…her hands were on her lap…is she sick? She is awfully pale…her eyes are bloodshot…not normal. His heart started to beat even faster. I tried to ignore the drumming in my ears. He noticed too much. He was paying more attention to me than I had anticipated. Cold skin was one thing, but icy skin, something else. It didn't help matters any that we happened to be watching a vampire movie. He might make comparisons. It was only logical. I shouldn't have to worry about that though. He was human after all. His mind would rationalize everything. There always had to be a rational, logical, maybe even scientific explanation for everything. After all, vampires were not, could not be…real. They were fictional characters created centuries ago by overactive imaginations.

We watched the rest of the movie in complete silence. I wanted to hear his thoughts now more than ever but at the same time, I was afraid. I was afraid this was it, the end. I realized, as much as I didn't want to admit it to myself, that I missed the companionship. No matter how much I took pride in being happy alone, I realized I'd been lying to myself. I hadn't expected this to feel so natural and comfortable. Now I sat here wanting to hear his voice, to answer his questions, to hear his laugh. I was tired of hearing disembodied voices spiraling around me yet never touching me.

It wasn't a romantic connection I felt, at least, I didn't think of it that way. It was more of a comfortable, talking to your best pal kind of thing. Sharing your thoughts and laughter with someone. Something I hadn't been able to do in many years. The truth was flooding my mind. It terrified me, yet, it was so simple…so human. I needed some type of a connection again, mortal or immortal, it didn't matter. The safest thing would be to seek out others like myself. They were out there. I knew that for sure. I had come across them in this city. The problem was that most were a bit territorial. Most were already in groups they did not want to add to, or take away from. We called them covens. I had never belonged to one for very long. Like I said, we were a bit territorial, if not possessive.

"Are you any warmer?" he asked, whispering it in my ear. I could hear his heart speed up as he leaned closer.

"Yes. Thank you," I lied. Of course, I didn't feel cold at all. The temperature didn't affect my dead body.

He looked at my face for a second, questions in his eyes, and then reached under the jacket on my lap to find my hand. I couldn't believe he was trying again! If my heart could have stopped beating it would have done so at that moment. What could I do at this point but sit still and accept it?

"No. You're still cold!" He took my hand out from under the jacket and cupped it in both of his, rubbing it between his warm hands. The heat from his skin felt like fire. It was a sensation I had felt many times before but only as I fed on my prey. As he rubbed my hand I could hear his heart speed more and his breathing was out of control.

God…I want this woman…feel her skin…her lips…all of her…

That did it. That was all it took. My future was planned, decided in a dark movie theater. I couldn't – wouldn't – hurt this man. He was innocent. I was a killer. The two did not mix. Ever!

It was simple enough in my mind. Make an excuse as to why I needed to go right to my apartment when the movie ended and just do it. Pack my things and leave. Very simple.

"That was pretty weird. Vampires and humans together. What did you think?" he asked as he dropped my hand and stretched. I was already on my feet, ready to bolt.

"Pretty outrageous. Good music though." I wanted to talk about something other than the vampires and the humans and the impossible, far-fetched romance.

"I liked the classical music especially," he said as he put his arms through his now cold jacket. I hoped he didn't notice that. I had mine on before he had a chance to help me with it. I didn't want him to feel any other part of my cold body. Even through clothing my skin was like ice…dry, cold, hard ice.

If he didn't start walking soon I would have to climb over him! My need to be out of there was so great. But, as soon as he found a break in the line of people filing out of the theater, he started edging his way into the aisle. I followed at his heels.

Wow! He was gorgeous…I would've done anything for him…

Don't know how that girl treated him like that…what a bitch…

Why didn't she force him to make her one of his kind? I would've forced him…couldn't live without him…so sexy…yummy…

I wanted to shout to these stupid people, "YOU HAVE NO IDEA WHAT YOU'RE SAYING! WHAT YOU'D BE GIVING UP. YOU KNOW NOTHING!" Of course, I didn't. Let them fantasize…idiots! I made the mistake a long time ago. There was no turning back now. I couldn't help but laugh at all the thoughts that were going through the minds of the people filing out of the theater. I had those dreams once. I wish someone had told me the gory details. But no. No one ever had. I couldn't save these people. I couldn't even save myself.

"What do you want to do next? Get some coffee maybe?" he asked as we walked back to the car, hands shoved in my pockets so there was no chance of him trying anything again. I couldn't believe he was still trying to spend more time with me…not scared enough.

"I think maybe I am coming down with something. I feel kind of strange. Maybe I should go to bed." I bit my lip, waiting. He seemed to hesitate for a moment but then agreed. Sleep was the best thing for me. I wished more than anything at that moment that sleep was an option, an escape, if only for a little while.

He opened the car door for me and let himself in the other side. As soon as he started the engine, he turned the heat on full blast. I appreciated his concern. I hated the fact that I had to end any sort of friendship with him just as soon as it had begun. Better sooner than later though, before he could get hurt.

Too bad she's sick…should've dropped her off at the door…probably made it worse…so much for a kiss…she looks sick…very pale…wonder if she'll let me take care of her…don't want to leave her tonight…

I only let myself listen so I could be prepared when it was time to say good night. He did want to kiss me. I had a feeling that was going to happen.

I started coughing. The harder I coughed, the less he should want to kiss me…right? That's how it should work anyway. Every time I coughed, he looked at me with concern in his eyes. I hated doing this to him. He was concerned about me. No one had worried about me in so long. It was kind of nice; sad, but kind of nice.

When we pulled up in front of our building, he sat there for a few seconds with the engine still running, prolonging the moment, afraid that it would end as soon as the motor died. I knew the feeling. I had no choice. My mind was made up.

He looked at me before his fingers were on the key in the ignition.

"I had fun tonight. I just wish you were feeling better. I don't have to work tomorrow so I'll check on you…if that's okay," he said, his fingers still not turning the key.

I swallowed hard. "Sure…I guess. I don't want to get you sick though."

"I don't care. I'll get you some soup and bring it up. Then you don't have to worry about cooking. Just rest." He turned the engine off.

As we walked up to the door, my hands in my pockets again, I felt an emptiness I hadn't expected. I somehow didn't want this to be the last time I saw him. I *had* enjoyed his company. Now it was over as usual. I needed to say something.

"I had a good time too. I'm glad we did this. We should do it again sometime." Anything but that. But I said it and I couldn't take it back, couldn't make it fly back into my mouth. I was giving him false hope and it was vicious of me.

"As soon as you feel better." His smile was so hopeful it lit up his whole face. If I had the ability to cry, I would have at that moment. This would be yet another memory to haunt me for the rest of my existence. Add it to the collection.

He walked me up to my door, as expected. He stood still as I unlocked it, his heart beating out of control. I threw myself into a coughing fit, bent over and everything. He patted my back before yanking his hand away. The cold again.

"I'll see you tomorrow. Bundle up and get some sleep." He squeezed my arm for a second then yanked his hand away, looking at his fingers. He was thinking he should take me to the hospital, get me checked out.

"I am sleepy. I'll be out in no time." I meant it. It wouldn't take me long to pack what little I had. I could be out within the hour. But if I didn't want him to see me, I had to wait. "Good night and…thank you. You are nice to talk to."

"Thank you. I'll see you tomorrow. Can't wait." He turned and started to walk away, stopped, looked back at me, and smiled with a sad look in his eyes. He raised his left hand and gave a little wave before starting down the stairs.

That's the last image I had of him, a sad wave as if he knew he would never see me again. I walked in to my apartment and headed straight for my closet and my suitcases.

❧ FOUR ❧

The clouds were gray and thick as I drove down the highway. Everything I owned was stuffed in the trunk and scattered all over the back seat. I had looked back at the building with longing as I drove away. This was the first place I had lived for a reasonable length of time. Any place else, alone or otherwise, had been brief. There was a time when, with *him,* I had considered myself a citizen of the world. We traveled through Africa, Europe, even South America. He, it seemed, was always in search of something. What that something was I had no idea.

I would miss the apartment building, I realized, as it became almost like a shadow in my rearview mirror. I could always come back and look at it. Maybe check on Clara…check on Jack. No! That would be impossible. Jack would be hurt enough by my sudden disappearance. I couldn't confuse him anymore by showing up and disappearing again. We had only known each other for a short time so I took comfort in the fact that he did not have the chance to get more attached. He would, hopefully, get over this fast. I laughed as I thought of what I had almost done, before I left. I had almost written him a note. What would I have said? Something like:

Dear Jack,
I am so sorry for hurting you. You deserve better. It's not you. It's me.
Take care of yourself,
Lily
P.S. By the way, the movie was good but you should read the book. It explains so much more.

Would he have gone right out and bought the book? Would he have made the connection? Impossible! Humans didn't think that way. The human mind was much too protected.

In a way, as I drove down the empty highway, I felt relief. Relief that I didn't have to open myself up to anyone again. I had the chance to start over in a new place. Starting over was something I was very good at. It was my specialty. Avoidance. I had become a pro at it. I could never let anyone into my world. How would I explain what I was? How could I possibly answer any questions? There was just no way. The only way to have anything close to a relationship was to stick to my own kind.

In the past, I'd heard there was a family of vampires living near the coast of Oregon. That's where I decided to go. It was worth a shot. I would look around and see what I might find. If I found nothing of interest, I could move on, even try another country. There was nothing to keep me in this one. I had been to Lima, Peru, once, many years ago. It was a large city with a growing population, busy, yet laid back. In fall and winter there was a constant haze and mist in the air. I wasn't sure what summer was like since we hadn't stayed long enough to find out. I wouldn't mind going back there and exploring. My Spanish was also getting very good, I was almost fluent. I'd been there with Ian. It was the first time in a long time that I thought of his name. It hurt. I had to stop this nonsense. He wasn't worth the agony.

I turned on the radio and let it scan through the stations. If I couldn't find something I liked, I could pull over and get my CD case from the back seat. I didn't like to be weighed down by material things so there wasn't much in the car. The things I did hang on to were small reminders of good times. I liked to keep things simple. I didn't stay in one place too long, mostly out of boredom. But I had stayed in Olympia. I had stayed for two years. Two years was a record for me. Two years before things started to get complicated. I had gotten so comfortable that I had, even if only for a second, contemplated the thought of getting myself a pet. What was next? A house with a picket fence?

The radio station I found was playing half-decent music and I found myself singing along to a Duke Ellington song. It had started to rain again and the wipers were making their usual squeak, squeak. Not an annoying sound but distracting enough to someone with super-sensitive hearing. I checked the clock and noticed I had about another hour and a half drive left ahead of me. Squeak, squeak. It was kind of odd, the mix between the music and the sound of the wipers, especially when I noticed they were keeping time with each other.

I sang along with the radio for a while before I let my mind wander back to Jack. I was glad I needed to be closer to hear someone's thoughts… glad I would not hear what he'd think once he realized I was gone. I don't think I could bear the pain and hurt I was causing him. He had done nothing to deserve it. The more I thought about it the more I wanted to turn around. Maybe there was some way we could be friends. If there was some way we could be friends without letting out the truth about me, I couldn't think of it. Maybe I should just turn around. Maybe if I gave it a little more time. Something could be worked out. But, no. He had other intentions. I could not ignore that. I needed to keep going…*had* to keep going.

Keep going…you're doing the right thing…keep going…

My fingers clutched the steering wheel with a death grip.

"Ian?" I whispered. "Ian?" My head turned to the next lane. Nothing. I searched in the rearview mirror, even turned my head to look at the back seat. Nothing. I was alone. The one car that had been behind me for a few miles had long ago exited the highway.

"No! It's impossible. You aren't here. You don't exist anymore…not possible," I said aloud. I'm going crazy. That is the only explanation. All my years alone had led to this. I searched around me, both with my eyes and ears. All quiet. I found the volume knob on the radio and turned it up as loud as it would go. I had to keep myself distracted. I did *not* want to hear that voice again. That commanding yet beautiful voice I had once loved. I needed to hate it now.

The rest of the way I kept my eyes straight ahead and my ears on the music. I was getting closer to where I wanted to go. Astoria. It was a pretty name. I liked the way it sounded when I said it aloud. It had promise. I planned on staying in a hotel for a while. I wanted to look around, listen to the town, before I made more permanent arrangements. If I found any of my own kind here I would start to look for an apartment. I wanted to see about classes at the community college. I still needed something to keep me busy. Besides, one could never have too much education.

I followed the lodging signs at the end of the exit ramp, slowing down a bit, to take in the scenery. It looked like a nice place, tree-lined streets and small businesses all locked up for the night. About a half a mile from the exit I found a promising hotel. I parked in front of the office and took a deep breath…first night in a new place…again. I stepped out of the car, locked it, and went in through the automatic door.

The lobby was very clean, typical with its pamphlet stand, arm chairs, and end tables piled with magazines. The breakfast area was to the right and the elevators on the left. Before the elevators was the reception desk. I walked over to it and noticed there was no one there. I hit the bell.

"Be right there!" a man's voice yelled from the other side of the door behind the counter.

"Okay! Thank you!" I yelled back. I heard the elevator ding. The door opened and a young woman, about my age, stepped out. She looked at me and quickly looked away but continued to walk toward the counter. She stopped in front of it and hesitated, noticing we were alone.

"He said he'll be right out." I could hear her heart beating like music in my ears. My mouth started to water. I hadn't realized I was thirsty. Her pale neck showed her veins. I could envision the blood flowing through them. My whole body tensed. I would have to find a place to feed and soon. I was distracted for the moment by the appearance of the clerk, a short, pudgy, balding man.

"Okay. Who was here first?" he asked putting on his glasses.

"You can take care of her first. Please." I said motioning to the girl. *Please take care of her and get her out of here. I can't take the sound of her heart.*

He nodded and stepped closer to where the girl was standing. She looked over and smiled. *I never liked when my food smiled at me.*

"Do you have change for the soda machine? It won't take my dollar bills."

She held up the bills for him.

"Oh, that thing is a pain...does it all the time. Here." He handed her change. She rushed back to the elevator, without bothering to count it. The scent that followed her was almost irresistible...mouth-watering sweetness. I closed my eyes and inhaled, letting the aroma flood through me.

"Do you have a reservation? Miss...do you have a reservation?"

"Um...no. Sorry, I don't." I hadn't been paying attention. I had been too busy dreaming about the taste of the girl's blood in my mouth. The warmth of it on my tongue.

"That's okay. We're not too busy this time of year. Too dark and gloomy for the tourists. Let me see what we have for you..." He looked at his computer screen while he spoke. "Is it just you?"

"Yup. Just me." *Always, just me.*

"I can give you a king size room for the price of a double. How's that sound?" He still looked at his computer.

"That sounds great. Thank you." I didn't care. I wouldn't use the bed anyway, except maybe to watch TV.

"And how long will you be with us?" he said looking up at my face. *Very pretty...looks too young to be here alone...no boyfriend? Sneaking him in the side door?*

"I don't know yet. Is that a problem?" I knew it wasn't a problem. Business was business after all.

"Not at all. If you'll just fill this out..." He handed me the form along with a pen. I filled it out, ignoring his thoughts, and handed it back to him, taking care not to touch his skin.

After all the technicalities were taken care of, he handed me a key card and gave me the hours for the continental breakfast bar. I returned to the parking lot to park the car. The experience I had with the girl at the counter was not the first time something like that had happened. She wasn't a criminal. I just needed to feed.

After the incident in the car, I didn't much feel like exploring the town just yet so my thirst would have to wait. I wanted to settle into my room and take some time to clear my head. Besides, tomorrow's weather forecast was just as co-operative as ever; cloudy with occasional drizzle. Beautiful weather! I carried as much as I could fit into my arms and used the back door to let myself in. From the directions he had given me, my room was near the back of the hotel anyway. I could just imagine the look on the clerk's face if he saw me walk in with a pile in my arms taller than I was. That would be pretty funny but also senseless, so I kept myself in the shadows.

Seeing no one in the lobby, I hurried to the elevator. Balancing the pile, I backed up and held my right leg up in the air. I used the tip of my shoe to push the button that summoned the elevator. Once inside, I used my foot, again, to push the number five.

After reading the sign outside the elevator, I found the door marked 513. This would be my new address. I placed the pile on the floor and opened the door. I got a blast of *hotel clean* in my face as soon as I pulled it open. All hotels smelled the same. It was better than the smell I had encountered in the elevator. It was the same elevator the girl had used and her sweet aroma lingered. I tried to ignore the thirst.

As promised, there was a king size bed with four pillows. There were also two dressers, a television on one of them and a desk with all the necessary connections for a computer. Next to the window were a reclining chair and a small table with a lamp. One of the nightstands on either side of the bed held the mandatory bible. I set everything down on the bed and went to check out the bathroom next. The toilet had a toilet strip across the top to signify it had been cleaned. I made sure I removed this right away, before I forgot, so the housekeeper wouldn't think it odd. So, having inspected every part of my new residence, I decided to unpack.

I put away my clothing and placed my shoes underneath the rack where the hanging clothes were. Next, I put my few toiletries in the bathroom. I put my sketch pads and notebooks on the desk. All of that took mere minutes at the speed with which I worked. I slowed down a bit when it came to setting up my laptop. I looked at the card on the desk to find out how to connect to the Internet. Oh…right…a password. What had he said about a password? I had been distracted by the girl at the desk…by the way she smelled. I replayed my conversation with the clerk, something about the key card…right. The password was on the back of the key card. I pulled it out of my pocket and flipped it over. Sure enough, *Hotel Guest 513*. How original! I turned on my computer and let it run through its start-up routine while I went to sit on the bed.

The only things left on the bed were the two boxes I used to keep under the sofa at the apartment. One had a lid and one did not, since I had shattered it. I picked it up. Did I dare look in it? Could I look in it without losing my temper again? There was nothing in that box but pain. I had promised myself, for years, that I would burn the contents. Of course, I still hadn't. I looked at it for a while without touching it, trying to decide if it was best to just push it under the bed. The more I thought I should, the more I wanted to touch it. The more I wanted to ignore it, the closer it seemed to get.

Pulling it closer, I took a deep breath. I had to see if it still felt the same. It had been so long since I had looked at anything in it. Maybe it wasn't so bad. Maybe after all these years I was still imagining a pain that wouldn't be there anymore. After all, these were only trivial things. It was a box full of bits and pieces of a past gone long ago. But were the pain and betrayal gone? I had to see.

I held the red ribbon in my hand, could still feel it in my hair, the one I'd worn the first time I set eyes on Ian. His eyes never left my face. I was walking in the park with my father. It was a cloudy spring day. It was warm enough to be outside without a jacket and I remember how we felt liberated. It was the first warm day of spring. It had just finished raining and everything smelled fresh. My father complained that I did not spend enough time with him since I was attending college. So, feeling like a little girl, I had worn that red ribbon in my hair just for him. It was his favorite color on me.

We had gotten ice cream cones at the shop on the corner and then found a bench in the park. We were enjoying our cones, his vanilla and mine chocolate, of course, when I saw a man leaning against a light post. When I looked his way he tipped his hat and smiled. I remember thinking how debonair he looked, like a movie star. I looked at my father, thinking maybe he knew him. He was looking the other way, watching a young boy throw a stick for his puppy. I looked back at the man, wondering if he had moved on by now but he was still there, smiling at me. I felt a bit awkward but couldn't take my eyes from him, couldn't force myself to look away. His eyes were like magnets. Then, as if I couldn't feel any more discomfort, his face grew serious. He stared with no expression, not a twitch. I fidgeted and played with my hands and all but hyperventilated but still couldn't take my eyes off of him. I couldn't look away from his perfect, pale face. It wasn't until my father looked at his watch and said he had an appointment that I forced my eyes away. My father was starting to walk the other way and I knew I had to keep up. I looked back toward the man, trying to at least smile but he was gone…just like that. He had vanished as quickly and suddenly as he had appeared.

I dreamed of him, my pale-faced admirer, for many nights. He became my fantasy for the next few months. He was my beautiful, pale-faced vampire.

I realized, in the middle of that memory, I was clutching the ribbon so hard in my hand that my fingernails were digging into my palm. I looked at the nail marks, dropping the tattered ribbon onto the bed. How could that first memory still cause so much pain? It felt like a band tightening around my heart causing my imaginary breath to explode from my mouth with anger and desire. I felt angry with myself. I was angry with him, angry for believing in him, for allowing him to destroy my world. He entered my life and ended it and I had been so willing. My body shuddered as if I was going to cry. I felt the pain in my stomach. I felt it in my head. If I could shed tears, I would be doing just that.

I threw the ribbon back in the box and kicked it under the bed. I couldn't deal with the contents right now. It was too soon. A hundred years could have passed and it would still be too soon. The wound he left still felt too fresh. I grabbed the remote and clicked the TV on. There had to be something to distract me. I wanted to wait until day break to go out. I wasn't in the mood to hunt tonight. I could go to any local bar and try to find someone tasty, but like this, I might even consider someone with a minor traffic infraction a tasty meal. No. I would wait. I had standards. I would wait until I calmed down, my mind clear enough to know the difference.

AFTER COUNTLESS HOURS of channel surfing, I pulled the curtain aside. It was definitely morning. The sun was not shining but there was light in the sky. People were stirring in the hotel. I was a little interested in what the girl from last night was doing. I scanned the rooms but did not hear her voice. She must still be asleep. Oh well.

I changed my clothes, anxious to get out for some air and see my new town. I would worry about hunting later. I had waited this long. I walked out to the front of the hotel and noticed it wasn't raining yet; walking would be good. I seemed to be close enough to civilization to explore without dealing with parking and one-way streets. Besides, I was in no hurry.

Deciding to stick to my usual charade of coffee and a park bench, I headed toward what looked like downtown. I passed a few small shops that were just opening. The owners were sweeping the sidewalk or cleaning their display windows; preparing for a day of business-as-usual. As I walked, I could smell coffee brewing. As usual, I let my senses guide me. A block to the left and across the street; there it was. A quaint little corner shop tucked away with its familiar newspaper stand just outside the door. A young man, with a newspaper tucked under his arm was walking out. He let go of the door before he saw me and hurried back.

"I'm sorry. I wasn't paying attention. Please...allow me." He smiled and held the door open for me. *She is really beautiful...idiot...should be watching...*

"Thank you," was all I managed to say as I entered. I looked back and saw him still standing there, shaking his head. Here we go again.

Besides the man that had just left, I was the only customer. I looked at the menu board and decided on a large mocha this time. It was funny to me to look at the menu and make a decision as to which size and flavor I should try that day, as if I was actually going to drink it. It was amusing anyway, pretending to be human. I ordered and then moved over to the end of the counter marked *pickup*. The man making the coffee was so quick, like he could do it in his sleep. He poured the shots and frothed the milk like an expert. I didn't even hear anything coming from his mind.

"Large mocha latte!" he yelled as if the shop was full of people. I laughed but he didn't notice. He was so into his routine that he moved like a robot.

There was a pile of magazines on the counter that lined the large front window and comfortable looking stools. I decided to sit there so I could pretend to read a magazine while watching the action on the street. I chose the stool farthest from the door and settled there to eavesdrop on whoever looked interesting. What better way to learn about this town than from the private thoughts of its residents?

I was paging through a fashion magazine when all the air left the room. *He* walked in. Not Ian, no…this was some other form of torture. He walked in looking at the floor, or maybe at the map in his hands, and went to the counter without looking around. In a deep, melodic voice I heard him order a large mocha latte and a blueberry muffin.

"Excuse me? Do you know where the college is? I think I'm close but I'm not sure which way from here." His eyes were on his map.

"You are close. Left when you leave here, five blocks, and then right on Maple Avenue. You can't miss it." The man answered without taking his eyes from the coffee machine. "Your large mocha latte." He handed him the cup and the napkin-wrapped muffin.

He took his cup and went to a table in the back. He set them on the table and unfolded the map. He looked at it, drawing lines with his index fingers. He was so intent on figuring out the map that he didn't notice me looking at him, even though I had to turn around in my stool to do it. I sucked in a gulp of air. I felt the muscles in my arms tense as I gripped the sides of the stool. His heart beat so loud in my ears that the sound was deafening. I wanted to hold my hands to my ears but I was afraid to move.

He made my mind reel! He was human, wasn't he? What could be even remotely extraordinary about him? He was dressed in khaki pants and a red sweater. His dirty blonde hair was combed neatly. He wore a watch on one wrist and a silver and black bracelet on the other. He wore no rings. Why I took notice of that I couldn't say at that moment. He continued to look at his map for a moment and then paused. He held his head very still for a second and then slowly lifted his eyes, his beautiful blue eyes. He must have felt me staring and yet, even though I had been caught, I couldn't make myself look away. He tilted his head slightly to the side and I saw a smile, a smile that made one of his beautiful eyes squint ever so slightly. My world had been turned upside down again, for the second time.

I finally made myself look away. The sound of his heartbeat was maddening. His scent, sweet yet musky, filled the air. I inhaled and then stopped. I couldn't breathe at this moment. I had to wait until I got back outside yet I couldn't force my legs to move. I couldn't command my hands to loosen the grip that held me to the stool. I heard him breathing behind me. I heard his heart speed up. I wasn't looking at him yet I pictured his face. I had already memorized it. What was wrong with me? This had only ever happened to me once, long ago. It had been a mistake; the worst mistake I ever made. But this was beyond mistake. This was a mortal man making me feel things I hadn't felt or wanted to feel in a very long time. This was a downright sin yet I felt unrepentant.

Somehow summoning enough strength to jump off my stool, leaving my coffee behind, I ran out the door. I needed to get out so I could breathe again. His scent was so powerful. I never looked back. I did not listen for his thoughts once I was through the door. I was afraid of what I might hear.

I ran, not caring that people might see, at a more reasonable speed than my usual vampire speed but still, I ran. I didn't know where I was going. I needed to be away from the possibility of seeing him again. The way his scent and his heartbeat had enveloped me, I was afraid I would hurt him. Why would I hurt this man? I didn't kill without merit. I didn't kill anyone who didn't deserve to be punished. Why this man? Why now?

Keep going…you can do it…keep running…faster…no one sees…

"LEAVE ME ALONE! Why are you doing this to me? Haven't you done enough?" I shouted and whispered, all in the same breath.

⤷ FIVE ↫

The beach was beautiful even in the gloom. The thick, dark clouds hung low. I knew that soon it would be more than a drizzle. I sat on the wet sand with my arms wrapped tightly around my knees. I felt safe wrapped up that way. I stared at the ocean and watched the white spray of the waves as they pounded over rocks. The sound was calming. The sound of a stream or a river had the same effect. The ocean was my favorite. It was peaceful despite the wind that blew my hair in my face, blinding me. There wasn't a soul around.

I pictured his face, the loving way he had looked at me. He didn't know me from Eve but I had seen love in his eyes or at least the capacity for it. I was losing my mind. My loneliness was making me imagine things. That couldn't have been love. He didn't even know my name, for crying out loud!

The rain was picking up, just as I had suspected. I unhooked my arms from my knees and let my body fall backward. Closing my eyes, I let the rain wash over my face. I would love to sleep right now. It would be such a welcome escape. But with sleeping came dreaming and I didn't feel I would welcome that. I kept my eyes closed anyway and tried not to think, focusing on the sounds around me. The waves crashed like thunder against the rocks protruding from the shore. Marine birds dove in and out of the water with a splash, in search of food. A distant foghorn called a warning to the boats scattered in the distance. I lay there for what felt like an eternity, my eyes closed until I heard a rustling sound. I looked around, holding my hair so the wind couldn't blindfold me with it. I saw no one. I propped myself up on both elbows and looked behind me, sand pelting against the side of my face.

That's when I saw her. A tall, slim figure walking toward me. She was taking her time, careful on the slippery stones before the small strip of sand. She looked hesitant yet curious. My body tensed. I listened. I could hear her breathing as she took very calculated steps but I heard no heartbeat. Maybe I wasn't listening hard enough. I closed my eyes to let my sense of hearing take over. Still, nothing. I let my sense of smell take over. I caught no scent except of the salty ocean and a dead fish decaying somewhere.

My body tensed and I sat up, ready for anything. I didn't want to get up and walk away. I wasn't ready to give up the peace I felt since encountering this vacant beach. I should leave though. Why wasn't I hearing a heartbeat? As thirsty as I was I should have been catching some kind of scent. Could it be? No. It couldn't be that easy. I planned on searching for others of my kind but it couldn't possibly be as easy as this. Had one of them found me?

Please don't run. It's okay. I mean you no harm…you are right…I am a vampire.

I took a deep breath and, waiting for her to approach, concentrated on relaxing my body to encourage her. As I watched her getting closer, I noticed how serene her face looked. There seemed to be no worry in her large, purple-blue eyes. Her damp hair framed her face in a mound of curls. She walked like a runway model; so graceful on the uneven ground and the strong wind. She stopped a few feet away from me and her full, red lips curled into a smile.

"Welcome. My name is Kalia," she said as she lowered herself to the sand. She tucked her long legs under her making that rustling sound again. She was wearing warm up pants and a windbreaker.

"Thanks. I'm Lily…Lily Dane Townsend." I extended my right hand. She looked at it for a moment and then reached her pale hand out to meet mine. Her skin was just as cold as mine.

"We've been waiting for you."

"Um…who are *we*?"

"Aaron, Maia, and myself…of course." As if I should've known that.

"How did you know? I didn't…"

"I'm sorry. Aaron saw you coming. He can do that. He's very talented."

"And Aaron is…?" I still had no idea who she was talking about.

"Aaron is my husband. We've been together for over a century."

I was surprised to hear that. Over a century was a long time. That was impressive.

"How old are you?" I asked bluntly.

"I'm going on two hundred years. Aaron is a bit younger than me," she stated.

"And who is Maia?" Now I was intrigued.

"Maia is a fledgling. She lives with us."

"You all live together?" I asked very curious.

"Aaron and I were alone until Maia joined us. Now it's the three of us. One big happy family!"

I couldn't tell if that was sarcasm or excitement. I looked at her in awe. It was unusual to see more than two vampires living together.

So, let's go get your things out of that hotel…that's no place to live.

I tensed again. Had she wanted me to hear that? *Why would I do that? I just got here…not sure I'm staying.*

You're staying. Isn't family what you were looking for? She got up on her knees.

I looked at her eyes trying to read the intention in them. *Is that really what you want? You don't even know me.*

You don't know us either. What better way? The more the merrier…right? With that said she was on her feet and extended a hand to me. I avoided contact and stood on my own. I'd had my share of physical contact for a while. A handshake was enough.

"Are you sure about this?" I asked aloud this time.

I wouldn't have asked if I wasn't. I never say anything I don't mean. It's what we all want. Oh, by the way, Aaron is not like us. He can't hear our thoughts so he gets a little irritated when Maia and I do it. I wouldn't recommend it if he's around.

That was good to know. I realized I hadn't accepted the offer but I don't think I had much choice. I was going to be their new housemate whether or not I agreed. I also realized I was following her.

She looked around and said, *Race you!* And she was off, a blur through the sand. I took off, whizzing past her, hitting the sleeve of her windbreaker with the tips of my fingers. I reached the stairs a few steps before her.

Wow, you're fast! And I got a head start! We both laughed. I knew at that moment I was going to like being around her. She had an easy nature about her. She laughed so comfortably, like she had known me longer than ten minutes.

We took her Jeep back to the hotel, passing the coffee shop where I had been that morning. I saw it to my right, even though she was driving at a ridiculous speed. My stomach did a little flip as we passed. *OH FOR CRYING ALOUD!* I thought to myself.

What was that? She looked over at me.

"Er…nothing. I…" Oops. I was going to have to be careful around her. That was going to take some getting used to. I was usually the intruder.

We went right to the front desk at the hotel and told them I was checking out. Of course, the desk clerk was worried something was wrong. I assured him my room was fine but that something else had come up. He seemed reassured and we went through the simple check out process. I paid and then went to the elevator. It would only take me moments to pack and I told Kalia she could wait in the lobby but she insisted she follow me, as she didn't want to be gawked at by the desk clerk or anyone else for that matter.

I packed my things while Kalia looked around the room. As soon as I was finished, we piled things into our arms and headed for the stairs. I had already told her we needed to go out the back door since my car was there. I left the key card on the desk for the housekeeper.

As we walked to the back stairwell, I inhaled the delicious scent from last night. The girl was walking down the hall in the other direction, toward the elevator. I held my breath for a while.

Wow…that's a nice scent…so hungry…

Kalia turned to look at me. She frowned a little. *Has she done something? I don't think so. I didn't listen to her. She just has such a powerful scent. We can always tell who is a criminal…so it must be something else… What then?*

*That, my dear, is the scent of an innocent, menstruating woman…*she chuckled.

Oh…I hadn't even considered that…wow.

Yes…it can be very deceiving. You have to be careful. Listen closely to the mind before you attack. Don't let the scent fool you. We were out in the parking lot by now and I led her to my car. I opened the trunk and let her put her pile down first.

That didn't explain my experience in the coffee shop. He was a man. Kalia watched my face for a moment but didn't question my thought. This was going to take some work.

"I'll get the Jeep and you can follow me. It's not far." She headed away from me toward her own vehicle. I arranged my things so they wouldn't fall off whenever I hit the brakes. By the time I got into the driver's seat, she was waiting so we pulled out onto the road.

She seemed much more comfortable behind the wheel and was a faster driver than I. It didn't take long, though, to realize I was hearing her thoughts. She communicated her moves, which made it easier to stay with her even when two other cars made their way between us.

She entered the highway, after advising me to do the same. We stayed together on the highway for a few miles and then she made her way to an exit. I followed as she drove away from town and entered a more isolated area. She had, however, slowed down a bit so I assumed we were getting close. *You're right…a blind driveway sign…that's us…*I prepared to turn.

We followed a narrow, tree-lined driveway. It was unpaved and a bit bumpy. I was glad I had arranged things on the back seat. I did not want to have to pick up the contents of the box with no lid. I wished I hadn't remembered to get that out from under the bed. I would have to burn it soon. As I looked ahead of me, I saw the house. It loomed high above the tree line. It was a huge, old, white, story-book Victorian with a wraparound porch. There were wicker rockers with plush wine-colored cushions, two on either side of the door. The house was beautiful.

"Welcome home, Lily!" She said, smiling as she saw the awe in my eyes. "By the way, how did you get Dane as a middle name?"

"It was my mother's maiden name. She wanted to keep it in the family," I explained. I stood next to her making no attempt to empty the contents of my car. That could wait. I was anxious to see the inside of this gorgeous house. I was, however, nervous about meeting its other inhabitants.

"And it suits you. Come on. I'll give you a tour," she said aloud again. Now that we were close to Aaron she spoke aloud. Was he that sensitive about his inability to read minds? I decided he must be and asked no questions. I didn't have to. Kalia looked at me with a smirk on her face and nodded.

She led me into the entryway. To my surprise, Aaron was already there. He must have heard us drive up. Aaron was a tall man, about a head taller than Kalia and she was quite tall. He had piercing green eyes and straight blonde hair, almost to his shoulders. He stood stone still, making no attempt to come closer. He wore jeans and a t-shirt but nothing on his feet. The skin on his face and arms looked flawless. I saw not one freckle. In his paleness, he looked absolutely perfect, like a painting. Though he looked very young, his eyes showed the wisdom of someone who had lived and learned for centuries. Kalia nodded and winked at him. Only then did he stretch out his hand. I could see who the leader of this coven was. I reached out to return his welcome. A brief handshake and I saw his body relax.

"Welcome home, Lily. It's good to meet you," he said and dropped my hand. "I'll let Kalia show you around and get you settled. I have some work to do; I'll be in my study." He turned and walked toward the back of the house, around the right side of the staircase.

"Did he say he has work to do?" I had never known a vampire that worked for a living.

"Yes. Aaron is a translator. He speaks nine languages. He works from here, on his computer. That keeps him pretty busy," she explained as I followed her in the direction in which Aaron had gone just a moment ago. She lightly tapped a door we passed along the way and held her index finger to her lips. "That's his study. We never disturb him when the door is closed. If he wants company, he will leave it open."

So that's how it could be done: earn a living without having to face humans…to face temptation. I found that a fascinating alternative I would need to consider in the future. Kalia took me on a tour of the rest of the house. She showed me the spacious, light and airy kitchen, with its many windows and hanging plants. The living room was very comfortable and decorated in Victorian-style furniture. All of it looked used. We went upstairs. Most of the doors were closed. She opened the first door and poked her head in. She stepped aside and motioned for me to take a look.

"This is our room. I wanted to make sure it wasn't a mess. Aaron can be very forgetful sometimes. He leaves clothes lying around." She laughed and rolled her eyes as if it was something endearing. I assumed that to her, it probably was. She closed that door and pointed to the one across the hall. "That's the bathroom. Plenty of towels in there. It's an old door so there's no lock. Sorry."

"This is our guest room. It doesn't get used much but we keep it free just in case. We have friends that sometimes pass through the area," she said this as she opened another door at the end of the hall. I noticed that all the doors were old. They had ornate, glass doorknobs on them. I doubted any of them locked. When she opened the door at the end of the hall, I saw another set of stairs. They were much narrower than the stairwell that led to the second floor. I followed close behind her. She stopped at the top of the stairs and I saw three more doors. How many rooms were there?

I looked at the door straight ahead as she said, "That's the way up to the attic. We just use that for storage. It's very dusty and full of spiderwebs."

She pointed to the door on the right. "That's Maia's room. She's not here right now…out of town. This will be your room." She pulled a door open.

I stepped in beside her, letting my eyes take in everything. The room was much bigger than I expected. Judging by the size of the staircase, I expected everything to be smaller up here. I was mistaken.

"Wow! It's beautiful!" I was surprised to see a four-poster bed in the middle of the room. It was dark mahogany and very intricate in its design. The bedding was, like the rockers on the porch, a dark wine color. The curtains on the windows matched. That seemed to be the color palette throughout the house, from what I had seen so far. The bed made me smile and she noticed.

"Just because we don't sleep doesn't mean that we don't still need a bed. Plenty of other things to do on it…if you know what I mean." She winked.

Of course, I thought, she had a husband.

I continued to look around at what would be my new home. There were two night stands, one on either side of the bed. One had a telephone on it but both were equipped with a small lamp. On one side of the room there was a vanity table; complete with what looked like a silver brush, comb, and hand mirror. There were also small glass boxes of different shapes scattered on the surface. One of them contained a handful of cotton balls.

"I didn't know what you would need so I took a guess. If you need anything else, anything at all, please don't hesitate to tell us."

"Thank you but I should be fine. You've done enough already," I said to her, looking her in the eyes so she could see how truly grateful I felt.

"These two doors…" She pointed to the doors on the opposite end of the bed. "Closet and your sitting room. We put a desk in there so you have a place to put your computer. We have a rule that when you are in your own private rooms, especially with the door closed, we make it a point to stay out of your thoughts. It's especially important to Aaron when he is working. So much of what he does is confidential plus it just annoys him. I think he feels left out."

"I will remember that."

"You can block us out whenever you sense Maia or me listening in other rooms. Sometimes we do it without thinking." She started to head to the door that led back into the hall.

"Block you out?" I asked. "I don't think I know how."

"Really?" She showed her shock. "I thought we could all do that. Oh well, we'll have to see. Let's go get your things."

I felt like I was in a dream. Last night I was in a hotel, as alone as I had been for many years and now I was in a beautiful house with such nice beings…well…the two I met, anyway. If I didn't know for a fact that I didn't sleep, I would be waiting to awaken at any moment and find it was all a dream. Everything felt so surreal to me at that moment…so good. I didn't want to spoil it by thinking.

Kalia led the way back downstairs and to the front door. I turned my head and looked down the hall. Aaron's door was still closed. He must still be working. I would get to know him later. I was already feeling more relaxed around Kalia. I had a feeling I soon would feel the same around Aaron. His eyes had shown so much warmth.

We carried everything upstairs and then Kalia excused herself, leaving me to my unpacking. She closed the door as she left, showing me that it was okay to be alone with my thoughts now. I wondered about this and waited. It was true. I received no answer in response.

I looked around the room and saw no dresser. That was odd…no drawers for clothing. I figured I would hang everything in the closet and walked over to open the door. What I saw when I pulled the door open took me by surprise. It was huge! It could have been another bedroom! That solved the drawer problem. There were two dressers in the closet. I couldn't help but laugh aloud. What else should I have expected? Things weren't as they seemed in this house. I barely had enough clothing to fill one dresser let alone two! There was enough hanging space for a whole family in here. One wall was lined with a built-in shoe rack that could easily hold fifty pairs of shoes. I stacked my three pairs on it; one pair on each shelf as if my shoes would feel overcrowded if I didn't give them space.

Once I finished with the clothing, I went to deal with my boxes of memories. I shoved one under the bed as far as I could. The other box I decided to place in a drawer in the closet's one empty dresser. I could use that to store anything that wasn't clothing. I had yet to inspect my new, personal sitting room. I never had one of those before and I was thrilled by the idea.

I turned the knob on the only door I had not yet opened, slowly, as I noticed it squeaked a bit. Again, I was surprised by what I found. They seemed to have gone to a lot of trouble to furnish this room and I couldn't help but wonder if it was something they had done long ago or if it was something they had done with me in mind. I made a mental note to ask later. I really needed to thank someone.

There was a desk in front of the window. In the corner was an overstuffed chair with dark flowered upholstery. Next to that was a small table with a lamp and underneath the table was a square basket full of magazines. One side of the room was floor-to-ceiling bookshelves. Most of it was already filled with books. Some of the spines were leather. I walked over to take a closer look and noticed it was a collection of classic literature. Others were mystery novels, romances, art books, and a few that looked like textbooks. I wondered whom the textbooks belonged to.

I picked up the first art book and went over to the chair. It was soft and my body sank into it. Since the curtains were closed, I switched on the lamp. I began to page through the book, without really bothering to focus on the pages. My mind had filled with the image of the man in the coffee shop. My stomach had knots in it as soon as I pictured his face… the beautiful smile. I could still imagine the sound of his heart beating in my ears. I could smell his sweet aroma in the room as clearly as if he had just been standing here. Why was I so intrigued with this man, this man that I would probably never set eyes on again?

Let it go…not a good idea…not a safe or sane one…

I stopped breathing and listened. Aaron? No. Aaron couldn't hear my thoughts. And I highly doubted Aaron would have just invited himself into a stranger's bedroom. It was definitely Ian. There was no mistaking Ian McGuinness' voice. And the fact that, even after all these decades, he still had a slight Irish accent, made it all more real. Was I inventing all this in my mind? Was I going completely and utterly mad, finally? After decades of not speaking to him, of not hearing a word from him or about him, his voice was as clear as if he were standing right in front of me. And it had been only for the last few days. That made even less sense.

I decided I needed to get out of the room for a while. If he spoke to me again Kalia would hear him so I headed downstairs. As I walked down the hall, I decided to take a peek at the bathroom. That was a door she hadn't pulled open. It was a normal looking bathroom except for the fact that it was furnished with antiques, complete with a clawfoot bathtub. I pulled the curtain aside and, to my relief, saw that it did have a shower. The sink was one on a pedestal and next to that was the toilet, complete with toilet paper hanging on the rack next to it. That, of course, made me laugh. As if any one of us had any need for that! I pulled open the small closet door and saw what Kalia had meant. The shelves were piled high with towels and wash cloths.

There was no noise coming from the main level of the house. I stood at the bottom of the stairs and listened but still heard nothing. I walked around slowly. Aaron's door was still closed so I went toward the kitchen. I looked in before I entered and saw Kalia. She had an easel set up in front of the back door and was painting something she saw through the glass. Trying not to startle her, I cleared my throat gently. She turned her head with a smile.

"Oh…I didn't hear you coming. I get so lost in what I'm painting I forget that anyone else exists." She set her paintbrush in a glass of water. "Did you settle in okay?"

"Yes. Thank you. Everything is lovely. I was wondering: did you set up that room when you moved into this house?" I looked over her shoulder at the canvas. She was painting the tree in the backyard. The fence and the bird feeder were also in the painting. It was a perfect depiction of what was through the door. "That's lovely, by the way."

"Thank you. I dabble. It gives me something to do and I find it soothing." She wiped her brushes in a handful of paper towels. "And to answer your question, no. We put some things in there when we moved in. We had set it up as a bedroom, just in case. The bed was in there and so were the night stands. But that's as far as we got. When Aaron saw you coming, or thought you might, we put the rest of the things in there. The dressers used to be from my sister's room. We had those up in the attic. Aaron sanded and repainted them. He was very excited at the thought of a new family member. I got you the chair as a homecoming gift." She set her brushes down and stepped back to examine her painting. Something about it did not meet her approval and she shook her head.

"I can't believe you went through all this trouble…for me…someone you don't even know. I don't know how to thank you." I looked down at the floor. I was suddenly filled with emotion I was afraid to show. She looked away from the canvas and turned toward me. She held her arms out. I walked slowly into them. She smiled just as I reached her.

"I…we…are happier than you know that you are here. Three is a nice number but I think four makes a family more complete, don't you agree?" She said this as she wrapped her stone cold arms around me; yet I felt strange warmth. She let one hand stroke my hair. I relaxed in her arms and laid my head on her shoulder. I let the warmth wash over me, comfort me.

"I am happy you found me. Thank you." I meant it. I could feel it deep inside. I could feel that they would be my family for many years to come.

"You're thirsty, aren't you dear?" She asked pulling her face back enough to look at my eyes. She could probably see the dark circles around them. The longer I went without feeding, the darker they became. As a vampire, I needed blood in order to stay looking like the age when I died. In the beginning, we need to feed much more often. After many years, we can go weeks without feeding. But just like a human, sometimes tragedy or conflict can suck the energy right out of our bodies, in which case, we need to feed in order to replenish it.

"I am," I said in a whisper. I was ashamed I had let it go enough to look so obvious.

"As soon as Aaron is done, we'll go out to dinner. How does that sound?"

"Sounds good to me. I'll go change." I thought it was odd, how she made it sound so human. She made it sound as if we were a human family going out for a human meal; like we would order from a menu and pay and leave a tip. The image of the three of us at a table with napkins on our laps made me laugh. Of course, Kalia laughed too.

"That reminds me. There are a couple of bags up in the attic full of clothing. Most of them were Maia's. She changed her whole look after she moved in so she doesn't want them anymore. She's about your size. There are a few things of mine…you could try them anyway." She looked at me, realizing how much smaller I was than her model-like stature. "I'll put them in your room."

I thanked her and excused myself to go change. As I walked past Aaron's door, I could hear him saying goodbye to someone on the telephone. I walked faster just in case he was finished working for the day. I didn't want to make my new hosts wait too long.

HUNTING WITH MY new family was an interesting experience. We went to a local bar, ordered drinks, and then pretended to drink them as we listened for our prey. Aaron depended on his hearing to get the invitation he needed. He would also point someone out to Kalia and wait for confirmation. She made sure that his intended victim was well-deserving. Not only was the relationship unique in that they worked together in the baiting of their victim but they also shared the meal. They needed to feed so sporadically now that one or two victims per feeding were satisfying enough. Once they left with their intended prey, they left the coast clear for me to work my magic.

The hunting styles between us were different. They were a little subtler, luring their victim into a trap, making promises they would not keep. I, on the other hand, fed my victims' minds with what they wanted to see happen and then quickly sprang into action. I rarely played with my food. I knew of some vampires that dragged their kill on for days. It made it more exciting and satisfying when their victims actually felt something for them.

I FOUND THE bags of clothing on the foot of my bed. Kalia and Aaron had gone into the living room to watch a movie and I told them I wanted to spend some more time in my room organizing my things. I began with the smaller bag of clothing. I picked it up with one hand and flipped it over so the contents spilled out onto the bed. There were some nice things in there. I couldn't imagine why Maia was trying to dispose of them. I immediately started trying things on. I put on a long, black skirt with a slit half way up the back and twirled in front of the full-length mirror. I wasn't one for wearing girlie things. I was usually more comfortable in jeans and a sweater but I had to admit to myself that I looked pretty good.

I tried on everything in the bags, including a couple pairs of pants that were obviously Kalia's, as I was tripping all over them. I couldn't help but wonder what the man from the coffee shop would think of me in this outfit or that. The image of his face kept popping so clearly into my mind. I could hear the soft sound of his voice. Instead of hearing his voice asking for a mocha latte, I could hear him speak my name.

I imagined his eyes looking into mine, his skin against mine, all the while waiting for Ian's warning voice. It didn't come this time. Had I been imagining that? Had I been feeling guilty about something? I couldn't imagine why. Ian walked out on me, without a word, when I needed him most.

The more I thought about the man at the coffee shop, the tenser my body felt. I wondered what harm it could do to find him, talk to him. There had to be some reason why my brain wouldn't let go of him. I could find him. I could find anyone I wanted if I set my mind to it. The only reason I hadn't been able to find Ian, and believe me, I had tried, was he didn't want to be found. He had blocked his thoughts from me. He had taken himself away from me completely. So completely that, until recently, I couldn't even remember how his voice sounded.

As I put my new things away, I thought about what I wanted to do. I would find him, or at least, I would try. What harm could it do? I was a vampire and he was a human. There was nothing in the world that could become of that and I knew it. He had said something about needing directions to the community college. Maybe he was a new student. The winter session would be starting soon. There was no harm in trying. At least, that's what I tried to convince myself…no harm.

⤜ SIX ⤛

"Isn't the winter session starting soon at the community college?" I asked as I sat in the kitchen with Kalia and Aaron. We were at the table sharing the newspaper. I had the leisure section, Kalia had the crossword puzzle (half done within minutes), and Aaron was poring over the police section. He had a pen in his hand and was circling some of the articles. Though I was curious, I decided not to question it.

"I think so," Aaron answered me without taking his eyes from the article he was reading. "Why? Going back to school?"

"I was thinking about it." I turned the page on my section of the paper.

"Have you gone to college before?" Kalia stopped working on her puzzle and looked at me with interest.

"Many times actually. I have a couple bachelor degrees. I was thinking of registering for something not too serious…something just to keep me occupied a couple nights per week."

"They have evening classes. I took a couple business courses there. It's a good school. I can drive you over if you like." Aaron finally stopped reading. His eyes lit up as if I was his child announcing I wanted to go to college after all.

"Thank you anyway but I think that's something I can do by myself. You've done enough for me already." I smiled at him, trying to sound sure of myself. The fact was that I was terrified. What if I didn't find him? What if he had only been there for a meeting or a delivery, something that would take him away as quickly as he had arrived? "I'll go today. I'll talk to someone, get a course catalogue."

"It's supposed to be this gloomy all day so it's perfect. I'll write down directions." Aaron was excited about this possibility. He looked over at Kalia and she got up right away. She went over to a drawer at the desk that held their computer and pulled out a pad of paper. She handed that and a pen to him.

As Aaron wrote, I ran upstairs to change my clothes. I was excited at the possibility of seeing him again. What would I do if I saw him again, if I was standing face to face with him?

Are you crazy? Lost your mind…have you? Have you thought at all about this?

"NO…NO…NO! You aren't real. You don't exist…not real." I spun around the room, my eyes wide. I thought I caught a shadow glide past in the corner of the room, next to the window. It had to be the light through the window…shadows from the rapidly moving clouds through the trees. I was letting my panic take control of my senses. I checked my appearance in the mirror once more and rushed out.

Kalia was just reaching the top of the stairs as I approached. She looked at me with concern in her eyes. "You look like you saw a ghost!"

"Oh…no. I'm okay," I hesitated and then asked. "Did you hear anything…strange?"

"Like what my dear?" She had stopped just below the top step. Even one step down she was taller than me.

"It was nothing. I just thought I heard…nothing." I had forgotten about their rule. Once I was behind my closed bedroom door, any listening came to a screeching halt. They obviously took that very seriously.

"All right. Are you heading out?" She asked with a pile of towels under one arm. She must have been doing laundry.

"Yup. I'm kind of excited about going back to school. I've always enjoyed being a student."

"Maybe you should consider becoming a teacher, if it's the classroom you enjoy." She walked past me and headed toward the bathroom.

"I never thought of that. Maybe someday." I smiled at her and ran down the steps and out the front door, yelling goodbye to Aaron. I didn't stop to hear his response before I was in the car with the engine roaring.

As I drove to the college, I realized I forgot to take Aaron's directions. If I could make it back to the coffee shop, I would be okay. I replayed the man's conversation at the counter back in my head. I heard word for word the directions he was given. I could find it. I could find him.

I found the college with no problem and followed the signs to the administration building. There was plenty of parking but I, nevertheless, chose a parking spot many rows away from the entrance. I enjoyed walking. It was something calming and relaxing and that's what I needed at the moment. The wind had picked up so I had to hold my hair back to keep it out of my eyes. I had decided to wear it down…just in case. I passed only two people on my way in. I smelled them before I saw them and it wasn't a scent that appealed to me. I wanted only one scent: his scent. I listened as I passed. Maybe someone had seen him or knew him. The only thoughts I heard were about being late for something and about the damned wind.

As I walked into the building, I saw the admissions office to the left. I turned the knob and walked in. I looked around, hoping, listening. No one was behind the counter. I could hear a woman's voice in the distance, muffled, talking on the telephone. I took a seat on one of the chairs next to the door and picked up a course catalogue that was lying on the table. I started paging through it.

I was looking for evening courses. I could register for day courses but then I would have to miss classes whenever the sun decided to make an appearance. I could always just invest in more makeup but the evening course idea was the most practical. Let's see…English…European Literature…took that already…no Mathematics…no way. What else was there? Introduction to Anthropology…took that already…hmm…Introduction to Archaeology…maybe. I flipped through a few more pages. There was always the foreign language classes…maybe art history? But Intro to Archaeology? That could be exciting. I turned back to that section. I had all the prerequisites. Please let this be an evening class…yes…that's it. It looked interesting, I had the prerequisites, and it was offered in the evenings; it was a sign. I should go for it.

"May I help you?" The woman had come back to the counter.

"Yes. I would like to register for a class? Am I too late?" I asked as I went to stand in front of her with the catalogue in my hand.

"No, just in time. Let's see…" She took the catalogue as I pointed out the class I wanted. She typed some things on her keyboard and then looked up at me over her glasses. "We are offering this class with two different professors. There is the morning class," she pointed at the first option. "With Professor Miriam Keller and the evening class with Professor Christian Rexer. Which one do you prefer?"

"The evening class please." I said to her, still looking at the name. Christian Rexer…I liked the sound of it.

"Evening it is. That one is two times per week." She started filling out the paperwork.

We began the protocol involved with registration. We filled out paperwork. She made copies of my transcripts then handed me a schedule, materials list, and map of the campus.

"The book store is open until 5 p.m. today." She smiled as she dismissed me. *She sure could use some sun…*

I heard her as I walked out the door. I was on a mission now and that was my only concern. I would be here two times per week. Hopefully I would run into him. I was already thinking of spending time in the cafeteria and the library whenever I could. After all, I was a registered student in the college and that should arouse no suspicion.

After I registered, I headed to the book store to purchase my supplies. I wanted to be ready for my first day of class as soon as possible. I only had one week and didn't want to take any chances.

I drove home thinking of nothing but him. I couldn't get his face out of my head…that enticing smile. I sighed as I thought of it and realized how silly I was acting. I was acting more like a nineteen year old than my true biological age. Oh well, it didn't matter. There was no harm in entertaining my fantasies. That's all they were.

As soon as I drove up to the house I could feel my body tense. I heard nothing from Ian during the drive home but I wondered what would happen once I entered my bedroom. Would he start antagonizing me again over my decision? I hoped not.

When I entered the kitchen, putting my books down on the table, I noticed the note.

Lily,
We went to run some errands. We won't be long. Please make yourself at home.
Kalia and Aaron
P.S. We are having some friends over tonight to meet you. Don't worry. Nothing formal.

They had friends! Their friends wanted to meet me? I wondered if they were human. They couldn't be, I decided. They would have warned me about that. They would have wanted me to be prepared. Now all my excitement about my upcoming classes was drowned by the unknown. I had no idea how this would work. Humans were difficult to be around but vampires were worse. All those talents and powers in one room! Reading each other's minds!

I flew up the stairs. I set my books down on my desk and plopped down on my soft chair. I wanted to think of a reason not to be present when they arrived. It would hurt their feelings and I knew it. They were trying to do something special for me...again. Didn't they know they didn't have to do anything? What they had already done was more than enough. I sat with my head back and my eyes closed, taking deep breaths. Vampires didn't need to breathe as often as humans but it felt cleansing. I didn't really understand what I was so worked up about, besides the fact that I wasn't very good at meeting new people. Whatever Kalia and Aaron were doing would be safe. They struck me as beings that would not take unnecessary risks. They had a family and a life here and they would not do anything to jeopardize that. I needed to relax and appreciate the fact that my new family just wanted to introduce me to the ones they cared about. That was all.

It was after 8 p.m. when the doorbell rang for the first time. I stayed in the kitchen with Aaron while Kalia, straightening her skirt, went to answer the door.

"There's no need to be nervous. Everyone will love you. You'll see. You're very likable." Aaron was standing across the counter, leaning against it with both elbows. He looked into my eyes as he said this and somehow, I believed him. Just listening to him made me feel more relaxed. "Shall we?"

I took his arm and we headed to the living room to meet Kalia and the first of the guests. It was a woman. She was almost as tall as Kalia but she had bright red hair and the greenest eyes I have ever seen. She was talking to Kalia as we approached and she suddenly stopped.

"Well, hello. You're just a tiny little thing, aren't you?" She smiled but her eyes swept over me. I extended my arm, expecting to shake her hand. She made no attempt to take it. Instead, she clasped both her hands behind her back. I looked from Kalia to Aaron. Kalia bit her lip and looked over at Aaron. Aaron nodded so slightly that the woman didn't notice.

She won't shake your hand yet...has to get to know you. She's afraid she'll send electricity through you. We'll explain later...after...

"Kalia my dear, have you forgotten I can hear you?" She said with a smile on her face.

"I'm sorry, Riley. I wasn't thinking," Kalia answered.

Riley looked over at me again and took a deep breath. She stepped closer and took my right hand in both of hers. I felt the hair on my arms stand up. "If I have the go-ahead from you, it's fine." She looked at Kalia.

"Welcome my dear. You must be Lily."

"That's me. Thank you. I appreciate you coming over. It's nice to meet a friend of Aaron and Kalia's." I felt much more relaxed once she dropped my hand.

"Any friend of theirs is a friend of mine."

"Shall we sit?" Aaron motioned to the sofa. Just as he did, the doorbell rang again.

"It's Beth and Pierce. I hear them. They brought you a gift Lily." Kalia went back out to answer the door again. The rest of us remained on our feet waiting.

"How was your trip Riley?" Aaron asked.

"It was a lovely trip…lovely night for a flight. The clouds are so thick no one noticed."

"Riley lives in Alaska. She doesn't get out here much any more. Not since she met Raul anyway." He smiled teasingly at her.

"You took a plane out here just for this?" I was honestly surprised.

"Oh, no. I hate planes. They're too stuffy and the passengers are too noisy."

That only meant one thing. She could fly. I had only met one other vampire with that ability. We had flown together; me in his arms, my head snuggled against his chest. It was a horrifying yet exhilarating experience. The thought of it made my stomach turn into knots. I could remember the feel of his rock-hard chest against my face…the smell of his skin. I shuddered. I had tried so hard to forget all these things about Ian and then lately he had been all around me.

"Hello, hello!" Beth walked in with her arms already outstretched toward Aaron.

"Hi Beth. Hello Pierce. Long time…" He took her in his arms, squeezing her so tightly that had she not been a vampire, she would have been in extreme pain.

"How do we get so busy that we don't see each other? We have to make it a point to change that. We live so close," Pierce said. He looked over at me but did not smile. The smile he had shown to Aaron became a frown as soon as his eyes reached me. He looked at Aaron and raised an eyebrow.

Pierce was a few inches shorter than Aaron. He had very dark hair, almost black, like his eyes. He had a neatly trimmed goatee and wore all black. He looked like one of those bohemian poets reciting poetry aloud in a crowded, smoky coffee shop. Beth, on the other hand, looked like a teenager. She had long blonde hair and her eyes took on a more violet hue. She looked like she was dressed to go out dancing, though I didn't know how someone would dance in stiletto heels that high. Her manner seemed too cheerful for the way Pierce acted.

"Pierce! Don't make Lily uncomfortable." She stepped over and embraced me. It startled me and I stiffened. I had been worried about the way Pierce glared at me.

With that, Pierce's face relaxed and he took a few paces back. He made no attempt to touch me. Riley and the newcomers all greeted each other cheerfully. Pierce didn't take his eyes from me. Once all the hellos were taken care of, everyone made their way to a seat. Aaron took a seat in the arm chair, with Kalia sitting on the arm and leaning into him.

"Pierce, why don't you give Lily what you brought her," Kalia looked at Pierce with encouragement.

"Oh yes, I had almost forgotten." He reached into the pocket of his black leather jacket and pulled out a small black felt box. He got up and walked across the room to stand next to me. Riley leaned closer to me on the couch, curious.

"You really didn't have to do this," I said with the little box in my hand. I hesitated, since all eyes were focused on me.

"It's not much. Please, open it." He went back to the love seat and Beth.

I lifted the lid and saw something round and silver. It looked like a charm. I touched it with the tip of my index finger, feeling the cool metal. I lifted it out of the box. It was a necklace, a rectangular charm with what looked like a lower case letter "n" on it, except that the bottom of the letter was a bit too open. It was attached to a silky black cord.

"Thank you. It's beautiful," I exclaimed still holding it my hand.

"You are always so thoughtful, Pierce," Kalia said smiling at him.

"I know what that is…do you know what that is, Lily?" Riley put her hand out toward the necklace, awaiting permission to hold it.

"Not really." I handed it to her.

"Explain it to her, Pierce. Don't leave her hanging," Beth said taking his hand in hers.

"It's Uruz, the symbol of rebirth and new life. I figured it was fitting considering…" He looked away from me and focused on Beth. "I should have chosen a different one. Next time."

"Oh no…please…I love it. It's quite fitting." Riley put it around my neck. I wanted them to know I appreciated the thought put into it.

"I should have given you one to protect you from…" He looked down at the floor and stopped speaking. Beth looked nervous.

"So Kalia…where's Maia?" She spoke before I had a chance to ask any questions.

"She's visiting some friends in England. She should be home soon," Kalia answered her without taking her eyes off me. She had a worried expression on her face. I wanted to ask her what it was all about but I was sure I would get an opportunity alone with her later.

Conversation filled the room for the next few hours. I learned so much about Kalia and Aaron's friends. Beth was the newest in the group. She had met Pierce at a carnival one evening and it had been love at first sight. I found out that Pierce once had a relationship with Kalia, before she met Aaron. It had been a difficult situation at first but over the years the jealousy had dissipated and the three of them were able to be friends. Aaron and Kalia had met Riley while on their honeymoon in Alaska. They used to make frequent visits to Alaska but that changed once Maia came along. Apparently, Kalia had made Maia an immortal out of her need for a child and Riley wasn't too happy with that.

Aaron told them the story of how I came into their lives. No one was surprised he had expected me to join them. He seemed to have the ability to know a vampire's move before the move was made, though he could not read minds. I didn't understand how that was possible but he said that it was just a feeling he got. He didn't know how to explain it either.

The discussion toward the end of the night turned to my attending college. They asked about the class I planned to take and my past schooling. They seemed genuinely interested in my choice of archeology. Beth had a master's degree in anthropology and Pierce had a doctorate in American literature and a master in journalism. He said he still did some freelance writing for a few newspapers and a magazine. What amazed me the most was that Riley owned a "gentleman's club" in Anchorage, Alaska. She was operating her own business, surrounded by humans. She told me she did have a few immortal employees, one of them being Raul. He was a bouncer. She had been doing this for the past twenty years and had met some very interesting characters. She suggested that I visit her there sometime, said her customers would love me. I laughed nervously at that idea.

All in all the evening was very enjoyable and by the end of it, I felt like I had made some new friends. I was glad I hadn't come up with an excuse to get out of it. The only one that made me feel unsure was Pierce.

He still wouldn't smile at me and looked at me as if he was worried about something. I tried to read his thoughts but was never able to do so. He was excellent at concealing them. It frustrated me that I couldn't just come out and ask him what was bothering him.

By the time everyone left, I was actually feeling kind of tired. I hadn't had that feeling in so long that I wasn't sure what it was at first. But then again, this was the most I had talked in years, before Jack...poor Jack. I felt sadness at the thought of his name. Kalia looked at me with concern. I looked away before she could question me.

As I was getting undressed to lie in bed and read a book, or maybe watch some television, there was a knock at my door.

"May I come in a moment?" Kalia poked her head in.

"Sure, come on in," I said and got under the covers, my knees up and my back against the headboard. I moved over so there was room for her to sit next to me.

"Tonight seemed to have been a hit," she said putting her arm around my knees. It reminded me of when my mother came to my room at night for our usual mother-daughter chats. The memory made me smile.

"Everyone was so nice. Thank you. I really did enjoy it...but," I bit my lower lip. "I couldn't help but notice that something was bothering Pierce."

"I caught that too. He wasn't himself tonight. He's usually a bit more cheerful than that. Not much, he's pretty serious. He has a rare gift." She took her arm from around my legs and turned herself, one leg on the bed, to face me. "He gets...premonitions...for lack of a better word."

"Like...he can see into the future?" I asked, now intrigued and worried at the same time.

"Well...sort of. It's hard to explain. He doesn't get clear images. He can't see clear pictures or anything like that. He seems to think there is some trouble in your future but he's not sure what it is." She watched my hand as I wrapped my fingers around the charm.

"So he thinks something bad is going to happen to me? I didn't hear anything...I tried...to read his mind but I got nothing."

"That's because he wasn't letting you. But no...he told me that on the phone today. I talked to him after you left for the college. He didn't get that premonition until today. He had already gotten you that charm. He thinks you need a protective charm instead. And believe me; he will make sure you have one. Pierce is a very interesting creature. He got the best of both worlds when he was *reborn*. He is not only a vampire but he is also a witch. He is extremely talented. I could tell you stories."

"Why don't you? I'd love to hear them," I said hoping.

"Maybe another time. We'll have plenty of time. Right now, Aaron is waiting for me." She smiled widely when she said this. If a vampire could blush, now would have been the time.

"Okay. Another time," I said, a little disappointed. "Good night."

⌁ SEVEN ⌁

I grabbed my books and stuffed them into my backpack, yelled good-bye to Kalia and Aaron, and ran out the door. I was anxious to get to class and wanted to be there early. I wanted a chance to walk around the campus. I needed to look for him. Traffic was light so I made it to the campus in no time, parked the car, and headed toward the library. Many people rushed by carrying books. I didn't bother to listen to anyone this time; I was sure I would get nothing I needed.

The library was larger than I expected and it smelled like old books, a smell I loved. Of course, the smell of blood was also strong, but I wasn't thirsty so I paid no attention to it. I was focusing on one smell, one scent in particular. It wasn't in the library. Disappointed, I looked around just in case I had somehow missed it. I saw a few people sitting at a table in the corner, with a pile of open books in front of them. I heard a heartbeat behind the case to my right but it was just a woman with a cart full of books, placing them back on the shelves.

Next, I tried the cafeteria. There were more people. Heartbeats came from all directions. I had just made it past the area where they kept the stacks of trays when I stopped dead in my tracks. I heard it: his heartbeat. It was a rhythm I hadn't forgotten. I sniffed the air. The sweetness filled my nostrils. I closed my eyes and inhaled deeper, taking it in. I was afraid to open my eyes, afraid that I was mistaken.

Why is she just standing there? Something wrong with her?

I opened my eyes and saw that a pimple-faced teen was standing behind me, afraid to walk around.

"Sorry about that," I said and moved to the side so he could pass. I hadn't realized I was blocking the entrance. I was so lost in the smell and the sound of him. He had to be here.

I looked around the room. There he was. Sitting in the corner, alone. He had a cup of coffee in front of him and he was reading something. I couldn't breathe. I couldn't walk. I needed to get something – anything – so I could go to a table. I looked at the cooler next to me and grabbed the first thing my hand touched: a Diet Coke. I paid for it and walked to the table behind him.

He looked up as I passed. I stopped breathing again. The hand that was holding the soda was shaking. He looked down at his pile of papers for an instant and then raised his head again. His eyes met mine. He looked like he wanted to speak but didn't. He just stared and I couldn't do anything. I couldn't make myself look away. I couldn't even remember how to walk.

"Don't I know you?" he asked. His sweet voice made my whole body shake or at least it felt that way.

"Um...I don't think so." Oh God. I sounded like an idiot. My voice was almost a whisper. Did he even hear me?

"I'm sorry. You look somehow familiar," he said and smiled that beautiful, breathtaking smile.

"It's okay. It happens," I said it without whispering this time. I went to sit behind him.

I could've sworn...where? I couldn't forget that face...those eyes...where?

I couldn't believe it. He remembered me. I felt so good about that realization that I couldn't stop smiling.

"Excuse me..." He was leaning out of his seat, toward me. "Weren't you at Café Java recently?"

He remembered! It wasn't just me that had been impacted by that. Maybe he was just good with faces. I tried to tell myself that it didn't mean anything.

"Oh...yeah. That's right. That's where I've seen you. I thought you looked familiar too." Okay. So now he knew I remembered him too. That was stupid of me.

"It would've driven me crazy all day if I couldn't think of it." He laughed, looking relieved. He was so close to me that I could see the blood moving through the veins in his neck. His scent was maddening. His eyes were mesmerizing. He never took them from mine as he spoke.

"I have that problem too." I swallowed hard. I could almost taste him; his scent was so strong and sweet.

"Well, I'd love to stay and chat but I'm afraid I have a class. Maybe we'll run into each other again." He gathered his papers, grabbed his coffee, and stood. As he moved I could hear the rhythm of his heart speeding. I could hear when he swallowed. I wanted to stay here all night…all night just looking at this perfect man. But I had a class too.

"Yup…me too. It was nice seeing you again," I gave him a reluctant wave as he started to walk away.

When he reached the entrance to the cafeteria, he looked back over his shoulder. He turned for a moment and smiled, one eye squinted slightly more than the other. *Wish I had time…wish I could ask her name…something…stupid move, walking away without even a name…*

He was gone. I couldn't hear his heart anymore. I had found him and I had let him get away. I had allowed him to just walk out because I was too chicken to do anything. I realized I actually felt sad now. I felt an emptiness that didn't make sense. I didn't even know him. I looked at my watch and noticed the time, in horror. I would be late if I didn't leave. I had to walk at a human's pace so I wouldn't attract attention. I shoved the bottle of soda into my backpack and headed out the door.

The science building wasn't far from the cafeteria. There were still students lingering outside the classroom. No one seemed to be in a hurry. Inside the room, people were looking for seats. Everyone seemed to be moving in slow motion. I wanted to just get this over with so that I could go back outside, hoping to see him again. This was going to be torture! Okay. Calm down. After all, this had been my idea and I was paying for this class so I might as well enjoy it.

I walked up the steps on the left, as the room was set up more like a stadium, and found a seat toward the top. There were many empty seats up there and I was able to avoid sitting close to anyone. The beating hearts in this room were easy to ignore after having dealt with his heart in the cafeteria. I had managed to do okay with that. These were just ordinary, dull hearts in comparison.

I looked around the room and noticed everyone had laptops open (I still preferred paper), when it suddenly grew quiet. I heard muscles tensing as everyone sat up straight. I looked up too, though I didn't need to. I heard him before I saw him, smelled the sweetness fill the air. He was here…in the same room again. I couldn't breathe. Good thing I didn't need to.

"Good evening and welcome. I am Professor Rexer, Christian Rexer. You may call me Christian. I'm not much for formalities." There was that smile again.

He walked over to the desk in the front of the room and set his papers down, along with his briefcase and coffee. He was going to be my professor! I couldn't believe my luck. I had registered for this class hoping to run into him sometime, somewhere on this campus and now this. What were the odds?

He'll have my attention all semester…that's for sure… The girl in front of me was staring at him, her head in her hands.

Smug son of a bitch…who does he think he is? The guy next to her wasn't very happy with the way she was staring at him.

"I have a syllabus for you. It explains the class objectives. It lists all the work, research and tests, everything we will be covering. I've also put my office hours and my office number on it, along with my cell number. As you can see, my office hours are limited and I don't always remember to check my voice mail, so if you really need me, the cell number is best." With that said he walked over to the first student in the front row and handed her the pile. She took one and passed the rest over. He started talking again before the papers had made it all around the room, his eyes scanning the room as he spoke.

"As you all know, this is an introductory course. Everything that is expected of you is in the packet. Please take a few minutes to look it over and hold your questions until everyone has a packet." He was looking around the room again, like he was counting…maybe.

I wonder where she is…maybe after class…

Was that about me? It couldn't be. He had to be thinking about someone else. It hadn't even dawned on me that he might be married. He might have some gorgeous, lucky woman waiting for him somewhere. That thought made me feel sad. He started digging through his briefcase. Once he found what he was looking for, his eyes scanned the room again. He looked at every face in every row, briefly. I held my breath again.

His eyes started at the other end of the top row. Still, I held my breath. Finally, he got to me. His face lit up…or was I imagining that? No. He smiled. His eye squinted a little again. I felt butterflies in my stomach. I didn't think that was possible since I became a vampire. I was wrong. I heard his heart go from normal to racing. He smiled and nodded. *You're here…really here…oh God…help me through this semester…wow…look at her…what is it about her?*

The rest of the class was pretty normal for a first class. We discussed the syllabus further. He answered questions that were posed to him. We learned that his father and grandfather had both been archaeologists and he had traveled with them, therefore, falling in love with it. He had been a history major with a minor in archaeology. He explained to us how the two went hand in hand. By the end of the class, we had begun the first chapter and he assigned the rest of it for homework. There was a summary essay due by the next class. Pretty basic stuff. Most of the time he spoke in the front of the class, his eyes were on me. I also kept my eyes on him, memorizing every detail. I wanted to remember the way his eyes had little crease lines in the outer corners whenever he spoke about something that he felt passionate about. He told us about some excavations that he, with his father and grandfather, had participated in on some of the Civil War battle fields in the U.S. His heart rate sped considerably whenever he spoke about anything to do with American history. History was his first passion.

Minutes before the class ended, he decided to take attendance. He had tried to count us before the start of the class but even I could see he hadn't finished. He started calling out names. As he said a name, the student raised his or her hand. I waited patiently for him to get to mine. As he was doing this alphabetically, I knew I would be toward the end. He had a bit of difficulty with some of the longer names in the class, as some students were of foreign descent. I could hear the expectancy in his voice whenever he called out a female's name. Finally, he called "Lily Townsend."

I raised my arm in the air and again my voice came out in a whisper. "Right here, sir." Sir? I called him sir! Oh what an idiot. He had asked us to call him Christian. I didn't need to call him anything. All I had to do was say "here" and leave it at that. Maybe he didn't hear me. I knew that wasn't true by his smile.

Would she do it? How do I ask? She'll think I'm crazy…should wait…a little longer…but I desperately want to…

He stopped and continued with his list. Only one student had been missing from the first class. Surprising. Most figured nothing important happened on the first class so why bother, right? I stared at him, very obviously, since he was now sitting at his desk neatly placing all his piles of papers into his open briefcase. Other students started packing up their things. He was done for the evening. He wanted to ask something…of me…possibly. I had no idea what it was. He was no longer thinking, just moving automatically. I listened as hard as I could to see if I could hear anything at all. But nothing else happened except that he thought he should set a syllabus aside for the student that hadn't been present.

People started to get up from their seats. "Professor, are we done for now?" I heard a male voice ask.

"Oh...sorry. Yes. We are done for tonight. See you all Friday," he said looking up from his briefcase.

People started to walk down the steps and shuffle out of the room. There was a lot of chatter on the way out. I kept hearing *He's too young to be a professor...must have graduated early...he is cute!*

I took my time putting my things away, wanting to be the last one out of the room. It was very difficult to move at the pace in which I was moving. I had to control every movement. Even when I was human I hadn't been this slow! I looked down and saw he was still at his desk, saying goodbye to students as they walked past. He looked toward me for a moment and went back to the other students. *Good...she's still here...can't do it...it's crazy...wrong...she's a student...how young could she be? Looks very young...I shouldn't but I want to...*

What could he want? He never finished that thought! How frustrating! It couldn't be that bad, could it? I waited a minute longer as two students were just making their way to the door after stopping at his desk to ask something. Finally, I left my seat and started at a snail's pace down the steps. They were wide stairs, like the kind in a movie theater with stadium seating. I had to take two steps on each stair at the human pace and it felt awkward.

When I reached the bottom, I turned my head to look at him. I raised my hand to wave goodbye, like most students had done, when he looked at me and his mouth opened a little, like he was going to say something.

No! Keep moving...out the door...keep going...don't be a fool!

What? Why would he...? It wasn't him. It was Ian again and he was really getting on my nerves. *Stop it! Now! You have no right...no right at all!*

"Um...Miss Townsend?" He said my name almost in a whisper.

I stepped closer to his desk and noticed he had underlined my name on his attendance sheet. None of the other names were underlined. I was hopeful then, sure that he wanted to remember mine.

"Yes?" Was all I could manage to say. I could see pink suddenly showing up on his face and neck. His aroma was intoxicating. I inhaled as deeply as I could without looking obvious.

"I was wondering if we could have a cup of coffee...maybe...tomorrow. I have something to do tonight but tomorrow?" He looked down at his desk, afraid to meet the shocked expression I no doubt had on my face.

"Um…" Was it supposed to be cloudy tomorrow? Did I know this? I couldn't remember…why couldn't I remember? I always checked the weather. "Sure…I don't see why not. Where?" I swallowed hard, still trying to remember the weather forecast.

"Café Java?" He looked up at me.

"Okay. When?" Please don't say in the morning…or afternoon for that matter…please.

"Two o'clock okay?" He smiled his squinty-eyed smile, the one that took my breath away since the first time I laid eyes on him. It wasn't long ago and yet it seemed like an eternity.

"Um…okay," I said trying to smile back. I was still trying to remember what the weather was supposed to be tomorrow. I could always do the makeup thing but I didn't want to take chances, not with him.

"I'll see you there. You have my cell number if there's a problem. Please feel free to use it…*any time,*" he picked up his briefcase and stood…all six feet of him. Absolutely perfect!

"Okay. I'll see you," I said and walked out the door without looking back. I just about skipped down the hall with excitement. I wanted to get out of there before one of us changed our minds. And I knew I should change my mind. I should turn around and walk back in there and tell him that I couldn't but I kept walking to my car without once looking back. I didn't want to change my mind but most of all; I didn't want Christian to change his. Christian. I said it aloud. I loved the sound of it.

You are making a big mistake…huge! You are going to regret this little stunt!

Shut up, Ian! You have no say in what I do! You are dead to me! Do you hear me? Dead!

I got into my car, threw my bag onto the passenger seat, and slammed the door shut. I wanted to shut him out. I was surprised the door didn't fall off from the force of my hand. I shouldn't take it out on my poor little car. I knew, of course, that shutting the door didn't shut Ian's voice out. I would be stuck with that for who knows how long. I needed to talk to Kalia and find out how to shut someone out of my mind. I never learned how, but then again there was a lot I didn't learn.

The rest of the ride home was quiet. Ian stayed out of my head. Maybe I scared him. Doubtful. I knew it would take a lot more than my yelling at him. He was never afraid of my temper. Ian was never afraid of anything. Me on the other hand…that's another story.

Driving home in silence was nice. I pictured his face constantly and replayed his words in my head. He was interested. He had to be, right? It wouldn't have been so hard for him to ask if he wasn't thinking about me as more than just another student. Okay. So if he was interested in me, what then? What could I possibly do it about it? Nothing. Absolutely nothing! He was human and I was not. The two did not mix. Not in the real world anyway. Maybe they mixed in books – or that movie – but not in the real world. I tried not to think of that as I neared the driveway. I needed to clear my mind of any thoughts of him before I entered the house. I wasn't prepared to answer questions just yet.

"OH, IT'S YOU," a voice I didn't recognize came from the living room. "I heard you in the car…something about answers?"

"I…um…was thinking about my class," I set my bag down by the bottom of the staircase and turned toward the living room. Maia was back. She stood in the doorway leaning against one side. She was breathtaking. She wasn't much taller than me and she also had long black hair. It was cut to frame her delicate face. Her face was small but her golden eyes were not. It's the first thing I noticed when I looked at her. The rest of her facial features were tiny in contrast. There was a sparkling coming from the side of her face and when she turned to the side I could see a tiny diamond stud on the side of her nose. Her small, yet shapely, lips were done in a dark wine-colored lipstick, very glossy and shiny.

"So I hear you started school. Don't know why…what good does it do you? Can't work anywhere…" She had an all-knowing look on her delicate face, her lips pursed.

"It's interesting. It gives me something to do besides sit around the house all day," I tried to smile at her. She was determined not to smile back.

"There's plenty to do. I do whatever I want whenever I want. I go all over the world. I have a lot of friends." She said this as if it was a contest. "Isn't that my skirt?"

I forgot I'd chosen the long black skirt for my first class. I wanted to look my best in case I ran into him. Little had I known…

"I guess so…Kalia gave it to me. She gave me a bunch of stuff she said you didn't want anymore." I felt like I was on guard, defending myself. For what?

"Well…it looks good on you. It was too big on me." She looked me up

71

and down. As if she was any thinner than me…please.

"You're both home!" Aaron called happily and walked out of his office, shutting the door as he left. "So nice to have you both here finally." He went over to embrace Maia, kissing the top of her head. She looked like a child standing next to him. How old was she? She couldn't be any older than what? Twenty at the most?

"I had an awesome trip! And guess what? I met somebody!" Maia never gave him a chance to guess. She still had her arms wrapped around him. She was looking up at him like he was some kind of god.

Aaron looked over at me before he spoke. He had a look on his face that showed he was apologizing for not having a chance to hug me too. "And who is this somebody?" He smiled at Maia again.

"Oh no. It's not that easy. I'm not telling everything. Not in front of…" She looked over at me and then back at Aaron. "Anyway, let's just say I met him in England. We spent most of my time there together but then he had to leave, said he had something important to do. I could tell he really didn't want to leave me. He said he'd come see me."

"Oh, I see. So does this somebody have a name?" Aaron teased. She still held on to him.

"I'm not telling. You'll meet him soon enough." She finally dropped her arms and stepped back into the living room. "I have gifts for you and Kalia. Come see. Where's Kalia?" She was already in the living room where her luggage was scattered about, some of it open.

"She went shopping for her girls," Aaron gave me a quick hug before entering the room behind Maia. "I want to hear all about your first day then Lily."

"That can wait. Can't it? I've missed you so much!" Maia said with a huge smile on her face just for him.

Oh please! I thought. She glared at me knowing Aaron hadn't been watching. He was busy closing the curtains. Oops. I forgot for an instant that she could hear me.

"I'll be upstairs. I have homework," I announced as I picked up my bag and headed upstairs. All the happiness and excitement I felt during my ride home was fading. It was obvious Maia didn't want me here. She didn't want Aaron's attention being taken away from her for a moment. *Spoiled little brat!* I froze at the top of the stairs and listened. I had done it again but she wasn't paying attention to anything but Aaron right now. That was a plus.

I walked into my room and shut the door. I went to my sitting room and threw my bag onto the overstuffed chair. Then I went over to the bed and threw myself onto it. Wow! What a day! Everything I had been dreaming about lately came true. He was not only there, at the college, but he was going to be my professor for the whole semester and he had asked me out! I sighed and propped myself up on my elbows. He was perfect, wasn't he? His voice. His face. The way he moved. His mind. Everything! I felt more *alive* at that moment than I had even when I was mortal. The only thing that was bothering me in the glow of that happiness was Maia…and of course, Ian. Ian wasn't a problem…not really. He was just in my head. But Maia! That was another issue. She didn't like me. I could tell from the moment she spoke. I could hear the disappointment in her voice when she said "Oh…it's you." I mocked her voice. I didn't care if she heard me. If she was listening she was breaking the rules. What was her problem?

Maia was not going to ruin my mood. I refused to entertain thoughts of her any further and forced my mind to go back to Christian…not that it was difficult. I couldn't help but think of him all the time. He was on my mind constantly when I was in my room, alone with my thoughts. What would it be like to sit across a table from him? To have his full attention? To look into those gorgeous blue eyes while his voice filled my ears? I rolled over onto my stomach and closed my eyes, wishing I could sleep to make the time go faster. I wanted it to be two in the afternoon on Thursday now. It was going to be torture to have to wait so long.

My eyes were still closed and I could smell him in my mind, inhaling his wonderful scent, when I realized I needed to check the weather forecast. I jumped from the bed and ran to turn on my computer. I carried it back to the bed with me. I waited impatiently while the computer went through its start-up routine. Come on! As soon as I saw that it was ready, I typed in the address for the weather channel and waited for it to connect. I went to Thursday's weather. Oh no! Why? To my horror tomorrow was supposed to be *partly* cloudy! I felt anger welling up inside me. I was angry at God. I was angry at Mother Nature or whoever was responsible for this.

I closed the computer and put it aside. I lay on my back and closed my eyes. There had to be something I could do. I knew there was no way I could change the weather but there had to be something…there was always makeup. But I wanted him to see me exactly as he saw me the last two times. I never quite felt like myself with stuff smeared all over my skin. I could call him. I could come up with an excuse, something I had forgotten about, and see if we could meet later. But what if he had other plans? What if he couldn't do it and I missed my only opportunity because of the stupid sun? It was worth a try.

I pulled the syllabus out of my bag and looked at the clock. Was it too late to call him? It wasn't after nine yet. I found his cell number and picked up the phone on my nightstand. I took a deep breath and dialed. It rang. One…two…three times. I was ready to disconnect, not wanting to leave a message, when I heard a melodic "Hello?"

"Um…hi. Christian?" I whispered again. Why couldn't I get my voice right?

"Yes?"

I felt a pang of pain at his question. He didn't know who I was. Oh… wait. This was the first time he was hearing my voice on the telephone.

"It's Lily. I'm sorry to bother you but…I have something to do tomorrow afternoon that I had forgotten about. I won't be able to meet you at two." I swallowed hard, holding my breath.

"Oh…it's okay. Maybe…" He sounded disappointed. That was encouraging.

"Are you busy later? Maybe around seven?" I crossed my fingers and waited. I could hear his breath coming faster. It sounded even more arousing over the telephone.

"No. Seven sounds good…but…" He hesitated. I held my breath. "That's more like dinner time. We could meet someplace else. What do you like?"

"Oh…I eat just about anything. You pick?" I asked. I couldn't wipe the smile off my face now.

"Do you like Japanese?"

I had Japanese once. A business man I had run into in New York. He had done some unspeakable things to women back in Japan…but that's not what he meant. "Sure. Sounds good."

"Lily…" he whispered.

"Yeah?" I asked, a little afraid he had changed his mind.

"Is this wrong?" He asked sounding sad.

"You have no idea. I'll see you tomorrow. Bye, Christian." I hung up before he could have a chance to question my answer. We made arrangements to meet at a restaurant downtown. He suggested picking me up at the house but I refused. I did not want to answer any questions yet.

FOOL!

Oh, shut up!

I had no patience for Ian right now. I was too happy. Besides, there was a knock at my door.

"Come in!" I yelled. I was hoping it was Maia; hoping I had misjudged how she felt about me. But it was Kalia that walked into my room with her usual big, warm smile. She was loaded with packages. "What's all this?"

"Please don't get mad at me. I just had to!" She said happily as she set everything down on the bed. She had been busy today. She had shopped for sheets, toiletries, even school supplies. She showed me everything with so much excitement that I couldn't help but feel excited. Her enthusiasm was contagious! The largest bag she saved for last.

"I noticed you don't have a printer. As a student, you will need one. I'm sure Aaron wouldn't mind sharing his but this way you don't have to wait. You'll have so many papers to do." She pulled it out of the bag. "How was your first day?"

"It was…fine. The usual first day type of thing. You know…" I couldn't help but smile as I said this. I hope she didn't notice I was hiding something. I was trying not to picture his face.

"Good. I'm so happy for you. Maia's home now and I have my two girls…together," She hugged me, squeezing me to her for a brief moment. "You and Maia will be friends in no time, trust me."

"I hope so," I said. Obviously Maia had said something to show her disapproval. "It would be nice."

"I know Maia is…a bit difficult. Give her time. She'll warm up to the idea of having a sister. You'll see." She squeezed again and stroked my hair.

So she really felt like a mother to the two of us. I took advantage of the moment to ask her what I had been curious about since I saw Maia. "Um…Kalia?"

"Yes, dear?" She pulled away to look at my eyes.

"How old is Maia?" I asked.

"She's eighteen. Just turned eighteen the day before…you know…" She stopped.

I nodded letting her know I knew what she meant. "I didn't get a chance to ask her."

She looked at me with concern in her eyes. "Everything will work out, you'll see. I promise and I never break my promises…well…almost never." She got up and walked toward the door. "Are you staying in here again all night?"

"For a while. I have some homework. I'd like to get it done right away. That's how I am," I smiled to reassure her nothing was wrong. "I'll be down later."

"Okay. I'm sure Maia has stories to tell. She always does." She left the room and shut the door behind her. Shortly after, I heard footsteps coming up…two sets of footsteps. I listened and waited. No one came to the door. It must have been Maia and Aaron taking her things to her room. I heard her door open and shut and then one set of footsteps descending the stairs.

I took everything Kalia had brought me and put it away. I set the printer on my desk, not bothering to take it out of the box just yet. That could wait. I went back to the bed and flopped myself on it again. I closed my eyes. I wanted to think of only him right now. Nothing else mattered.

I pictured his face, his eyes looking into mine. I pictured his lips…what they would feel like…hot…moist. I imagined his hand touching mine, the heat of his skin burning me. His hand would slowly go up my arm to my neck. His hand on the back of my neck…so hot…pulling my head back. His lips parted, his breath warm, touching my neck. I shuddered all over just imagining his lips touching my cold, pale skin. I sighed. I felt an ache in a place where I hadn't felt anything for so long. His lips moved up my neck, his breath coming faster and faster…hotter and hotter. His lips parting again, slowly moving up my face to my waiting lips…so hot…so moist. The image sent shivers through my body. My breath coming faster and faster until I felt that I couldn't keep up with it. I would suffocate. I couldn't stand it. I opened my eyes and jumped up, startled. What was wrong with me? My God!

I flew out of bed and out the door to the bathroom. I started the shower without even thinking about it, my breath at a pant now. I needed to calm down, relax my muscles under the warmth of the water. I checked the temperature and then undressed, letting my clothes drop where I stood. I stepped into the water and put my head under the stream. How was it possible? He was awakening things in me I didn't think existed anymore. No one had that kind of impact on me…not since…

The running water was soothing. I didn't bother to shampoo my hair or soap my body. I was afraid to even touch my own body at the moment, afraid those same feelings would come rushing back. Once I started to feel more relaxed, I turned off the water, wrung out my hair, and stepped out. In my rush to get in the shower, I had forgotten to grab a towel out of the closet. Could I make it to the door without dripping all over the floor? I started to reach my arm out toward the closet door when I heard a noise. The doorknob turned and the door flew open.

"Oops…sorry. I forgot someone else was up here. Not used to sharing the shower," Maia said with her eyes wide as she looked me up and down.

I wrapped my arms around me the best I could. "I understand. I forgot to put a towel on the rack by the tub." I looked at her expectantly, as she was standing in front of the closet door.

"Here. Let me." She opened the closet door and reached for a towel. I couldn't believe she was doing something to help me.

Absolutely…wow…try to get that image out of my head…

"Here," She handed me a towel. "I'll come back later."

Was she thinking about me? Nah! Couldn't be. She had to know I could hear her. Was that admiration I detected in her thoughts? Again, I shook my head as I dried my arms and legs and then wrapped the towel around my body. I picked up my clothes from the floor, turned off the light, and walked out the door. I went to my room as quickly as I could, not wanting anyone else to see me like this. I needed to go to the store and get a bath robe. I lived alone for so long that I didn't have use for one. I was able to walk around my apartment stark naked if I wanted. Not that I really did that, but I could have.

I decided to get dressed and join everyone downstairs. I threw on sweat pants and a sweat shirt, some socks, and then toweled my hair dry. After I combed it out, I pictured his face one more time, knowing I had to be careful downstairs. I saw all of him instead, standing in front of the class as he had tonight. I sighed. What felt like a shiver ran through me. I hurried out of the room, afraid Ian would start harassing me.

As I walked down the stairs, I heard laughter coming from the living room.

"Oh, hi Lily!" Kalia exclaimed, her face lighting up. "Come join us… sit." She motioned for me to sit on the floor, the way they were, around the coffee table. They had a board game spread out on the table in front of them. I didn't know human families that still played board games together and here were these vampires, gathered around the coffee table, looking all cozy.

Maia huffed a bit but moved over to make room for me. She was sitting with her back against the sofa. Aaron was at the head of the table and Kalia was across from Maia and me. There was a chest full of what looked like more board games at the other end of the coffee table. I would rather have sat there.

"Thank you, Maia," I said sitting next to her, my legs crossed under the table. "What are we playing?" I didn't recognize the game board.

"Oh, it's new. This is the first time we're playing. Someone will have to read directions. Volunteers?" Aaron looked at both me and Maia. Maia didn't move.

"I'll do it," I offered and heard another little huff out of Maia.

"Oh, and, no mind reading!" Aaron added.

SURE ENOUGH, AS promised, the next day dawned bright and sunny. As I was sitting at my desk near daybreak, I watched the clouds slowly scatter. By the time it was about eight in the morning, I had to close the blinds so the sun didn't burn my eyes. We had stayed downstairs all night, playing game after game. All the time Maia bragged about her trip to Europe. She excitedly talked about the *wonderful man* she met, all the while being careful not to let his name slip. She refused to answer any questions about him that Kalia or Aaron tried to ask. The only one she did answer was that yes, he was a vampire. She made sure we all knew she would pay no attention to a human. Humans were so dull and weak, according to her.

Close to 6 a.m., I excused myself to go to my room, saying I had school work to finish, which was true. I just didn't want to listen to anymore. She talked so much she was making my head spin! Shortly after I went upstairs, I heard the front door open and close. I looked out the window and saw Kalia and Maia walking down the driveway, both wearing sunglasses. Maia had said she had so much energy that she needed to run. Aaron suggested I accompany them but I declined once I caught a glimpse of the look on Maia's face. It was clear this was a ritual she had with Kalia and she didn't want me interfering. They ran together sometimes and if the situation was right, they hunted together. I was better off in my room where I could think about Christian – my Christian – without being bothered.

I tried to concentrate on the chapter I was reading, using the highlighter that Kalia had given me, but it was no use. I put that aside and went to the bookshelf, looking for anything I hadn't already read. Nothing looked interesting. I decided to go to the closet to try on some outfits to see what looked good. I tried different shirts with different pants, shoes, skirts, all of it. I couldn't decide on anything and now I had a mess to clean up. If it hadn't been so sunny, I would have gone out shopping. I heard

Kalia and Maia return shortly before the time people started leaving their houses, on their way to school or work. They came in laughing and then I heard Maia across the hall, closing her bedroom door.

All was quiet downstairs. I figured that Kalia would be painting, probably in the kitchen, and Aaron was most likely in his office. I went back to putting away the clothing I had scattered about. I looked at a red pair of pants I hadn't even tried yet. I had just tossed them on the bed, thinking they were too bright of a color for me. Hmm. Maybe I should try them.

I slid my sweats off again and pulled the pants on. I buttoned and zipped them and then walked over to the mirror. They felt good. I looked at my image. They looked good. But the color…I wasn't sure about the color. Too bright? I couldn't decide. At least these weren't Maia's. She didn't seem at all happy about the fact that Kalia had offered her discarded clothing to me. No…these were mine. I bought them a long time ago, on a whim. I thought the color would be good with my pale skin but then I had been unsure and never bothered to put them on. Maybe with my black sweater. I took that out of the drawer and put it on. I went to the mirror again. I turned, backed up, and tried to see myself from all angles. Yeah. That worked.

Do you have any idea how ridiculous you are being? Leading that man on…can't do anything but kill him in the end…

And there it was! It had been too quiet and I knew it wouldn't last. Where was he? Could he be close enough to be sending his thoughts to me whenever he wanted? I shuddered at that thought. I wasn't afraid of much in this world but seeing him again? That was scary!

I tried to ignore him by acting as if I had heard nothing. I didn't want to give him the pleasure of knowing he was bothering me. Not today…I was too happy. I wanted to find something to do to occupy my time until I could leave the house. Maybe I would do what I was supposed to do for my class. After all, it was *his* class and I planned to give it all I had.

I decided to take my book and my notebook down to the kitchen. If in fact Kalia was painting in there, I doubted she would mind my company. Vampires did tend to get lonely on sunny days. We had to stay indoors and make the best of it. I ran down the stairs and past Aaron's office as I headed into the kitchen. I could hear him speaking French as I passed. Wow!

Kalia was standing at the back door, her hair up in a ponytail, working on the painting she hadn't finished the other day.

"Hey, Lily!" She said with a smile.

"Hi. Do you mind if I work down here?" I asked standing next to the table, not wanting to sit until I had her approval.

"Of course not! Don't be silly. I'd love the company. Aaron is working and I think Maia went out again." She was looking through her brushes for a different one.

"Maia is out? On a day like today?" I was shocked. I figured that she was up in her room.

Kalia laughed and nodded. "Nothing stops Maia from doing what she wants. She just wears a lot of makeup…more than usual, anyway."

"I do that sometimes but only when I have to. I don't like the stuff." I pulled out a chair and set my things down.

"And you don't need it. You are absolutely stunning without that junk on your face," She found the brush she wanted and was busy mixing colors on her palette. "Did Aaron tell you we have a cabin?"

I thought about it for a minute before I answered, trying to recall. "No, I don't think anyone mentioned it."

"We go up there several times a year. It's deep in the mountains, in the center of the state, no one in sight for miles. We can be out in the sun all we want. You're welcome to use it anytime. It's yours now too…remember that." She was still working on her colors.

"How do you feed when you go out there?" I was curious about this. I would love to take her up on her offer sometime. I did love nature and sometimes I also missed the sun.

"We usually hunt whatever is around at the time, black tailed deer, mule deer, elk, sometimes even raccoons. I honestly don't like those much but they'll do. We went up there and stayed for two months once, when Maia first came." She gave me a knowing look.

I knew she meant it was when Maia was first made. Fledglings, or *new* vampires, can sometimes be pretty wild. They have to be taught things, just like any child. "I do know what you mean. That was a good idea, to keep her away. Is she any better now?"

"Oh much better. Better than she was anyway. Maia is still a bit… *wild*…but I have a feeling that is not something we'll be able to change, no matter how much training we give her, I'm afraid." She started painting again so I decided it was a good time for me to start reading.

With Kalia painting and me at the table, silent, I finished the chapter and wrote out an outline for my summary. The rest I would finish later… after. I was too anxious.

"By the way, Kalia, I'm going out later. I shouldn't be too late," I started to gather my things again.

"Oh? Anything you want to talk about?" She looked at me so warmly that I felt bad. I had been prepared to lie. I had been prepared to tell her that I had some things I needed to research at the library but I couldn't lie to her.

"I'm not sure what it is yet but I don't think I'm ready to talk about it… if that's okay?" I looked at her and smiled as warmly as I could manage. Warmth wasn't something that came comfortably.

"Of course it's okay. I just want you to know that I am here any time. Same with Aaron, okay?" She had her hand on my shoulder and was waiting for a reply.

"Thank you Kalia. I will remember that, I promise." I said it but I knew there were some things I could not tell her. I couldn't tell her about Ian McGuinness and what my short experience with him had been like…how he had made me and then left me to fend for myself…alone and uneducated. How many times had I wished I still had a mother to talk to? Now I had one, in Kalia, but I was clamming up as usual. There wasn't anything to talk about yet though. It was my crazy obsession with a human. For all I knew, he just wanted to talk or ask me to assist in class…or something.

"Would you like me to water the plants for you?" I asked not only to keep myself distracted but also because I noticed she stopped painting and was about to fill her watering can.

"No thanks. I love doing it. I talk to them when I give them water. It keeps them healthy. Talking is a good thing…you know." She had one eyebrow up and looked at my eyes.

I had been thinking about Christian in front of her! I had to learn this blocking thing and learn it soon. "It's nothing."

I was halfway out of the room when I heard her whisper "Christian… huh…" I couldn't believe I had been so careless. I didn't want anyone to know anything yet because it was very possible it was nothing. But then why was *nothing* making me feel like this?

Standing in front of the mirror, I adjusted anything that needed adjusting and made sure every hair on my head was in place. I decided to wear it up, in a slightly messy bun, with tendrils hanging down around my face. I looked at the clock and moaned. It was only a little after five. I couldn't stand two more hours! The sun wasn't even down yet. Damn the sun!

You are going to regret this…big time, my love.

I spun around the room, almost losing my balance. He wasn't here. But where was he? He had to be close to be talking to me like that. I couldn't stand it anymore. If I left now, I would just have to wait in my car or find someplace where I could wait indoors. I was halfway down the stairs when I remembered we were going out for dinner. My purse...I forgot my purse. I ran back up the steps. I was in such a hurry to grab what I needed and run back down the stairs that I threw my bedroom door open and left it open. I went straight into the closet and pulled it off the shelf. I opened it to make sure it didn't still smell like pizza...well...maybe just a little but not too noticeable.

I heard the stairs creaking in the hall.

You want to keep him safe, don't you? Then don't do this! I'm warning you!

"Lily, is there someone here?" Kalia was at my door, peering in, a basket of clean clothes in her arms.

"No...just talking to myself...I guess," I was still frozen in the same spot, sunglasses in my hand.

"I could've sworn it was a man's voice...okay then. Do you have anything that needs to be washed?" She looked around my room, confused.

"No thanks. I was just about to leave," I said as I gained my composure and closed the closet door.

"What? No makeup?" She looked surprised.

"I'll be indoors til sundown, don't worry," I tried to give her a look like a teenage girl would do. She smiled so I guessed it worked.

"Have fun then. You have a cell phone. Use it if you need it," she was headed into Maia's room as I flew down the stairs.

Ian was making threats and Kalia heard something! What a relief. I wasn't crazy after all. I laughed as I got into the car and drove down the driveway.

ᴇ Eight ᴇ

The restaurant parking lot was crowded so I parked on the street. The windows on my car were tinted so I felt safe sitting here. I had decided that since I had been lucky enough to find a parking spot right in front of the building, I would wait here until Christian arrived. I really didn't want to walk in first.

I was listening to a CD, trying to keep my mind occupied, when something hit me like a bomb. Boom! My happiness faded…just like that. So what if I wasn't crazy? So what if Kalia had heard Ian's voice too? He was making threats against Christian. My hands balled up into fists and a growl escaped from my throat. How dare he? How dare he come waltzing back into my life and take control? What game was he playing? I was digging my nails into my palms again and I didn't care. Ian didn't want me, and hadn't for many years, but if he didn't want me, no one else could want me either? "YOU SON OF A BITCH!" I screamed. I slammed my fists into my legs. I felt no pain, just pure anger.

A couple walking past, arm in arm, obviously heard me because they jumped away from the car and picked up the pace. I needed to calm down before Christian arrived. I wasn't going to ruin this or let him see me like this. He would be scared enough later, when he would start to wonder what I was. I would worry about Ian later. He obviously didn't feel like talking now…did he?

I listened to the CD and tried to let myself get lost in the music. I tried to relax as best I could, under the circumstances. The sun was fading and the clouds were getting thicker. *Soon,* I thought. *Very soon now.* I rested my head against the seat and cleared my mind. Suddenly the hair on my arms stood on end. I heard it: the beautiful rhythm of his heart. I couldn't smell him because the windows were closed but I remembered his scent as if he was in the car with me.

He stood by the door of the restaurant with a single white lily in his hand and looked around nervously. He was a little early and I couldn't get out of the car yet. I was afraid to take a chance. The sun seemed to be setting but it was hard to tell from where I was. It could be all the buildings creating shadows. I looked at him and sighed. I could barely breathe. I wanted to jump out of the car and into his arms. But I couldn't...not yet. I had to give it another minute just to be sure. I relaxed a bit as I watched him walk into the building, forgetting for a moment that he couldn't see me.

I looked out through the windshield. Close enough. I took a few deep breaths, grabbed my purse, and jumped out the door.

"Good evening miss. Table for one?" A slender Japanese woman greeted me at the door with a menu in her hand.

"Um...no...I'm meeting someone," I looked around for him. I could hear his heart but couldn't see him.

"Gentleman over there waving?" She pointed with her menu.

"Yes, thank you. That's him," I said still looking at him. He had taken a table in the corner, half hidden by one of those ornate screens.

I followed the hostess, trying not to run her over in my haste to get to him. He stood as we approached. He smiled his beautiful smile, the one that took my breath away.

"Thank you," I whispered to her as she handed me the menu. I practically stumbled into my seat because I couldn't take my eyes off him and he smelled absolutely delicious.

"This is for you. I hope you don't think it's cheesy." He handed me the lily.

"Oh no...it's lovely," I said and inhaled the flower's aroma.

"Not as lovely as you are." He looked away when he said that, as if he was embarrassed.

"Thank you," I whispered again. Why couldn't I get my voice to come out when I was around this man? I knew he had chosen a lily because of my name but it was far from cheesy. I didn't think this mortal man was capable of cheesy. I was intrigued by him and all he had to do was sit there and look at me.

"Thank you for agreeing to meet me. I hope I didn't take you away from anyone..." He was trying to find out if there was someone else but was afraid to come right out and ask. That little shyness made me smile.

"No. But you did take me away from my summary," I joked with him. Something was definitely going on with me. I had surrounded myself with humans and vampires lately. I was focusing more on my appearance. I was joking. So many years of trying to stay away from the world and it had all changed in a matter of weeks.

"Oh don't worry. You have a very easygoing professor. I know him." He smiled so warmly that I felt more relaxed.

He ordered for both us, since I told him I had never been to a Japanese restaurant before. I liked that he took a chance. If he only knew what kind of chance he was actually taking. At that moment though, he didn't seem to suspect anything and I was more than willing to cherish our time together as long as possible.

We talked easily for what seemed like hours. I learned he had never been married; he had come close, but it didn't happen. He described the relationship with a hint of bitterness in his voice. Apparently, she had wanted monogamy but only from him. She had wanted her freedom to do as she pleased. He said it wasn't for him. He wanted to give his heart to one woman and one woman only and wanted those feelings to be reciprocated.

He asked if I had ever been married and I told him I had never been asked – not yet anyway – that I was only nineteen years old.

"You don't act nineteen. There seems to be wisdom in those dark eyes of yours; wisdom that belongs to someone much older." He had his hand on the table, his napkin balled up in a tight grip.

"I think I was born in the wrong century or something…I don't know. I'm not as wise as you may think." I stared at his eyes as I spoke and didn't look away. It felt comfortable, as if we had done this many times before.

He told me about his education, how he started out college studying English and then changed his mind junior year. History had always been his passion. As he spoke, he relaxed his grip on the napkin. His hand started to slide closer to mine. I was sure he was doing it on purpose but he didn't seem to skip a beat as he spoke. His voice and the sound of his heart and breath were so soothing. As his hand moved closer, my brain screamed at me. *What are you doing? Don't let him touch you! Never touch you!* Yet, I couldn't will my muscles to move. I saw it coming and yet…I froze. His fingertips touched the side of my open hands. I looked at his face. His eyes were wide, questioning. I yanked my hand away. I couldn't breathe. I had to search his thoughts.

Okay…calm down…it's okay…breathe…breathe…

"Well…let's get out of here. Shall we? It's a nice night. I thought maybe we could take a walk by the ocean?" He pulled out my chair.

I couldn't believe it. What was that? What was he thinking? I never expected that reaction. I had never gotten that reaction from anyone. I wanted to ask him but I couldn't. I couldn't let him know I was listening to his mind. He didn't seem afraid but nervous about something else. As far as I saw, he didn't seem to notice how much food was left on my plate. I had, as usual, taken the opportunity to dispose of food in my purse when he excused himself to go to the restroom. Then, of course, I had excused myself to go to the ladies' room and disposed of my meal in the toilet.

As we walked, I could hear his soft, yet rapid, breath on the back of my neck. It was warm and the scent so sweet. When we reached the door, he held it open as I passed. His hand touched the arch of my lower back. It was a polite touch but still, it sent an electric shock through me.

"Why don't we put your lily in the car?" He asked, pausing and facing in the direction of his vehicle.

"Sure. If it's not out of the way," I whispered again. I needed to concentrate on my voice with him. He would feel like he was going deaf trying to hear me if I didn't calm down. I didn't remember ever having this problem in the past, not even with Ian.

"Not at all. It's just over there." He pointed across the street, not far from where I had parked.

We walked to the car in silence. He glanced at me from time to time, like he wanted to say something but was unsure. I tried to behave myself and stay out of his thoughts. I was letting him surprise me every time he opened his mouth. It wasn't much fun when you knew what people were going to say before they actually said it. We reached the car, a black SUV of some sort. When he opened the passenger door, to set the flower on the seat, I noticed the back seat was full of books. It looked like he had a mobile library in there! A laugh escaped my lips.

"What's so funny?" He locked the door as he gave me a sideways glance.

"Read a lot?" I asked.

"Every possible moment. Most of those are books I bought recently at used-book sales. I haven't gotten around to unloading them yet. I haven't quite finished setting up my apartment. I know I need more bookshelves." He started walking down the sidewalk, away from the car. I followed, enjoying the sound of his voice.

"So you just moved?" I asked, wanting to not only learn more about him, but to lose myself in the sound of his voice.

"I came here about a month ago. I found a place to rent and then went right back to Pennsylvania. I had to get things settled there before making the actual move. It took a little longer than I expected." He was walking a little slower…a little closer. Our arms were almost touching. I had to keep reminding myself to breathe; not that it did any harm if I didn't but it could be noticeable. "I hope you're up for a little climbing."

"What do you mean?" I asked, looking around.

"Just downhill a little. We can get to the water that way." He pointed down the street where there seemed to be no more buildings. "It might be a little hard to see but I'll help you."

"Sure, I'm game," I assured him. I knew I would have no problem. I could see in the dark as clear as if it were sunny. It was him I was worried about but I didn't let on. I trusted him to know where he was going. I did listen to his mind after he suggested it and I gathered that he had been down that path once before, memorizing its terrain.

He led the way, stepping into the clearing first, and we started walking downhill. He extended his hand out behind him, to help me down, but I made no attempt to take it. Instead, I kept my head down, as if I didn't see his hand at all. Suddenly, I felt his whole body against mine. I was so busy watching the ground that I didn't see him stumble slightly and stop to catch his footing. The sand and stones were loose. I froze, feeling the heat against my body. I inhaled and held my breath, his scent was so overpowering. My throat tightened. He stayed totally still. He wasn't breathing. I heard only his heart beating.

"I'm sorry…I…must have stepped on something…" he was whispering now.

"It's okay. It's very rocky." I jumped back as soon as my muscles responded to the commands from my brain. "We're almost there."

He started walking again, finally exhaling. I could still feel the warmth of his body, the infernal heat. What was I doing? How could I have agreed to be alone with him in the dark, not a soul in sight? No one to hear his scream. Could I control myself? I should have fed again before seeing him. I really hadn't thought of his scent as food in the past…but now…mixed with the smell of the water…the night…

We reached the bottom of the hill. I could hear the water's soothing sound. The rocks protruding from the ground, in and out of the water, looked eerie in the darkness. The wind blew unfastened strands of my hair and his sweet aroma into my face. I felt my mouth water. I could feel the sharpness of my teeth against my tongue. This wasn't good at all. I needed a distraction…now.

"Have you been down here before?" I asked, following his lead and sitting on the sand, cross-legged a few feet away from him.

"Once, when I was here in the summer. I just had to see where the trail led so I followed it. Isn't it nice down here? It's a little different during the day, of course. I was wondering something…" He hesitated a moment. I turned toward him. "Is there some unwritten rule or something that women can't eat in front of a man?"

His smile was so childlike that I couldn't help but laugh. I wondered if he could see my face the way I could see his, in the darkness. "Not that I know of. I said I eat just about anything. I just didn't say how much." It was true. I never said that.

"You are so very right." He was still looking at the side of my face. I was trying to keep my eyes straight ahead. I could see distant lights, very faint and small. I heard him move and I turned to look at him. He was raising himself up on his hands as if he were going to stand but instead, he moved closer to me, the side of his body touching mine. My breath caught in my throat. My head was spinning. I tried desperately not to invade his mind. How soon before he ran? How soon before he realized there was something not right?

I continued to stare straight ahead, only listening to the speed of his heartbeat. The heat of his body was burning through me. I was breathing faster and faster. I needed to say something! I *had* to say something!

"Christian…" I whispered, my voice so hushed I wasn't even sure he even heard me. "I…"

"I'm sorry. Am I making you uncomfortable?" His face was turned toward me now and I could feel his breath on the side of my face…so hot.

"Um…no…I don't know…I…" What was I even going to say? I couldn't think.

"Lily?" His voice was so hushed, so sexy. As if he could get any sexier.

"Yeah?" I asked though I was afraid to hear anything.

"I haven't been able to stop thinking about you since the day I saw you, when I was lost. Your face has been popping into my head ever since. I don't know…maybe it's just me…crazy…but I thought I saw something in your eyes that day." He seemed so much closer now though he hadn't moved.

"I know. I saw something too. I thought about you, every day, but…"
What was I saying? I had started to play this game, knowing it couldn't go
anywhere. Now what? How could I walk away?

I felt him move. His body pushed against me slightly, hotter. His hand
searched in the dark for mine. I wanted this. I wanted him to touch me.
I had to be crazy. He would be disgusted as soon as he felt my skin, yet I
couldn't stop him. I moved my arm closer, making it easier for him to find
what he was seeking. I felt the heat of his skin before he touched me. He
let out a long-held breath as soon as his hand made contact with mine. I
held my breath, waiting for the inevitable reaction.

"You're cold…here…let me," he whispered, taking both my hands in
his. He cupped both of them in his and brought them to his face. He
pulled them closer to his mouth and exhaled warmth on them, all the
while rubbing my skin with his. It was maddening! The heat of his skin,
his breath, the smell, the spinning of my head, all of it!

I pulled my hands away from his and, without giving it a second
thought, I turned my body toward him, grabbed the back of his neck, and
pulled him to me; so hard, in fact, that I was afraid I hurt him. I heard his
shock as he gasped. The heat beneath my lips was like a flame. The taste,
the moisture…very hot. As soon as his arms went around the middle of
my back, I panicked, came back to reality…for a moment. I tried to pull
away, not hard, but he held me to him. His mouth locked on mine. I felt
the sharpness of my teeth brush his bottom lip and I fought hard not
to clamp down to taste him. He kissed me with so much force that we
tumbled sideways, onto the sand. I could feel his weight on me, so hot
and wonderful. *You'll be sorry. You'll be responsible for his death…I warned
you Lily!*

I pushed with as much strength as I could. He rolled a few feet away
like a rag doll. I sat totally still, trying to gain my composure, trying to get
my head to stop spinning. I had to concentrate on calming myself. I knew
I should make sure he was okay but I was afraid to move yet. I was afraid
to look in his direction. What I was most afraid of was that I may see Ian
standing there, ready to make true on his threat. I kept my head down and
looked at the sand surrounding my legs.

"Lily, I'm sorry…please…" He was apologizing to me! I was the one
that had grabbed him, kissed him, and then practically threw him across
the beach.

"Christian, I'm sorry. I am so sorry for all of this." I wanted to make him believe me. I knew this was the last time I would ever see him. I wanted him to truly believe me before he died, and I knew he would. What else could Ian mean? He wanted Christian dead and it was because of me. I couldn't stop Ian from killing. I had never been able to do that.

Christian knelt next to me now, looking down at the darkness. I ached to wrap my arms around him, to say goodbye as quickly as I had said hello. I didn't know what to say to him, how to make it okay. He continued to stay next to me, though I could feel him shaking. I could hear his heart drumming in my ears.

"Lily?" He sounded so unsure of himself.

"What?" My voice shook as it came out in its usual whisper.

"I'm sorry I got carried away. It's just…I want you. I have since the moment I laid eyes on you and I'm not ashamed to admit it. There. I said it." He plopped himself back down on the sand.

I couldn't help but laugh. At a moment like this I couldn't believe I was laughing.

"How could you? What are you thinking?" I was looking at his face, at his eyes that looked so hurt.

"What do you mean?" He asked.

"Didn't you notice…something? Anything?" I asked in disbelief again.

"I don't know. Maybe. All I know is how I feel. I felt like I was hit by a wrecking ball the first time I saw you and I can't forget it. I was going to try to find you somehow but then you…" he was staring ahead again.

I looked at his perfect profile. His lips were in a pout. I just wanted to kiss him again and make him smile but I didn't dare. Not again.

"I need time to think. It's been so long since…" I couldn't think of how to explain anything to him. I did know I didn't want to make it final by telling him I wanted nothing at all, though I knew that was exactly what I should have done.

He turned his face, forcing a smile. There was a glimmer in his eye as he reached up to touch my face. His heat made me feel like I was going to jump out of my skin. I wanted to feel his lips again. "I will be patient. I promise."

"Thank you…" I started to tell him that I was glad he understood until I felt his lips brush mine, gently. My breath came fast again. I wanted this man with every fiber of my being. I wanted all of him: mind, body, and soul though I didn't know why.

"I need to go home…now please." I was already standing and walking backward away from him. I had to be away from him before it was too late...before...

We walked back toward the car in silence. I didn't speak but his mind did. I had given myself permission to listen, considering the fact that he had not once reacted to my skin the way I had expected.

I love the way she smells...her hair...her breath...so cold...so pale...so... doesn't matter...does it?

I kept a safe distance, trying not to look at him. I walked slowly though because I didn't want my time with him to end. He looked over at me from time to time, but remained silent. He gave me space.

How can I make her understand...I could love her...all of her...so fast... I don't even know her but I need her...she needs me too...I can feel that somehow...

That last thought made my head jerk toward him. He looked at me, startled. What did he mean by I need him too? What did he know? He couldn't have meant anything by it. He couldn't possibly know. I didn't need anybody at all, especially not a human, so much weaker and fragile. He wanted to take care of me...was that it? That was so far from reality. I was going to have to take care of him, protect him from Ian.

"Lily?" He looked at my eyes as he spoke. I had to look away or I would melt. I paused as we arrived at my car. "I will give you all the time you want. I promise to act normal in class tomorrow. Again, I'm sorry."

"I'll see you tomorrow," I nodded, as I got into my car. I opened and closed the door so fast that I was sure he had seen how quickly I moved, but I didn't care. I did care though, that in my haste to get away, I had forgotten my lily.

∽ NINE ∽

I spent every moment I could in my room, hoping Ian would start making his threats again. I hated that he had access to my mind. I had no idea where he could be though I felt he was close and it terrified me. I was scared for myself but most of all for Christian.

"Ian? Are you here?" I asked aloud. It was worth a try. "Answer me! I know you can hear me! Damn it!" I waited. The only noise I heard was out in the hall, as Maia's door opened and closed. To my shock, I heard a knock at the door.

"Come in!" I yelled. Maia was in the room before I actually saw her move.

"Maia…what's up?" I asked expectantly.

"Are you going to be home tonight?" She asked snidely, looking around the room. I realized she had not been in this room since I'd moved in. "You don't have much, do you?"

I ignored her second question, thinking it was none of her business.

"I'll be home after my class. Why?" Why would she be asking me that? She had made no attempt to talk to me let alone spend time with me.

"I have company coming tonight. Don't you have anything to do?" Her voice was mocking.

"Not really. Does it matter?"

"I guess not. Do I have a choice? You do live here now. It's just that I wanted everything to be perfect but…" She glared at me.

"I'll stay out of your way. Who's coming?" I couldn't help but be a little curious.

"It's really no concern of yours…is it? Kalia and Aaron know. They're the only ones that matter." With that said, she spun and exited.

She tried my patience. She was infuriating! Had I not gotten so close to Kalia in the last few days, I would have packed up my things and left. Christian would be safe if I left. Aaron would probably be hurt, though I didn't get to know him quite as well as Kalia. He was a little distant in comparison.

I looked at the clock on my nightstand with shock so I shoved my things in my backpack, grabbed the finished summary, and ran out the door.

The entire way to the campus my stomach felt as if it was in knots. I would see him soon – very soon – and I didn't know how I would react. I'd spent most of the night thinking about him. I could still feel the heat of his lips, the warmth of his body; picture his face, his eyes pleading with me for forgiveness for something he hadn't even done. I was the one that grabbed him and kissed him and then threw him off me like a used napkin. Yet, he had apologized to me! I wanted to apologize to him, say, "I'm sorry. I didn't mean to push you away. Let's forget about that part, start over from the kiss." I wanted that badly but I knew I couldn't. It could kill him.

Even though I was afraid to face him, I ran to class. Drawing attention to myself by walking in late was the last thing I wanted. As I approached the room, his sweet aroma filled my nostrils. He was leaning against the wall, outside the classroom, talking to the pimple-faced boy I had seen in the cafeteria. Christian stopped mid-sentence and looked my way. A smile lit up his eyes. As quickly as the smile appeared, it disappeared and his eyes filled with confusion. I heard his heartbeat increase. I nodded as I walked through the doorway and sprinted up the stairs to my seat.

As soon as he walked into the room, his eyes went to the back row at the top of the room. He was looking for me. He paused a moment, no expression on his face this time, and went to his desk. Most of the class went smoothly. Every once in a while, I could see him looking at me. I tried to avoid his eyes, looking away before he could see. I was listening to his thoughts more and more, wanting to know when he was going to look so that I could turn away. I couldn't bear looking at his eyes. They showed the pain I had caused by acting so impulsively.

Instead of lingering to be the last one out of the room at the end of class, I rushed to be the first one out. As I headed to my car, across the dark parking lot, I heard rapid breathing behind me and the sound of feet pounding the pavement. I fumbled with my keys and dropped them. As I bent down to pick them up, my backpack fell off my shoulder. I picked that up too, giving him enough time to catch up.

Christian bent over, hands on his knees, trying to catch his breath. I didn't think it was possible for a heart to beat that fast and not explode. "My…God…you…walk…fast!"

"Sorry. I didn't know you were there. Why didn't you call out?" I asked, concerned about the way he was breathing.

"Would…you…have stopped? Honestly?" He asked, his heartbeat slowing a bit.

"Probably not," I lied. He asked for honesty but I couldn't give him that. I *would* have stopped. I would have run to him if he had called my name. I couldn't resist the sound of his voice and I knew it. There was immediate hurt in his eyes.

"Fair enough. I did ask for honesty. I have a favor to ask…just this once."

"Okay, ask," I said sharply. Too sharply by the shocked look in his beautiful blue eyes.

"Can we at least talk? Nothing else. I promise." His eyes looked hurt but pleading.

"Um…I don't know. When?" I wanted to say yes immediately just to be by his side.

"I was thinking now. We could go for a ride." His eyes searched mine.

"I guess we could for a little while," I said. Maia didn't want me around tonight anyway. I didn't want to be alone with him but I didn't want to go home either. His face lit up.

"Thank you. Let's take my car. Want to put your bag in yours?" He asked finally smiling.

I unlocked the car door and threw my bag in. I couldn't believe he had been running after me in the parking lot! Had anyone seen him? Any of the other students? He didn't seem to care. We walked to another parking lot behind the library in silence. He opened the door for me when we reached the car. His proximity as he held the door brought all the feelings from the night before rushing back like a tidal wave. I felt my legs weaken as I stepped in. He closed the door and walked around to the other side and got in. I could hear his heart beating so rhythmically, so intoxicating…like a melody being played by the finest of musicians.

We headed out of the campus and onto the road in silence.

*She's here…really here…how do I start? Does she hate me…like me…I don't know…*I wanted to tell him I did not hate him, that it was the furthest from the truth but I kept my mouth shut and listened. *Love at first* *sight, huh…could it be? How do I keep her? Maybe…I don't know…*It was frustrating. His thoughts were incomplete, jumbled. I wanted so badly to tell him I didn't hate him. Why couldn't he just ask?

He drove on a dark road along the coastline. I watched his hands on the steering wheel, watched the concentration on his face as he focused on the curves in the road, and I found him even more attractive. As if that were possible! His brow crinkled as he drove. I looked ahead but didn't recognize anything. I hadn't been on this road before. I wondered where we were going, why he wasn't saying anything yet. He had wanted to talk, right?

On the left side, I saw buildings start to appear. We passed three of them before he turned left. I looked at the building. It looked like a house.

"I know I said we would go for a drive but it's hard to drive on these roads and have any kind of conversation," he explained as he pulled into a parking spot.

"Where are we?" I asked looking around. I heard him inhale deeply before he spoke.

"This is where I live. We'll stay out here, in the car. I live upstairs." He pointed to the second floor. It looked like it had been a house at one time but it had been split into apartments.

"Looks nice," I said, my eyes still focusing on where he pointed.

"Lily, I need to ask you something. It's serious." He turned his body so he could face me. I could smell his sweetness every time he moved.

Oh my God. Here we go…he knows something. I held my breath, waiting, looking at him.

"Um…" he inhaled deeply again, "are you afraid of me or something?" He looked into my eyes when he said this.

Or something was more like it. I was afraid; not of him but for him. How could I possibly tell him that? "No, it's not you. I'm just afraid to get hurt again," I said. It was true, in a way. I had been hurt before and it had been very bad. That was a reason he could understand. "I just don't want to go through anything like that again."

"Do you want to talk about it?" He said softly, worry in his eyes.

"No!" I snapped much too harshly. He jumped, felt the sting of my words.

"I'm sorry. It's just that…well…" His breathing was getting faster again. "I would never hurt you. I promise. I know you've probably heard that before but I mean it."

"Why? What makes me so special? Why do you want me?" I asked, honestly wanting to hear the answer.

He thought for a moment. "I don't know how to explain it exactly. There's just something different about you. Something I've never seen before…anywhere. I can't explain it."

I sure could, explain it, that is. I was sure he had never seen anyone like me before. I doubted that he got involved with vampires. I sat still and said nothing, couldn't think of anything to say.

"I feel like I knew you before…like in another life, maybe. I know it sounds crazy." He was leaning the side of his head against the head rest, his eyes on me. He looked so peaceful at that moment, with the street light shining on the side of his face, like an angel. He looked into my eyes again and as usual, I felt the butterflies. "What color are your eyes, anyway?"

"Dark brown." I opened my eyes wider as I said this.

"They look more like black to me. I've never seen eyes as dark as yours before or skin as white…like porcelain." His breathing continued to speed, keeping pace with his heart. His head was still on the head rest, eyes still on mine.

"I have my father's eyes. His were very dark, especially in the winter," I explained. Of course, I made up the winter part.

"His eyes *were* dark? I don't…"

"My parents died in a car accident many years ago. It's okay," I lied again.

"I'm sorry. Can I ask you something else?" He looked away, as if unsure of himself.

"Sure, go ahead." I tried to sound as calm as I could.

"Do you share my feelings?" He was looking right into my eyes. Obviously he had gotten his confidence back.

I took a deep breath. I listened to the sound of his heart, trying to relax before I blurted something out. "I…I do. I'm just confused, scared. I don't want to feel that pain again. I'm so used to being alone."

"As long as you feel something there's hope for me." His smile lit up his whole face. "Can I kiss you?"

I couldn't believe he asked! I hadn't been at all prepared for that. He sure had gotten his confidence back!

"Yes! I want that…" I blurted it out before I could think about it, already leaning closer. I inhaled his sweet scent, his breath, the smell of his clothing, his hair, everything. He shifted himself a bit so he could get closer to me without hurting his ribs on the steering wheel. His breath was hot on my face as his lips neared, his eyes locked on mine before they closed and our lips finally touched. It was a soft kiss, lips parted slightly, very gentle. It wasn't the desperate hungry kiss from the night before. It was a bit more guarded yet I could feel the emotion in it. My cold hand reached for his. He jumped but didn't pull back. I traced the top of his hand with my index finger and felt him shudder. Still, he made no attempt to stop. Finally, I backed away. As I moved, I paused to inhale the breath from his still-parted lips. I wanted to hold it inside me for the rest of the night, to have a part of him with me.

He moved back toward the steering wheel, gripping it with both hands. He looked straight ahead, toward the wall of the building. He was still breathing very rapidly. *Wow…that's just incredible! So cold…icy…incredible…how does she do that?* I sat very still listening to the rhythm of his heart, waiting for it to slow back down to normal. He looked over at me with so much emotion in his eyes that I felt like I was going to melt.

"I don't want to be away from you. But I need you to be patient with me, please," I said. I couldn't stop myself.

"I'm glad you don't want to be away from me. I understand though. I will prove to you that you can trust me. Oh, by the way," he said, reaching into the back seat, heat radiating from his stomach, his chest, and every part of him that was close enough to touch. "You forgot your lily."

"I did. Thank you," I said as I took the flower from him. He got back to his seat and started the engine. He must have been getting cold because he was adjusting the heat. Or maybe he thought I was cold.

"By the way," I said. "I don't even know how old you are."

"No idea?" He looked at me as I shook my head. "Guess."

That was so not fair but I did it anyway. "Twenty-six," I said.

"How did you know?"

"I don't know…wild guess?" I laughed and shrugged my shoulders, innocently.

"Do you think I'm too old for you, honestly?"

"Not at all. Age doesn't matter to me." I laughed under my breath. If he only knew!

We rode home happily chatting. I felt happier than I had in a very long time. I knew I would regret this but I would wait until later for that. I wanted to relish the moment, the mood. We agreed to see each other tomorrow afternoon, Saturday. It was supposed to rain so he was taking me to an indoor antique market he thought I would like. I did like antiques, but not for the same reasons he did.

He gave me a quick, sweet kiss goodbye as he pulled into the spot next to my car. I drove home feeling nothing but happiness, at least that's all I would allow myself to feel. As I pulled into the driveway and up to the front of the house, though, I couldn't breathe. It felt like there was a weight pinning my body to the seat, heaviness so great that it was suffocating. I couldn't move. I looked at the house with horror, a growl emerging from my throat. The house looked like it always did: lights on, inviting, beautiful, but something was wrong. I wanted to turn the car around and get as far away as I could. I listened carefully.

Maia tells me you travel around the world often? It was Aaron's voice. Silence again.

That's fascinating! That was definitely Kalia's warm voice. Silence again.

Tell them about Africa. They'll love that story. Maia's excited voice said. Again, silence.

Someone was in there but I couldn't hear! I couldn't hear anything they said! Who was it? I was suddenly shaking, afraid to move. I knew something horrible was going to happen when I walked through that door. I just didn't know what.

Once I finally got the muscles in my body to let go of the fear that kept me paralyzed, glued to the seat, I left the safety of the car and inched my way to the door. I turned the knob, as Kalia and Aaron didn't believe in locking themselves in. Someone had to be stupid to attempt to rob this house, with four vampires inside. I walked through the doorway and all went silent. I heard movement coming from the living room but the conversation stopped. I waited, afraid to go any further.

"Lily? Is that you?" Kalia called from the living room.

"It's me." My voice cracked as I answered.

"Come on in here dear. There's someone we'd like you to meet."

I walked, calculating every step. I realized I wasn't breathing as I moved, that I still felt the heaviness I had felt in the car. When I finally reached the doorway, I kept my eyes on the floor…scared for what reason? I didn't know.

There was a familiar but unpleasant scent in the room. It was a scent that brought all sorts of emotions rushing back, like a flood gate was opened. My body stiffened and I bared my teeth. I didn't even need to look around the room to know Ian was standing there. I could feel him.

I could feel him in every muscle, every pore. I raised my head to look at him. I didn't know what to expect. It had been so many years since I had last laid eyes on him. The year 1940 if I wasn't mistaken.

He stood in front of me, tall and gorgeous. His violet eyes fixed on my face with a sly smile on his lips. His hand, with those long cold fingers, extended toward me. His hair was still long, past his shoulders. Maia stood glued to his side, her arm clamped tightly around his free arm, glaring at me.

"It's nice to meet you, Lily," his husky voice said. He gripped my hand so tightly that I felt like I would fall to my knees.

"Um...you too..." I saw all eyes on the two of us. Kalia and Aaron smiled. Maia glared. They had no idea! He told them nothing! He stood here and pretended to meet me for the first time. What kind of game was this? I had to follow along with it. What choice did I have? Worry Kalia and Aaron? Not acceptable. I would not involve them in whatever it was that Ian was doing.

"So, you're the famous Lily Maia's told me so much about? How's your archaeology class going?" As soon as he let go of my hand I grabbed it and rubbed it. I couldn't bring myself to inflict that pain back...not in front of them. Obviously they didn't know and I planned to keep it that way. It was safer that way.

"I like it. Thanks," I answered, looking at Kalia as I spoke. So, Maia talked about me? That was curious. I felt his eyes burning into my skull as I continued to look at Kalia for strength, I think.

Aaron was the first to make a sound. He cleared his throat, obviously noticing the situation was becoming uncomfortable. "Shall we sit?"

"Yes. We should all talk together. I would like that. You, Maia?" He said never once taking his eyes off me.

Suddenly, I felt sick. I felt pain in the middle of my abdomen. It shot through me like a bullet. I grabbed my stomach and my body bent forward. How could I be feeling pain? There was nothing alive in my body... was there?

"Maia!" Kalia rushed to my side, stroking my back. "Stop it now!"

Maia stomped away and threw herself on the sofa, extending her arms to invite Ian. The pain slowly subsided as Kalia rubbed my back. Aaron was standing in the same spot he had been since I entered the room. He was leaning against the fireplace, one arm on the mantel, face furious, eyes darker than I had ever seen them aimed at Maia. Why all the anger at Maia?

"Are you okay? Is there anything I can do?" Ian asked his voice as sweet as pie. I wanted to yell at him, scream at him, that he had done more than enough but I could barely get out enough voice to whisper.

"Be all right…no help…going upstairs," I started to turn toward the stairs but Aaron was at my side in an instant. He swept me up in his arms as if I weighed nothing and carried me toward the stairs.

"Good night, sis," Maia called from the living room. I wished I had had something to throw at her at that moment. As if Ian's being here wasn't bad enough. I had to deal with her too.

"Good night, Lily. Hope to see you again soon," Ian's voice rang as we reached the middle of the staircase.

Aaron's eyes were so soft on my face. I saw real concern when he looked into my eyes. I laid my head on his chest as he carried me into my room. I wanted to cry at that moment, cry like I had never cried before, to just let it all pour out on this man's shoulder but I did not have the ability to shed a single tear. It infuriated me not to have that release. Instead, I clung to him. I wanted to whisper to him, ask him to help me. I said nothing.

He walked across the room toward my bed and gently laid me on top of the covers. He went to the bottom of the bed and started removing my shoes. It shocked me at first and I almost pulled away until I realized: he was being a father. He was treating me the way a father might treat a sick child. I was overwhelmed with love for Aaron at that moment. He set my shoes at the foot of the bed and came around to my side.

"Do you want to be under the covers?" He asked bending down, ready to pull the covers over me if I wanted.

"No. I'm okay like this." I smiled at him, trying to reassure him.

"How are you feeling?" He nodded toward my stomach.

"It's almost gone. I don't know what happened…"

"I do but don't worry. You'll be fine. Never again…" He bent down toward my face, his lips reaching my forehead. They lingered there a moment and then he pulled his face away. "You're safe here. It'll be fine. I promise."

I reached for his neck and pulled him toward me, sitting up just enough to hug him tightly. "Thank you Aaron. I mean it."

He smiled before he left the room. I had not expected such fatherly tenderness from Aaron. He spent so much time working that I hadn't had the chance to get to know him. I was gushing with love for my new father when…Ian was downstairs. Here! In this house! In my life!

I rolled over onto my side, feeling just a hint of pain in my stomach. As I concentrated, I heard laughter once in a while and the creaking of old floorboards. I could hear the minds of the immortals in the house but never Ian's.

Of all the men for Maia to bring home! Why did it have to be *him*? It had been almost sixty years since I last set eyes on Ian. Why did it have to be now? Now that Christian was in my life and I wanted to keep him there. Had Ian come here to stop me? Was he that intent on ruining me and everyone I loved? I lay on my side, curled up into a ball, wishing again that I could sleep. I looked at the clock on my nightstand. It was just after ten. When would he leave? I couldn't relax until he was out of the house. As I lay thinking, I heard a low humming sound coming from the floor by my bed. I leaned over the edge of the bed and looked around. My backpack was lying on the floor, next to my nightstand. Cell phone. I jumped out of bed so fast I almost stumbled, ignoring the pain.

"Hello?" I said, not looking at the caller ID in my rush to answer before it went to voicemail.

I heard a loud sigh on the other end. "Lily? Hi. Did I wake you?" It was Christian's sweet voice.

"Not at all…still up," I said sounding as surprised as I felt. "What's up?"

"I just wanted to hear your voice one more time before I go to sleep. I hope you don't mind." He said it so softly that even with my sensitive hearing I had to focus.

"I'm glad you called. I wanted to hear you too, before I go to sleep." The lie was only in the part about sleeping.

"I can't wait to see you tomorrow. It can't come soon enough."

"I feel the same." I meant what I said but I also wanted to take it back. I knew the danger I was putting him in.

"By the way, I don't know where to pick you up," he said.

"No!" I snapped, fear welling up inside me. "I can drive. I remember where you live. I'll be more than happy to pick you up." I could absolutely not allow him to come here with Ian so close. There was always the possibility he would be here tomorrow afternoon and I was not willing to take that chance.

"Well, okay, if you feel that strongly about it. I'll be looking for you around one-thirty. If you want, you can just call from the car and I'll come down…unless…you want to see where I live…" He sounded very unsure.

"That's okay. I'll come up and get you. I'll see you tomorrow. Good night," I said not really wanting to get off the phone but I knew I needed to pay attention to what was happening downstairs.

"Good night. And Lily…" He hesitated.

"Yeah?" I asked curiously.

"Nothing. Never mind. See you tomorrow. Sweet dreams." I heard the click as he disconnected.

I let out the breath I realized, again, I had been holding. He had called me just to hear my voice! I didn't think anyone would ever feel like that about me again. Even in the past, it hadn't been quite like that. My relationship with Ian had been…I don't know…different.

I listened again to see if anything had changed. I heard footsteps on the stairs and then the sounds of Kalia and Aaron's voices as they entered their bedroom. I listened harder but heard nothing else from the first floor. I was very uncomfortable knowing Ian was still in the house, especially since Kalia and Aaron knew nothing. He had made sure they knew nothing of his threats. He wanted me to be on my own with this one…defenseless and alone. Little he did know, I was no longer the fledgling I was when he left me; an inexperienced, untrained vampire. Though I hadn't quite *lived* a century yet, I had learned many useful things in the time since I was reborn. I knew my own strength, my own power. Still, I needed to learn how to block someone out of my mind. That would be extremely useful. I had to ask Kalia and Aaron to teach me.

The front door opened and I jumped out of bed and to the window. I pulled the curtain aside just enough to be able to see. Maia was on the front walk with Ian. He was talking. I could see his lips moving, but of course, couldn't hear anything. He was keeping his voice so hushed that he knew I wouldn't be able to hear him, especially with the window closed, no matter how overdeveloped my sense of hearing may be. Maia was just listening. She looked like she was leaning toward him, or at least trying to, but he didn't notice. He was very focused on whatever he was explaining to her. After a few more minutes, I saw Maia start to back up, toward the porch. Ian reached out, squeezed her arm, and started to back away himself. I heard the front door open again and I saw Ian's head tilt upward. His eyes found my window. I let out a gasp and released the curtain. I stumbled backward against the bed.

Panic soared through my body. Every muscle tensed and I felt myself become totally rigid. I listened for footsteps. Where was Maia? Why wasn't she coming up to her room? She seldom stayed downstairs when everyone was in their rooms. As I sat still, like a stone, I heard the door open and close again. I ran to the window and pulled the curtain back. Maia was getting in her car. Was Ian with her? Was she driving him somewhere? I couldn't see into the car – bad angle. I was angry with myself for not staying at the window and watching him. I had no idea if he was gone or if he was out there…waiting.

I sank to the floor on the side of the bed, leaning my back against it. My head dropped to my bent knees. I wrapped my legs in my arms as tightly as I could, wanting to feel safe, inside a cocoon. I felt so helpless. Had I known Ian would waltz back into my life, had any kind of a warning, I could have been prepared. But now, I felt like a deer in headlights: completely paralyzed. I threw my arms back on the bed, stretching my tense muscles. My hand hit something hard. My phone. Christian…I wanted to talk to Christian…hear his voice…lose myself in his breath. My fingers started to scroll through my incoming calls when my brain screamed for me to stop. What would I say to him? I would wake him up to tell him…what?

Frustrated, I threw the phone across the room. It bounced off the carpet and landed right back in front of me. Worried I had broken it, I grabbed it to inspect it. All the lights went on when I opened it. No damage on the surface. I put it back on the bed behind me. I pulled myself up to the bed again and lay on my back, closing my eyes. I needed a plan…

My breath froze in my throat. A screeching noise came from my sitting room. I froze, listening. I let out a gasp of air. I was imagining things now, panicking. I laughed at myself for getting so worked up over a little noise. Probably a bird or branch. I jumped out of bed faster than I have ever jumped before, crouching on the floor on the opposite side, low growls coming from deep in my throat. Every muscle in my body was stiff… ready.

"Shh…" He whispered, holding his finger to his lips. *Don't want to scare the whole house, do you?* He stood in front of my sitting room door, which he threw open with a bang.

What do you want, Ian? He cringed when I said this. He heard the poison in my mind, the hate with which I pronounced his name.

Is that any kind of welcome? Why so bitter? He mocked, floating closer, his feet just inches from the floor.

Stay away from me! I...AM...NOT...AFRAID...OF...YOU! I warned, glaring at him, growls still emerging from my throat.

Do you have any idea how sexy you are when you're angry? He laughed, throwing his head back. He was squatting on the floor, still not close enough to touch me. *Oh, but you are afraid of me. You are very much afraid of me. I don't buy the tough-girl act. I know you better than that, Lily.*

*You don't know anything about me. You know nothing. You...*I leapt through the air; everything in the room was a blur. I landed on the opposite side of the bed, as far from him as I could get. He still laughed.

Impressive! Keep that up and you'll be flying in no time. You've been practicing I see. He made his hands do a silent clap. That infuriated me even more, being mocked by him. *I've missed you so much, my love.*

I cringed. I felt my teeth against my tongue, the wetness in my mouth. Every muscle in my body tightened as anger welled up inside me. He smiled, enjoying himself.

You always were a passionate one. He licked his lips like he was savoring the memory. His hand reached up to wipe the moisture from his lips. *Bet you still have that...for me. I'm here now.*

I felt sick, if that was really possible. I looked around, trying to find something to throw at him. He tilted his head and laughed.

It's useless, my love. You can't hurt me. You wouldn't hurt me. He was gliding toward me, around the bottom of the bed. *You love me. You always loved me. You know that. Look at me Lily...please...*His pleading sounded so sarcastic.

I did as he said. I raised my head, still crouched and ready to attack, and looked right at his violet eyes.

Why? Tell me why that would make any difference? I demanded.

Because you loved me once and I know you still do. You just don't realize it but you will. I have patience. His voice sounded calm now.

Well...you're wrong. You couldn't be more wrong. Besides, I have no patience for you. Not anymore! I looked away from his eyes, feeling the anger all over again.

Oh but you do...love me, that is. Can't you see? I belong to you just as much as you belong to me. It'll always be that way.

Before I could even hear or see anything, his body was right in front of me and his hands gripped my arms. He pulled me up in the air. His mouth was on mine, cold, wet, and hard, pushing, bending my head backward. My mind froze for an instant, at the familiar sensations, the well-known force and passion of his kiss. I fought myself not to kiss back, not to lose myself in the moment because no matter how much I told myself I hated him, no matter how much he disgusted me, I knew I had loved him once…worshipped him. I would have done anything for him, anything at all. Die for him. I felt my lips starting to part and I saw the blue eyes I loved looking sweetly and warmly at me…NO!

I lifted my legs off the floor, pulled my knees up, and kicked against his body in one smooth movement…so fast. My body crashed against the floor, bouncing slightly off the plush carpeting. I heard a loud thump as his body hit the wall by the door. He was down for a moment, a wild look in his eyes, a growl escaping his parted lips, teeth gleaming, bared!

You will regret this! I swear to you…

He was up again, this time his whole body off the floor, flying over the corner of the bed toward me. His arms were stretched out, hands ready to grab, his hair flying wild around his face. I jumped to the side but there was no place to go. I was in the corner of the room. I felt a burning pain on my neck as his fingers encircled my throat. I knew he couldn't stop me from breathing – not that it mattered anyway – but he could and would break my neck. I didn't know what that would do to a vampire. I wrapped my legs around his body and squeezed my muscles with all my might, all the while flailing my arms, trying to make contact with his head. His eyes stared lovingly into mine! I hit the floor hard, landing with one leg bent behind me. He stood, frozen to the spot. His arms still outstretched.

"Lily?" I heard Kalia's voice calling from outside my door. I looked up at him, panicking.

Answer her…carefully…

I nodded. "Yes?"

"Everything okay in there? I thought I heard…" She hesitated.

He put his finger to his lips and nodded his head toward the door. I felt him move behind me, over the bed.

"I'm okay. Sorry. I was just…rearranging and I…dropped something. Sorry," I yelled, panting.

"Do you want some help?" She asked, her wedding ring clicking against the glass doorknob.

I looked around the room wide eyed. He was gone.

"No thanks. I'm done…going to do schoolwork now," I held my breath, waiting for her to come through the door at any moment.

"Okay. See you later," I heard her footsteps descending the stairs.

I used the wall to help me pull myself up. I could just imagine what a sight I was. Kalia would have known, hair tangled and all over my face. I tasted blood on my lower lip. I slid my tongue along my lip to clean it off.

My legs shook as I staggered to the sitting room. He must have gone to hide in there. He couldn't have left that easily, not without whatever it was he wanted. The door was still open and the room was dark. I focused my eyes. It only took seconds for them to adjust to the darkness. I could still smell him…that…odor. The window was open and the curtain was blowing inward with the breeze. The room was empty. I grabbed the curtain and pushed it aside. I yanked the window down with both hands and flipped over the lock. It made the same screeching sound I had heard when Ian had entered through it. I laughed. Lock the window? Like that would stop him.

∽ TEN ∽

The sky had grown lighter but dark, gray clouds lingered over the house. Raindrops already started falling and I breathed a sigh of relief, knowing that I would be able to walk among the living today. I couldn't endure staying in the house all day after everything that had happened. I wanted to see Christian. I wanted to smile again, feel the happiness I felt when we were together. I didn't want to wait until this afternoon. I wanted to leave now.

I looked at the clock. It was only a little after nine. Would he be awake yet? I paced back and forth, trying to decide, trying not to jump out of my skin. I had to be out of the house before Ian came back and I knew he would. Maia had dug her claws into him and she wasn't going to let go. No, he wasn't going to be out of the picture any time soon. The more I thought about the situation, the more I wanted to be near Christian. The more I wanted to be with Christian the more afraid I felt for him. I was afraid for Kalia, Aaron, even a little for Maia. What lies had he told her? How much had he manipulated her? Did she have any idea of the damage he could cause? How could she? After all, he had done the same thing to me. Told me lies, made me promises, and then had taken my life without thinking twice about it.

I grabbed another pair of jeans from the closet and slid them on. I put on a sweater and a pair of boots and went to the nightstand for my cell phone. Not even bothering to look at the clock, I ran out the door and took the steps by twos. Just as I reached the door, I heard Aaron's voice coming from the living room.

"Lily?"

He was sitting on the sofa, his legs stretched out across the coffee table, the remote control in his left hand. That struck me as odd. Aaron in sweat pants, stretched out on the sofa, watching television? All I had ever really seen him do was lock himself in his office and work. I didn't think he knew how to relax.

"Hey, Aaron," I said backtracking.

"Can I talk to you a minute?" He patted the sofa.

"Sure." I looked around the room. "Where's Kalia?"

"She went to see Pierce."

"Oh…" I said and walked over to sit by him. "Something wrong?"

"No. I just think I need to explain about last night."

Did he know something? Had Ian said something?

"About what?" I asked, anxious.

"About what happened to you…the pain you felt," he turned to face me.

I expected him to go on about what Ian had done to me. His next words came as a shock.

"The pain you felt was real. I have seen it before but…only humans," he explained. "I never saw it happen to one of our kind."

"I don't know what you mean." I was getting impatient. I wanted to leave.

"The pain you felt was one of your organs being squeezed," he whispered this information, as if someone might overhear.

"What? I don't get it!"

"One of your organs – I don't know which one, I'm not a doctor – was being squeezed. I've seen her do it before. I told her I don't like it but it's her prerogative. It's how she hunts. She squeezes things inside human bodies, immobilizing her prey."

"Are you saying that…? Maia?" I felt my jaw drop.

"Yes. Maia did that. I have never seen her do that to another vampire. I didn't know it was possible." His head dropped into his hands. He looked ashamed.

"But why?"

"From what I gathered, she didn't like the way Ian was looking at you."

I cringed at the sound of that name coming from Aaron's lips.

"Are you kidding me?"

"Maia has a little problem with jealousy. She also has a problem with self-control. We have been working on that for the last eight months but," he explained, shaking his head. "We don't seem to be getting anywhere."

"So, I'm the first vampire she was able to do that to?" I was now in shock. Disbelief.

"As far as I know, yes. As you can see, she spends a lot of time away so we have no way of knowing. We only know what she tells us." He seemed a little calmer but still looked like a father ashamed of his spoiled, bratty daughter.

"Thank you for telling me and for helping me last night. I will do what I can to stay away whenever he's here." Gladly, I thought. "I will probably be away most of today. I'll see you sometime tonight."

I stood up again, ready to leave. He looked up at me with a pained expression.

Just remember…if you think about leaving us…I love you…Kalia loves you…

I couldn't help but smile at that unexpected display of emotion.

"I love you, too," I said. I gave him the warmest smile I could, trying to reassure him that I intended to come back.

I left him sitting on the sofa, smiling but with pain still in his eyes.

Driving to Christian's apartment distracted my mind for at least a little while. Last night, in the dark, was the first time I had been there, and needed to remember where it was. I tried to picture the roads as they had looked then. I remembered the curves, that there were no buildings, and then they started up again. I found them and then counted…one…two…three…and I turned left.

I felt the smile on my face at the sight of his car. I pulled up next to it. As soon as I stepped out of my car, I could smell his hypnotic sweetness and knew I was exactly where I wanted to be.

I stood on the top step looking around for any doorbell to push but did not find one. Then I noticed the door was partially open. I looked in through the opening and saw that it was just a foyer. I pulled the door open. To my right, I saw a brown wooden door with a small colorful wreath hanging. A child's scooter leaned against the wall. That wasn't his door. He didn't have a child, besides, he said second floor. I looked to the other side of the small enclosure and saw a narrow set of stairs. I wondered how anyone managed to get furniture up those. I started to head up and about half way, I could hear it: the melodic rhythm of his heart. It was almost like it was calling my name.

The door to his apartment was painted white. A simple brass knocker hung in the center. There was no peep hole. As my hand shook slightly, I lifted the knocker and let it fall twice. I held my breath and waited. For a few moments, I heard nothing besides the sweet melody coming from his chest. Then I heard rushed footsteps.

"Lily! Hi! What time...what is it? What's the matter? You..." He opened the door wider and stepped aside, motioning with his arm for me to enter. "You look like you've seen a ghost."

Great! As if I wasn't white enough!

He shoved the door closed with his foot as I stepped inside. He grabbed me and pulled me to him, squeezing me in his arms. I let my body go limp in his embrace. I hadn't noticed when he opened the door but my face was on his bare chest! The warmth and the aroma were indescribable! My mouth started watering instantly and my arms found their way around his waist. I tried to ignore the thirst I started to feel with every fiber of my being. I breathed in his scent, holding my nose against a patch of soft, light-brown hair.

"You're shivering! And you're cold and wet. Let's get you warm," he said still holding on to me.

It had been drizzling on the drive to his apartment but it started pouring when I stepped out of the car. Now my hair was wet and sticking to my face. He walked sideways, still holding me, and aimed my body toward a love seat. I didn't want to let go of him.

"Sit here. I'll be right back...getting a towel." He rushed down a hallway.

There was a coffee table in front of the sofa where I sat, magazines neatly piled on one side of the table, mostly *National Geographic.* On the other side was an open notebook with a pen on top. I glanced at the neat handwriting on the page and saw my cell phone number at the top. He had also scrolled my complete name underneath, including my middle name. Under that, he had written down the month and day of my mortal birthday: March third. I smiled at that discovery. He had gotten that information from my enrollment paperwork. I jumped back to how he had left me when I heard him returning.

He had put a black t-shirt on so I could no longer see his chest. He was carrying a towel in one hand and a blanket in the other. His expression was a mix between happiness and worry. He rushed to me and instead of handing me the towel, he gently wiped my face and then my hair. When he was done with that, he threw the towel on the floor and picked up the blanket. He laid the blanket on my lap and looked at the other cushion on the sofa then back at me.

"Do you mind if I sit there?" he asked.

"Of course not. It's your sofa," I said, looking around the room. This was the only place to sit. The living room contained a sofa, a coffee table, a three level bookshelf, and a floor lamp. That's all.

He sat down and picked up my legs, turning me enough to rest my legs on his lap. The warmth of his skin felt like fire burning through me. He took one of the laces on my boots and looked at me. I nodded. He untied my laces and pulled off my boots then wrapped the blanket loosely around my feet.

"So…are you going to tell me what's wrong?" He looked at my face now.

I pulled the wet strands of hair away from my face before I spoke.

"Nothing's wrong. Why?" I tried to sound as indifferent as I could.

"For one thing, you're early. For another, you look like you've seen a ghost. I know your skin tone is usually very light, the lightest I've seen, but you look paler, even wan…" He said this with such tenderness that I could not possibly take offense to his use of the word *wan*.

"I'm fine, really. I just couldn't wait to see you. I couldn't wait until this afternoon," I said, biting my lower lip.

His face lit up. He gave my feet a gentle squeeze.

"You're so cold. Are you sure you're feeling alright?"

"I really am. I feel healthy as a horse. I must have poor circulation or something because I'm always cold. I've always been this way. Nothing to worry about," I said convincingly because he dropped the subject. "I'm sorry I came early without checking with you. I hope I didn't interrupt anything."

"Not at all. Do you have any idea how happy I am that you are here? I didn't think I could make it. I was fighting with myself to keep from calling you." He looked down, hanging his head to show his shame. That made me smile. I was more relaxed already. I couldn't, however, get the image of his bare chest out of my head!

"I'm happy to be here, honestly. I couldn't wait anymore. I picked up my phone so many times and then set it down. Then, impulsively, I guess, I found myself in the car and on my way." I liked this version of the story so much more than the reality. The fact that I had wanted to see him still remained just that, a fact, but there was so much more attached to it, so much horror.

We sat for a few moments in silence. I was enjoying the heat of his body, even through his jeans. It felt so comforting. I listened to the musical sound of his breathing, his heartbeat.

I want so badly to tell her…could I? I'll scare her…can't do it…not yet… but…

I couldn't listen anymore. It was wrong. He was obviously struggling with something and I had no right to intrude. If he wanted to talk about it, he would, on his own time. In the meantime, I had struggles of my own. How long would it be before Ian found Christian? He knew where I went to school, where I lived. How long before he picked Christian's address right out of my head? I couldn't handle that possibility. We couldn't just sit here and wait for it to happen. I would need to keep Christian moving if he was going to remain safe while in my presence.

"Still want to go to that market you told me about?" I asked, trying to sound cheerful.

"If you still want to. But they don't open until three," he replied.

"Oh. What do you want to do until then?" I looked at the clock. It wasn't even ten yet! That meant we had to wait five more hours. Five more hours alone in this apartment…together!

"We could stay here. Are you hungry?" he asked.

"No thanks. I ate when I got up," I lied. I remembered the human routine well enough to know humans were usually hungry first thing in the morning.

"We could watch a movie," he suggested.

I looked around the room nervously. There was no television in here! I hoped he wasn't suggesting going to his bedroom. I couldn't even imagine that…temptation.

"Um…there's no TV…"

"Oh but there will be. Wait and see…" He lifted my legs, and pulled himself out from underneath. As soon as he was standing, he set my legs back down and disappeared down the hall. I heard some things being moved around and then he walked down the hall, pushing a metal cart. The cart contained a television and what looked like a DVD player. I laughed at the sight. He looked like a teacher pushing a television into a classroom.

"That's…interesting…" I said.

"Simplicity! Why have more than one set when I'm the only one here? I can move this anywhere I want. I have a cable hook-up over there," he pointed to the white cable along the far wall. I hadn't noticed it when I looked around since it blended in with the wall. "And I have one in the bedroom."

"That's good logic, professor," I joked with him.

"Why thank you, Miss Townsend," He went over to the far wall, where the cable wire was lying, and plugged everything in. He squatted on the floor trying to get the wires straight. "Now of course the tough part: what to watch…"

I didn't care what we watched. I didn't care if we sat and stared at a blank screen just as long as I was with him. What was happening with him was incredible, feeling things I hadn't felt in such a long time, things I had only ever felt once before. But the timing couldn't be more wrong. Even if Ian wasn't harassing me, it just couldn't happen, me and Christian. How would that be possible? Unless…no! That could never happen! If we came together, as a couple…no way. He would continue to age, change, and I would stay exactly the same. Would he want to be like me? Would he ever want to give up his life for me? And if he did, would I dare? I didn't think I knew how. I had never tried it, never found anyone worth spending a lifetime with.

He went over to the bookshelf filled with DVDs and started to read the titles to himself.

"What are you in the mood for? Comedy, drama, action, horror, Civil War, more Civil War, romance," he paused and turned to me. "Yes. I have romance."

"Whatever you feel like watching is fine with me. I'm not picky when it comes to movies." That was the truth. I gave anything a chance.

"Why don't you come over and see? Lots to choose from," he said and went back to looking at the titles in his collection.

I took the blanket off my lap and went over to join him. I squatted beside him and read the titles. With every breath I inhaled his scent, his proximity so close now. Our shoulders were almost touching. He turned his face to look at my profile and I could see a smile form. I could hear the speeding of his heart. I kept my eyes on the movies, reaching out to touch a couple of the cases, so he would think I was concentrating on choosing. That was so far from the truth, though, my mind swimming with his intoxicating aroma. I felt him moving closer, felt his hot lips lightly brush my cheek. My breath caught in my throat. I turned my face and caught his eyes.

"I couldn't go much longer without kissing you." He smiled.

"I was wondering when you were going to do that," I admitted. It didn't feel so wrong to admit the truth to him. It felt...natural.

He kept his eyes on mine and he was no longer squatting but sitting, cross-legged on the carpet, facing me. I followed his cue and did the same. We kept our hands on our own legs and just stared into each other's eyes. It went on like that for what felt like an eternity. His breath was coming faster with every moment that passed, his heart keeping pace. I realized my breath seemed to be keeping pace with his. I waited, allowing him to make the first move, while trying desperately to stay out of his mind.

His right hand moved, ever so slightly. I wasn't even positive I had seen that movement except that his heart changed its rhythm. He took a deep breath and raised his hand. I mirrored his movement, raising my left hand. Our fingertips touched, fire against ice. The sensation was indescribable. He didn't flinch at the temperature of my skin. He seemed to have accepted the poor circulation excuse. Within moments, our fingers intertwined. He looked away from my eyes and gazed at our hands. His lips parted as if he wanted to speak but didn't dare.

After a few moments, his eyes returned to my face. He studied my lips, which made me a bit self-conscious so I automatically licked them. He shuddered when I did that, as if he'd gotten a chill. His eyes met mine again and his left hand came to rest on the back of my neck. I felt myself stiffen. I felt his hand tighten as he pulled my face to his. While looking deep into my eyes, his face moved closer. I felt like the world suddenly stopped, everything frozen around me. My head was so deliciously dizzy. I inhaled deeply just before I felt the burning heat of his lips, finally, reach mine.

My head spun out of control. He moved his body closer but never dropped his hand from my neck, nor did he drop my hand, which he tightly grasped now. I realized I was gripping his fingers as tightly as he gripped mine, if not tighter. He didn't seem to notice but I knew I could easily break every bone in his hand so I loosened my hold just a little.

His lips devoured mine, his tongue following along. I was so intoxicated by the taste and smell of him that I hadn't realized, until that moment that my legs were wrapped around him, our bodies so close I was practically in his lap. I was feeling things happening in my body that I couldn't control, didn't want to control. I felt drunk with passion. His lips did not move away from mine and I had to wonder how he was breathing. My free hand went up to his face, my finger tips burning under the heat of his cheek, his chin. I could feel the corner of his open mouth with my fingers as he kissed me. He took a deep breath, still not moving his face away from mine. His lips kissed me for a few more seconds and then pulled away, still holding the back of my neck. His forehead rested on mine, eyes closed.

It took him some time to catch his breath but he did not move; did not open his eyes. His heartbeat, however, did not slow down even a little bit. His lips parted again.

"I…I think I'm in love with you," he whispered, keeping his eyes shut.

I stopped breathing. I felt something that I had not expected: complete and total terror. It was too late, I realized. I had been denying what he felt for me, thinking he was just lonely and wanted someone to spend time with. I realized also, to my complete and utter amazement, that I felt the same. Maybe not quite the same because I *knew* I was in love with him… completely and madly. He had only said he *thought* he was. Before I could stop myself, before I could come up with any sort of argument, I said it. I said the line that would condemn him to an early grave.

"Christian, I am in love with you. I can't stop it," I whispered. He opened his eyes. "I love you, desperately."

His kiss was passionate, filled with such tenderness. He wrapped me in his arms. As my head rested on his chest, I listened to the beating of his heart – my heart – as I knew I now needed to do whatever it took to make sure that heart continued to beat.

You stupid…little…moron! His blood will be on your hands…his death on your conscience…remember that! It's a promise! Ian was in my head again. I had hoped Maia would be able to keep him distracted but it was no use.

No! Please leave him alone! Let me be happy…finally. I thought, I pleaded but I knew it was useless. Ian was determined to destroy me and that was how he was planning on achieving it: by destroying the man I loved.

I pulled away from Christian's body and looked at his face. The happiness in his eyes was unmistakable. He looked into mine, still smiling.

"Wow! I wasn't expecting that," he said. "I thought it was just me. I was afraid to tell you, afraid to scare you but now…"

"I meant what I said. I do love you…more than you can imagine," I admitted, again.

"I figured what would really scare you is how soon…how quickly this happened. I thought you would think I was crazy."

"No. Oddly enough, that didn't even cross my mind." It was the truth. I already knew there was something he wanted to say to me, something he struggled with, but I had no idea it would be something so life-changing. "I don't think time has anything to do with it."

"I do love you Lily, I know I do. I just didn't want to scare you so I said…"

"I know what you said but I also know how you feel. I can tell. Please, you don't need to explain." I could feel his love. He didn't need to come right out and say it.

"Thanks. Did you still want to watch a movie?" he asked, starting to raise himself from the floor. I followed.

"Actually, I'm getting a little hungry," I lied. "Why don't we go out and get something to eat?"

Getting him out of the apartment was my first priority. I hadn't for one second forgotten Ian's rude interruption during such an important moment between us. I couldn't think of anything else to say so I said what came to my mind first. Of course, I realized I hadn't bothered to bring my purse in my rush to get to him.

"That actually sounds good to me too. Can you give me a few minutes?"

"Sure. I'm not going anywhere," I said smiling.

"Be right back…" he said kissing the top of my head before turning to walk down the hall.

As I watched him walk away, I felt an instant emptiness. I was shocked at emotions I didn't understand. So many years of trying to avoid any type of emotional tie to anyone, of trying to avoid love, trying to protect myself, and now this! And with a human!

I heard a toilet flush and then water running. Shortly after that, as I was still looking in the direction he had gone, he emerged again and I felt myself exhale. Why did I hold my breath so much when I was around him? It was ridiculous!

He walked in wearing a gray V-neck sweater over his black tee shirt. He smelled like his usual sweet self but there was another scent mixed in with it. It was a pleasant scent…kind of musky. It must be cologne. Regardless, it did nothing to cover up the mind-boggling aroma of his blood.

He took me to a small yet quaint pizza shop. It was the kind of place that still used red and white checkered tablecloths. I ordered a chef salad and a Diet Coke. I figured it would be easier to dispose of bits of salad and cold cuts than it would be a slice of pizza. He ordered a cheese steak and fries. As he talked, I carefully threw pieces of salad under the table. As he didn't take his eyes off my face, it was easy to do. From time to time, I imitated chewing motions, just to make the charade more convincing. Before we left the restaurant, I even remembered to excuse myself to use the ladies' room, just in case he wondered how I could go so long without it.

We walked hand-in-hand around the antique market for a couple of hours. The only time he let go was when he reached into his pocket for his wallet. He paid for a dragonfly charm on a silver chain he had noticed me admiring. As he fastened it around my neck, he noticed the necklace I was already wearing. I started to explain to him, as I had been told, that it signified new life, rebirth, energy, but he stopped me.

"Believe it or not, I know what this is. It's a rune...a 'u' rune to be exact. Where did you get it?" He asked, still holding it in his hands.

"I got it from an uncle. He gave it to me when he found out I was planning to go back to college...you know...new life..." I replied. I hated to lie to him but I didn't have a choice. I couldn't very well tell him that I had gotten it as a gift from a *vampire slash witch*...could I?

"It's very nice," he said setting it against the skin of my chest. "Do you want to save mine for another time?"

"No way! I can wear both. Put it on, please," I cried. "I love it! Thank you."

As soon as he finished closing the clasp, I threw my arms around his shoulders and gave him a kiss on the lips, right in front of everyone. He seemed surprised at my reaction but as usual, did not flinch from the feel of my icy lips. I was beginning to get used to the fact that neither my skin, nor my paleness, seemed to trouble him. I wondered how long before he would catch on to other things that were different about me; like my inability to cry, sleep, or eat, my super human strength, my mind reading, the fact that I didn't age.

We spent a joyful and relaxing afternoon together. Let Ian try to interfere, I'd slam the door on him. Knowing Christian loved me gave me all the strength I needed.

The drive back to his apartment was full of chatter as we discussed the things we had seen at the market. I noticed that he mostly admired colonial style furniture and anything from any of the wars. His favorite appeared to be the American Civil War, of which he had a large collection of movies. As he drove, I couldn't help but watch his face. So full of emotion. When he smiled his whole face lit up.

We agreed to spend the next day together. We could start out at his apartment and then go someplace if the mood struck or maybe actually watch a movie this time. I already knew the weather was supposed to stay the same so I didn't have to hesitate when I agreed to drive over whenever I got out of bed the next morning. Slipping into melancholy, he asked me to stay but I made excuses. I needed to think.

When we pulled into his driveway, he stopped his car next to mine. He turned off the engine and then just sat there, staring straight ahead, his hands still on the steering wheel.

"What are you thinking?" I asked, trying not to invade his mind.

"I just don't want to say goodbye. I hate it!" He answered, looking at me with sadness.

"Then don't. Say, 'I'll see you in the morning'," I suggested.

"How important is what you have to do at home?" he asked.

I didn't know how to answer. I should be able to think, regardless of where I was, but I knew I couldn't…not with him. I was too distracted when I was around him. All I could focus on was him.

"I can come over early, really early if you want." I didn't try to explain what I needed to do. His eyes lit up again…a little.

"I guess I can live with that. Hey, if you're still tired then you could… never mind," he said, looking away again.

What? I could what? I had to listen to his mind to get an answer to that. I had a feeling I knew what he wanted to suggest so I let myself enter his thoughts.

What I wouldn't give to just lie in bed with her…next to me…hold her in my arms…feel her…her coolness drives me crazy…maybe soon…maybe…

I felt my eyes widen. That couldn't be possible. What he was thinking couldn't happen. I didn't think I could control myself with him, under those conditions. I could hurt him – kill him – if I got carried away. I couldn't take that chance, not like this, not while he was still human.

"What's wrong?" he asked with a worried look.

"Nothing. I don't want to leave you either. I promise I will be here bright and early. I'll even bring coffee." I leaned over to him and planted a kiss on his cheek. He turned to face me.

"Okay. I'll behave and not beg," he replied, touching his cheek where my lips had been.

I was beginning to think the coldness of my skin was not only something that didn't scare him, but that it was something that maybe…turned him on? He walked to my door and opened it, giving me his hand to help me out and then went to my car and opened that door.

Before I could get in, he raised his hand to the back of my neck, finding his way under my hair, and pulled me to him. His lips burned mine as soon as he reached them. I felt an instant flutter in my stomach.

"Until morning then. Remember…I love you," he said with his face still only inches away.

"And I love you, Christian."

I started the car as soon as I was in my seat. I backed out of the driveway, with his help as he watched the street for other vehicles. As I turned onto the street, I could see in my rearview mirror that he was still standing there, with a smile on his face.

Eleven

The kitchen was alive with activity as I opened the front door. Two voices I recognized immediately and one was somehow familiar but did not belong to Ian. I closed the door behind me, making as little noise as possible. Of course, Kalia heard anyway.

"Lily? Could you come into the kitchen please?" she called.

When I walked into the room, Aaron was sitting at the head of the table with Kalia to his right and Pierce to his left.

"Oh…hello Pierce. It's nice to see you again," I said, surprised. "Is Beth here?" I looked around.

"It's nice to see you, too," he said, seriously. "Beth had another commitment."

"Please sit, Lily. We'd like to talk to you." Aaron pointed to the seat next to Kalia.

With a lump in my throat, I did what I was asked. Kalia smiled at me, taking my hand in hers under the table, trying to reassure me. Pierce's expression was unreadable. Aaron looked as calm as ever. I swallowed hard and waited.

"We have reason to believe you may be in danger. Pierce has seen things…vague things…" Aaron said. Pierce looked at me with his soft eyes, yet something about his expression scared me.

"What do you mean? What kind of things?" I asked.

"Well…as you know, Pierce sees things…things in the future," Aaron explained. "He has seen death and it has something to do with you."

My jaw dropped. I looked at Pierce, wondering why he wasn't explaining this to me himself. He just sat there with that same blank expression. I turned my attention back to Aaron, feeling the security of Kalia's loving touch.

"Of course, we have no details yet. As you already know, I cannot read minds. Kalia has not been able to hear anything from Ian but she has, of course, listened to Maia. It's been just bits and pieces of Maia's thoughts but we get the impression that Ian knew you before last night."

I sat frozen for a few seconds. He was watching my face, waiting for some kind of confirmation or denial to what he was saying. With Kalia and Pierce in the room, I had no choice but to speak the truth. I swallowed hard and cleared my throat, gathering courage.

"You're all right. I do know him. I wish I didn't but...I can't change that," I admitted.

Pierce and Aaron looked at each other, confirming what they'd guessed. Kalia squeezed my hand tighter.

"Do you want to tell us about it?" Aaron asked.

"I haven't told that story in so long. I don't know where to begin," I explained. They all stayed silent, waiting for me. I took a deep breath.

"It was in 1938 that I first saw Ian. I was human then, only eighteen years old. Ian was a mystery from the beginning. I was mesmerized by his looks, by his darkness..." I dropped Kalia's hand, stood, and paced the room. Everyone else sat motionless.

"I mean darkness in a totally different way...let me explain.

"When I was younger, I was fascinated by vampire stories...horror stories in general but vampires were my favorite. I created my own world, filled with them, and then there was Ian...my prince. I was sitting on a bench, at the park with my father, eating an ice cream cone. My fantasy leaned against a light post. He tipped his hat but, in a flash, he was gone.

"I didn't see him again until five months later. He came into my parents' store, somehow enchanting my father, making himself out to be a successful businessman, traveling the country. He knew how to put on an act.

"I was away at school and only came home once every two months and for holidays. My father wasn't happy about the fact that I was going to school. He believed a woman's place was in the home. Of course, he never really came right out and said, hoping I would 'get it out of my system' as he put it, but it was obvious how he felt. Behind my back, he had made up his mind that Ian was the man for his little girl...perfect for marriage.

"When I came home for Christmas, my father made arrangements to have Ian over for dinner. He knew what he was doing. He didn't, however, know I had already set eyes on Ian, had been thinking of him...fantasizing about him for months.

"Imagine my surprise when Ian walked into my house a couple days before Christmas! My mother told me we were having a guest, even mentioned his name. Of course, I didn't know his name before that night. I just thought of him as the mysterious stranger in the park, the one I imagined as a vampire. Anyway, I was totally captivated by him. He seemed to feel the same about me. I knew from the start that there was something really different about him.

"We saw each other every evening I was home during that holiday, but only in the evening. When I invited him to a picnic, he said he had business affairs to attend to and could not see me during the day. I believed him, of course, as I had no reason to doubt him. After all, he had my father fooled. My father couldn't stop talking about him. My mother had nothing but good things to say, and why not? He brought her flowers every time he came to call." I took my seat again, wringing my hands on the table.

"One night, while we were sitting on the front porch, enjoying the moonlight and hot tea that he never seemed to touch, he confessed his love for me. I was beside myself with joy…I had been waiting for it. I knew I loved him too but…there was my education to think about. I wanted to be a writer but I couldn't see myself without this man. He asked my father for my hand the very same night. My parents were ecstatic! It was their dream come true: their little girl married to someone so successful. My father wanted that more than anything.

"I managed to convince all three of them to give me some time. I agreed to marry him but I wanted to go back to school and at least finish the semester. Ian promised I could continue school, after we were married, if it was still what I wanted. It would have to be in Ireland, however, as that is where Ian was born and raised.

"Our relationship continued through letters. We saw each other rarely, as neither of us could seem to match our schedules. I didn't think much of the fact that he had never laid a hand on me, figuring it was his Catholic upbringing. At that point, I was no longer consumed by vampire fantasies, having matured somewhat since starting college.

"The more time passed, the more I missed him. I longed to be by his side every possible moment. I was sick of just reading his letters…sleeping with them under my pillow. During my next trip home, I wrote him and begged him to come for me. I confessed to him that I did not want to be separated from him any longer, that school wasn't as important," I looked around the room again. They sat stock still listening intently. I sat down and Kalia began tracing circles on the top of my hand with her thumb, feeling my melancholy.

"He was more than ecstatic at this news and, believe me, so were my parents. He came for me almost immediately. We made arrangements to go to Ireland. They did not like the idea of me going with him before we were married but he was so convincing in his argument that my father relented.

"We were in Ireland for only days when I noticed things were not as I expected. I noticed things I take for granted now: his lightning speed, his lack of eating and sleeping. When I asked him about the wedding, his face would grow angry and he would tell me he had too much to do to worry about that at the moment. This continued for many months. By that time, I was nineteen.

"One night, we were sitting in front of the fire, looking at some photographs I had brought with me. I decided I had waited long enough, that it was time I at least knew what it was like to kiss the man I was about to marry. So I did it...went for it. I climbed up on his lap as he sat on the sofa. His reaction wasn't as I had expected. I had expected surprise or maybe anger that I had taken it upon myself to make the first move. Instead, he grabbed me and kissed me furiously. I tried to pull away. I had never kissed a man before and that amount of passion scared me...terrified me. His lips were like ice, his hands were like ice as they groped any bare skin on me he could find. I couldn't stop him. He was so strong! My mind knew...knew something was terribly wrong. I was thinking about all the things I had noticed about him...that were strange about him...when I felt it. The horrible, burning pain at my throat. I heard the ripping sound of my skin. I felt myself getting weaker with every breath I took," I looked at Kalia. She nodded as she laid her other hand on mine, encouraging me to go on. I swallowed hard before continuing. This was a memory I did not want to relive.

"As I lay dying, he stayed away. I screamed for him, unable to move the pain was so horrible, but he never came. I saw him standing in the doorway a few times, but he never came near me or tried to comfort me. I knew what was happening to me. I knew deep down what he was all along and yet...I still loved him, still wanted him.

"Once my body was finished dying and I was born into what I was destined to be for all eternity, I realized I wanted him even more. The love and desire I felt for him seemed to have intensified, along with all my senses. But, he stopped wanting me. I tried to get him to show me the kind of physical love I wanted, even though he did sometimes give in, his mind was already elsewhere.

"We spent some time traveling the world, sampling 'foreign cuisine' as he called it. Not a night passed that we didn't kill some innocent human just for pure enjoyment. It was his way, and since I loved him enough to do anything for him, it became my way. He taught me how to kill, reckless and brutal, leaving the bodies discarded in dark alleys. He didn't worry about their families, their loved ones. He believed we were superior…we were meant for population control. He didn't see us as the monsters we are.

"I learned nothing from him, except to kill. He never answered my questions, no matter how gently I asked them. I had no idea where he came from…who made him. He refused to tell me, becoming violently angry whenever I brought up the subject. After a while, I stopped asking. I found out bits of information from other vampires we met throughout our travels but it was never enough. Those vampires lived much in the same way Ian and I did, from place to place, never settling anywhere, always preoccupied with their next meal.

"As time passed, Ian withdrew more. He left me alone to wander city streets, while he disappeared for hours, sometimes days at a time. I could, of course, not question him on his whereabouts. I was just happy he came back to me. The more he withdrew from me, the more I wanted him. He would tell me I was weak and helpless whenever I begged him not to leave. It went on like this for a long time.

"We were in Lima, Peru in 1940, when we found another coven there. We spent most of our time with them…well, I did, as Ian was leaving for days at a time again. One night, he came back for a few hours. He was actually affectionate with me, which both shocked and confused me. But of course, since it was what I craved…always craved…I took advantage of it, not questioning him. That night, alone in an abandoned apartment he found, he showed me more passion than he had ever shown before, more love. I was so happy that finally he was as in love with me as I was with him. I had never been more wrong." I sighed when I finished and turned to look at Aaron and Pierce. Both looked at me with their eyes full of questions. Kalia softened her grip on my hand but still held it affectionately.

"When I started to pack my things to leave, I found wads of bills in my suitcase. A lot of money. His payment for loving him. I felt like a whore. That was the last time I saw him...until a few days ago."

Aaron was the first to break the silence that followed.

"Wow! I had no idea...I'm sorry, Lily, I didn't..." He shook his head as if in disbelief.

"Where did he go?" Pierce asked, his voice as calm as ever.

I shook my head. "I have no idea. He just walked away and never looked back. For a while I feared he had been destroyed but I knew deep down that wasn't a possibility. Ian was the strongest vampire I had ever known. As far as I was concerned, he was indestructible," I explained, feeling sadness. I remembered the anguish I felt when he didn't return. How was it possible that I had once loved him so much, enough to give him my life?

"Anyone can be destroyed, Lily. Even the strongest and oldest of our kind can come to an end," Pierce explained.

"That's true dear. It is possible, not easy but, possible," Kalia added, reassuring me.

I thought about it. I had never heard of any vampire being destroyed. I couldn't imagine how.

"It takes fire, Lily. Simple as that," Pierce explained. "The hard part, of course, is getting to that step. A vampire isn't just going to stand by and allow himself to be carried off and thrown into a pit of fire. I know I wouldn't."

"So, why do you think Ian is here now? I don't think it's a coincidence that he met Maia." Aaron said and looked at Kalia. "And when I introduced him to you neither of you said anything."

I bit my lip before I could say anything. I didn't know what to say, except the truth.

"He scares me. That's all there is to it. Lately, he's been talking to me in my mind. I thought I was going crazy at first but it was real," I explained.

Kalia's eyes lit up as if something big had just been revealed.

"Remember when I thought I heard something? Talking in your room?" she asked.

"I remember. He was talking to me then. I'm sorry I lied to you. I didn't want you to worry," I replied.

"So..." Pierce started, straightening himself up. "Was there ever a wedding?"

"There was never meant to be one. That was just a ploy to get me away from my parents."

"What happened to your parents after you went to Ireland?" Aaron asked. He leaned against the table calmly, his head in his hands.

"I never saw them again," I practically whispered. "When my father died, I received a telegram from my mother. I was devastated, of course, but I knew I couldn't be there. I couldn't allow myself to be seen by anyone from my former life, not like this, not as a monster. Ian made excuses for me. I couldn't even talk to her myself; afraid she would notice something in my voice. My mother died shortly after, as I knew she would, since they had never been apart. I wasn't there for that either. I was too afraid. At the time, I didn't know the possibility of being outside before nightfall existed. Ian had led me to believe we could only roam at night. It wasn't until after he left that I met others like myself who knew it was possible only when the sun didn't shine."

"You were never told?" Kalia asked, surprised.

"No. There was a lot I wasn't told. I didn't know about the sunlight thing, or that it was possible to go for periods of time without the need for fresh blood. Ian killed every night and I followed. I had no idea it was possible to survive from animal blood, though I prefer the evil-doer. I didn't know my own strength, both physical and mental. He left without teaching me anything useful."

"I don't understand. What does he want? What could he possibly want after so long? Was there something *unfinished* between you?" Kalia asked.

"Nothing I can think of. He has ignored me completely since he left. I don't know why now," I lied. I had an idea why he was here. I pushed it out of my mind. Kalia was very quick to catch my thoughts.

"He has to be after something. He's taken a lot of steps to be here. He made sure he found Maia and then came all this way with her. That couldn't have been easy, befriending Maia. She's not the easiest to get along with, as you know," Aaron said.

"He's definitely after something. I just don't know what it is yet," I admitted. I knew there was no way to convince them that this could possibly be a coincidence. Kalia, for one thing, was too observant and Pierce, well…

"What can we do?" Kalia asked.

"Yes. Please let us help. You know you are part of the family, right?" Aaron asked, putting his hand over mine.

I looked, first at him, and then at Kalia and Pierce, who sat watching me.

"I don't think there is anything to do right now. He seems to be keeping his distance," I lied, as usual. "Maia is keeping him occupied. I will be on the lookout though and I promise to tell you if anything happens."

"Oh, that reminds me," Pierce said, rising from his chair. His hand went up to his shirt pocket. "I have something for you."

He pulled another one of those small boxes out of his pocket, like the one he had given me the first time I met him. He pushed his chair away and came around the table. I looked at him confused.

"This is the right one for you," he said as he placed the black felt box on the table in front of me. He returned to his seat. I caught the blur out of the corner of my eye. All eyes were on me as I took the box in one hand and lifted the lid with the other. My eyes must have shown my confusion because Pierce started to explain before I could say anything.

"That is Raidho, or "r"-rune. It's for your protection. Please wear it always," he explained.

He watched me as I lifted it from the box to examine it. The charm was very much like the last one he had given me. It was made of metal and was hung on a silky black cord but this one had what looked like a capital letter 'R' in the middle of it, except the rounded part of the letter was more like straight lines, like a triangle. I saw Kalia and Aaron exchanging looks of agreement.

"Thank you. It's beautiful. I will wear it always." I put it over my head. It hung at the same level on my chest as the first one he had given me. I felt my chest to make sure both were visible and my fingers felt the dragonfly. The dragonfly Christian had given me was shorter, more like a choker, and I felt the emptiness I felt whenever I was separated from him. Kalia looked at me with a faint smile on her face. I dropped my hand and looked away from her eyes.

"So where is Maia now?" I asked, wondering if Ian had heard any of our conversation.

"They went to Washington for a couple of days," Aaron replied.

"Washington? What on earth for?" Kalia asked.

Obviously she hadn't known. I also wondered why they would be going to Washington but didn't ask. I was just happy they were out of Oregon, even if it was only for a couple of days.

"Are you sure you are okay, Lily? It just seems there should be something we can do for you." Aaron looked at me with so much warmth in his eyes that I wanted to tell him everything that happened lately. I bit my lip to keep myself from speaking or thinking.

"You would tell us anything was bothering you, right?" Kalia asked.

"I told you I would. I'm fine. Other than my shock to see him, nothing else happened. Please don't worry about it until...*if* something does happen." I realized I almost slipped there, almost said I knew something was going to happen. I needed to be careful. I needed to keep them safe.

They looked at each other, my three protectors, and said nothing else. I sat and waited, patiently. I looked at them, one at a time, and fought to keep my mind clear. I couldn't be careless, not now.

"I better get back...lots to do," Pierce said rising from the table again. "You know how to reach me if you need me." He winked at Aaron when he said this, as if there were some secret between them.

"Thank you, Pierce, for everything," Kalia said taking him in her arms. She gave him a warm squeeze before letting him go. Aaron walked over to him and did the same. Pierce slapped a hand on Aaron's back.

I stood close by, waiting to shake Pierce's hand but before I could do anything, Pierce wrapped his arms around me. With his mouth touching my ear, he whispered, "We'll be looking out for you. You *are* in danger, more than you know." He released me. I stood frozen to the spot. Kalia looked at me but said nothing. I knew I wasn't the only one who heard his words.

As Kalia and Aaron walked Pierce to the door, I took the opportunity to run up to my room and close the door. I wanted more than anything to be alone. As much as I loved and admired my new family, I couldn't help but feel like I had been ambushed. I told them things I had sworn to myself I would never utter again. That had taken an unbelievable amount of energy and strength. I felt famished now. I needed blood worse than ever.

CLIMBING UP THE tree to my sitting room window, as I suspected Ian had done that night, I let myself in as quietly as possible. I left through the window, not wanting to talk to anyone. I wanted to drive to Christian's place to check on him but I needed to change my clothes first. Feeding on two humans instead of one tonight, which gave me back the energy I had lost, had been a little messy. I had a few blood spots on my shirt, which was something I never did. I prided myself in the fact that I never spilled a drop of blood. But tonight, probably due to my exasperation and exhaustion, I had been sloppy. I had even gone as far as to dump the bodies in the Columbia River.

Stuffing the dirty shirt in the clothes hamper, I went back into the closet to pick out a clean one. I felt the warmth in my cheeks, as the fresh blood coursed through my veins. I decided to wear a white sweater to show off the new color in my face. Christian will like that when sees me. I looked at myself in the mirror. My face had a humanlike blush to it.

"Lily? May I come in?" Kalia called from the hall.

I hadn't heard her knock. All I wanted to do was get in the car and race over to Christian, keep him safe as he slept. But Kalia was outside my bedroom, asking to come in, and I couldn't refuse her anything.

"Yeah, come on in," I said, taking a deep breath.

She pulled the door open only enough to squeeze her slim body through. She walked right over to my bed and sat down on the edge. She patted the mattress next to her and smiled. I hesitated briefly but walked over and did as she requested. I knew what was coming but I waited in silence.

"We need to talk about something, don't you think?" she asked. She kept her voice calm and sweet as honey.

I took a deep breath. I was wondering how long it would take her to hear something I was trying desperately to hide. I nodded.

"What do you want to know?" I asked, figuring it was easier to answer her questions than it would be to spill my guts again.

"Who is Christian?"

Slap! She came right out and asked.

"Um…he's my professor," I answered, keeping my eyes down.

"Is that all?" she asked, taking my hand in hers and squeezing it gently. "You can talk to me about anything."

"What do you want to know?"

"Are you in love with this man?" she asked.

Another slap in the face. Kalia did not tip toe around an issue. I bit my lip.

"Madly!" It actually felt good to say it aloud.

"Okay, okay…I can understand that. You are an adult, after all. Just one more question: is he human?"

"Yes, he is!" I snapped. "Didn't you know that? Didn't you pull that out of my head?"

She flinched as if she had been slapped in the face. I regretted the harshness of my own words.

"And what do you plan to do about that?" She was back to her usual relaxed posture.

"I don't know. I don't know anything. All I know is that I spent so many years trying my hardest to avoid feeling anything for anyone and this man comes into my life and I can't even breathe when I'm around him. I can't control myself…I…I…" I was ranting now. It was all pouring out of me. "I love him so completely. I want him."

She put her arms around me but I sat stock still, refusing to let myself be comforted.

"Does he feel the same?" She whispered.

"He does. That's the hard part. If it were just me, I could walk away. But knowing he feels the same makes it so much harder. He's like a magnet, always pulling me to him," I whined, my hands in tight fists on my legs. She held me for a few more moments and then pulled away.

"What does he think? Who does he think you are?"

"I try not to listen to his mind but, sometimes, I can't help it. I get curious when he gets quiet," I explained, a little more serene now. "He seems to like my cold skin. It excites him for some reason. I told him I have poor circulation and he accepted that explanation. He says my skin is like porcelain."

"Have you…you and him…you know?" She seemed embarrassed now.

"Oh God, no! I couldn't! I would definitely hurt him…or worse." I couldn't even begin to imagine that with him. Something that was supposed to be so beautiful between a man and a woman was nothing but deadly between a vampire woman and a human man. The need for blood was so strong then.

"Do you have a plan?" she asked.

"Not really. This is so new to me. I thought about…" I hesitated. She looked at me and knew.

"Lily, no! That's not an option. That's not fair to him. Think about that, please. Think about what you would be doing to him, condemning him to this. It's not for everyone."

"I know it's not but I don't want to be without him," I insisted. "I can't lose him. I feel like he was made for me, intended just for me. Please don't ask me to give him up."

She closed her eyes. I could see she was deep in thought so I gave her privacy.

"You're considering making him like you then?" she asked outright.

"That thought has crossed my mind," I admitted.

"I could list all the reasons why you shouldn't, but I won't. You're a smart girl, you know the reasons yourself. And besides, you know he may run like hell if he discovers what you are. But I just want to tell you one thing," she said and took my hand in hers again. "Just promise me that if you do make him, you are absolutely one hundred per cent sure that's what you want, what you both want. Make absolute sure he loves you the way you love him."

I nodded, not quite sure what she meant by all this.

"Newborn vampires tend to be completely attached to their makers, subservient, almost. He will be loyal to you through eternity. Pierce made me, as you know. Pierce is a wonderful, intriguing, and fascinating being. He is well respected in the vampire community. I adored him, worshipped him if you will. But…he met Beth and was head over heels in love with her at first sight. Where did that leave me? Out in the cold, you could say. When he left me, and he told me he needed to go, I went almost completely mad. I tried to destroy myself. I roamed the mountains and the countryside, barefoot no less, looking for anything that would end my misery. I didn't think it was possible to survive without him. Of course, after only a few years, I got lucky. I found Aaron…or I should say Aaron found me. I was curled up on the ground in a field trying, in the pouring rain, to light the haystack next to me so I could burn with it. If it wasn't for the fact that the rain was working against me and that Aaron happened to be hunting in the area, I would not be here right now," she finished.

Her eyes looked sullen after that revelation. She was breathing faster and I could tell speaking of that period in her existence hurt.

"All I'm trying to say is make sure you both really want that, one hundred per cent. Make sure the love you feel for him is the love he feels for you. Because, come to think of it, I wasn't madly in love with Pierce, not like I am with Aaron. But I still felt like my world came crashing down when my maker left me." She laughed a little.

"I promise I will think of all of that before I make any decisions. I don't know how to do it anyway so it wouldn't be any time soon."

"We have a strange situation, if you think about it. My maker, his lover, my husband and I…all friends. I never thought that would be possible but now, after a century, it happened." She stood up and started walking back and forth, along the side of the bed. "There is a kind of bond, between a maker and a newborn, something not easy to break. It's almost an owner-ship."

"What do you mean *ownership?*" I asked still confused.

"Yes, an ownership. Even though I wasn't as in love with Pierce as I should have been, to spend eternity with him, I was devastated when he left. And even after Aaron found me, once I knew I loved him, it still bothered me to know Pierce was with Beth, that he was spending his eternity with someone who was not me. Does that make more sense?" she asked, pausing in front of me.

I thought about it for a moment. She was saying that even though Ian didn't want me, he didn't want anyone else to want me either. I was shocked at that possibility. It was so human, this jealousy!

"So you're saying you think it's possible Ian is here because I found Christian?" I asked in disbelief. Even though the thought had entered my mind before, it had been just that, a thought.

"Actually, I was talking about making sure that Christian and your feelings are concrete before you decide to make him one of us but you may have a point," she replied, sitting back down on the edge of the bed. "That is a very good possibility. Have you been even remotely interested in anyone since you and Ian separated?"

"No, not at all. I did my best to avoid it." She could very well be right, though I guess it was me that came to that conclusion.

"Hmph, we could have something very useful."

"What were you getting from Maia that made you worry, anyway?" I realized they never told me what they knew.

"It wasn't any one thing in particular. I was getting bits and pieces from her, all fragments. I knew she was angry with you. I knew there was jealousy from the beginning but more so after she brought Ian. She was thinking, again very fragmented, about both of you at the same time. That's when I decided to talk to Aaron about my suspicions. He agreed with me that Ian was putting on an act the "first time" he met you. So, of course, we worried," she explained. "I hope you're not angry with me for bringing Pierce into this, it's just that I value his insight."

How could I be angry with her for caring about me?

"Kalia, you have been nothing but a mother to me ever since the first time I met you. There is no reason I could be angry with you or Aaron for caring," I explained and took her hand in mine. "I know I haven't said this and it still sounds strange coming from my mouth but, I love you. Thank you for all you do."

She took me in her arms and held me for a few moments.

"Still strange coming from you? Does that mean you've told Christian you love him?" she asked releasing her arms from around me and leaning away to look into my eyes.

"Yes, he knows," I said looking away from her. I got the feeling that was the wrong answer.

"You'll figure something out...we'll figure it all out." She stood and started walking to the door but just as she got to it she paused. "I didn't say anything to Aaron about Christian yet. You know you'll have to talk to him soon."

I nodded.

"And, by the way, next time you need to feed in such a hurry, please use the door." She smiled as she said this so I knew she wasn't angry. I smiled back before she closed the door behind her.

⤜ TWELVE ⤛

I sat across the road from Christian's apartment, the car idling. The darkness that surrounded me felt uncomfortable. The building was complete darkness, except for the foyer. I listened but heard no voices. Everyone was asleep. The dark clouds overhead covered the moon, allowing it to make an appearance only briefly, before it was surrounded again. I could see no stars and knew Sunday would be as wet as always.

Another car parked on the side of the road, not far behind me. I caught sight of it in my rearview mirror as I drove, but didn't give it much thought. Though I tried to focus my eyes, I could see, even from this great distance that the vehicle in question had the darkest tinted windows I had ever seen, impossible to see through. I tried to clear my mind, just in case. It was, of course, very possible the vehicle had nothing to do with me. I had, after all, been looking at Christian's building so I could have missed the driver exiting the vehicle and entering a building. Yes, that was a possibility. I told myself to relax and just concentrate on keeping Christian safe.

Settling back in my seat, hands on the steering wheel for comfort, I listened and watched the building, concentrating on any movement. I saw a squirrel run along the lawn and take a flying leap at a tree next to Christian's car. I watched him run up the trunk and disappear into a round hole just before reaching the outstretched branches halfway up. My eyes shifted to the building. I watched for what felt like hours, looking around the yard, the driveway, and at all the windows I could see from this angle.

Lily…please don't…don't go…don't…

I bolted straight up in my seat, my hand already on the door handle, ready to run to him. Just as I pulled on the door handle, my body relaxed again, realizing that Christian must be dreaming. I smiled. He was dreaming about me, saying my name aloud in his sleep. I could just imagine how he looked right now, curled up in his covers, eyes closed, and a look of serenity on his face. My body ached as I pictured him like that, ached to be curled up next to him, in his arms.

A sound startled me out of my fantasy. I saw headlights behind me, bright and blinding in the rearview mirror. My body stiffened again in defense, ready to do whatever I needed to protect him. As the car rolled away from the curb, my body went into alert mode, muscles rigid, hands balled into fists on my lap, fangs protruding. The car continued toward me. I sat up straighter, ready to fight if it came to that. As it came closer to me, I heard low growls coming from my own throat. I was ready to kill if need be. The car paused next to me, the dark window still closed. I thought about my own car, my windows also tinted, and realized the driver couldn't see me either. Then what was it doing next to me?

While I held the door handle in my left hand, ready to jump out and defend myself, the car sped away. Its rear lights disappeared in the distance around a bend. I had not caught a glimpse of the driver or his thoughts… nothing…no heartbeat. It was another vampire. It had to be. A human couldn't block thoughts like that. But who? Why was I being followed? I didn't get the feeling that it was Ian, didn't feel the sense of panic I felt when he was near. He was supposed to be in Washington with Maia. I knew she wasn't about to let him out of her sight. I took a deep breath and tried not to worry about it, for the moment, anyway. I could have followed the car but I didn't want to leave Christian.

Faint light pierced the thick clouds with promise of a new day. As I was looking at the sky, I caught a light out of the corner of my eye. A small window on the side of the building, on the second story, was now dimly lit through the blinds. That must be his bathroom. My stomach did a flip as I watched. He must be awake enough to go to the bathroom. A smile flashed across my face. My hand went to my neck, feeling for the dragon-fly. I held it for a moment, trying to decide if I should go to the door. It was too early, I knew, but I ached to see him. I let go of the dragonfly and felt for the other ones, the ones Pierce gave me. The protection charm still hung around my neck, feeling oddly heavy in my hand.

I tapped on the door and waited. If he had gone back to bed, he would not hear me. I heard his footsteps nearing. I could hear the rhythmic melody of his heart. He pulled the door open.

"Lily…hi," he said sleepily. He was wearing a pair of black and white checked flannel pants and nothing else! I inhaled his sweet aroma.

"Hi, Christian. I hope you don't mind, I couldn't sleep," I answered, stepping through the door as he moved aside.

"No, not at all. I just woke up…to use the bathroom. I doubt I can go back to sleep anyway." He smiled, flicking on the living room lamp.

"I'm sorry. I couldn't get you coffee. They weren't open yet," I lied. I had forgotten about my promise in my rush to get to him. Thinking about it, I didn't think it was much of a lie. They wouldn't be open for business yet.

"That's okay, you're forgiven. I do have a coffee maker. Would you like some?" he asked, motioning for me to follow him into the kitchen.

"Um... sure," I said, not thinking about what I was going to do with the contents of the cup.

"I'm glad you're here now. That gives us more time together," he admitted. "Can you excuse me for a moment?" he asked, leaving me in the kitchen as he stepped into the hallway.

"Sure, go ahead," I replied, leaning against the counter. I heard a door close and then water running. Brushing his teeth, I thought. I had, after all, caught him just as he was waking up.

A black two-slice toaster and black coffee maker sat on the counter. A microwave, kind of small, was in the corner. On the side of the refrigerator, a black towel hung on a metal hook. The stove was sparkling clean, like it was rarely, if ever, used. It was certainly a bachelor's kitchen, nothing looked used: no dishes in the sink, no spices on the counter, not a spot of anything food-like anywhere. The only thing that did look used, since it had a few water spots on the carafe, was the coffee maker. He was back in the kitchen with a wide smile, his blue eyes full of life.

"Okay, much better," he said walking toward me. "Now I can kiss you."

His lips were hot on mine and my arms instantly went around his neck. He kissed me passionately for a few moments and then stopped, backing away, looking at my face. His head tilted to the side.

"You look different," he said, a confused look on his face. "Are you wearing makeup?"

It was the color in my cheeks. He had never seen me so soon after feeding.

"Just a little blush," I lied. What else could I say?

"You look good." He smiled and then set out to make the coffee.

I watched as he took a paper filter from the cabinet and placed it in the coffeemaker. He went to the refrigerator, pulled out a foil bag of coffee, and poured it straight in from the bag without measuring. He then went over to the sink, turned on the water, and filled the carafe, all the while looking at me. The water started spilling over the top and all over his hand.

"Oops!" He jumped back.

I grabbed the towel from the side of the refrigerator and while he held the pot up, I wiped the bottom. He started laughing, a laugh so contagious that I couldn't help but join him. It was so easy, to be almost human with him. He poured the water in, set the carafe on the burner, and pushed the button. Almost instantly I heard gurgling sounds.

"What would you like to do while we wait?" he asked, putting his hands on the counter on either side of me.

"I don't know. Whatever you'd like," I said, inhaling him.

"We could go watch TV in the bedroom," he suggested nervously.

My breath raced at the thought of us in the bedroom. I must have looked as uncomfortable as I felt because his gaze dropped to the floor.

"Or I can move the TV set into the living room again," he said, not raising his eyes.

"No. That's okay. We can watch in there," I said sternly, trying to be adult about it. "Should we get coffee first? There's enough in the pot for two cups."

"Yeah, sure. Good idea," he replied and went to open another cabinet. He pulled out two mugs and I could see his hands shaking. He poured two cups and managed not to spill any.

"Sugar?"

"No thanks, just black."

He opened the refrigerator and pulled out a half gallon of milk. After adding two heaping teaspoons of sugar, he poured in a little milk and stirred. He lightly banged the spoon on the side of his cup before depositing it into the sink. He put the milk away and walked back to pick up his steaming cup.

"Shall we?" he asked, putting his hand out for me.

I saw a shiver shake his body as my fingers touched his. I nodded and went with him down the hall.

His bedroom was as sparsely furnished as the living room. A queen-sized bed sat against the far wall, with a nightstand on either side. The covers were still rumpled in a pile in the middle of the bed. Four pillows rested against the headboard. Only one of the nightstands had a lamp on it, the other was completely empty. His TV cart was against the wall, directly across from the foot of the bed. Next to the window was a chair, piled with books and next to that a bookshelf, which I noticed, did contain books, unlike the one in the living room. The other wall contained a chest of drawers. There were no pictures on the walls, no curtains on the window, just a cream-colored plastic blind. It was closed to block out the faint light from the street.

He let go of my hand and went over to sit on the side of the bed, the side that had the table with the lamp on it. He patted the empty side next to him and smiled.

"I don't bite," he joked.

"I might." I wasn't joking.

I went to the other side of the bed, and after setting my cup on the empty table, I made myself sit. I pulled my legs up, wrapping my arms around them. I sat very still while he watched me.

"You can get comfortable, you know. Pull the covers up and relax. Why not take it easy and do nothing today?" he asked. He leaned back against the pillows, legs stretched out in front of him. "Would you feel better if I put on a shirt?"

"No. I'm okay, really," I said, trying to convince myself.

He reached to his nightstand and grabbed the remote. Then he jumped up.

"Oh! I have an idea. There's a movie I want you to see. I'll go get it." He sounded excited.

In an instant, he was gone. I could smell him all around me, all over the bed. The shape of his body was left indented on the mattress, on the sheet. I took the pillow he had been resting against and inhaled his aroma. I put it back, not wanting to be caught.

"This movie reminds me of us." He squatted in front of the TV cart, inserting the DVD into the player.

"What is it?" I asked curiously. I lifted the coffee cup from the table and held in my cold hands, allowing its heat to warm them.

"It's called *A Walk in the Clouds*. Don't laugh at me but it's a romance." He came back to sit beside me, a second remote now in his hand. "I think you'll like it."

He looked at the remote trying to find the correct button to push. As I looked at him, I had a sudden and overwhelming urge to lie next to him with my head on his chest. Could I do that? What harm could that do? He looked at me as I thought about this.

"You don't have to be so far away. I told you I don't bite," he said with a sly smile on his lips.

I smiled back at him. I moved closer, stopping next to him before my body touched his. He put his arm up on the headboard, just behind my head, his palm open, inviting me. I hesitated but moved a little closer. His arm went around my cold shoulders. My head was being pushed forward by his arm but I didn't want to say anything. I felt uncomfortable enough by his closeness. I knew I needed to control myself but didn't know how long that would be possible. Finally, he pushed the play button on the remote.

A few minutes into the movie, he reached to his nightstand for his cup. He leaned his body forward and took a sip, put his cup down, and looked at me.

"You don't look comfortable."

"I'm okay," I assured him but he was right. My neck was not comfortable with his arm situated where it was. I hesitated but not for long. I decided it couldn't possibly hurt, so I scooted myself down on the bed and laid my head on his chest, my arm draped across his bare stomach.

"This is nice," he said with a sigh. His breathing became just a little faster. His arm wrapped around me, squeezing.

"Yeah. It is," I admitted. I dared myself even further and draped my leg over his. I waited, perfectly still, to gauge his reaction. He sighed again.

We continued to focus on the movie, laying perfectly still, both of us breathing in sync. I watched the television screen but my mind was concentrating on his breathing, his scent, his warmth, the incredible heat of his body. I didn't realize, until he sighed, that my fingers were entwining in the soft hair of his chest, willing themselves without my control. I stopped but did not remove my hand. He sighed again. His right hand was touching my now immobile one, as if wanting me to continue. As soon as I returned to what I had been doing, he removed his hand, letting it drop off the side of the bed.

I paid attention to the movie some more. A woman on a bus, dumping a suitcase all over the aisle, was talking to a dark-haired man, an actor I recognized. My eyes were watching but my mind did not understand anything I was seeing. I was preoccupied.

"Why does this remind you of us?" I asked.

"Because they come from two different worlds and yet they find each other," he whispered as if we were in a movie theater.

The sound of his voice, in a whisper at that moment, was more than I could handle. Before I knew it, I found myself on top of him, straddling his body, my fingers circling his wrists. I held him down tightly, much too tightly but he didn't seem to care, except for the shocked expression in his now wide eyes. His breath came faster as my face neared his, taking my time to inhale his sweet scent.

I kissed him hungrily, animal-like, not giving him a chance to breathe. His legs bent at the knees, pushing me closer to him. As soon as I let go of his wrists, putting my hands under his head to bring him closer to me, his hands went to my back, tracing up my spine. His grip was tighter, more demanding. I kissed him like I had never kissed anyone before, feeling every bit of the passion that had been welling up inside me for so long, releasing it finally. I flinched when I felt the heat of his fingers on my skin as his hands found their way under my shirt. I couldn't control my breathing any longer.

I felt myself lifted, suddenly, as I realized he was now taking control. He had thrown me off him and I was lying on my back, his body on top of mine. His hands were exploring the skin on my stomach as his mouth continued to devour mine. As I tried hard to control my breathing, his lips traveled to my neck, covering every inch of my cold skin with what felt like hot lava. My body arched in response, trying to get closer to his. The pounding of his heartbeat was deafening in my ears as his kisses traveled, from my neck down to my collar bone. I heard a soft moan escape my lips before I could stop it.

My hands felt the heat of his body as I clung to his shoulders, wanting to stop him, yet pulling him closer. His fingers were lifting my shirt, his lips reaching the bare skin on my stomach, the heat making my body arch out of control. He nibbled on my rib cage as more moans escaped my lips, no matter how hard I tried to stop them. I wanted him...wanted him more than I had ever wanted anything in my life. I wanted to have all of him, be one with him. I envisioned it, felt it, and desired it with all my being.

"NO! YOU HAVE TO STOP! NOW!" I yelled. I threw him off me with a swift move of my arm. I heard the thump of his head on the head-board.

I tried to get a hold of my breathing, to slow it, as I turned to look at him. Luckily, he landed on the empty side of the bed and had not gone further. He rubbed the back of his head, the shocked look on his face beyond words. He looked like he had just been slapped. He stared straight ahead, his eyes wide, his heart pounding furiously.

"I…I…Uh…" I tried to say something, anything that might make this alright. "I'm sorry…it's just…"

"It's okay. You don't have to explain," he said sternly, a little angry.

"But I do," I replied. "I have to say something. I owe you that, after what I did. Is your head okay?"

"Yeah, fine, but…Lily, you don't owe me an explanation at all. It was me. I was moving too fast and I'm sorry. It's just I love you so much it hurts. I can't stand to be without you and sometimes I feel like you're not close enough, even when you're right next to me. Does that make any sense?" he asked, finally turning to look at me.

"It does…perfect sense. I love you too, more than you'll ever know but I'm just not ready…not yet," I explained, trying to keep my voice gentle. I was angry, but not with him. I was angry with myself for losing control. I didn't want to think of what I could have done to him, the damage I could have caused. As it was, I hurt his head but more than that, his feelings.

"I understand. I'll try harder," he said seeming to relax a little now. "I gotta tell you though…you're really strong!"

He had no idea!

He inched his way closer to me, looking at my expression as he did so. I moved my arm out of the way so that he could rest his head on my chest. I wasn't thinking when I did this. I was still worried about calming my body, my instincts, my craving for his blood. His warm head was on my chest, his right ear pressed against me, his arm across my stomach. I froze, becoming rigid, waiting.

"Um…Lily?" He said, lifting his head slightly.

"What?" I snapped. I knew what was coming. I feared it.

"I can't hear your heart…why can't I hear…?"

I was off the bed and out the door before he could finish his question. I heard him running after me but I didn't stop. I was down the steps in one bound and out the front door, jumping in my car and starting the engine before he could reach the exit. As I sped out of the driveway, tires screeching in reverse, I saw him standing on the walkway, still bare-chested. I could see a single tear falling down his cheek as I sped away, turning the car onto the road that would take me away from him forever.

I drove home in complete silence except for the constant squeaking of the windshield wipers. My body shook with sobs that didn't come, couldn't come. I felt like my short-lived happiness had come to a screeching halt and it had nothing to do with Ian this time. It was all due to my selfishness. I had wanted Christian so badly that I hadn't stopped to think how that would be possible. He had accepted the paleness of my skin, the deathly temperature of it, without much problem. I should have known that at some point though, sometime sooner rather than later, he might notice my heart didn't beat. I had been so stupid! Stupid enough to get so wrapped up in the moment that I didn't hesitate when his head came to rest on my hollow chest. And to top it all off, I hurt him, physically! His head banged off the wooden headboard as I had tossed his body aside. He said he was okay, and I believed him, but it still happened. I shuddered at the thought of how I could have hurt him, killed him even, if we had continued to fulfill our passion.

The worst thing of all was how I'd hurt him emotionally. As he stood there watching me, I had seen that tear streak down his face. I hated myself for being the cause of his pain. He did not deserve that. He deserved everything good in his life, everything I could not give him.

My phone vibrated in my back pocket. I kept the car steady with one hand on the wheel as I reached with the other to retrieve it. I flipped it open to look at the caller ID. Christian! I looked at it for a moment and tossed it onto the passenger seat. What could I possibly say to him? How could I even begin to explain my actions? I would have to tell him what I was and then I knew that would be the end anyway. No! It was better this way. I had his sadness to remember but I would rather have that than his complete and utter disgust. Yes, it was better this way.

∽ THIRTEEN ∽

"Lily! I need to see you!" Aaron yelled from his office.

I closed the front door and started down the hall. My breath was suddenly stuck in my throat. What could he possibly want? He never called me into his office.

"Hi. You wanted me?" I kept one hand on the door as I poked my head in through the opening. He sat at a large, intricately carved, wooden desk.

"Yes. Come in and close the door please," he said, not lifting his gaze from the documents in front of him. "Sit."

I sat in the chair he motioned to. This room, which I had never entered before, was full of books, mostly foreign language dictionaries. Some sort of audio equipment was placed on a small table in the corner by the heavily curtained window. Paintings hung on all available wall space, oil paintings, I think. I wondered if they were Kalia's but didn't ask. I could tell by the expression on his face that he didn't call me in here to exchange pleasantries…not today.

He cleared his throat and looked up at me, taking the documents in his hand and setting them, face-down, off to the side. His eyes looked full of pain.

"Let me first start by saying, Lily, that you have no reason to feel uncomfortable here. We are merely talking," he explained with a slight smile on his face I knew was for my benefit.

I tried to visibly relax my body, for his benefit, but I knew it was no use. I felt as tense as I must look.

"I will, first, apologize for having you followed last night," he said and looked down again, as if ashamed. "That was Pierce in the black car. I wanted to make sure you were safe. That is my first priority, keeping you and my whole family safe. He followed you while you fed, also. I must admit…impressive…two in one night for someone of your size." He laughed, shaking his head.

"But I went out the window. I didn't see anyone…" I admitted.

"Pierce went on foot. By the time he realized you were on the move, it was too late to take his vehicle. He would have lost you, so, he ran behind you, concealed by the trees." He watched the surprise in my eyes. My throat had a lump I couldn't manage to swallow. I knew what was coming.

"Who is Christian Rexer?" he asked. He didn't wait for an answer. "Never mind. I know who he is. After Pierce came back to report what he saw, and to tell me that you were, at the moment, in no danger, I talked to Kalia."

He sat still and waited, for what I wasn't sure, but I said nothing.

"Okay. Like I said, I talked to Kalia. Let me just start by saying that I do not, in the least bit, approve of what you are doing…or thinking, for that matter. Love, between a mortal and a vampire is not possible. Making that mortal a vampire is not acceptable."

He stopped talking and gazed at me, waiting for my reaction. He laid down the law and was expecting me to say something. I said nothing. I continued to sit still, hands folded on my lap.

"Do you love this man, Lily?" he asked.

"More than anything," I admitted in a whisper.

"Then let him live."

This talk was going to be easier than he had anticipated. He had no knowledge of my most recent decision.

"It's done. His heart still beats and it will continue to beat until his time comes…naturally," I replied. This time I had my voice. I wasn't nervous anymore because I knew I had made the right decision, one that Aaron would approve of. "I won't be seeing him anymore. I will not be returning to the college. I will stay completely and forever away from him."

"That's good to hear but I was not expecting that. Something happen?"

"Yes. Something I couldn't explain. I didn't know how so…I ran. I ran away as fast as I could without saying a word to him." My words came very fast in my frustration.

"May I ask what this something was?" He looked at me with sympathy.

"He couldn't hear my heart!" I snapped.

"Oh…is that all? I imagined worse."

"What do you mean *worse*?" I asked in disbelief. What could be worse than that, besides his death, of course?

"I thought maybe you got carried away enough to give in to...passion. There's an overwhelming desire for the taste of your lover's blood while in the middle of...you know...there's nothing like it," he said softly, his eyes focusing on his desk while he spoke.

At least I knew I wasn't the only one embarrassed by this sort of talk coming from him. I had felt it and I was thankful I had not given in to my desires, my instincts. I could have killed him right then and there, without even meaning to.

"I never made love with a human," I admitted, shocked that I got that out of my mouth.

"I see."

"Why is making him one of us not acceptable?" I needed to hear his reasons. I had no intention of doing that...not anymore. I loved him too much to take his life away, but I needed to know why Aaron felt this way.

"We are not gods, Lily. I don't believe it's our choice to take life away and then to replace it with this...eternal half-life we lead. Besides, it's complicated. There is much involved, much at stake," he explained as he leaned forward in his seat, elbows on the desk.

"Have you ever done it?" I asked.

"No. I will not...ever."

"Then Maia...what about Maia?" I asked.

"That was not my decision. That was Kalia's. It's what she wanted. Kalia lost a child once, when she was mortal, and she never quite recovered. To tell you the truth, I am a sucker when it comes to Kalia. I cannot deny her anything," he explained. His eyes softened as he spoke of her, full of love.

"So you don't even know how. Do you?" I asked, shocked.

"I know the logistics of it. Kalia did it when I was not present. It's how I wanted it," he said as his hands reached for the documents again. "Now...I need to get this finished. I have a deadline."

"Oh...okay," I said as I stood.

"Promise me you'll stay away from this mortal. Promise me you will allow him to live the life he was meant to live."

"I promise," I said, biting my lip. I had to promise him but most of all, I had to promise myself. I could tell by the documents in his hands that our conversation had come to an end. I was dismissed.

IN THE SOLITUDE of my room, I paced the floor at the foot of the bed. I couldn't get the look on Christian's face out of my head. I pictured the tear running down his face and felt his pain. It was completely inappropriate to think it but it broke my heart. I wanted to call him, say anything to make it better, make him smile again but I knew I couldn't. I also realized my phone was on the passenger seat of my car.

How was I going to stand the pain and emptiness I would feel day by day as I stayed away from him? It was an agony I dreaded not only for myself but for him. I heard the front door close as I walked into my sitting room, toward the window. Aaron walked to his car, a brown manila envelope in his hands. He must be going to mail the documents he was working on. I listened to the rest of the house and heard nothing. I didn't see any other cars outside besides my own so I figured I must be alone. Maia must still be away, with Ian, and Kalia was probably out shopping. She seemed to like to do that on Sunday afternoons. She almost always came home with something for me, some little trinket she thought I would like.

I sat on the edge of my bed, trying to relax. I thought about the conversation I'd had with Aaron, how true it was. He was right, we were not gods, but…if we didn't make our own companions we were limited to choose only from the few already existing vampires that populated the world. That did not give us much choice. Compared to the human population, we were outnumbered. I jumped as the telephone on my nightstand rang. I didn't move, didn't reach for it, though I wanted to. I wanted to hear his voice, know he was okay, that he didn't hate me. It took all the self-control I possessed to keep my hand from reaching for the receiver. After four rings that seemed to go on forever, it stopped its taunting.

I jumped off the bed as I heard the sound of my window opening. Before I could get in the room to stop it, Ian stood in front of me, a satisfied look on his face.

"What the hell are you doing here?" I snapped, standing with my body frozen, my fists balled up at my sides.

"Is that any way to greet someone? How rude!" he said with a mocking smile on his face.

"Where's Maia?"

"Oh, she's still in Washington. She doesn't mind when I leave for a day or two…she's the same way. We get along well that way. I see good 'ol Aaron took the bait, huh?" He was leaning against the doorway to the sitting room, looking relaxed, like he was chatting with an old friend.

"What is that supposed to mean?" I snapped, glaring at him.

"Those documents he was so tediously working on – rush delivery – to an address that doesn't exist," he laughed. "He'll be gone for quite a while."

"Why would you do something so…so YOU?" I realized it was exactly the sort of thing he would do.

"I wanted time alone with you; after all, I've missed you." He smiled his warmest smile, only when he did this, it was mocking and sarcastic.

"I don't want to see you, or talk to you. Don't you know that by now?" I asked in disbelief. I thought I had made that perfectly clear the last time we had a confrontation.

"Oh, but you do want to see me. You need to see me. After all, I come bearing news," he replied, no emotion in his voice.

"What on earth could you have to say to me that would be of any interest?" I asked, trying to hide my fear.

"Well, I have a proposition for you, one I think you won't want to pass up," he said as he walked to the side of the bed and was bold enough, as only he could be, to sit down. He patted the mattress, inviting me to accompany him. I shook my head, disgusted.

"Well, get on with it!" I made no attempt to mask my annoyance.

"Come with me. Live with me like you were meant to do and in return I will allow the rest of your loved ones to live. Take it or leave it."

I stopped breathing, the air caught halfway down my throat. I was thankful breathing was not a requirement.

"What do you mean…the rest? What have you done? Where's Kalia?"

"Oh, Kalia's fine. She's out spending Aaron's money. Don't you worry about her…yet. Jack on the other hand…" He smiled and shook his head.

My body went weak and I dropped to my knees.

"What did you do?" I screamed, banging my fists on the carpet.

"You've got quite a temper, little lady," he chastised. "Let's just say Jack is no longer hurting after you. He won't be worrying about your abrupt disappearance anymore."

"How could you?" I was growling, I realized, instead of speaking. "Why? Why him?" I shook my head in disbelief, still trying to make sense of what he was saying.

"It wasn't easy, let me tell you, he put up quite a fight and the dog, well, Maia took care of that minor inconvenience."

"You killed Jack?" I shook my head as I stared at the carpet below me. I couldn't believe what he was saying, didn't want to believe what he was saying.

"The funeral was this morning. Google it if you don't believe me," he announced. "Maia is quite…helpful. So anyway, you either come with me, or, one by one, they die."

I couldn't speak. I couldn't move. All I could do was sit crumpled on the floor and stare at the carpet, hoping that maybe I was able to sleep and this was some sort of a bad dream, some horrible nightmare.

"I would of course, save the best for last. Maia is useful to me, so not her, not right away. Aaron and Kalia I have no use for. Your beloved and wonderful Christian, he's the prize I'm after…unless you choose correctly, that is." His face was serious as he came down to the floor, to my level, trying to make eye contact. I knew without looking at his eyes that he was dead serious.

"No! You leave them alone! I will do what you want. You just leave them out of it!" I rose, my legs shaking, my vision blurred as I tried to focus on his face.

"Good choice, my love. You won't regret it," he said as he stood.

He stretched his arms out to me, watching my face in silence. I couldn't look at his eyes…not now. I walked into his arms and let my body go limp in his embrace. I saw nothing around me as we left the room, my face tucked into his chest, my eyes closed. I only felt the cold air rush past us as we flew out the open window of my sitting room. The only thing I could think of while we were in the air, still above the house, strangely, was that my cell phone was on the passenger seat of my car, about fifty feet below us.

THE COLD WIND flew past us as we climbed higher, Ian trying to get just above the clouds to avoid being seen. I clung to his hard body, not because I wanted to, but out of fear. I was never comfortable with heights. I felt numb. My thoughts were going in circles, nothing made sense. I pictured Christian's face, the tear I had caused, and sighed. I pictured Jack, his sweet face, his innocent eyes, and I wished I could cry, mourn for him the way humans did when they lost someone they cared about but…

Forget about Christian…as long as you are with me, he will be safe… living his happy little life. What were you thinking, anyway, a human? What on earth possessed you to fall in love with a human?

I ignored his question and continued to cling to him, my face buried in his chest, my eyes closed.

Where are you taking me? There was no emotion in that question.

You'll see when we get there. You just keep your eyes closed. I know how much this scares you.

He did remember that.

Don't you think someone will be looking for me…eventually?

Why should they? We left no trace, no clues. They won't know you're with me. Besides, as much as you move around, they'll just assume…

He was probably right. They may think I just couldn't face everything that was happening and just reacted like a coward, leaving everything I owned behind. But Maia would return…and then maybe…I stopped that thought as soon as it reached my mind.

Too bad you're so scared. It's a gorgeous view over the clouds, but that's okay. I'll keep you safe…

His arms tightened around me. I welcomed the embrace, out of fear and hurt, regardless of whose it was. I had been in this position many times in the past, flying through the air surrounded by Ian's strong, hard arms. The difference was that, this time, I was doing it out of necessity, not love.

I still love you, Lily. I always did…all that time apart…I never stopped loving you or wanting you.

He was listening. I needed to be extra careful.

You have a funny way of showing love. First you leave me, then you kill someone I cared about, then you threaten to kill the ones I love, then you take me prisoner! Did I forget anything?

I had no choice. You gave me no choice. Maybe one day you'll understand. I will make you happy this time, I promise.

Understand what? I know nothing! I have no idea why you left me in the first place!

One day soon I'll explain. For now, just let me show you I love you, that I never stopped…just let me do what I should have done all along.

I couldn't wait to hear this! Whatever explanation he would give, I couldn't imagine. I buried my face closer to his chest, trying to block the wind with the collar of his jacket. He took that as a sign, one I hadn't meant at all, and I felt his grip grow tighter, squeezing me to him. Without realizing it, I intertwined my legs with his, to keep them from dangling as we soared through the air. I was surprised, and repulsed, at how safe I felt in his arms.

The wind was bitter cold as we continued to soar, just below the clouds now as the sky was losing light. I clung to him, trying not to look below. My legs were starting to feel stiff. I hoped we were nearing wherever it was he was taking me. We could not continue like this much longer, me clinging and him supporting my full weight. It wasn't as windy now and he seemed to have slowed down a bit so I tried my voice.

"Where are we going?" I asked. It wasn't easy to speak with the amount of air and rain still hitting our bodies but it was somewhat better.

"Back home," he yelled against the wind.

"Are you crazy?" I yelled back. "Do you mean to tell me that we are flying – like this – all the way to Ireland?"

"Oh, no, even I wouldn't attempt that, not carrying you, anyway. We're going to New York and catching a flight to Dublin," he explained.

"How is that possible? Did you realize I don't happen to have anything with me, even a passport?" I asked in disbelief.

"That's all taken care of, don't you worry about it. Your things are waiting at the airport," he yelled.

"How? When? I don't understand…"

"I took the liberty of packing a bag for you and getting your passport, no worries," he chuckled.

"You broke into my room when, when I wasn't home?" I was dumbfounded.

"I did, I confess. By the way…" he started.

"What?" I snapped, furious at the thought of him going through my things.

"If you hate me so much, like you claim to, then why do you still keep all the things I gave you? All those memories of us?"

"Because I'm a glutton for punishment, I guess! I have no other reason!" I yelled.

I honestly hadn't given the reason for that any thought. Many times I had taken that box, ready to burn it, only to shove it back its hiding place. I was never able to bring myself to actually destroy it. For the longest time I clung to the thought that something had happened to him, something horrible to keep him away from me. I refused to believe the idea that he could just leave me. I always had hope that he would find his way back to me. Little by little, that hope started fading away, along with my love for him and yet, I did still cling to those memories. Hmm…

"I'm sorry, I know you hate when I do this but are you saying you don't love me at all anymore?" He asked, squeezing me a little tighter to his body.

"No. I mean yes; that's what I'm saying. I don't love you anymore. I haven't for a long time. You are wasting your time! You belong with Maia. She obviously wants you," I snapped at him. "Can't you stay out of my head for even a minute?"

"I could but I won't. It was never easy to communicate with you. I have to listen to your thoughts to get the truth from you. You don't talk!" he scolded.

"Where are we? Shouldn't we be close to New York by now?" I ignored his accusations. I couldn't stand the stiffness in my legs much longer. I needed to stretch them out, walk a little. I also wanted more than anything to be free of his embrace, the icy cold, hard embrace, so the opposite of Christian's.

"Haven't you noticed we've been descending or are you too busy being scared? No wonder you can't fly!" He laughed.

I opened my eyes, just a slit, and turned my face away from his chest. He was right; we were much lower, just above the rooftops. I turned my face back and shut my eyes.

"Where are we landing?" I yelled.

"Not sure yet. I'm looking. We can land on any one of these buildings with tenant roof access and use the elevator. We'll take a cab to the airport," he explained.

"How long have you been planning this?" I dared.

"Ever since the day I left," he answered. I knew better than to insist on a better explanation, to anger him…not at this height.

It was only a matter of minutes, though the way my body ached it felt more like hours, before I felt the thump of his feet. As soon as his feet hit the ground, I felt our bodies straighten. He ran slightly, with me still in his arms, before coming to a complete stop. We finally stood still, his arms still around me. He loosened his grip, making sure I could stand on my own, before dropping his arms to his sides. I was afraid to take a step for fear that my legs were permanently shaped to the way they had intertwined with his.

He stretched his arms straight up and arched his back, trying to loosen his muscles. I followed suit and tried to do the same, stumbling forward a few steps before I realized I was, again, in his arms.

"Easy there…slowly. You're not used to flying. You have to be really stiff. You had a death grip up there." He laughed as his arms tightened around my waist, supporting me.

"Yeah, guess so. I can do it now. Let go."

He held on to me still, one hand reaching up to stroke my hair. I started pushing away from him but realized my arms felt like rubber. It was no use. He pulled my head back, grasping my hair, and looked at my face. If I hadn't known better, I would have sworn I saw compassion in his eyes.

"I will never make the mistake of letting you go again. I swear it," he whispered before his lips touched mine. I stood helpless for a few seconds, unsure of what to do; after all, we were still really high. Suddenly, I found myself kissing him back. Disgust set in and I pushed him away, trying to find some strength in my numb arms. He stumbled backward two steps and froze with a hurt expression on his face.

"I'm sorry, Ian, but you have to give me some time. It's been way too long. I need time to get used to all this," I explained, trying to smile.

"You're right, my love. I'll try harder," he said smiling back and nodding. "Stay put. I'll go find a way into the building…" He went around a corner.

I stood, looking up at the darkening sky. I'm so sorry Christian, so sorry for what I am about to do. I didn't know if I meant to kiss him back or whether it had been just an instinct but, what I did know was I was going to have to do some of the best acting of my life. I was going to play Ian's game, his way.

⤳ FOURTEEN ⤳

We landed in Dublin, Ireland, sometime close to dawn. I wasn't paying much attention to the time. Having been from New York to London to Dublin, it all became a blur. I played my role, very well I might add, throughout the rest of the trip. I rested my head on his shoulder and even allowed him to hold my hand through most of the flight. We talked a lot also but I decided not to bring up anything touchy. I would get the answers I wanted later, one way or another.

Ian had a suitcase and my passport waiting for us in an airport locker in New York. I was shocked, however, to discover that I had another bag, a small duffle. It wasn't a bag recognized. I looked at him with surprise and he smiled.

"It's the contents of the box under your bed. I figured it would be easier to carry this way since it had no lid," he explained.

"Oh, thanks. Good idea."

He rented a car in Dublin and began the one-hour drive to Maam. Maam, or Maam Cross as it was known, was not where Ian was born and raised, but, conveniently enough, it was one of the darkest and rainiest places, and therefore the best place to be when one was a vampire. I sat back in the seat and looked out the window as Ian sped through curvy roads. I wasn't much in the mood to talk, feeling exhausted from the confrontation with Ian and all the traveling. What I wanted more than anything at that moment was to think, to think about *him*, but, of course, I didn't dare.

Ian drove silently, concentrating on the road ahead, possibly considering my need to rest. Every once in a while, I couldn't help but glance over at him. He looked gentle and serene when he was deep in thought. He glanced over and smiled at me. I turned my head.

"What were you looking at?" he asked, his eyes back on the road.

"You. It's just been so long. I was trying to remember, the way you looked back then." It was true, I was reminiscing, trying to remember what exactly had been so intriguing to make me fall so hard.

"You don't have to stop. I like it. I missed it," he said with a sigh.

"I...um...it just doesn't seem right," I explained. "We've been apart for so long and now I'm just supposed to sit here, with you? I don't know what to say or how to act. I don't know what to do."

I twitched at the touch of his skin on mine. I looked down at my hand before I realized he was holding it in his. His touch felt wrong, yet so familiar. His thumb traced circles on my skin the way Kalia's did when she was trying to calm me. The thought of Kalia hurt. What would she think when she discovered I was gone? What would Aaron think? And Maia? Christian's beautiful face flashed into my mind. I felt the angry squeeze.

"Ow! Let go!" I hissed.

"I'm sorry. Truly, I am. Just have some respect, please," he said without taking his hand away. He only loosened his grasp.

"Respect? What do you know about respect?" I yelled as I tried to pull my hand out of his.

"I'm sorry...again. Let's not start off this way. I hoped this could be a fresh start for us," he pleaded, looking at me with a hurt expression.

I swallowed hard and stopped struggling against his iron grip.

"You're right. No more fighting,"

As I looked out the window, I noticed we were surrounded by nothing but fields. There was no sign of civilization in any direction. The breeze blew through a wheat field, making it a maze of ripples. I kept my eyes on the road ahead, realizing it was now a dirt road.

"Where are we going?" I asked. I hoped we were stopping soon. I needed some distance from him, even if it was just for a matter of minutes.

"We're almost there...patience," he replied. He looked at me and smiled. I saw it from the corner of my eyes, his self-satisfied smile. I refused to acknowledge it, keeping my eyes straight ahead.

The road came to a T ahead of us. I felt the car slow and we turned left. This dirt road was much narrower than the one we were on previously and he drove much slower. I noticed many more trees farther ahead, on the right side. They were so close together they seemed to form a wall. As we approached the tree wall I noticed a break where we turned down another narrow dirt road that led us to a small stone cottage that seemed to have appeared out of nowhere. The cottage had a red wooden door. A black iron lantern hung just above the door, still lit, despite the fact that there was now light in the sky.

He stopped the car just a few feet away from the front door. I looked out the window, wondering if there was enough room for the car door to swing open and not hit the house.

"We're home," he announced. "Isn't it beautiful?"

"I don't know. All I see is a red door."

"Yeah…sorry 'bout that. Bad habit," he said and came to my side to help me out.

I let him take my hand and help me out of the car, letting go as soon as I found my way between the car and the house. I walked toward the trunk to get my bags. He grabbed my arm, stopping me.

"Don't worry about our stuff. Fergus will get it later," he informed me as he pulled me through the door.

"Fergus? Who is…Fergus?" I asked.

"Fergus is a…friend. He lives here too," he explained.

I looked around the small cottage, shocked at the size of it, and wondered how anyone else could possibly live here.

"No…not in the same house. They live in the back, just at the top of the hill."

"They?" I asked.

"Three of them. They're with me…Fergus, Ryanne, and Fiore. You'll meet them soon enough," he said and pulled me into his arms. "For now, it's just you and I."

Just what I wanted!

His arms were around me, squeezing me to him. His hands stroked my hair. He leaned his face onto the top of my head and I heard him inhale. I closed my eyes as hard as I could, trying not to let images of Christian flood my thoughts.

"I've missed that scent so much," he inhaled again. "I've always loved the smell of your hair, your shampoo."

He continued to sniff my hair, his hands on the back of my head. After what felt like hours, though I knew it had to be only seconds, his lips made their way to my forehead. I closed my eyes even tighter, briefly remembering the feel of Christian's lips on my skin, fire. Ian's felt nothing like that so it was easy to push Christian out of my head, at least for the time being. Ian's skin was the same temperature as mine so there was no shock to the feel of his touch. Except, that it was him.

His mouth found mine, devouring. I pushed at his chest with both hands not even budging him. Instead, he held me closer to his body. I kept my mouth as stiff as possible, not responding to his demands. My mouth started watering, feeling the hunger that came with excitement. I pushed at him harder.

He lifted his face enough to look at my eyes. His expression was unreadable.

"What is the problem?" he asked, his voice still soft.

"I...I'm not ready for this...not yet," I said, trying to catch my breath. It had taken all my strength to push him a little bit.

"I can't take it anymore. I have done nothing but want you since I saw you again. Now I have you in my arms, finally, and you're telling me no?" he asked, still holding on to me.

"Ian, I am not a robot. You can't come waltzing back into my life after almost sixty years and expect me to jump right in with both feet!"

He dropped his arms, but not before kissing my lips once more. I backed away, looking around for someplace to sit. I saw an armchair in front of the window and headed to it. I let my whole body drop on it.

"Okay. We'll do this your way...for a while, anyway. You want me too. You just need to remember that. I can only be patient for so long, my love," he said and turned away. He walked through a door behind him, disappearing.

I looked around the room. There were two armchairs, both in front of the window with a round table in between. Across from that was a love seat with oversized cushions. An oval area rug laid in front of the sofa, colored in earth tones. The only other thing in this section of the room was a fireplace. Ash covered the floor in front of it.

Behind the sofa was a very small kitchen. Everything looked extremely clean, like it was never used. Of course, vampires had no need for food, but most of us did use the kitchen. Kalia had her plants, and of course her paintings, all over the kitchen. Aaron usually read his morning newspaper at the kitchen table and that is where we sometimes sat to talk or read mail. This kitchen didn't even have a table!

I assumed the door Ian disappeared through must be his bedroom. I wondered if there was a bathroom in this place. I had the sudden desire to take a shower, a long, hot shower, to wash Ian's scent off my skin and hair. I slid myself down in the chair and stretched my legs out. I threw my arms up over the top of the chair and took a deep breath.

What now? I was going to have to play my part and had absolutely no desire to do it. All I wanted to do was to get back to Christian, explain what I had done, and ask his forgiveness. But, I knew that was impossible. Not only did I have to deal with Ian but…what possible explanation could I give? I had nothing and I knew it! It didn't matter whether or not I would be able to get away from the predicament I found myself in; I still could not see Christian again!

"Ugh!" I yelled out of frustration.

"Did you say something? Sorry…I was on the phone," Ian said as he came out of the room carrying two folded towels in his hands.

"No. Just stretching. I'm sore. Are those for me?" I asked, thankful he had been on the telephone and not listening to my mind.

"Uh, yeah. Figured you might like a bath…long trip. Freshen up a bit and you'll feel much better. We should eat soon, too," he said as he handed me the towels. "This way…"

I followed him to the open bedroom door. Just as I walked in the first door, there was another door to my left. He turned the knob and pushed it open.

"Everything you'll need should be in here. If you need something else, let me know. I'll come running," he said with a sheepish smile.

"Yeah…thanks," I replied and closed the door before he could say anything else.

It was a normal bathroom, a bit small but otherwise normal. I set the towels on the closed toilet seat. I stood in front of the sink and looked at my image in the mirror and felt suddenly disgusted. His hands in my hair, on my neck, even my face. I saw no trace of that in my reflection but I still felt it all over my skin. I glared at my own eyes: dark as night, angry, hateful. Why did I have to be such a coward, even when I felt so furious with him? I could have fought, should have fought…somehow. He was not much older than I was when he made me. His strength couldn't be that much more than mine. Could it?

I started the water and sat on the side of the tub to adjust the temperature. The warmth felt good, relaxing, on my cold fingers. I watched my fingers, the water running over them, through them, and the image of his beautiful face filled my mind. I could smell him, his sweetness, as soon as I closed my eyes. I saw his deep, warm, blue eyes looking lovingly into mine. I sighed as I thought of him, feeling the emptiness his absence caused when a loud bang made me jump, right off the narrow edge of the tub and onto the wooden floor.

"Lily!" Ian's voice screamed through the door. "What are you doing?"

"Taking a shower! What do you think I'm doing?" I yelled back through my teeth.

"That's not what I'm hearing! You need to learn respect when you're in my house!" he screamed again, his face pressed to the door, his voice a bit muffled.

"What do you expect? I asked you to give me time. Do it!" I yelled. I started the shower. "I'll be out soon. Give me *some* privacy…at least in here!"

I heard his footsteps pounding away. I stood up and dropped my clothes onto the floor. I realized that in my haste to get away from him and close myself in the bathroom, I hadn't thought to bring any clean clothes with me. My bag was still in the trunk of the rental car. Panic set in for a moment until I heard his footsteps outside the door again. I threw myself against it and grabbed the knob. I could hear him breathing on the other side but he made no attempt to speak. Suddenly, panic struck again as I felt the doorknob shake.

"What do you want, Ian?" I asked, keeping the door shut with the weight of my body since the knob had no lock.

"Here…your things," he whispered from the other side. He pushed the door open as my feet slid on the floor. I let go of the knob and wrapped my arms around myself, trying to cover as much of my naked body as possible. He stood in front of me, my bag dangling in the hand of his outstretched arm.

I instinctively thought to reach for it but my mind caught on quicker. I wrapped my arms tighter around myself.

"Drop it!" I snapped.

"Just trying to help. Relax…" he said and continued to dangle my bag in his hand. His head tilted to the side. "Still as beautiful as ever."

I backed away as he stepped forward, but only a couple steps. The way I was glaring at him must have something to do with his hesitation. It wasn't like Ian to stop himself from taking anything he wanted. I squinted, trying to look at him with as much anger as possible. A slight growl escaped my throat.

"Okay, okay. Here…I get it," he said. He unwrapped his fingers, one by one, from the handle and let it fall to the floor. His sarcasm made me want to pound my fists on his head. I pictured the pained look on his face at the possibility of me causing him damage. His eyes still locked to mine, he closed the door behind him.

I took a deep breath as soon as the door was closed again. I had expected more of a challenge, perhaps a fight, to get him to leave and yet, he had gone before it turned to that. Could I have possibly put that angry image in his head? Umm…that could be useful. Many years ago, when I finally realized I had the ability to impose my mental images into the minds of others, I was already separated from Ian. Ian never experienced my imposed visions, until now. But, how could I use that to my advantage? There had to be a way. I would figure that out later, when he wasn't hovering.

With a towel wrapped around my hair, piled high on my head, I put on a clean pair of jeans and a long-sleeved cotton shirt. Ian packed exactly three of each—jeans, shirts, socks, underwear, bras. He put one extra pair of shoes in the bottom of my bag. I pulled those out before I put the clothing back in. As I prepared to leave the bathroom, I picked the shoes up in one hand and the bag in the other. Turning the knob with the hand as I held the shoes and the bag wasn't easy so I dropped the shoes. The fall loosened the objects I normally stored in that pair. How convenient, that in his rush to pack my things while I wasn't home, he grabbed that particular pair, the one that contained my credit cards!

I did not, usually, carry a purse and since I rarely shopped, I stored my credit cards in a pair of shoes I seldom wore. They were a bit too tight. I shoved the cards back into the shoe. I had a way out! If I could figure out a way to get away from him, I wouldn't be totally helpless. I had money!

I heard the front door open and then voices.

"Hello. Come on in. Where's Fiore?" Ian asked.

A low male voice answered, "She's still gathering dinner. Should be back soon."

"Where is she?" a female voice asked.

"Should be out any minute. She was showering," Ian answered.

I held my breath and paused where I stood. I took the towel off my head and ran my fingers through my wet hair, arranging it quickly so it did not hang in my face. I figured it must be Fergus and Ryanne in the living room. Great! Time to meet Ian's puppets. I took one last look in the mirror before hanging the towel up on the shower curtain rod. I heard two thoughts coming from the living room this time.

We will be at our best...won't let her...we promise. The first was the female.

We have always been loyal...without you, we'd be nothing... The male voice this time.

I listened, holding my breath. As usual, I heard nothing from Ian. I waited a few moments to see if there would be more but all was quiet so I made my entrance.

"Lily, feel better?" Ian asked with a smile on his face.

"Yes, I do. Hello..." I said to the rest of the party.

The female was tall and slender. Her long, curly, red hair hung to the middle of her back. Her green eyes, wide as she looked me up and down, were an indescribable shade of green. She wore a simple long, flowing white dress accented with dozens of silver bracelets on her pale arms, the black boots a contrast to her white hem. The male stood at her side. He was much shorter than Ryanne. His dark hair disheveled and dusty looking, hung just to his shoulders. His eyes were like onyx. I read thirst in his sunken pallor.

"So, here you are at last," Ryanne said with a hint of sarcasm.

"I suppose no introductions are needed. Lily has the gift too," Ian said looking at his guests, then back at me. "Fiore should be here soon. We are having a dinner party in your honor."

I couldn't imagine what that meant, nor did I have the interest to ask.

"Here...let me take that from you. I'll put it in our room," Ian said taking the bag from my hand. He walked away with it.

Our room? Great!

Ryanne tilted her head, looking at me. Of course she heard my brief thought. Damn! I was going to have to be careful around all of them apparently.

We stood still, the three of us, not bothering to speak. When Ian came back out of the bedroom, he went straight to the living room and sat, motioning for us to follow. Ryanne and Fergus did so. I stood still a moment longer, hesitating, seeing Ian had sat on the loveseat and had his arm already resting along the back, waiting for me to join him.

"Lily!" he said with a commanding tone. The other two looked at me.

I made my way over, wishing there were more chairs in the room, not that there was sufficient space for them. I sat, slower still, and leaned forward, avoiding his arm. He grabbed the back of my shirt, and with a laugh, pulled me back. His cold arm rested along my stiffened back, his fingers touching the upper part of my arm. How different it felt compared to Christian's hot fingers. I jumped as his fingers closed on my arm, snapping me out of that painful thought. Fergus and Ryanne smiled, baring all their glistening teeth. They seemed to have gotten some sort of enjoyment from my discomfort.

"Now then…" Ian said, holding me closer to his side. "This is more like it."

"When are they getting here? I'm famished," Fergus said. He was leaning forward, his elbows on his knees, eyes on the door.

"It should be very soon. She has the car. I told you not to go this long but…no. Do you ever listen?" Ryanne laughed.

"You'll have to excuse my friends. They have been fighting with each other for almost two centuries. They won't change that just because there is someone new here," Ian explained.

I looked at them. Two hundred years! Wow! I hadn't imagined they were together…but two hundred years…

"Yes, we have been together for what seems like forever. We met in England. I was immortal, he was not. I had been searching for over a hundred years when I found him," Ryanne explained, glancing at Fergus and smiling at him.

"So that makes you what? Like three hundred?" I asked in disbelief.

"Three hundred and twenty-one, to be exact. Does that surprise you?" she asked, leaning forward in her seat, looking intently into my eyes. I snapped my eyes away.

"Well…yes. I don't know too many that are as old as you," I admitted.

"How right you are! We are far and few between…" she said, stopping mid-sentence when Ian's face turned toward the door.

A shockingly beautiful vampire entered first. Dark hair curled in ringlets around her small, dainty face. Her almond shaped eyes were a deep, brown color with yellow flecks, glowing in the light of the lamps. She was fashion model thin with jeans so tight they looked painted on, black highheeled boots, and a red cowl necked sweater—a reflecting pool for the intense scarlet of her full lips. She tossed her hair aside, baring her perfect, slender neck. I couldn't take my eyes off her!

"Hello all," she sang as she stepped to the side, still holding the door open.

I caught a scent that made my mouth water. Fergus sat up straight in his seat. Ian dropped his arm from around my shoulders and stood. The only one that didn't move was Ryanne.

"I brought guests…two of them. Come on guys!" she said as she looked outside. She herded two men into the room.

The men stood, silent, waiting for Fiore to make a move. She closed the door and then turned to Ian. She stepped over to him and gave him a peck on the cheek. I saw her lips moving rapidly as she did this. Ian nodded his head so fast I doubted the two men noticed. Their scent filled the room. My mouth watered.

"Hello. Welcome," Ian said looking at the men. "I'm Ian. This is Lily, Fergus, and over there is Ryanne."

He pointed to all of us and Ryanne and Fergus jumped to their feet, stepping away from their chairs.

"Please, sit," Ryanne said, motioning to the empty seats.

The men took a quick look around the room and then made their way to the chairs. One of them, the one directly in front of me, was very small, thin. He smelled a little like…flowers? The other man, the one to my left, was slightly bigger. They were common looking men, nothing special about their appearance. They sat with their hands on their laps, fidgeting.

Fergus, Ryanne, and Fiore all made themselves comfortable on the floor, leaning against walls. The men looked at Fiore with admiration in their eyes. I also noticed them looking at me.

Wow! Beautiful women in this house…

I smiled as the smaller of the two sat admiring us. Ian squeezed my arm possessively now that he was seated next to me again. Fiore and the men made small talk as Ryanne and Fergus looked on. Fergus looked almost as if he were in a trance, his eyes blank. I waited for something to happen, for someone to explain why these men were here but no one did. I decided I wanted to find out.

"Ian, can I see you in the bedroom for a minute?" I asked with my eyes still on the two men that now chatted with the other three.

"Sure," he answered sweetly, rising from his seat and holding his hand out to help me up.

I stood, pretending I hadn't noticed his hand. I followed him to the room. Once there, he closed the door and sat on the bed. I took a deep breath and cleared my throat.

"Who are those guys? Why are they here?" I whispered.

"They, my love, are dinner. Fiore finds them in the city and brings them to us," he stated as if it was nothing unusual.

"Are you kidding me?" I snapped, a little too loudly. Ian's index finger flew to his lip, to hush me.

"It's how we do things around here. They drink, they chat, they flirt, and then they're ours. No harm done," he whispered, his face so close to mine I could feel his breath. "I suggest you forget the way you do things. You're with us now. You play by our rules. No more evil-doers only diet for you so get used to it, beautiful."

"We'll see about that!" I whispered back, showing as much anger in my hushed voice as possible.

He took my hand and led me back out of the room.

They were seated as before, but now they all had wine glasses in front of them. As the night dragged on, the laughter got louder as the humans got drunker. I sat back glumly and listened, speaking only when spoken to and even then my answers were short. I wanted to think of a way to save these men, innocents, but couldn't do much thinking with Ian hovering. At one point, I tried to vividly picture what would happen to them in my mind, only to have one of them, the drunker one of the two, look at me for a moment and shake his head in disbelief, as if trying to shake a hallucination out of his mind. Of course, Ian noticed what I was trying to do and, again, squeezed my arm so hard it stung for quite a while.

The night dragged on, with me sitting on the sofa, next to Ian, watching the whole charade. I knew better than to attempt anything to save them again. It didn't make a difference anyway. There was no way they could avoid being killed by four fierce, thirsty vampires. I knew it was hopeless so I just sat, stiff and still, watching and waiting.

The drunker the men became, the more Fiore and Ryanne flirted with them. As Ryanne flirted, I watched Fergus for any sign of jealousy; instead, I saw admiration and lust in his wild eyes. His fangs showed every time he smiled but the inebriated men noticed nothing. The party continued.

Finally, after listening to the slurred speech of the two humans for what seemed like hours, Fiore made the first move. She walked over to the smaller man, the one seated directly in front of Ian and me, and climbed onto his lap. The smile on his face made me want to scream *run as fast as you can!* My mind pleaded with him, with her, with all of them. Ian held me tighter, one arm around my shoulders, and one hand holding my hand. His hand squeezed mine every time I flinched. Fiore was now kissing the innocent man passionately. His friend looked on with envy. He glanced at Ryanne with lust. Ryanne took the bait and stood to walk over to him. She kneeled on the floor in front of his legs and made her way to his face.

I looked away, burying my face in Ian's cold chest. He wrapped both arms around me and held me tighter, enjoying the closeness. Moments later, Fergus stood and walked to where Ryanne was kneeling. I peeked with one eye, afraid to really see but curious anyway.

Ryanne was holding the limp man in her arms, still kneeling on the floor, as Fergus bent over his face attaching his hungry mouth to the man's neck. I looked at the other man just as Fiore was backing away from his neck, wiping her mouth daintily with a napkin she pulled out of her pocket. She looked at Ian.

"He's all yours. Enjoy…it's very sweet. Good choice in wines tonight," she said stepping away from the man who was now slumped over the side of the chair. She straightened her sweater as she walked toward us. "Ladies first. Lily…"

She stretched her hand out toward me. I looked at her, lifting my head from Ian's chest, my eyes wide with horror.

"I'm not thirsty. I drank just before…too much, I think." My voice cracked.

"Your loss," Ian said as he stood and reached the slumped body before I could even move out of his way. He bent over the body and drank.

Once they'd had their fill, it was Fergus's job to dispose of the bodies. He took both, one over each shoulder, and headed out the door, which Ryanne held open for him.

"Well, Lily…it was good to finally meet you. I think we'll call it a night. Good party, as usual, Ian," she said kissing Ian on the cheek before nodding to me and following Fergus out into the darkness.

Fiore left shortly after them, kissing both Ian and I goodbye. I stood, frozen to the floor, not saying a word. I felt nothing but disgust for what had happened. Ian stood next to me, a wide smile on his face.

"Shall we?" he asked, holding his hand out to me. "Shall we go rest a while?"

I let him take my hand and lead me to his bedroom. I walked without saying a word, my steps automatic, and my mind blank.

⤳ FIFTEEN ⤶

It was hard to believe three weeks had passed since my ordeal began. I now spent every moment of every day stuck to Ian's side. Every time I tried to get away from him, even if it was only for mere moments, like when I walked the perimeter of the woods surrounding the cottage, he sent someone looking for me. Because of their feeding habits, my survival depended on animal blood. I couldn't adapt to their way. Ian tried to talk me into it, giving me his usual population control speech but I refused.

So far, I managed to ward off Ian's advances. When we went to the bedroom to *rest*, we lay side by side on the bed and he tried to get close but I always managed to stop him. He didn't insist. He seemed to be walking on eggshells and relented when I requested more time. I usually started some sort of conversation to occupy his mind. I wanted to know so many things I was afraid to ask. I was afraid not only of his reaction but also of my reaction to the answers. I wanted to know what he had done to Jack. Had Jack suffered? Had he known what hit him? I also wanted to know how much he knew about Christian but I didn't dare ask.

I remained as friendly and contented as possible, with all of them, biding my time. I knew Ian couldn't stay by my side too much longer. This was totally out of character for him. Sooner or later, he would need to leave to do whatever it was he did when he disappeared for days. He would have to leave me with his little coven of loyal servants. And when he did, I would have to act fast.

I decided to go for a walk through the fields and the woods one afternoon. The sun was out on and off. I was bored and could find nothing to occupy my time. I dabbled with writing again, read as much as possible, and watched television to keep my mind from wandering to thoughts I needed to keep protected. As I was about to turn the doorknob, I heard

Ian leaving the bedroom.

"Where are you going?" he asked.

"Just for a walk," I answered. My hand was still on the knob, waiting, hoping he would let me go alone. If he wanted to, he would send a message to the mind of one of his slaves, telling them to follow me. I didn't mind Fiore so much. She usually walked with me, talking to me. The others just kept a safe distance, watching from afar.

"Good idea. I will go with you. I'll get my shoes," he said and headed back to the room. "You know the sun is shining today."

"I know but there's no one around. There never is," I explained.

We were isolated. It was very seldom a car passed on the dirt road at the end of the property. Regardless, there were plenty of trees to duck behind if anyone did happen to venture out here and I sincerely hoped no one did…for their sake.

I waited for Ian to return, discouraged that I couldn't have as much as a single moment alone with my thoughts, my memories. I would rather have Fiore's company. She was easy to talk to and she didn't insist on answers. Sometimes we walked in complete silence, enjoying our surroundings. I did, however, learn much about her during our walks. I learned she came from Italy and didn't remember her maker. They parted ways not long after she transformed her and it was so long ago that what memories she did have were hazy. I also learned, interestingly enough, that Fiore was not only the oldest of the foursome but she had been with them the least amount of time. Something in her tone as she talked about her new coven told me she had not yet made her decision to stay.

"Ready?" Ian asked with a wide smile as he approached me, interrupting my thoughts but making no comments about whether or not he had been listening.

"Yeah, ready," I said, leading the way.

I started walking up the hill, like I usually did, past the other cottage on the property. He walked behind me until we made it to the top then made his way next to me, holding his hand out. I hesitated a moment, but after seeing the peaceful look in his eyes I gave in. He grasped my hand at once, giving it a gentle squeeze.

We walked in silence for a while, past the cottage, the abandoned stone barn, and across a field. When we got to the edge of the trees, Ian suddenly stopped, eyes scanning the area.

"What's wrong?" I followed his eyes.

"Nothing. I want to show you something. I just have to remember where it is," he explained.

He looked right and then left, deciding on a direction. I walked beside him, my hand still in his, being careful not to trip over branches strewn about. Every time we came to something that blocked the way, he stopped and assisted me, whether it was moving something out of the way or helping me climb over it. I wasn't used to this type of behavior from him. He usually treated me with the least amount of attention possible; at least, that was how it was back then, in another time. The less he had to do for me, or anyone for that matter, the better. Now he was acting like an attentive boyfriend.

As we walked deeper into the woods, I could hear the sound of water in the distance. I tried to block out the sound of animals scurrying from the sounds of our footsteps. The closer we got, the more clearly I heard it. Moments later, smelled it. It was an earthy smell, like the way a ball field smells after a sudden downpour. I smiled at that thought. I always loved the sound of running water.

"You like that?" He smiled.

Rays of sun that managed to find their way through the dense trees shone off his glistening teeth. I could see the blood running beneath the pale skin of his face.

"You know I do. What is it?" I asked, trying to sound lighthearted.

"It's the prettiest little brook. You'll see," he said. "I haven't been here for a long time. It shouldn't be much further."

We walked on, following our senses, led by the sound and the smell of the brook. In a matter of minutes, he stopped, his grasp on my hand a little tighter, maybe from the excitement.

A narrow brook flowed curving through a lush, green bank. Just in front of us, on the edge of the bank, a tree had fallen, long ago by the looks of it, creating a perfect seat. Wildflowers, along with long blades of grass grew all around it. The water looked cool and refreshing. A bird flew over the water before flying high to rest on a tree branch, directly across from where we stood. He looked at us for a moment, tilting his head to the side, before flying away with a loud screech.

"It's beautiful."

"I come here sometimes when I want to be alone," he said, leading me to the edge of the water.

When we stood in front of the fallen trunk, I saw it was farther away from the edge than it looked from the other side. He pulled me to the ground and instead of sitting on the trunk, we sat on the grass and leaned against it.

"I can't believe I never found this before," I said looking around, admiring the serenity of the scenery. "I usually go the other way and circle around back to the cottage. Fiore didn't tell me about it either."

"As far as I know, she doesn't come here. She doesn't usually walk the grounds. She's more of a city girl. She never used to go for walks in the woods until you came along," he explained, leaning against me.

He continued to hold my hand on his outstretched legs, tracing circles on the top of my hand with his index finger and watching what he was doing. He seemed so calm and serene now that I was afraid to move for fear that his mood might change. This calm, peaceful Ian was not someone I knew.

I leaned my head back against the moss-covered trunk and closed my eyes. I inhaled the freshness around me and sighed, for once relaxing in his presence. The breeze blew through my hair and felt so relaxing that I felt almost positive I could sleep.

"Lily," he said almost in a whisper. His voice sounded sad.

"Yeah?" I said, not bothering to open my eyes.

"Are you ever going to forgive me? Is it ever going to be the same between us?"

I hesitated, not knowing what to say. I kept my eyes closed and focused on the feel of his skin on mine. It was so familiar, almost comfortable. It scared me. Christian's face flashed in my mind. I felt Ian stiffen, growing tense. That gave me the answer I was looking for.

I turned my head and looked into his eyes. I stared at him for a moment, not moving. Then, I closed my eyes, took a deep breath, and thought, *perdoname*. I knew Ian didn't speak Spanish. It was something he hadn't bothered to learn, even though we spent time in South America. He thought it was a waste of time. Before he could question what I thought, I pushed myself away from the trunk and climbed, both legs straddled around him, onto his lap. I took his face in my hands, seeing the shock in his eyes, took a deep breath, closed my eyes as tightly as I could manage, and leaned toward his lips. I let his passion take control so that later, I could take control.

***

In the days following the intimate moment between us, Ian seemed to relax a little more. He didn't question me much when I took a walk with Fiore and was sometimes gone for hours. He didn't seem to bring up the issue of my choice in diet anymore. He did, however, still hover when I was in the cottage, never leaving the room for long. I acted as affectionately toward him as my conscience would allow, hoping he would trust me more, enabling him to leave me, like he did in the past.

According to Fiore, Ian still disappeared for long periods of time, never informing anyone of his whereabouts or the length of his absence. I was trying to prepare him for that, trying to make him believe I would still be here when he returned, that we could be a couple again. I didn't know if it would work but I had to try.

One afternoon, months after arriving in Ireland, I sat on the sofa reading when Ian came to sit beside me. I closed the book but kept it on my lap. He sat, silent at first, and then looked at me with sadness.

"I need to talk to you about something," he said, his eyes now on his lap.

"What is it?"

"I'm trying, Lily. I really am, believe me."

"I know and so am I," I answered. "Talk to me."

"I know it hasn't been easy for you. I know I've done many things, things I'm not proud of but..." he looked down at his lap again. I didn't interrupt.

"I don't blame you if you say no but I need to ask your forgiveness, for everything," he said looking at me again, waiting for an answer.

"My forgiveness? Why? Does this mean..." I asked, confused. I wished I had a way into his mind.

"Oh, no. I'm sorry. I can't let you go. I won't, let you go. I love you too much," he said with a sigh. "I mean for everything I've done in the past, including recently, with your friend in Olympia and all."

My breath stopped in my throat. I had been trying not to think of poor Jack who died because of me. I hated myself for that! I had been fighting with myself to keep from asking questions about it, to keep from imagining how dreadful his last moments must have been. I forced myself to breathe again and swallowed hard, trying to clear the lump in my throat so I could speak.

"Why are you doing this? Since when do you ask my forgiveness?" I snapped.

"Because I think we can't have an honest fresh start unless you can do that. Forgive me. I know how I feel about you but I don't know how you feel about me. I haven't been able to get into your head. I don't know why but I can't."

Since we arrived here, I tried hard not to think about anything he might be able to use against me or might anger him. Unfortunately, painful memories did pop into my head from time to time and I stopped them as quickly as I could, trying to focus on something else. I found myself doing that more often. I felt guilty for what I was doing with Ian, though I knew there was no way possible I could go back to what I really wanted. Had I really been able to stop Ian from his mental invasions? If so, how?

I changed my thinking back to the present conversation, though my fingers still played with the book on my lap. I looked at his eyes again; he simply waited for me to speak. He hadn't heard me.

"I will forgive you. God knows I shouldn't but, you know me, I can't hold grudges. I think we deserve a fresh start."

"Thank you, Lily. You don't know how happy that makes me," he said, his eyes glowing. "One more thing: how do you feel about me?"

I bit my lip and told myself to relax. I could do this.

"I love you, Ian. I never stopped. I was angry with you but, I never stopped loving you," I answered.

His eyes filled with so much happiness that I almost felt guilty. Almost. After all, he deserved it. He was the inventor of lies. That much I had learned from him.

He wrapped his arms around me, clinging. I returned his hug, wrapping my arms around his back. When he leaned back to kiss me, I didn't hesitate. I allowed him to kiss me for as long as he wanted. I let myself get lost in it, not wanting to think at all, just respond. When he finally pulled away, I felt a longing I hadn't expected. Somehow, I didn't want him to stop. I decided to let it go for the moment, analyze it later. I wanted to keep things as peaceful as possible.

"We should celebrate!" He jumped up, excited. "I know! I'm taking you out for dinner. I promise no innocents. You have to be starting to feel weak from nothing but the blood of animals. You need a human."

"I guess I am. Animal blood is hard to get used to," I smiled at him as carefree as I could manage. "I'll get ready."

THAT NIGHT, WE fed mostly my way, but a little Ian's way too. I picked the human, a woman, using my mind by finding her faults and then painting enticing pictures to lure her. My way was a little more subtle, a little gentler. I lured my prey, played up to what I painted in their minds – to an extent anyway – then took the plunge. Ian had a habit of wanting to plunge right in, no regard for the victim's fear. He cornered them and then went straight for the kill, no subduing images fed into their subconscious to ease their panic. It was brutal the way he did it but I said nothing because, after all, it was at least someone with a criminal history.

Days later, I decided to go for a walk through the woods again. The sun was hiding behind dark clouds, though it was not yet raining. Ian was busy with something (what it was I did not bother to ask) so he suggested I take Fiore. I would rather have been alone, trusted by now, but I didn't argue his demand. Fiore was the one being I truly didn't mind spending time with. So, as Ian demanded, though he made it sound more like a suggestion, I went to the larger cottage, in search of her.

Fergus opened the door and peered out before I actually reached it. He looked as if he was expecting me.

"Hello, Fergus," I smiled. "Is Fiore in?"

"Yes, Miss. She told me to tell you she will be right out," he replied, blocking my view into the cottage with his slim figure.

"Can't I wait inside?" I asked. I was never inside this cottage and I was a bit curious to see how they lived.

"Umm…she'll just be a minute. I'll hurry her along," he said as he rushed away. I heard him turn the bolt on the door.

I stood in silence looking at the door. He went back inside with such haste, locking the door behind him, that I hadn't been able to catch even a glimpse of the interior. Why was I not allowed inside? I pondered that for a moment when I heard footsteps approaching. I backed away from the door, trying not to look conspicuous. The bolt was turned again and Fiore emerged from the other side, pulling it shut behind her.

"Hello." She smiled radiantly at me. Her face looked like the face of an angel when she smiled like that, eyes glowing.

"Hi. Were you busy?" I asked, looking for some kind of answer as to why I couldn't come inside.

"Oh, no," she said with a worried expression on her face. "Ryanne and Fergus were…cleaning. They don't want you to see the house the way it looks now. They are very thorough. They move everything." She started to walk toward the path we usually walked when we went out together.

I stopped her, touching her arm.

"Let's go that way today," I said, pointing to the path Ian and I had taken.

She looked nervous at first, eyeing the path I pointed out. She looked back at me and her expression looked instantly more relaxed, her brows smoothing out again.

"Do you know what's over there?" she asked.

"Well, of course. Ian took me. There's the most beautiful little brook. It's so peaceful and relaxing. I loved it," I explained. "I would love to sit there again. Have you been there before?"

"Only once. That's a place Ian likes to keep to himself," she explained. "But if he's taken you there, then I guess it's okay. Let's go."

I followed her lead, staying close to her heels. We strolled, admiring the greenery and the fresh air. We didn't talk at all. We maintained a comfortable silence. It wasn't until we got closer that she suddenly spoke.

"Did you go to the fallen tree?"

"Yes. We sat there for a while," I answered nervously. The images of what happened between us that day came rushing into my mind.

Fiore looked at me with shock on her face. She turned away, as if embarrassed; she had intruded on something so private. Suddenly ashamed, I looked at the ground as we continued toward the brook that would appear at the end of the path.

Once we arrived, I stood still just behind the fallen tree. I closed my eyes and let my other senses take over. I inhaled, allowing the fresh, clean scent of the running water to fill my lungs. My ears caught the sounds of small creatures scurrying for cover as they heard our approach. Birds called to each other in the trees above our heads.

"No wonder he likes to keep this place to himself," Fiore said, breaking the silence. "It is magical."

"It sure is. If I ever attempted to write again, this is where I would do it," I stated.

I stepped up on the tree trunk with one foot and hopped off the other side. I settled down in the grass, leaning against it as Ian and I did that day. Fiore looked around for a few more moments, then came to my side and settled herself down. She stretched her long, graceful arms above her head and sighed.

"This is heaven," she said still looking at the water.

I nodded, sure she saw it through her peripheral vision. Then, I saw her face turn toward me. She had a serious expression, her eyes searching my face.

"I was wondering…" she started in a hushed voice.

It was strange how none of us used our minds to communicate with each other. I assumed they only felt the need to do that when there were humans present.

"What is it?" I asked a little afraid of what her question would be. I wasn't sure I would have an answer for her, at least, not an honest one. I was trying my best to be as careful as possible with all of them but with Fiore, it was becoming more and more difficult. I found her so easy to like.

"You and Ian. Do you still love him?" she asked looking right into my eyes.

I knew if I lied she would be able to pick up on that. I knew if I told the truth, it could have dreadful consequences.

"Sometimes," I said. "There are days I feel like I do love him and there are days…I'm not so sure. I'm still confused."

That should be an acceptable answer, even if it got back to Ian. He couldn't possibly blame me for my confusion.

"That makes sense," she answered. Her fingers were playing with a blade of grass she had plucked. She held it in one hand and ran it between her thumb and index finger with the other.

"It's hard," I explained. "I thought I would never see him again. In fact, I had resigned myself to that, thinking he had been destroyed."

"I have been with Ian for so long now. There wasn't a day that went by that he didn't speak of you. The thing I find odd though is it wasn't until recently, in the past few months, that he indicated he wanted you back," she said. "What do you think that's all about?"

I thought about it for a while, looking at the water and watching the patterns it made as it rolled over stones. She sat silent, waiting. Could I tell her what I suspected? That I suspected he was doing this because I finally fell in love with someone else? Someone I could never have anyway? I decided against it, for the time being.

I turned my face toward her again and looked at her expression, wondering if she caught any of my thoughts. If she did, there was no point in lying. Her expression was exactly the same as it was when she asked the question. I saw no sign that she had gotten her answer from my mind. That made me curious and I decided to avoid her question for the moment.

"Fiore, please be totally honest with me," I said. She nodded. "Did you just get anything from my mind?"

"I saw the water. The rocks with the water running over them, making odd patterns. Why?" she asked.

"No reason. Just wondering." I looked at the water again.

"So…about my question. Any idea?" she asked standing now. She held her hand out to me in invitation. I reached for it and she swiftly pulled me up.

"Sorry, no. I've thought about it but I don't have a clue. I never could figure him out," I lied, not really considering it a lie since it was just speculation. He never came right out and said it.

"Have you walked up along the brook yet?" she asked, obviously satisfied with my answer.

"No. You?"

"Yeah. A bunch of times. I don't come to this spot but I do wander up further, along the side of the water. I want to show you something up there. I think you'll enjoy it." She smiled again and that made me relax.

We walked, single file since the narrow path along the stream didn't leave enough room for both us. The trees and shrubs were a bit overgrown to our left side so she had to move branches aside as she approached, holding them for me to pass. As we walked, I looked at the ground and concentrated on every detail in the path: the dirt, the stones, the fallen branches, and the moss on the rocks. I wondered if she was tuning in to my mind. She had not caught my dilemma earlier, as she asked a question I was not sure how to answer. I was concentrating on the water then, as I thought of how to answer. I was thinking about two things at once! That was it! It had to be. She had not tuned in to my verbal thoughts. She had only been able to see the images. Could broadcasting images hide my words? I decided I would experiment more with that…later.

We walked for many minutes before the path started to incline.

"Will we end up close to the cottage again?" I asked, trying to get my bearings.

"Close. We can go out to the field and walk that way," she said with a slight giggle. "We don't have to go all the way back the way we came if that's what you're worried about."

"No, of course not. I enjoy walking."

She looked over her shoulder at me as she continued forward.

"Okay…maybe not through the shrubbery though. I'm more of a city girl," I admitted.

We reached an area where the trees were much taller than the ones we had been passing. She pointed to one specific tree, just on the edge of the water, its branches growing lower than the ones on the other trees.

"Yeah. A tree?" I said, stopping behind her.

"Wait till you see the view from up there. It's incredible!" she said as she jogged, heading straight for the tree.

Panic ran through me as my body stiffened, keeping me from following her. She stopped a few feet ahead and looked back.

"What's the matter?"

"I…I can't. I'm…afraid of heights," I admitted, suddenly ashamed of myself. Vampires weren't supposed to have such silly fears, weaknesses.

"I'm sorry. I didn't know," she said gently. "I figured since you flew with Ian…."

I shook my head. I still couldn't move.

"Well, try it. You can stay on the bottom branches. This is the perfect tree for climbing. I do it all the time," she said, trying to ease my mind. "Trust me. It's very strong."

"Okay. The bottom branches only," I replied, my voice cracking. "You can go all the way if you want but closer to the ground is where I'll be."

I forced myself to walk toward her, focusing on her gorgeous face and avoiding glancing at the tree. She seemed to notice and her expression grew softer, soothing, encouraging. Once I reached the place where she was standing, she smiled and nodded. Her hands reached up to the nearest branch and she effortlessly pulled herself up, as agile as an Olympic gymnast. Her move was so graceful that she made it look easy. I can do this, I told myself. Just not too high.

I looked above my head, at the branch she had first grasped, and took a deep breath, extending my arms above me.

∽ SIXTEEN ∽

Higher and higher she climbed, like there was nothing to it. Her movements were agile and smooth. As for me, I had only just reached the second branch, my legs shaking every step of the way. I straightened my body from a squatting position, clinging to the branch above. I realized I wasn't that high off the ground. Not much of a view from here. I looked above, trying to spot Fiore amongst the greenery.

"I'm up here. A little to your right," she yelled. She saw me looking for her.

"I see you!" I yelled back.

I spotted her, sitting on a branch, her legs dangling, swinging back and forth as if she was sitting on a porch swing. Her eyes had an expression of awe, her head revolving to admire the view.

"You can see everything from here. It's gorgeous!" she exclaimed.

Curious, I found myself pulling my weight up to the branch I was holding on to. I made my mind concentrate on my movements and not on the height. I calmed myself by telling myself that I, too, would enjoy the view. If she said the tree was strong, then the tree was strong. After all, this wasn't the first time she'd done this.

I kept climbing, taking deep breaths before each new branch. I looked above as I steadied my feet on the last branch reached and saw Fiore was only about five branches up. I decided to stay on the left side, as Fiore was on the right. I wasn't sure the branch she sat on would hold the weight of both of us.

As I pulled my weight up on the branch I had just been holding, I accidentally let my eyes see beyond the tree. The world began to spin. My legs began to shake. My grip felt weak. I shut my eyes, trying with all my might to hang on, to stop myself from shaking. I managed to get up onto my feet one branch above, four branches below Fiore. That was enough. This was as far as I was going. I held onto the trunk while lowering my body to sit.

"I am so proud of you!" Fiore yelled. "Relax and look around. You're safe."

"Just one question," I said with a shaky voice. "Can you fly?"

"Not at all," she said with a smile.

"Great! Just great! Neither can I."

She smiled and pointed to something in my direction. I followed her finger, still trying to catch my breath. I looked straight ahead; it was easier than looking down. The view did take my breath away, not because of fear, but because of its beauty. The fields looked like a tapestry. It was something I hadn't imagined when I walked through them. Off in the distance, I saw a building. I focused harder on it, adjusting my eyes, and noticed it looked like a house, maybe an old farmhouse. To the right, I spotted a stone barn, ivy covering one whole wall and part of the roof.

"Is that a farm?" I asked, still focusing on the structures.

"It is. They're our closest neighbors," she replied. "We don't really know them though we do exchange greetings when we pass on the road."

I didn't realize anyone lived so close. I wondered how far that farm was from the cottage. I looked for the cottage, aiming my eyes below, which really took my breath away. This time it was from fear. I could really see how high we actually were. I held on tighter than I already was. My eyes scanned the area, spotting what had to be the roofs of the cottages on Ian's property. They looked so small and insignificant from this altitude.

I looked at both roofs, spotting Ian's, on flat ground, and then moving my eyes to the other, which sat on the hill behind it. I saw movement coming from the front of Ian's cottage. I focused my vision on that, trying to make out the small figure. Ian! He was leaving the cottage. I looked at Fiore, to see if she was watching. She was not. Her eyes focused straight in front of her, on the other side of the brook.

Ian walked to the other cabin but glanced around him with every step. He approached the door just as it opened. He obviously warned Ryanne and Fergus of his visit. It was Fergus that appeared, jumping out of the way. Ian's head turned as he scanned the area once more. Assured that no one was around, he entered. Fergus also looked around before he shut the door. I wondered what they were doing. After all, it was Ian's property and they were his friends. Why wouldn't he go see them?

Moments later, the door opened again and all three of them emerged. They stood just outside the door. They seemed to be having a conversation. I tried to block the sounds of nature, hoping to hear the three vampires below. As expected, I heard nothing from Ian and only bits and pieces of unfinished thoughts from the others.

He's weak but fine...

Don't worry...we watch...

There was silence for a moment, as I suspected Ian was now doing the communicating.

Go in peace...we will...

Ryanne helped assure Ian. *Will be at our best...*

The three of them stood for a while before Ian turned his back and strode away swiftly. Ryanne and Fergus re-entered the cottage.

Go in peace? What in the world did that mean? Who's weak? Fergus? Was something wrong with Fergus? Was that even possible? I had so many thoughts running through my mind that I attracted Fiore's attention.

"What's wrong? Who's weak?" she asked.

"Um...the tree. I was just wondering if any of it was weak...just in case. How do we get down?" I asked, trying to disguise my true thoughts.

"Same way we came up," she said. "I'll start down so you can watch."

As she started down, as agilely as she had climbed up, I rose to my feet, holding the branch above me. Something cracked. I froze.

"What was that?" I panicked.

"Could have been anything," she assured me. "Could have been an animal walking over a twig. Things sound much louder to us."

A bit reassured, I made my way closer to the trunk, trying to turn my body so I could step down to the next branch backward, the way Fiore was doing it. Again, I heard a snapping sound. The branch I was holding on to above my head shook. I moved my feet, positioning them so I could turn, when I felt the branch beneath quiver. My fingers slid. I froze. When I didn't hear anything else, I started lowering my body to a squatting position. Snap!

There was no more branch under my feet, as I realized with horror that I could see it falling, hitting lower branches, on its way down. My first thought was relief that Fiore was on the other side, she would not get hit. My next thought was there was nothing in my hands, or below my feet, my body was falling!

A blood-curdling scream escaped my lips as I almost hit a branch. It felt like I was falling in slow motion. I arched my body in the opposite direction of where the branches were, trying at all costs to avoid the impact. I fell through the air in shock…especially because I saw the tree to my left, not touching any of it, somehow clearing the branches I should have hit. I saw Fiore watching in silent horror.

The ground below looked hard. I tried to brace myself for the inevitable impact that would probably not kill me but would be painful anyway. I kept screaming, all the way down, my arms and legs flailing. I realized, to my horror, I would hit the ground on my back. I could no longer see it below me. I had somehow altered my position with the flailing of my weightless limbs.

"Lily!" Fiore screamed. "Turn your body! Stop flailing!"

How could she say that? I was about to hit the ground very hard! And she was giving me orders? Shouldn't I have hit the ground by now? Was my fear and panic causing my brain to make it seem like I was in a slow motion fall, like in some action movie?

"No! You're flying, Lily! Get your feet down! Come on! Turn!" She kept screaming commands at me.

Flying? Not possible.

I concentrated on righting myself and turning so my legs would be below me, instead of straight out. As I tried, it felt like my body was slowing down. I could finally see the ground again. I was close. I would hit any moment. The grass had more detail now that I was close enough to focus on it. I put my arms straight out in front of me. The rest of my body followed. I no longer fell straight down but floated ahead, aiming toward the direction of the cottages. Wow! My body felt weightless, like a feather in the wind, just hovering above the ground.

My arms were back at my sides as I looked down at what looked like a soft patch of grass, a good place to land, considering I didn't know how.

My feet made impact with a thump, shooting pain straight up my legs and into my hips. I stumbled, two, three, four steps, not able to stop myself from running and rolled to the ground. Fiore was at my side in an instant.

"Are you okay?" She knelt next to me.

"Um…I think so," I moaned as I tried to move. I shifted, making sure all my body parts were still where they should be. Pain shot through my right leg, which hit the ground first. I flinched.

"Your leg?" She was already reaching under the leg of my pants to get a better look.

"Ow!"

"Sorry! I'm sorry. Nothing looks broken," she assured me as she touched my leg in different places. "I think it was just from the impact, probably be sore for a while. You'll learn to land on both feet."

"What do you mean? You think I'm going to try that again?" I asked in shock.

"Lily, don't you know you were flying?" she asked, pulling my pants leg down again. "You weren't falling, I mean at first, yeah but then, you flew. Your body took over."

I sat still, trying to focus on her words. Me? Flying? That didn't make any sense. But I should have fallen a lot faster, closer to the tree. I should have hit branches on the way down that should have thrown my body in different directions, causing a lot of damage. Instead, I cleared the tree, willingly, though unknown at the time.

"Guess I did. Don't expect me to try that again any time soon." She helped me up, holding me close to her side so I could lean against her.

"Can you put weight on it?" she asked.

I tried. The pain was there but it was bearable. She released her hold. I took a couple steps. Pain shot through my leg with each step. I forced it out of my mind.

"It hurts but I can walk. I'll soak in the tub." I headed toward the cottage but she did not follow.

When I paused and turned, she smiled.

"Just making sure your pain is not obvious. How would we explain that to Ian?" she asked and started walking again.

I didn't answer her question, knowing it was a rhetorical question. She wasn't going to tell Ian. She looked at me and nodded, still smiling. I didn't bother to ask why she was doing it. I just walked, still in shock, by her side.

We said goodbye at the door, embracing each other as we normally did when we parted, only this time, it felt different somehow. We had a secret. We had formed an unspoken bond. As we embraced, her hand came up to touch my hair, holding my head close to her face. Her lips parted, as if she was going to say something but she closed them again, taking a couple of steps back. She smiled as she looked into my eyes. Then, she nodded, so quickly I almost missed it. She turned and walked away.

I watched until she disappeared. She wasn't walking in the direction of the cottage she shared with the others but back toward the forest instead. Once I could no longer see her, I took a deep breath and turned the knob.

"Lily? Is that you?" Ian's voice came from the bedroom.

"Yes!"

He was standing by the bed arranging things in a suitcase!

"Going somewhere?" I asked, trying to hide the excitement in my voice.

"Yes. Something came up and I have to leave. I shouldn't be long," he explained not looking at me, still busy with the suitcase.

Now was my chance to put on a very convincing act. I watched every move of his hands while I thought about how to start, hoping I was able to block his mind, the way I had discovered today with Fiore. I looked at his back a moment, waiting for him to say something about what I was thinking but he didn't.

"You're leaving me here?" I tried to sound sad.

"Yes," he turned and I could see the shock in his violet eyes. "Only for a little while. A few days at the most. Besides, you won't be alone. Ryanne and Fergus will be here and you always have Fiore. I know how much you like her."

I walked closer to sit on the edge of the bed. I looked down at the floor, trying to look disappointed.

"But why can't I go with you? I just got here and we just…" My voice trailed off. I held my breath and waited.

"Aww," He sat next to me and took my hand. "Are you saying you'll miss me?"

"I guess I am." I kept my eyes on the floor. I wasn't sure I could pull it off if I was looking into his eyes.

"I would but it is business. You know better than to ask questions. I think you've known me long enough. Besides, I won't be gone long," he said, his calm voice trying to convince me.

"Okay. I know. No questions. But what about me? You pulled me out of school to bring me here and now you're leaving?" I snapped. I surprised myself with that part.

He started pacing in front of me. I raised my head and looked at him. His hands were clenched at his sides. I angered him so easily!

"You want your money back?" He snapped at me. "I'll give you your money back. Make a list! Class, supplies, books, everything! I'll leave it on the nightstand!"

Ouch! I repressed a laugh. Money was not what I had meant by that but I wasn't going to argue.

"Okay," I replied. I bit my lip. "I'll miss you."

He stopped pacing and looked at me, relaxing his clenched hands. He walked back to the side of the bed and sat. He took both my hands in his this time.

"I love you, Lily. I will be back. I promise," he said looking into my eyes.

I was afraid of that.

I smiled and leaned to kiss him. I focused on his face the whole time, trying not to let him see my happiness over the long-awaited opportunity he was giving me.

"When are you leaving?"

"I need to leave by three a. m. to make it to the airport before sunrise," he answered. He took the bag off the bed and set it against the far wall, closest to the bathroom. "We have plenty of time to say goodbye properly."

I was more afraid of that.

THAT NIGHT, DURING the few hours we had before he left for the airport, we spent our time alone. I was getting used to putting on an act for him, showing him I truly did love him. It didn't feel so wrong anymore. I told myself actors did it all the time. They were affectionate and loving with other people while their spouses waited at home. I had to talk myself out of feeling guilty over Christian; after all, I had a part to play if I was ever going to get out of this in one piece. Besides, I had already resigned myself to never seeing Christian again. I needed to let him live his life, as a human.

As the moment approached for Ian to leave, I tried to appear sadder. I assured him, again, that I would miss him. He seemed to believe my words and I knew it eased his mind. He would feel no need to keep me locked up. He believed I would be here, waiting for him, when he returned. I smiled.

Ian looked around the room, making sure he wasn't forgetting anything. Then, he went to his dresser and pulled the top drawer open. His hand reached under the neatly folded pile of underwear on the left side of the drawer and pulled out a small, flat object, an object in a deep wine color. I looked at it for a moment. My eyes lit up and I turned my back so he couldn't see. His passport! He was taking his passport, which meant he was traveling outside of Ireland. He would be going somewhere far, where his mind couldn't reach me.

In the beginning, Ian had only been able to read my mind if I was within the same general location as him, on the same property or even under the same roof. In time, he had developed that skill to within a five- to seven-mile radius and it seemed to have stayed that way. It seemed to be that way for most of us. The mental connection faded the farther away our subject got. This meant that, while he was communicating with me in Washington and most recently in Oregon, he was very close. I might have known if I hadn't thought I was imagining it. But now he would be too far to use his skills to invade my mind and keep tabs on me. That gave me an idea.

"Ian, you're not by any chance going to South America, are you?" I asked.

"No. Why do you ask?" he said, one eyebrow rose.

"Well, remember when we were in Lima? That park we went to in Miraflores, the one with all the people and the flowers and the street vendors?" I asked hopeful.

"Um…oh, yeah. I remember. Lots of food carts and musicians. Always seemed like there was some kind of carnival going on even though there wasn't," he said remembering. "Why do you ask?"

He took the bait. I put on my best persuasive face.

"I remember we were there on a Saturday night and they had all these artists painting in front of the church, the one with all the stray cats. They were selling their paintings on the street. I was admiring some of those paintings, especially the ones of women working in the fields, with their layers of colorful tapestries, their skirts and black hats. I regret that we didn't buy one. It would look really good in the living room, on the mantel of the fireplace, don't you think?"

He thought about if for a moment and gave me a sly smile. His eyes grew softer.

"Well, maybe. You never know where I could end up," he replied.

He hadn't given me a straight answer but I knew the seed had been planted. He would do everything in his power not to disappoint me at this critical stage in our *relationship*; after all, he was trying to buy me back. Going to Peru to shop for paintings would not only keep him away longer but, it would keep him at a safe distance.

"Well, just in case you want to get me a gift," I said, my eyes glowing with hope and excitement, I hoped, anyway. "I especially liked the ones with those women, you know, the ones in typical dress, with the llamas in the picture. If you can find one, I would love it!"

He nodded and smiled, amused at my childish begging. I knew I hadn't seen any paintings like the one I just described, women in the field and llamas, in one painting. I may be sending him on a search, I realized. The longer, the better.

I stood watching him put on a jacket, tucking his plane ticket and passport in the inside pocket. He looked at his suitcase but ignored it and walked to where I stood. Once he reached me, he put his arms around me and squeezed. His lips kissed my forehead first, then my lips. Goodbye again, I thought. Only this time, he had every intention of returning. I was strangely sad to be parting with him again. Maybe it was the familiarity of him that kept me somehow bound. We could have been good together—very good, if he wasn't always playing games, if I hadn't fallen head over heels in love with someone else in his long absence.

"Take care of you," I said, still keeping my arms wrapped around him. I realized at that moment that I felt sorry for him. He was destined to always be alone.

He breathed in the scent of my hair, his nose on the top of my head, inhaling.

"Behave while I'm gone. Fergus was told to help you with anything you may need. The others will be here too, close by, always," he assured me.

"I know. You still don't trust me," I said. "I understand though. Don't worry about me. I'll be just fine."

He kissed me once more, hard on the lips, then picked up his suitcase and left the room. I realized after he left that I shouldn't have said the "trust" thing. It might have delayed his departure if it had caused an argument between us. I had, regardless, saved myself by saying I understood. Thankfully, he had left on time. Soon, very soon, I would be free to think, to plan.

∽ SEVENTEEN ∽

The first thing I wanted to do, before I could even think about leaving, was practice flying. I needed to gain control over it. Flying could be my only means of escape, my only salvation. I had to find out how long I could do it without resting.

I knew one of the three musketeers would come knocking on the door soon and hoped it would be Fiore. I knew they wouldn't leave me alone for any extended period of time, having received orders from Ian. Sure enough, about two hours later, I heard someone approach before I heard the knock.

"Hey!" Fiore sang. "First day of freedom. What should we do?"

"I don't know," I said. I wasn't sure how to take that comment; she was, after all, in Ian's employ. "Did you have something in mind?"

"I thought we could go into the city, maybe shopping?" She went over to one of the chairs in the living room and plopped herself down, looking very much like a carefree teenager.

"That sounds good. We'll have to wait until later. Nothing will be open for a while," I said. Though, this gave me an idea. "Actually, let's leave while it's still dark."

"Why? Like you said, nothing will be open for a while."

"Maybe I could try my hand at flying," I suggested.

"Whoa! Wait a minute! First of all, it would be your first time. Secondly, did you forget I can't fly? Which means you would have to hold me! What makes you think you could handle that?" She sounded afraid.

"You're not afraid, are you?" I teased.

"Of course not. It's just that…well, you're not used to it."

"I'll never know if I don't try, right?" I tried to sound sure of myself. "How else do we learn? I'm willing to try a short distance at first. If I can't do it, we'll take the car."

She sat silent for a few moments, giving my words some consideration. Then she looked at me with a smile on her perfect lips. "Okay. If you insist. Just don't drop me!"

I laughed. I knew I would miss her. If the circumstances had been different, if I hadn't been kidnapped, she and I could have become the best of friends. The circumstances being what they were though, I knew that was impossible. Once I was free from here, I would never see her again. I felt sadness at that realization.

"So where do we go shopping?" I asked trying to keep the mood light.

"Limerick, of course," Fiore said as if I should know this. "It's only about two hours by car. Why don't you humor me and we take one of those?"

"A car? Please…" I said trying to sound hurt. "Why don't you humor me and let me at least try. Like you said, it's only a couple hours by car so it should be an even shorter flight. By the way, what's the weather forecast for today?"

"Rainy again! I already checked. I figured you would want to do something besides sit in this dreary cottage," she said. She stood, looking a little anxious. "Okay. We'll try it your way. Let's go. The sooner we do this, the better."

I ran to the bedroom to get some money and put on something that would better shield me from the rain. I also grabbed my passport. I was glad I had distracted Ian enough lately that he hadn't thought of hiding or destroying it. Without it, I would have been stuck here for sure, knowing myself well enough that I dared not even attempt to fly that distance. Once I had everything I needed, I rushed back out to meet her. She was already standing outside the door, looking up at the sky.

"Ready!" I said excited. Finally, I was leaving the cottage I had been stuck in for months, even if it was only for a day. "Oh…what about the others?"

"They won't care. They know you're with me. They're not happy about having to babysit you anyway. Ryanne especially doesn't like it. She's wanted to go visit her sister, who's also a vampire, by the way, and Ian hasn't allowed it since he brought you here. She sort of resents you for that," she explained as we walked toward the path leading to the water's edge.

"How far does her sister live?" I asked curiously. Two vampires in the same family…what are the odds?

"About five hours I think. I never asked. I know they like to make a weekend of it when they go," she explained.

"I have an idea!" I announced. "Why don't we make a weekend of it, in Limerick, I mean. That way, they can go and stay for a couple of days and not have to watch me and I'll be with you the whole weekend!"

She stopped walking. She looked thoughtful for a moment, like she was considering the possibility. I held my breath and waited, keeping my fingers crossed behind my back.

"I guess that's not a bad idea. I could suggest it. I know she hasn't seen her in a long time. Hmmm…" she thought again.

I thought it was a brilliant idea, a vacation for everyone. An opportunity for me.

"I'll talk to them. Just one thing…" She looked at me with a slight smile on her lips. "If we do that, go for the weekend I mean, let's take the car. We'll need to pack some things and we'll need the cover of the tinted windows, just in case the sun…"

"Okay. You win," I didn't give her a chance to finish. "Car it is."

She walked toward the other cottage, her strides long and elegant. I followed close by her side. Once we arrived at the door, she looked at me with worry in her eyes.

"You'll have to wait out here. Actually, why don't you head back and pack some clothes, enough for the weekend. I'll meet you up there with the car. I need to throw a few things into a bag myself," she said trying to convince me.

I nodded and stepped back. Again I wasn't allowed in their cottage. It couldn't possibly be that they were cleaning again. They were hiding something. What else could it be? I lingered just outside for a few moments, trying to listen.

I could make out very fast hushed voices. Finally, I caught a thought.

What do we do about him? Tie 'em up? It was Fergus.

Why not? I don't see a problem with that…feed him first though… Fiore thought as she walked away from them, her thoughts now on what she needed to pack.

As I walked back to the cottage, I thought about what I heard. What did they mean "tie him up?" Who? Tie who up? Feed who? Did they have an animal in there? Not possible. Most animals did not fare well around vampires. Somehow, they knew what we were and were fearful and defensive. I had to know what was in that cottage, the reason they kept me out of there.

Packing my duffle bag, the contents of which I had dumped out onto the closet floor, I realized my escape wasn't going to be as soon or as easy as I had anticipated. I planned to return to this place. I needed to know what they were keeping secret and I only had two days to do it, two days to get away from Fiore and find my way back here. I zipped my bag and headed back out the door. Fiore was already there, sitting in the driver seat of the car, tapping her fingers on the steering wheel. I threw my bag in the trunk.

"I hope you don't mind my choice in music." She smiled and turned up the volume on the radio as she pulled away from the cottage.

Her car was small, black and sleek. The windows were tinted so dark I knew it would be impossible for anyone to see us, even if we had the interior light on. It smelled fresh, like a new car, I mused. I wondered how long she'd had it.

"Not quite a year, I think," she answered, reading my mind. "Do you like it?"

"I do. It's comfortable and fast," I said as I held on for dear life as she rounded the turn onto the main road. "Do you always drive this fast?"

"Most of the time. I like driving. It's relaxing," she answered in a sincere tone. "Do you drive?"

"Yeah. I move around a lot and most of the time I live in places where public transportation is not convenient," I explained. "Like Oregon. I needed to drive to get to my classes."

She laughed and looked at me for a moment. "Now you can fly."

"Yeah…I suppose I could if I really wanted to fly with a backpack full of books. Besides, I've lost the semester," I explained glumly. A sudden sadness washed over me. She noticed.

"There'll be none of that sadness on this trip! This is supposed to be fun. Just us girls getting away for a weekend of shopping and indulgence. No sadness whatsoever!" She turned the volume up louder and floored the gas pedal, the interior of the car vibrating from the bass in the speakers.

The scenery flew past the windows like a blur. I had difficulty focusing my eyes on any one object. With Fiore driving, we would arrive at our destination in no time. I was excited about spending time with her but at the same time, I was in turmoil over what I had to do and how I should proceed. I looked at her and she seemed to be concentrating on the music, her lips moving along with the lyrics. I knew she wasn't paying attention to my mind but I also knew I didn't want to do any serious thinking, not right then and there, anyway. Sitting back and enjoying the adrenaline rush her daredevil driving was causing was more than enough to handle for the time being.

When we arrived at our hotel, Fiore checked us in while I stood by her side at the counter, trying to ignore the stares. Men's hungry eyes lingered on us, taking in the sight from head to toe. Women permitted themselves only several envious glimpses. As humans, we had been good-looking or beautiful, some of us. Once transformed, our beauty was enhanced, making us irresistible to our prey. Most of the time, I wished it weren't the case. I didn't like the attention.

"Good," Fiore said as we walked away from the counter, having turned down the clerk's offer to have a bell-boy carry up our bags. "We're on the top floor. We'll have a nice view from there."

I followed her to the elevator and stood at her side as we waited for the door to open. To my relief, it came down empty and we were the only ones to get in it. I watched her finger press the number seven. I noticed there was one more button above it marked with "PH." PH? What did that mean?

"That's the penthouse," Fiore explained. "I tried to get it but they said it was reserved. Just as well. We'll be busy shopping anyway."

The door opened and we looked at the sign on the wall just outside the elevator. Following the arrows, we started walking to the right. She paused in front of a door at the end of the hall and took the card key out. "This is us."

It was your typical hotel room. King-sized bed, night stands, two dressers, an armoire that contained a flat-screen television, a desk, and a small round table with two chairs. The bathroom had a deep, whirlpool bathtub that looked promising. I wondered if I would be able to squeeze in time to enjoy that before going forward with my plan, whatever that was.

"What do you want to do first?" Fiore asked as she drew the curtains aside. "It's early yet and we have plenty of cloud coverage. We could do anything."

"I don't know. I've never been here before. I trust you. You pick." I walked over to stand next to her and admire the view. From where we were, it did not look like too large of a city. I looked over the rooftops as I let my mind wander to what I needed to do.

"I think I'll get my hair done," I suggested. "I know it only takes a couple days for it to grow back but it's relaxing anyway, especially when they wash it."

"That sounds like a good idea," Fiore said, walking away from the window to the luggage rack.

"No! You don't need a hair cut. Your hair is absolutely gorgeous," I argued. "I wouldn't change a thing if I were you."

"Really?" she said looking at herself in the mirror.

"Really. I'll find a place to get mine done," I said, desperately thinking. "I saw there's a theater nearby. There was a sign in the lobby. I looked at it while you were checking us in. I haven't been to a show in so long…"

"Come to think of it, neither have I. That would be a nice change of pace," she said as she changed her shirt. She took off the long-sleeved, red t-shirt she was wearing and put on a white turtle neck sweater. The contrast between the white and her jet-black hair was stunning.

"Why don't you go and see about that? Get us tickets while I get my hair trimmed. It shouldn't take long," I explained. I crossed my fingers behind my back. Hoping. My chances of her leaving me alone were slim, I knew, but it was worth a try.

She seemed to be deep in thought as she walked back and forth at the foot of the bed, running her fingers through her hair. Staying out of her head was hard but I did it anyway.

"That way, we will be sure to get seats. No sense in wasting time," I insisted.

"I guess maybe that wouldn't hurt. We have plenty of time for shopping," she said, finally standing still. "Do you care where we sit?"

"As close as possible. I always have problems in theaters. Everyone's taller than me." She laughed. "Do you know where the nearest salon is?"

"No, but there's a phone book," she said. She walked over to the desk to retrieve it and started paging through it.

So far, my first plan was working. I doubted I was going to get any time alone but to my surprise, it was easier than I thought. I did, however, hate lying to the only friend I had here. I would have to make it up to her some day.

"Here's one," she said with her finger keeping her place in the listing of salons. "According to this address, it's about five or six blocks that way." She pointed to the left side of the window.

"I'll find it," I said. "The theater is that way. I can see it from the window." I pointed to the right.

"Okay. That's the plan then. You get your hair done and I'll get tickets.

We'll meet back here." She handed me the second key card for our room. "Try not to get lost." She also handed me a small piece of paper with the salon name and address.

We chatted as we went down to the lobby in the elevator. We made plans to go shopping for clothing before the show and also tomorrow. I didn't like shopping but I agreed with her enthusiastically.

Once we stepped outside, she pointed me in the right direction. "Okay. See you in about…an hour, I would guess. You'll be longer than me."

"Probably. If it's too long of a wait, I'll do it tomorrow." I told her as I started walking away.

"Sounds good." She turned her back and hurried away.

I walked in the direction she pointed and turned the corner. I was heading away from the salon. My only objective now was to find a pay phone. I knew that would be a difficult thing to do in the age of cell phones. If I could find a bus station or maybe a train station…I kept walking, looking around. I saw some men, about three blocks away, carrying duffle bags and walking swiftly. I decided to follow them. With bags in their hands, I assumed they would be traveling, therefore, headed to a station of some sort. Hopefully, they hadn't just arrived, I thought as I looked around.

They continued walking through an alley and then back out into the busy street. Finally, I saw the sign for the train station. I paused while they got further ahead though they hadn't noticed me following.

I stepped into the train station and began looking for a phone. A frail old woman, possibly in her early eighties, or maybe late seventies, was leaving the station as she watched me stop to look around.

"Are you lost, dearie?" she asked, looking up at me with gentle eyes.

"I'm looking for a pay phone. Do you know where I can find one?"

"Straight ahead and to the right," she said pointing. "You'll see an opening on the wall…a big one. The bathrooms are there and in the middle, on the wall, two phones. Only one of them still works though." She smiled.

"Thank you ma'am," I said and hurried away. I noticed the woman was still watching me. She stood by the door until I disappeared into the bathroom area.

To my relief, both phones were available. I walked over and took the receiver off the phone on the left, closest to the men's bathroom. I held it to my ear and heard nothing. Oh, right! I grabbed the other phone and I heard a faint dial tone. As I held the phone, my hand reached toward my pocket until I realized I had no change. Okay. Don't panic. I can call collect. I just prayed someone, other than Maia, would be there to answer. I had no idea if there was a time difference between Ireland and the United States. I hadn't thought that far in advance. I dialed zero and held my breath.

"May I help you?" A monotone voice said on the other end.

"Yes. Collect call to the United States please," I said.

After giving her the telephone number and my name, she told me to hold on and then the phone rang. One…two…three…please! I was about to hang up, before the answering machine could pick up, when I heard a male voice answer…a very comforting male voice.

"Aaron? It's me, Lily!" I practically yelled.

"My God! Lily! We've been so worried…"

"I know. I'm sorry. This is the first chance I've had…"

"Where are you?" he blurted.

"Ireland. It's a long story. I can't get into it but I'm trying to get home."

"Is Christian with you?" he asked.

"What? What makes…why would you?" I asked, confused.

"The police were here. Apparently, he hasn't been back to teach his classes," he explained calmly, as only Aaron could do.

"Why? I don't understand…"

"Some of the students saw you with him, in the parking lot. So when he didn't show up for class and the college couldn't reach him at home or his cell, they checked here…" he paused. "Are you okay? Lily? What's wrong?"

I realized my breathing was coming at a pant. He could hear that through the phone, though the connection left much to be desired.

"I'm not with him but I have a feeling…" I tried to explain but I could barely get the words out.

"Does this have something to do with Ian?"

"It has everything to do with Ian!" I snapped, my voice almost at a growl. I tried to take a deep breath and calm myself down. "Has anyone checked his apartment? I mean, has anyone been physically in his apartment?"

"I honestly don't know. We told the police we didn't know where either of you were. They seemed to have been satisfied with our answer but they left a card. In case we hear anything," he explained.

"I'm coming home. I'm not sure exactly when or how…" I started.

"What can we do? Tell me…anything."

"Just be ready. Be ready for my next call. I have a feeling…" I started to say and then stopped.

"You have a feeling what?" he asked. Now he sounded as if he was starting to lose his patience.

"I have a feeling I won't be coming home alone. I may know where Christian is. If I'm right, and I pray I'm not too late, I will need your help."

"Whatever I can do, any of us, let me know."

"Where's Maia?" I asked. I held my breath as I waited for his answer.

"She's in Europe again. She needed time alone, she said. Apparently, something went wrong with Ian. She came back from Washington alone and then left right away. She wouldn't tell us anything else."

"Okay. Thanks. I will be in touch again, soon. I promise," I said and hung up. I didn't even give him a chance to say goodbye.

~ EIGHTEEN ~

I stood as if glued to the spot and I was starting to feel light headed and dizzy. The realization of what was happening was making its way to the front of my thoughts. Christian was missing, had been missing for as long as I had.

Gathering all my strength, I walked away as if in a daze, willing myself to take one step after another. I walked past groups of travelers, loaded with luggage. I knew eventually I would find the doors leading out of the train station and onto the busy street.

Once outside, I was surrounded by the noise of cars and people. I couldn't get over Aaron's words. They played over and over in my mind. Christian missing...the police...not teaching his classes...students saw us in the parking lot. What did it all mean? Okay, I needed to think. I needed all the pieces so I could begin to put them together.

I went over everything in my mind. Ian made a deal with me. If I went with him, Christian would live. So I did. Yet...Christian has been missing for as long as I have. The cottage...their cottage...I was never allowed in there. I always had to wait outside. Whenever I did knock on the door, someone hastily closed it behind them and came outside. That door was always locked. Ours never was. The bits of conversation, the pieces I heard while Ian was there, the time I was in that tree...they weren't talking about some animal! Christian was in that cottage! But how? That didn't make sense.

"Watch it lady!" A female voice startled me out of my thoughts. Her hand gripped my arm hard.

"What?" I asked, confused.

"You want to get hit by a car?" she asked as she pulled me back onto the sidewalk. A car beeped its horn as it flew past us.

"Oh…sorry. Thank you," I mumbled, still confused. The woman looked both ways before she crossed, shaking her head as she went. Others were standing there, watching me and whispering to each other. I looked around, trying to figure out where I was. I had no idea which direction I had taken once I made it through the doors of the train station. I looked around again and saw only one building sticking out, high above the rest. That must be it so I turned myself around and started walking toward it.

If Christian was in that cottage, wouldn't I have smelled him, heard his heart beating? But why would Ian bring him here? For what reason? He would have just killed him if he weren't planning on keeping his word. Why bother bringing him here? And, he couldn't have brought him here himself. Ian had flown with me! That meant someone else kidnapped Christian and brought him here. But who?

Standing outside the doors of the hotel I couldn't decide what to do. I needed to act like nothing was wrong. I needed to face Fiore and pretend we were still on a happy shopping trip! Damn it! I didn't do anything with my hair. Oh well. I would tell her the wait was too long and I would get it cut another time. I knew I needed to get back to the cottage and see what they were hiding. Fergus and Ryanne were supposed to be at her sister's house. It was the perfect time. All I had to do was get away from Fiore.

I took a deep breath as I pushed the button to summon the elevator. I tapped my foot on the floor as I waited for the elevator to make its way down, like a snail. As soon as the door opened, I jumped in, not waiting for anyone to get out. Good thing it was empty. I pushed the button to our floor and watched the lights climb. It stopped on the fourth floor and the door opened. An elderly couple stood outside.

"Going up," I said and pushed the button to close the doors.

"We have seats for the eight o'clock show," Fiore sang as I opened the door to the room. "It's none other than The Phantom of the Opera! We lucked out."

"Good," I said trying to put on a happy face. "I haven't seen that one on stage yet…saw the movie though."

"Your hair…" she said.

"Oh yeah…they only had two stylists working. The list of names was long so I didn't even sign in. It's no big rush. I just thought…while we were here…" I walked over to the window. Which direction would I need to head in?

"Well, I meant to tell you…you don't need to do anything with yours either. We got lucky in the hair department. Most women would kill to have hair like ours." She laughed. She was standing next to me in front of the window, her arm across my back. I would definitely miss her.

WE WALKED AROUND town while we waited for the time we needed to be at the theater, going into a few small shops to look around. I was admiring a beautiful quilt, hanging on a wall, as Fiore was looking in a glass enclosed display case. I wasn't paying attention when she went to pay for something. When we were back outside, she handed me something small.

"What's this?" I said as I held my hand out, still closed around the object.

"Just a little something to show you how much you mean to me," she said, sounding a little sad. "I know I'm supposed to be watching you but I can't help but think of you as a friend. Look at it."

In my hand, I held a beaded bracelet. The beads were crystals and there was a charm hanging on it. I studied it closely.

"It's a peacemaker. See?" she said pointing to the charm. I saw two doves with hands in the back where their tails should be. Yes. That was it.

"It's beautiful! Thank you," I said and wrapped my arms around her. I hated myself for what I was about to do to her. A small part of me wished I could talk to her. I knew, though, that it was impossible. I couldn't put her in that position. She was following Ian's orders. That was her job.

"You're very welcome. Put it on," she said taking it from me and opening the clasp. She fastened it onto my wrist. "We should head to the theater now. The line will probably be long. We have tickets so that should help."

As we walked I could feel the weight of the bracelet on my wrist, could feel the coolness of the crystals and the metal of the charm against my skin. I reached my other hand out to touch it. I felt an aching sadness. Regret. Regret for what I was about to do to someone I could so easily have had an eternal friendship with. Somehow…someday, I *would* make it up to her.

As we approached the theater, we saw the line wasn't long at all. There were only three couples already waiting and they, too, had tickets in their hands. I wanted to see the layout of the theater as soon as possible. I needed to see how dark it would be, not that it would make much of a difference to a vampire anyway. I needed to make my escape, from this theater, on this night. I didn't know what I would find once I got back to the cottage but I didn't want to take any chances. Maybe it was nothing at all, but, time could be important.

We walked down the center aisle and Fiore had our ticket stubs in her hand so I didn't know our seat numbers. I just walked behind her until she stopped two rows from the front.

"This is us," she said as she stepped aside and pointed for me to enter the row first. From where we were, we could also see the orchestra pit. I wished I didn't have to do what I had to do. I made a mental note to leave some money at Fiore's cottage as repayment for this weekend.

"Good seats," I said to her as I looked around the theater. The way it was set up, inclined and in levels, I would have been able to see no matter how tall the person in front of me was.

We chatted idly while people filed in, laughing and talking as they looked for their seats. There was a lot of chatter coming from all directions in the theater. Everyone seemed to be excited about the upcoming performance. I was excited for other reasons and had a difficult time sitting still. I fidgeted as much as a human does, turning my head as I scanned the area. Fiore didn't seem to notice. She went on talking about other shows she had seen in the past, in different countries. She talked about how different things were in the theater two hundred years ago. I had seen many changes in my lifetime but not nearly as many as she had.

Once everyone was seated and settled, the lights finally dimmed. Music began to fill the room, softly at first, and then growing louder and louder as the dark maroon curtains parted. The only things – other than the music – that could be heard now were faint whispering and the beating of about two hundred hearts. Fiore sank into her seat and crossed her legs. She glanced at me and smiled. I could see the excitement in her eyes. I smiled back, squinting in the process. My right hand automatically went up to my eye.

I rubbed it, making it water.

"Are you okay?" she asked, leaning closer.

"Yeah…I think so," I whispered, still rubbing my eye. I was sure it was red and irritated by now. "I think I have something in my eye."

"Here…let me look," she said leaning closer to me.

"It's too dark. I'll go to the ladies' room and look in the mirror. Be right back," I said and started to rise from my seat. Fiore stood and stepped out into the aisle to let me through.

"Want me to go with you?" she asked.

"No. It's fine. I won't be long. You can tell me what happens while I'm out," I said. I had a sudden urge to wrap my arms around her but I walked away before I could make mistakes that would give away my intentions. When I was near the entrance to the lobby, I paused and looked back. She was back in her seat, eyes on the stage.

I did not stop again. I walked straight out the door and in the direction of the hotel. Once outside on the sidewalk, I broke into a jog. Even at a jog, I was flying past the few people that happened to be still walking in the rain. The rain fell lightly but it was still annoying as it hit me in the face. Flying, intentionally for the first time, was sure going to be interesting. I reached the hotel in a matter of minutes and got right on the elevator. I went straight into the room and grabbed my passport from the bottom of my bag. I shoved it into the inside pocket of my jacket. I shoved my cash and credit card into the back pocket of my pants.

Walking back to the elevator, I began to panic. I wondered if anyone was in the penthouse. I needed access to the roof and I didn't know any other way. I crossed my fingers as I waited for the elevator to take me there. I pressed the button but it didn't feel like I was moving at all. Strange… why not? Maybe I needed to do something else. It was possible the elevator opened right into the penthouse and I needed a special key to access it. Okay…think. There had to be stairs. In case of fire do not use elevator popped into my head. Of course!

I exited the elevator on a lower floor and searched the stairs. I saw the exit sign at the opposite end of the hall. I sprinted for it. I ran up the stairs taking them two at a time. I passed a door that had a sensor for a keycard. That must be the penthouse, I thought. The stairs continued, to my relief but to my dismay, when I reached the top, the door was pad-locked, chain and all. I took a deep breath and told myself not to panic. I had enough strength to break a chain like that, no problem. My only concern was someone might hear me. I leaned over the railing and looked down, feeling instantly dizzy. Great! And I was about to leap off a nine-story building. What was I thinking? I could have just taken a cab but…

After several attempts at pulling the chain, causing my face to scrunch and grunts to escape from my mouth, the chain finally gave. The metal links slammed against the heavy metal door creating a loud bang that echoed in the staircase. I held my breath for a moment and listened. I heard nothing. After deciding no one heard, or at least no one cared, I pushed the door open. The wind hit my face as soon as I stepped out, causing my hair to fly around. I reached into my jacket pocket, hoping I had left a hair tie in there, and was relieved when my fingers touched a bit of cloth. I pulled it out and tied my hair into a ponytail. It was going to be scary enough to fly, especially taking off from this height; it would be absolutely terrifying if I had to do it blind. I walked over to the edge of the roof, wind blowing my ponytail straight up. I paused a few steps before reaching the edge.

Looking around at the lights and buildings, I tried to figure out in which direction I needed to head. Usually, I was good at figuring out where I was and somehow always found my way to where I needed to be. However, I couldn't take chances now. Time was of the essence. When Fiore figured out I wasn't coming back, if she hadn't already, she would start looking. I doubted she would go back to the cottage though. She would probably head to the nearest airport.

Straight ahead. I needed to fly straight ahead. So I took a deep breath and walked the last few steps to the wall. I knew if I thought about it, if I actually stood there and contemplated what I was about to do, I would change my mind. I would lose precious minutes if not hours trying to come up with a different plan. My left leg went up automatically as I reached the wall. My right leg followed. I was standing on the edge of the wall that surrounded the roof. Because it was cold and rainy, I felt assured that no one would notice a person leaping off.

Dizziness took over as soon as I had both feet firmly planted on the edge of the wall, my body swaying both from the size of the ledge and the wind. I closed my eyes and pictured Christian…his beautiful face, loving eyes, his sensual smile that made one eye squint just a little. I felt an instant ache where my heart once beat. How could I have ever thought I could stay away from him? I was crazy! With that thought, and my eyes still tightly shut, I leapt.

The wind swept through my hair, and my clothes, as I fell. Rain pelted me in the face, hard. I could feel my body going down fast. I concentrated on straightening, leveling my arms and legs and the rest of me to be positioned horizontally from the ground, not vertically as I was now. The more I concentrated, the easier it became. I no longer felt like I was plummeting. It was more like…soaring. I forced myself to open my eyes. I blinked hard and fast against the raindrops that seemed to be aiming purposely for my eyes. I saw cars below, most of them parked and empty. Humans walked up and down the streets but never bothered to look up.

What had I been so afraid of for so long? My body still felt the anxiety, complete with dizziness, but I could get used to it. Maybe that only came with the fear of falling and now that I knew I wasn't falling, well, I was in control now.

Little by little, the lights below became less. I was leaving the populated areas and flying above more wooded areas. I spotted the highway below. Hopefully, it was the same two-lane highway that had brought us here. After several more minutes of following that road, I saw nothing but trees clumped in some areas and fields spread out over the rest. I had to be on the right path...I just knew it. Finally, I saw what looked like the farm of the nearest neighbor, the one with the old stone barn. I held my breath and felt a wave of excitement take over my body.

Once I passed the farm, I prepared myself for landing, looking for an open space, maybe something soft. I landed once before but not well. An open field, the one that spread out between the two cottages, which I could now see and which was, thankfully, completely dark, lay below me. Okay...vertical now, I told myself. I tried to get my legs down but I was already too close to the ground. Luckily, I remembered "tuck and roll" and that's exactly what I did, tucked myself into a ball and rolled, after hitting the ground a tad more softly than the last time. When I finally came to a stop, I was dizzy, this time from spinning. I sat still for a moment on the muddy ground, trying to see if anything hurt. Nothing did.

Taking slow, quiet steps, I looked around to see if there were any signs of movement. I saw and heard nothing but the raindrops, lighter now, hitting the roofs of the two cottages. There were no vehicles on the property and everything was dark. My eyes adjusted to the darkness so I made my way to the cottage the three vampires occupied. I paused in front of the door and waited, listening. Normally, Fergus had the door open before I could knock, hearing my approach. The door stayed closed. I heard no voices from within. My hand went up to knock. I stopped it before my knuckles could hit the wood. On second thought...

After knocking two times, I waited. I still heard nothing. I took a deep breath and turned the knob. It was locked, just as I expected. They kept it locked when they were in there; of course they locked it when they were out! I looked around to make sure nothing changed, just in case. I lifted my leg and pulled it in to my chest. I kicked the door hard, not losing my balance. The whole thing fell off the hinges with a loud bang. If anyone had been around, they definitely would have come running. To my relief, no one did.

The aroma that filled my nostrils made my head spin. My breathing came at an uncontrollable pace. I heard his heart beat in my ears, though it was very faint. My fists clenched as I entered what was their living room. Christian was here! I knew that scent anywhere. There was no mistaking it. I turned on a light in the kitchen and started looking around. I smelled him all over this cottage, though I didn't see him; at least, not in the main rooms.

Flinging the bedroom door open hard, so hard the knob made a round hole in the wall behind it, I stepped in. I could smell him here too. I looked at the sofas – two sofas instead of beds – and saw nothing but folded clothing on one sofa and just some throw pillows on the other. I knelt on the floor trying to see underneath but there wasn't enough room to even get a hand under there let alone a whole man.

I threw open the closet door. No signs of him there either. Nothing in the bathroom. There was no place left. These cottages were small. Where?

I went back to the living room and started pacing. I could still hear the faint heartbeats…a little too slow. I looked around anywhere I could, even opening cabinets. I slammed the doors shut. My fists were clenched and I felt the anger and desperation in me taking control. Maybe outside? I ran out. I was only a few steps from the cottage when I realized I couldn't hear his heart anymore. I ran back in. The sound was music to my ears. I searched the bedroom again, this time throwing the folded clothing across the room. I didn't care!

In the closet, I started knocking boxes over, spilling their contents out onto the floor, mostly old photographs. I started pulling clothing off the shelves when my foot slid on the glossy photographs scattered all over the floor of the closet. I grabbed the shelf to steady myself when…the shelf came crashing down. It hit me square on the head, spilling sweaters all over me. I grabbed a pile of sweaters and shoved them over so I could move the shelf and get out from under it when my hand felt something plastic in between a couple of wool sweaters. I pulled the flat object out to examine it.

I flipped the pages of the passport I held in my hands. Christian Alexander Rexer. Christian's picture was on the page. I held Christian's passport in my hands! I couldn't believe my luck. Ian had given it to them to hide. He knew it wouldn't be safe in his possession because I would have access to it. It was too hard to conceal anything in such a small area. Yet, they were concealing something alright. A whole person!

Back in the kitchen, I looked out the window and saw nothing outside had changed. Fergus and Ryanne were not due back until Sunday. Fiore was probably at the airport now or driving through the streets of Limerick, looking for me. I honestly couldn't think of any reason why she would think I would come back here before making my escape. I let myself relax just a little…enough to think rationally, anyway.

A small, round table sat in the middle of the kitchen, complete with tablecloth and a vase filled with flowers, and four chairs. I pulled a chair out and sat. I felt the top of my head to see if there was a lump. There was. I put my elbows on the table and rested my face in my hands, pouting. Where could he be? How could someone be hiding in this small place? I inhaled the air around me, letting his scent fill my lungs. I kept myself from exhaling as long as I could, feeling him closer to me because of it. His faint heartbeat still sounded in my ears. I shifted my legs under the table and caught the rug with the rubber sole of my shoe. Annoyed, I bent down to move the rug, to flatten it again so I could move my foot.

In an instant, I was on my feet, tossing the four chairs across the room, crashing them against the wall. I heard a window shatter but didn't even bother to look. I grabbed the rug with both hands and gave it a yank. The vase toppled over and rolled off the table, bouncing off the rug before spilling its contents onto the wooden floor. It didn't break. I picked it up and threw it against the wall. Just as I suspected, a trap door concealed under the table. I grabbed the metal loop to pull the door open. It fell flat against the floor. I stared down at the pitch blackness that greeted me. His heartbeat was louder in my ears but…much too slow, weak.

I walked down the creaking, wooden steps slowly, hoping they would hold my weight. My breathing came faster as I neared what I thought should be the bottom. Even with my enhanced vision, it was darker than dark. I could barely make out the shape of my own hand in front of my face. I knew I was at the bottom because I let my foot do the exploring and I could feel no other step, just level ground that felt like…dirt?

"Christian?" I called, my voice cracking. No answer.

With my arms out in front of me, I felt my way with my foot to where I thought the sound of his heart was coming from.

"Christian? Are you down here? Please answer me…" I pleaded, still walking slowly until…my foot hit something. I froze. I pulled my foot back.

"Christian please…" I felt around with my foot, as softly as I could, trying not to hurt him if it was indeed him. I felt it again. Something softer than the ground and…warm. I dropped to my knees and felt around with my hands, wishing I had thought to bring a light down with me. I felt nothing but dirt at first and then…warmth, softness and warmth.

"Oh thank God!" I sighed. "Christian? Can you hear me?"

I touched him again. I explored him with my fingertips. I could tell he was lying on his side. His head was to my left so it must have been his chest I was hitting with my foot. I bent down closer, running my fingers through his damp hair. I felt him flinch.

"Please talk to me…please." I tried to pull him toward me so I could position him on my back. I needed to get him upstairs, where I could see him and check to see how badly he was hurt.

As I pulled him onto my back, holding on to his wrists so I could carry him, I heard a slight moan. I walked as fast as I could through the darkness. At least I could see the light from the kitchen above the trap door.

"Just hang on. I have you. You're safe now." I tried to soothe him as I made my way up the old steps with his weight on my back. As heavy as he felt now, I realized I wasn't going to be able to fly with him like this, not until he could co-operate enough to hang on to me.

In the living room, I laid him down on the sofa and then rushed to turn on a lamp. I was no longer worried about anyone seeing lights. I rushed back to his side. He took my breath away. Despite the fact that he looked like he had been through hell, his hair was dirty and damp and matted to his face, his eyes were closed and he had what looked like bruises underneath, he looked pale and thin, his lips white and dry, despite all of that, I felt the excitement I felt the first time I set eyes on him.

"Christian…please open your eyes. Please look at me. Talk to me," I pleaded kneeling by his side. Beside his usual sweet aroma, I could smell sweat and earth on him. I held his dirty hand in mine, relishing in the intense heat of his skin. Just then, I saw slight movement. I took my eyes off his hand and looked at his face. His eyes were open just a little.

"Hi…Can you hear me?" I whispered in his ear.

His lips started to part but it looked like he was having difficulty. They looked so…white! I ran to the kitchen and found a glass – for guests, I'm sure – filled it with tap water and went back to the living room. I picked up his head with one arm and brought the glass to his lips.

"Drink…please. You'll feel better. Please open your eyes again…drink," I begged as I held the rim of the glass against his dry bottom lip. His lips parted and he got a mouthful of liquid when I tilted the glass, some of it spilling around his chin, down his neck, and onto his ripped t-shirt. When the cold water hit his chest, his eyes really opened.

"Wha…" he whispered, his voice hoarse. His beautiful blue eyes were trying to focus on my face, blinking rapidly. I realized then he was having a hard time with the light. He had been in the dark for so long. I put his head down and turned off the lamp.

"Christian…it's me…"

"Lily?" he asked before I could finish, his voice low and weak.

"Yes." I couldn't help but laugh from both happiness and relief. "It's me. I found you."

"Why?" he whispered. "Why?"

Why did I find him or why was he here in the first place? It didn't matter. Not now.

"I'll explain later. Right now, we have to get out of here. We have to leave. Do you understand me?" I watched his face. He was fighting to keep his eyes open. His heartbeat, though louder, was still slow in my ears. He nodded slowly and I could see his lips trying to form for "yes."

"I need your help though, Christian. I need you to help me. I can't do it all myself. Can you try?" I asked. His eyes closed again. "Christian?"

"Ye…yes," he whispered. He opened his eyes again, slightly, but kept them open longer. I thought I saw the hint of a smile starting to form on his lips. I shook my head…couldn't be.

"Do you think you can stand? With my help, maybe?" I stood and held my hands out to him. "Please try."

He looked at me, focusing longer on my face. Yes. There definitely was a smile forming on his lips. How could he be smiling at a time like this… after all he'd been through? I helped him get his feet on the floor and his body into a sitting position. Then, again, I held my hands out to him.

"Take my hands. I'll help you up," I encouraged. His hands reached out for mine and it took him a moment to find them, still trying to focus his eyes. His grip was better than I expected. That was a good thing.

I walked holding his body weight against my side while he concentrated on keeping his balance. Every step he took seemed labored, as labored as his breathing, but…he was walking.

"Okay. You're doing fine," I told him. "We're almost out."

We walked around the back of the cottage, toward a path that led to the woods. He did better with every step he took. He seemed to be stretching out muscles that hadn't been used lately. Every once in a while, I could feel him staring at me. His eyes burned through my skin, or it felt that way at least. I concentrated on the path we followed, my eyes being able to better see in the darkness than his.

"Are you still thirsty?" I asked.

"Yeah…I am," he said in a hushed voice. Though we were now in the middle of the woods, alone, we whispered.

"There's a brook somewhere over here. It's clean and cool," I whispered, looking at his face from the corner of my eye. I couldn't believe how good it felt to have him so close again. It was as if the part of me that died when we parted was suddenly brought back to life. Even though he could probably manage to walk without my support, I didn't want to let him go. We continued walking, with me helping him climb over obstacles until I heard the sound of the water.

"I hear it," he said.

"Yes. We're not far. We'll rest there." I continued walking toward the sound, helping him along the way.

We sat on the wet grass just on the edge of the flowing water. He crawled closer to the water and cupping his hands, began to take long drinks. I wondered how long he had gone without water, or food for that matter but, I didn't ask. I was afraid of whatever questions he would ask. Terrified, in fact. When he seemed to have his fill and crawled back to sit by me, his face finally turned toward mine, his eyes glowing in the darkness from the moonlight that had started to break through the clouds.

"Now what?" he asked. It wasn't the question I was expecting but I was relieved. He was focusing only on the situation at hand.

"We need to get to higher ground. Somewhere high, like a cliff or a ledge or something…"

He looked around, trying to see past the darkness. "There has to be something around here. The water is flowing rapidly, downhill. We need to follow it in the opposite direction," he explained.

"Can you do it? Are you ready to move on?" I asked.

"Ready if you are. I may need to take breaks once in a while. I'm pretty weak. I haven't…"

"They starved you too?" I snapped.

"Among other things…"

"Let's go. When you need to stop, just tell me," I said, cutting him off. I didn't want to hear any more, not right now. I needed to get us as far away from here as possible. If I listened to what he had to say, I might change my mind. I might decide, in my anger, to wait for them to return. There was no telling what might happen then.

We followed the path along the brook, climbing higher. We passed the tree I had taken my first flight from and I wondered if he could climb. Deciding against it, because of how weak he was, I didn't mention it. I needed a high place I could take off from, with him in my arms. How was I even going to explain this? I found it odd that he still wasn't asking questions. I heard rocks being displaced just as I realized he had stumbled. He had been following behind me as the path had narrowed.

"You okay?" I asked.

"Yup. Just a bit clumsy in the dark," he said but continued moving.

I reached back for his hand. As soon as I gripped it, I heard him inhale deeply. His skin felt so good against mine. He didn't flinch at my coldness. His thumb started making circles against my fingers. It took my breath away. We continued on, walking in silence until we came to a place that looked promising.

The path had veered away from the water and was now along the edge of what looked like some kind of road. To the left, there was a mountain, or maybe just a big hill, the road seemed to wind around. To the right, the incline was slowly making the sight and the sound of the running water disappear. There was no guard rail along this road and I wondered how anyone drove on this at night. The more we walked, the higher we got. Finally, we reached a place where I could see the valley below. It looked really far from where we stood. I stopped.

"Are you ready?"

"For what?" he asked, not taking his eyes off the valley below.

"Quite possibly the craziest thing that's ever happened to you," I admitted. "If you trust me, I promise I will explain everything to you later. But…you have to trust me."

He took a deep breath, turned his face toward me, and smiled.

"I trust you completely!"

How could he say that? After everything that had happened, trusting me was the last thing I would expect him to do. But right now, it was the only thing I needed him to do.

"Then hang on. And…close your eyes if you need to," I said walking to stand in front of him, my back toward him. I held my hands up behind me so he would know I meant for him to get on my back. He did. He clasped my hands and squeezed.

"Ready!" he said and then I heard no more breathing. I jumped.

"OH…MY…GOD!" he screamed. It sounded more like the scream of someone on an amusement park ride than the terrified scream of someone who was flying through the air on the back of a female half his size. I heard noises coming from his throat, as if he was gasping for air because of the wind hitting our faces.

I was already level above the ground, not finding it any harder to fly with him clinging to my back than alone. I looked below for any light clusters that might resemble a town. I knew I needed to get us as far away from here as possible but I couldn't keep this up too long. Not only for me but because of how weak and exhausted he was. I knew if I flew east, we would be in Dublin in less than an hour and a half. It's not like we would run into traffic where we were.

"You okay?" I yelled so he could hear me over the sound of the wind in our ears.

"Yeah…sure. I do this all the time. No big deal," he yelled with a nervous laugh. He buried his face in my back.

"I should tell you," I yelled. "I haven't quite mastered landing yet. This is only my third time."

"Oh sure. Only your third time…no problem. We'll figure it out when we get there," he yelled back swallowing gulps of air. At least we weren't getting pelted in the face by rain.

We flew quietly for what seemed like hours, though I knew better. Finally, a much larger cluster of lights appeared below, still at a distance. This was a cluster three or four times the size of others we had seen so I knew we were where I wanted to be, close to Shannon Airport.

"Lily?" he yelled, breaking the silence.

"Yeah?" I yelled back.

"You still love me?"

Shocked by his question and the fact that he was asking it now, as we were flying through the Irish skies, I hesitated.

"Yes. I do. You?" I asked, not sure I wanted to hear the answer.

"More than life itself!" he yelled and then buried his face in my back again, feeling the shift in my body as I prepared for our descent.

∽ NINETEEN ∽

We landed in someone's back lawn on the outskirts of town, in a more residential neighborhood. Given the late hour, I wasn't worried about someone seeing us. I made a sloppy landing, him jumping off my back and rolling to the ground as soon as he saw we were close enough. I rolled on the opposite side of the lawn and then, after brushing ourselves off, we met in the middle. We walked toward the street without another word over what had just happened, my hand resting in his, my mind reeling over what he just said to me. How could he still love me?

After walking for a while, we found ourselves in a more populated area. People still walked the streets, despite the hour. Not as many people as one would see at this time of night in New York City but still, people. As soon as we came to a hotel we stopped, relieved. I checked us in while "my sick husband…poor dear, must have caught a bug," waited on a sofa in the lobby. I told the woman behind the counter we were traveling through but decided to stop until he felt better. She asked no questions, only showed concern, and then handed me the keys.

We entered our room and Christian went straight into the bathroom. I had forgotten and hadn't bothered to ask him if he needed to stop. I locked the door behind me and went to look out the window. I wasn't sure what I was looking for. No one knew where I was. No one had been there yet, I was sure, to notice I had taken Christian. Still, I looked and then closed the curtains. In a city this large, it would take them a while to find us. By the time they would start looking, we would be gone.

When Christian walked out of the bathroom, I was already sitting on the edge of the bed, with the phone in my hand.

"I'm calling Aaron. He's waiting to hear from me. Do you have anybody you need to call?" I asked before I dialed.

"The only one I would call is already here," he said and settled next to me. He was sitting for seconds before he let himself fall backward, exhausted. He put his arms over his head and stretched out. I didn't even want to imagine how long he had been lying down there alone, on the dirt floor of a dark basement.

"As soon as I'm done, I'm going to get you food. As far as something to wear...everything is closed. We'll think of something," I told him, keeping my hand on his leg. Now that he was next to me again, I didn't want to lose a moment, afraid if I let go he might disappear.

He closed his eyes and kept his arms over his face as I dialed Aaron. He was glad to hear from me but not surprised. He was expecting my call and said he had no doubt I would be in touch. After asking about Christian and the name of the hotel and city we were in, he told me to stay put. He would be on the next flight out. I argued that there was really no need, I could easily put Christian and myself on a flight home, but he wouldn't hear it. He said he would see me as soon as possible and that was that. I hung up the phone.

"You awake?" I whispered trying not to disturb him if he wasn't.

"Of course. How could I sleep? I just flew through Ireland on my girl-friend's back. It's not every day I get to say that," he replied, taking his arms away from his face to look at me. I could see the smile on his face.

"I told you. I will explain, I promised. Just not now. Too much to do," I answered. He called me his girlfriend! I realized that was the first time he had used that term with me and now of all times...

He sat up and looked at me, turning his face so he could look into my eyes. I waited, holding my breath. He grinned and looked down at his feet.

"You realize I won't kiss you until I get a toothbrush, right?" he said. I smiled.

"I'm on it. What are you hungry for?" I asked, already on my feet. God it was so good to look at his face again!

"Anything. If there's nothing downstairs then I don't care if it's some-thing from the vending machine. I could eat a horse!"

"Let me see what I can do. I'll see what's in the bathroom, make sure we have what we need to at least clean our bodies; as for our clothes, that's another story," I said as I headed into the bathroom. "Be right back. I'm taking the key," I yelled as I headed out the door.

LATER THAT NIGHT, after he ate what I got him from the convenience store down the street, gulped his cup of coffee and started on his soda, he was ready to take a shower.

"Oh…look," I said reaching to grab the paper bag I had left on the floor by the bed. "Clothes. Some, anyway. I asked the woman at the desk if there was anything open, telling her our bag had been lost by the airline, and she told me not at this hour. When she saw my disappointment, she said I could look through the lost and found. Apparently people leave things all the time, even at the laundry." I handed him the bag. He dumped it out on the bed.

"Wow! Clean socks, a shirt…looks a bit big but it'll work, and hmm… someone left without their boxers?" He held a pair of boxer shorts up. "Would you wear someone else's boxers?"

"They have a tag from the laundry. They've obviously been washed. If it bothers you, go without," I teased. He laughed. I still didn't understand how he could act so lighthearted after everything that had happened to him unless…he was in shock.

"I'll stop being a baby and wear them. Aaron won't be here until sometime tomorrow, right?" he asked.

"Yeah. Not sure when but it will be quite a while. It's a long flight. Go take a shower. I'll be right here. Your toothbrush and toothpaste are on the sink. I got them downstairs," I told him as I propped the pillows on the bed and got comfortable in front of the television.

While he was in the shower, I couldn't help but feel nervous. I felt like a schoolgirl awaiting her first kiss. I still couldn't get over how well he was reacting to all this: the kidnapping, the starvation, the dark basement, flying on his girlfriend's back. If I were in his shoes, I would be ranting and raving and demanding answers. But he didn't pursue anything. It made no sense. I flipped through the channels not really paying attention, just pushing buttons to make the time pass and keep my hands occupied. When I heard the shower shut off, I got butterflies in my stomach. Shortly after, I heard the water in the sink. I realized I had forgotten to ask for a razor downstairs. I should have thought about it when I got the toothbrush. He had a full beard. I told myself to remember to do that first thing in the morning.

The bathroom door opened and Christian stepped out, wet hair and boxer shorts. He took my breath away as usual, even though upon close inspection I could see he was thinner and paler than normal. He threw the towel down on a chair as he came over to the side of the bed where I was lying. I moved over to give him room.

"I hope you don't mind I'm wearing just this. I have to save the rest for the trip home. My jeans are filthy though. Maybe we can get them washed in the morning…" He leaned closer to me, looking at my eyes. "Lily… thank you."

"For what?" I asked.

"For getting me out. For getting me away from them…from *him*," he said still looking into my eyes. My stomach turned at the mention of *him*. I knew, somehow, he wasn't talking about Fergus.

"You don't need to thank me. You wouldn't have been in this mess if it weren't for me in the first place. You should be running away from me… running for your life," I said but couldn't finish.

His lips were on mine and I felt the fire in them. My hands reached for his hair as he kissed me hard and with more hunger than I had ever felt in him. My body arched toward his with a moan escaping my lips. He kissed me harder. I closed my eyes and let the feeling take over my body and mind. My hands slid down the sides of his face. The beard, soft and coarse at the same time, tickled my senses as I stroked his face. I felt the touch of his breath as he exhaled a sigh, his hands seeking the cold flesh beneath my shirt. He moaned as fire coursed through me.

My fingers were on his collarbone when I felt it, something that made me suddenly freeze and push him off me, again.

"What?" he said, struggling to catch his breath. "Did I do something wrong?"

"Let me see your chest," I demanded. I turned the lamp so it was angled more toward us, shedding light directly on him.

"It's nothing…really," he said, holding both hands up to his chest, covering the spots where my fingers just left. I moved his hands aside. His expression changed immediately to sadness and…shame?

Just along his collarbone, where a shirt collar would cover them, were six or seven puncture wounds. They looked scabbed over and some were still bruised but, they were there, definite puncture wounds! I felt like I was hyperventilating. My breathing came so fast it felt like I had no control over it. He put his arms around me and patted my back as he buried his face in my neck, trying to calm me.

"I'm okay. Really…"

I jumped off the bed, pushing him away unintentionally. I walked back and forth in front of the bed, still trying to catch my breath, my hands balled up into tight fists. I felt the wetness of the blood my fingernails were drawing. My body trembled as I paced, shaking my head as if trying to deny it. He stared at me with a pained expression on his pale face, the palest I'd ever seen him.

"WHO DID THIS TO YOU? WHO FED OFF YOU?" I demanded, my voice much too loud. I didn't even give him a chance to answer before I rattled more questions at him, trying to keep my volume down this time. "Did they all feed off you? How often? How much? Did they *give* you blood? Tell me!" I screamed. He sat there, tears in his eyes, shaking his head. I realized at that moment I was scaring him but I couldn't stop, my anger was so out of control.

"You have to tell me!" I screamed. "You have to tell me who did this to you!"

"Please, Lily. Please calm down," his tear-filled eyes pleaded. As I looked at him now, finally stopping long enough to focus on his face, I could see the purple circles under his eyes. I thought they were from exhaustion, from the stress of his ordeal. I could see now they were almost as dark as mine, if not darker. They were due to blood loss, nothing else. It was normal for mine to look like that, I was dead, but his?

"Did they make you drink from them? Did they?" I screamed again. Every time my voice came out harsh, I saw him flinch. He lowered his head. I stood still, though still trembling, waiting for an answer, watching him.

I knew he was still alive…that much I was sure of. I heard his heartbeat and smelled the intoxicating sweetness of his blood. I also felt the warmth of his body. Though he did just devour human food, he was still weak, dizzy when he was on his feet. I continued to watch him, still waiting for some sort of a response. He remained silent and kept his head down. A tear fell from his eye, tracing a tortured path down his cheek. An aching feeling in the pit of my stomach snapped me out of my rage. I walked over to him, sitting next to him on the bed. I held my breath, waiting.

After a few moments, the tears stopped and he raised his head, wet eyes locking on mine.

"It was only one," he whispered, his voice shaking.

"Which one?" I asked, trying to stay calm. The last thing he needed was for me to take my anger out on him. I knew that, yet…it was more difficult than I could have imagined. I wanted nothing more than revenge at that moment.

"The tall, blonde one. The man...Ian."

My hands clenched again, the anger bubbling to the surface. Christian reached out and grabbed my wrists, gently, pulling my hands to him. I clenched them tighter, feeling the moistness of the blood.

"Please don't...you're hurting yourself," he whispered, pulling my arms toward him. "Please relax. We can talk about this. We can fix..."

He gasped as I opened my hands, seeing the blood. My nails had dug into my skin. It scared him. I pulled my hands away and put them behind my back.

"Did he make you drink from him?" I asked, not sure I wanted to hear the answer.

"No," he muttered. Now I was the one looking down.

"I'm so sorry..." I raised my head to look at him, really look at him. I looked deep into his eyes. "I will get you safely back to the States. I promise you that."

Worry took over his expression now, not fear, as I had expected.

"What do you mean? Me. You're coming with me, aren't you?" he asked.

"I don't understand," I said shaking my head slowly in my confusion. How could he want me with him after all this?

"I'm not going anywhere without you, Lily...EVER," he said firmly. I flinched at that last word.

"How could you say that...knowing what you know? How could you want me anywhere near you? Don't you know what I am?" I asked, jumping off the bed and pacing all over again. "Don't you know what I can do?"

"Lily...I wish you would sit still for a minute. You're making me dizzy," he pleaded, a look of resolve on his face. How could he be so calm? I didn't get it but I listened to him. I went over to the bed and sat on the edge, facing away from him.

"Talk," I demanded. He seemed to be more in control at the moment than I was.

"I do know what you are...I think, anyway. The point is, I love you and I refuse to be separated from you again."

I was dumbfounded, speechless...for a moment.

"You know? You think?" I asked.

He nodded. "Yes. I've been around. I'm an archaeologist, don't forget. I didn't spend all my time in a classroom. In fact, this is my first year in a classroom."

"What?" I couldn't believe it. I pictured him always the way I saw him, in front of a class full of eager students.

"It's true…my first time. It's a requirement…working toward my PhD. I traveled the world with my dad and my grandfather, on digs. I saw many things. I've been to places people only dream of. I'm not totally ignorant, you know…" A slight laugh escaped his lips.

I turned to look at him. I needed to see his eyes when I heard him say it. I took a deep breath and summoned all my courage.

"So…what do you think I am then?"

"A vampire," he said. He looked straight into my eyes when he said this and his voice didn't falter. He was so calm and I felt like I would go to pieces at any moment!

"And you're…okay with that?" I asked in disbelief. I was expecting him to burst out laughing at any moment, telling me he was just joking. He didn't. He remained calm, never taking his eyes from mine.

"Yes. When I said I loved you, I meant it. I don't care what you are. I love you, my Lily," he said as he took my hands. He turned them over to examine my palms.

I couldn't breathe. I couldn't move. I was waiting for him to do something, not this strange acceptance.

"You're not bleeding anymore. I don't see any marks," he said as he turned my hands over and then back again.

"I'm lucky like that. We are pretty resilient," I explained, still waiting for some kind of reaction. Nothing. He sat, calm and peaceful, holding my cold hands.

"That's why you're always so cold. That's why your skin is so pale and your eyes are so…deep. That's why you hide food in your purse when we go out to eat, or don't drink anything, though you do like to hold cups of coffee for some reason. That's why your heart doesn't beat. Why you have the strength you have. Remember when I hit my head?" he asked.

I was shocked. I couldn't believe he noticed all these things. No one ever noticed these things, at least not that I was aware of, and if they did, they didn't dare say it. I thought back to that beautiful, yet painful, day.

"How could I forget," I admitted.

"It was nothing. I was paying attention to you…all of you," he whispered. "I love you more than I've ever loved anyone in my life."

No. This couldn't be happening. This wasn't how it was supposed to go. When I imagined telling him the truth, I imagined him running away or at least laughing at me, maybe calling me crazy but…not this.

"Doesn't it bother you that I could kill you? Doesn't it bother you that I *do* kill on a regular basis?" I asked. His grip tightened on my hands and concern filled his eyes.

"I don't even think about you killing me. You told me you love me. You wouldn't kill someone you love." His eyes shifted away from my face. "As far as others…I don't know. I don't think I want to know about that…yet."

"Well, in my defense, it's not as bad as you might think," I said. "You're right. I do love you." He turned toward me again.

"Also…humans don't fly. Didn't you notice I wasn't freaking out about that?"

He was right. I had taken him on my back and flown to safety with him. He had been shocked at the experience but not at the reality of it.

"Now that you mention it, yes. I just thought maybe you were in shock."

"I've come across a lot of strange things in my life. I saw people in Egypt that fit the vampire description very well. I did extensive research on it, of course, but I dismissed it as folklore. I think I always kept the possibility in the back of my mind, tucked away." He smiled and his eyes lit up. "You are the first one I have known personally."

"I can't believe it," I said, shaking my head in disbelief. "Now what?"

He thought for a moment. "Now I love you."

"That's it? Now you love me?"

"Yes. That's it. It's that simple. Now I love you. I will continue to love you for the rest of my days," he said, looking sad all of a sudden.

I felt sadness too. For the rest of his days…I didn't want to think about that. Not right now.

"How often did he drink from you?" I asked later, trying not to lose my temper at the thought of Ian's cold, hard lips taking blood from Christian's warm, perfect body. We were lying on the bed, him on his back and me on his chest, the television on a channel that was playing an old black and white movie, though what it was I couldn't say.

"Almost every day, once a day. I think it was every day. It was always dark and I slept a lot so I lost track of time," he explained. His hand stroked my hair. I felt so relaxed in his arms, listening to his heart beat, that I didn't think I could lose my temper anyway.

"Did they give you food, water, anything?" I asked. My fingers were twirling around the soft hair on his chest.

"I had a jug of water. They filled it whenever I needed it. It tasted like…dirt. But it was wet so I didn't complain. I got bread once in a while. Sometimes crackers. They mostly stuck things in my mouth and I just chewed and swallowed."

"What do you mean they stuck things in your mouth?"

"They had my hands tied behind me, for a while. Then…Ian finally untied me one day after he made me promise I wouldn't try to run. I promised him. I told him I knew there were others above my head. I could hear them. Sometimes I could swear I heard you, though I didn't tell him that part." He kissed the top of my head. I sighed and closed my eyes.

"I was outside sometimes…to see Fiore. They would never let me in. You must have heard me then, in the few seconds the door was open," I explained, thinking back.

"That's what kept me hanging on…thinking and hoping you were out there, somewhere close."

"Had you not been underground, with no windows, I would have smelled you. I would have heard your heart. That's how I did find you, when they left. As soon as I broke the door down, your scent filled my nose and I knew you were there." I shuddered when I remembered my desperation.

"I have a certain…scent?" he asked.

"Yes. Only you smell that way to me. Sweet, intoxicating. It's mouth-watering," I admitted. I felt him flinch slightly.

"Mouthwatering?" he asked, flipping me onto my back and supporting himself above me. "You want to eat me?"

"You have no idea," I said with a nervous laugh. He really had no idea.

He looked into my eyes for a moment and it was as if the whole world melted around me. There was no one else but us. He lowered his face to mine and kissed me, with so much passion and so much fire that I could think of nothing else but giving in to it. I wanted him at that moment. I wanted him more than I had ever wanted anyone, or anything, before. But I knew I couldn't, not without danger and consequences. I tried to turn my face away from his, to stop his lips from devouring mine.

"What's wrong, Lily? Why are you so afraid of me?" he asked, looking into my eyes with new pain.

"It's not you. It's me. I'm afraid to lose control. I can't. Not with you."

"What's the worst that could happen? Honestly," he prodded.

"I could…bite you," I said.

He smiled. I knew what he meant by that. He had been bitten on a daily basis and it was no big deal to him. I felt disgusted at the thought of Ian doing that to him.

"There's no one I would rather be bitten by. I love you," he said, kissing me gently. "I want you," he kissed me again. "I need you," he kissed me harder.

I kissed him back. I kissed him harder than I had ever kissed him before, even that first time on the beach. I let him take complete control of me. I lost my mind in his kisses, his caresses, in the heat of his body. I lost myself in his eyes, his soul.

Time stopped as we went on kissing, touching, pausing only long enough to look into each other's eyes. The more he touched me the more I wanted him to touch me. It took me a while to realize at some point that he had taken off my shirt. Still, I couldn't stop, didn't want to stop. I kissed him with more hunger, savoring the sweetness of his breath, the spinning of my head. Every time he took his mouth away from mine, whether to look into my eyes, or to catch his breath, I pulled his face back down, demanding more. My lips continued down to his jaw line, his breathing out of control. I kissed his face, tasting his salty skin, hearing his heart beating in my ears, when I made a crucial mistake. Exactly what I had feared was about to occur. I let the passion and the wild desire I was feeling take over all my senses, and apparently my sense of reason went with it. I wrapped my lips around the soft, hot skin of his neck and let the tip of my tongue taste that too. I inhaled his musky scent, letting it fill me. I felt my fangs against his skin at the same moment that I felt him jump, his body stiffening, keeping his distance from me.

"What? I'm sorry. I didn't…I mean…I…I wasn't going to…" I stammered.

He took a moment to catch his breath, his eyes wide with fear. I felt angry again but this time it was with me. He moved his body away from me and sat by my side, wrapping his legs in his arms.

"I know, I know. It's just that…well…you know. I wasn't expecting that. I pictured someone else when I felt your teeth. I'm sorry," he said sadly.

"Here you go apologizing for something you didn't do again. You're good at that," I explained, trying to make my voice sound soothing and not angry. I understood why he panicked. Ian had fed on him and that was what he related the feel of my teeth to. But, regardless, he said he wasn't afraid of me. It didn't seem that way now. "I thought you weren't afraid of me?"

He thought about it for a minute before answering. "I'm not afraid of you, exactly. I don't know what it is. I don't know how to explain it."

"It would be easier to believe you are afraid than to believe you're not," I explained. "I am a vampire, remember? I would be afraid of me."

"It's not you I'm afraid of, it's…death."

⤳ TWENTY ⤳

Most of the night, we talked about his childhood, his career, and about how the school would react if we came back, suddenly, together. We decided that wasn't a good idea, though we had a good laugh over what other students may be speculating. After all, how would we explain this? We avoided any difficult subjects, for the moment, sensing each other's exhaustion though he did finally ask me my age.

"Can I ask you something personal?" He was lying on his side, his head leaning on his hand, his elbow bent. His blue eyes looked tired and blood shot, the circles around them darker.

"Sure…anything," I said, though I really didn't mean it. There were many questions I wasn't ready to answer yet.

"I know it's never polite to ask a lady this but…how old are you?" he asked, as usual trying to lighten the mood. I relaxed when he asked, having expected something much more complicated.

"I'm ninety," I replied. His eyes grew wide.

"Wow! You look damned good for your age," He teased. "Do you know others that are older?"

"Well, let's see…Kalia is about two hundred. Aaron is two hundred thirty."

He thought about this for a moment, trying to grasp the impossibility of it. "How old is he? All of them…there were four, right?"

I was afraid of that. I didn't want to think of them at the moment, afraid to feel rage again and lose control in front of him.

"Ian is one hundred five and Fiore is three hundred," I explained. It hurt to say Fiore's name aloud. "I just know the other two were together for two hundred years."

After that, he was deep in thought for a while and then I noticed he was fighting to keep his eyes open.

"Go to sleep for a while. You need it," I whispered to him. "I'll be right here, next to you."

"You don't sleep, do you?" he asked, moving his head to my chest. My fingers went to his hair, feeling the rich softness.

"No, unfortunately. Believe me, I would love to. It would be a nice escape once in a while," I confessed. He reached up to kiss my lips and then settled back down on my chest, his arm across my stomach, one leg over both of mine. Seconds later, I heard the soft, even breathing of sleep. I envied him for that.

While he slept, I let my mind wander. I thought about the last time I had seen him, with tears in his eyes, as he stood in the street and watched me drive away. I panicked and fled because he'd noticed I had no heartbeat. And now, here he was, sleeping comfortably on my silent chest. We had been so close to making love tonight, and again, I panicked. It should have been him panicking. He had, in a sense. He panicked when he felt my teeth against his skin, though I had no intention of killing him. I didn't realize my fangs were even out until he flinched. I was so wrapped up in tasting, feeling, smelling, and kissing his fiery skin. Would I have sunk my fangs into his flesh? I didn't know for sure, but, I doubted it. At least, that's what I wanted to believe.

Would I be able to convince him to go back with Aaron? Would I be able to let him go without me…to do what I needed to do? What I *had* to do? I doubted it but I had to try. I didn't think Aaron and Kalia would mind keeping Christian safe for me until I returned. I knew deep down they would do anything for me. I wondered, also, how they would react to the fact that Christian knew the truth about us.

Now that we were together again, how did we proceed? How could we be a couple when we couldn't even make love like a regular couple, without the fear of me drinking his blood in the heat of passion? He would continue to grow older and I would stay the same. He seemed so terrified…said he was afraid, of death. And me, I wanted to kill him and then…bring him back to me, to be with me through eternity. Did he want that? Did he even consider it? Had he given any thought at all, to *eternity*? Aaron would be furious if he knew what I was thinking.

As dawn approached, I came to a decision. I would take what comfort I could and let the final act play out. It was the best I could do…for now.

"Hey…" he said in a sleepy voice. He lifted his head to look at me, his eyes still unfocused from sleep.

"Hi. What are you doing awake already? Something wrong?" I whispered to him though I was happy to hear his voice again.

"I'm okay but…" He sat up and shook his right arm. "My arm's asleep and I have to go to the bathroom. You know…those pesky human things." He laughed. I couldn't help but laugh too.

He walked into the bathroom and closed the door behind him. Shortly after, I heard the sound of him brushing his teeth. When he came out, he looked a little more alert.

"It's early yet," I said. "Don't you want to go back to sleep for a while?"

"Are you kidding me?" he said as he climbed back in the covers. "I don't want to ever sleep. I don't want to miss another minute with you."

He kissed the smile right off my face. He held me in his arms for a while and didn't say anything. I hated the thought of parting with him again, even though I expected it would not be for long. Now that we were together again, really together, I didn't want to be away from him at all. I wished he had learned the truth from me and not while lying alone in the darkness putting the pieces of the puzzle together, experiencing what Ian was doing to him.

We dressed in cast-off clothes and then walked downstairs to find a restaurant so he could eat breakfast. This time, I knew I didn't have to put on my *human act*. I didn't order anything from the menu. I just watched, keeping him entertained by talking about some of the countries I'd visited, while he ate his eggs and bacon and drank his coffee.

"So…how annoying was I in my sleep?" he asked when he was finished. He pushed his plate aside and drank the last of his coffee.

"Not at all. You didn't even move," I assured him.

"I didn't snore or talk or drool or anything?"

"Nope. I wouldn't have cared if you did. It's not often I get to watch a human sleep," I explained. "The only thing you did was squeeze me once in a while, like you were trying to hug me or something."

"See? Even in my sleep I don't want to let you go." He reached across the table for my hand. "Lily, can you promise me something?"

"Anything," I said. His eyes looked dead serious right now. I knew whatever was coming was important to him. I swallowed hard.

"Please, promise me you won't ever leave me again." He held my hand firmly, squeezing it a bit. I knew I had to leave him, for a while anyway. That couldn't possibly be what he meant.

"I won't leave you again. I'm not afraid anymore, not of you being disgusted anyway. I was so afraid of how you would react when you found out the truth about me. But the truth is out."

"Good. I needed to hear you say it. There's no reason for you to run again. You don't have to run off to some far away land again…"

I interrupted. "Wait…you think I ran away to Ireland? You think I came to *him*?" I asked, shocked. I hadn't considered he might think I came here willingly. He nodded, confusion in his eyes.

"When I ran away from you that day, from your apartment, I went home. He came to me. It was either come here with him or…" I couldn't say it. I couldn't finish the sentence before I felt sick to my stomach.

"You mean he threatened you?" he asked in a hushed voice, looking around to make sure no one heard.

"Yes. It was either this or your life. I had no choice. It wasn't just you I was scared for, either," I explained, trying to get the words out before my anger flared again. "It was anyone I loved. Kalia, Aaron, even Maia… *anyone*! But most importantly, I had to save you."

He squeezed my hand tighter, sensing my emotions. His eyebrows furrowed as he started to speak.

"Who are those people anyway?" he asked.

"You don't know? Ian never spoke to you?" I asked in amazement. I couldn't imagine Ian not bragging about himself to someone, especially someone he was holding captive, who had no choice but to listen.

"Ian is my maker. He's the one that made me what I am," I said, trying to pull my hand away from him. I wanted to get up. I wanted to get out of the restaurant. I didn't want to talk any more, or think for that matter. Christian sensed that and didn't say anything else, though I could tell he was shocked. I could tell he had many questions I was leaving unanswered.

We walked up to the counter and I paid the bill. After we left, we walked, hand in hand, to a department store three blocks away and went in search of the essentials we needed. I had gotten him a few necessary things from the lost and found at the hotel but unfortunately, there had been nothing in there for me. I paid for our things and then we headed back to the hotel to take showers and wait for Aaron's arrival.

LILY IT'S ME. I'm coming up the hall.

I heard Aaron's warning and ran to open the door. I was thankful he sent me his thoughts, otherwise, I would have panicked at the knock. As soon as he was through the door, I threw myself into his arms, all but knocking him over. I didn't realize until that moment just how much I had grown to love and respect him.

"It's so good to see you!"

"It's good to see you too, Lily. Kalia is ecstatic! You have no idea." He stepped back to look at me.

"Where is she?" I asked, expecting her to appear behind him.

"She couldn't come. She had things to take care of…preparations to make," he said. He was looking around the room, for Christian, I presumed.

"He's just getting out of the shower," I said. We got involved in some movies we both liked and decided to shower afterward. "What do you mean…preparations?"

"She's getting the cabin ready for you, both of you. We'll hide you there for a while, until things blow over," he explained.

"The cabin? Why?"

"You don't expect to go back to business as usual, do you? He'll come after you. We have to take care of things," he explained. He sat on the edge of the bed. I was pacing.

"We don't need to hide. Christian is going back with you. I'm staying until…until it's done. You don't mind if Christian stays with you until I return, do you?" I asked.

"What are you talking about?" he asked, his face wrinkled with worry. I explained what I needed to do. I assured him I would be able to eliminate Ian. I told him I wasn't worried about the others, they only followed Ian's orders and once Ian was gone, they would move on. He was not happy with that idea.

"Does Christian know? Does Christian know about your insane plan?" he asked, anger in his voice. I shook my head, unable to speak. Aaron had never spoken to me that harshly before. It shocked me. "You cannot face him alone. Even if you do, what makes you think you can destroy him?"

"I…I want to see him burn in hell! Do you know what he did? Do you have any idea what he did to the man I love?" I screamed. Christian came out of the bathroom then, a terrified look on his face.

Aaron looked at him and put his hand up in the air, reassuring him he meant no harm. Christian nodded and stayed in the doorway.

"I can just imagine but Christian, obviously, is very much *alive*. And you are in one piece. Let's just get you both out of here," he reasoned. He looked at Christian again, analyzing his face. "I take it Christian knows about us?"

"Yes," I said. I stood still finally but with my arms tightly folded across my chest. I didn't know what else to say. I didn't know how to win an argument with Aaron.

"Think about it Lily. Ian is your maker. No matter what happens, when it comes down to it, you will always feel a certain loyalty to him. You may be angry now. You may feel like you hate him. You don't know what will happen when you are face to face with him. You are both close in age. Your strength is pretty evenly matched. It may be a battle you can't win. Is that what you want?" he asked. I said nothing. I just pouted. "Do you think that's what Christian wants?" he asked, looking at him.

That did it. That brought me back to reality, at least for now. "No."

Christian looked lost. He had no idea, though he may now have an inkling, that I had planned to go back to the cottage and destroy Ian myself.

"You said you wouldn't leave me. Remember?" he said as he walked to my side.

"Damn it!" I yelled. "How am I supposed to get my way if the two of you are going to gang up on me?"

Christian put his arms around me though he didn't take his eyes off Aaron. Aaron stood now and waited. Once Christian released me, Aaron held his hand out to Christian.

"It's good to finally meet you." He shook Christian's hand. Christian looked at me as soon as his skin made contact with Aaron's. It must have been incredible for him to be face to face with yet another vampire.

✑ TWENTY-ONE ✑

Aaron had already made reservations on an evening flight and a rental car waited in the hotel parking lot. We departed for the airport as soon as we were ready. We were in for about twenty hours of travel, flying into London and making another connection to San Francisco. From there, the last flight would take us to Portland. We wouldn't be arriving until the next evening. Once we arrived in Portland, Aaron would drive us straight to the cabin, where Kalia was waiting.

The airline seemed a little concerned we had no luggage but when we checked out clean through security they had no choice but to dismiss it. Aaron booked us on business class so we were able to board first. He thought that would give us more room to stretch out and also a bit more privacy. Our first flight departed on time, which I was grateful for. Now that I had decided to follow Aaron's advice, even though I had argued, it was a welcome relief to be away from Ireland. I had no idea where Ian was at the moment but I knew we were headed in the opposite direction. I wondered if Ian knew we had escaped yet. Surely Fiore was back home and had gotten in touch with him. It was also quite possible a search party had already been organized.

"What time are we supposed to be landing in Portland?" I stretched across the aisle to ask Aaron. Christian and I were sitting together with Aaron across the aisle. There weren't many passengers on the flight so talking was easy.

"5:30 p.m.," he said. "Kalia has our itinerary. She has her cell phone. I told her to be on alert just in case I got there and something had... changed."

"We can't leave the airport until the sun goes down."

Christian had been looking out the window but now turned to face me, eyes filled with curiosity.

"We'll have to get something at the airport in London. That's one thing I overlooked," Aaron said looking a little embarrassed.

"The sun?" Christian asked.

"Yes. We need to get something to cover our skin before we leave the airport in Portland, otherwise, we'll have to wait until dark," I explained.

"Does the sun...hurt you?" he asked.

"Oh no. Just our eyes and well...we kind of reflect light. It's noticeable."

His jaw dropped and I heard a chuckle from Aaron. He quickly turned his face when I looked at him, pretending he was interested in the magazine he had pulled out of the compartment in the seat in front of him.

"None of the stories you grew up with are true. We don't burn in the sunlight. We can see our reflections, we don't spend the day in coffins and garlic just stinks. "

"Wow." Was all he managed to say before he put his head on my shoulder and closed his eyes.

"What are you going to do about him?" Aaron gestured toward Christian.

"I'm going to keep him safe as long as I can. I'm also going to support him, considering he lost his job because of me," I started.

"That's not what I'm referring to," he said. "I mean, long term. Do you have a plan?"

"No. Not really," I lied. I knew what I wanted. I wanted it more than anything, but, I also knew how Aaron felt.

He shrugged but said nothing further. I knew he was giving me time to reflect on it.

"Did Christian tell you how he got to Ireland?" Aaron asked, closing the magazine. He arranged the blanket the flight attendant had given him around his legs. I had already arranged the blanket around Christian's shoulders, making sure he was comfortable and slept soundly until we landed in London.

"No. I didn't ask for all the details yet. I wanted to give him time to adjust. He was in darkness and alone for months. Ian was feeding on him almost daily. He's weak and exhausted," I explained.

"If anyone can nurse him back to health and keep him safe it's you," he said with a smile of assurance.

"It's my fault this happened to him in the first place. I feel so guilty."

"Lily, listen to me," he said reaching across the aisle and taking my hand. "You did the best you could. I mean, how could you have known Ian would take him anyway, even after you went with him? You risked yourself, your own happiness, to keep Christian safe. He knows that. We all know that."

"It wasn't enough, obviously," I said, thinking about all the things Christian had to endure, the loneliness, the hunger, the darkness, the fear.

"You figured out where he was. You got him out of there and you did it alone, with no fear for yourself. That's more than anyone could ask."

He gently squeezed my hand, trying to reassure me. I didn't feel reassured. I felt that somehow I could have stopped this. If only I would have stayed away from him from the beginning. If only I hadn't given in to my temptation, then, none of this would have happened. He would be living his life as usual, sharing his talent and devotion to his science with the world. Instead, he was unemployed and on the run, fighting for his life. Just as I was feeling lower than I had in a long time, I heard him whimper.

"Lily…Lily…please stay…pl…" His voice was soft and sweet, even in his sleep. Aaron turned to look at me. A knowing smile on his face.

"As much as I may be wary of your relationship with a…human, at least I thank God it's with someone like him. I hope you know how much that man loves you," he said.

"I think I do," I said, trying not to wake him.

"I don't have to read minds to know how he feels about you. He worships the ground you walk on. He knows you're a vampire and yet, he loves you all the more. You could have three heads and that man would think you're the most gorgeous creature on earth."

My jaw dropped and I knew it. I felt it. I couldn't believe what Aaron was telling me. He only knew Christian for a very short time and he noticed all that.

"I can look at his face and see his feelings for you, the way he looks at you, the way he inhales the air around you, like it's scented with roses, the way he hangs on your every word. Anyone would be a fool not to see it," he said as he reclined his seat back and picked up the magazine again. It was his way of dismissing the subject, of giving me time to revel in my own thoughts.

At that moment, I could swear I was the happiest woman that ever walked the earth, and, the luckiest. I turned my face and took a deep breath, taking in his sweet scent, taking in his soul.

We landed in London, on time. Once we were in the airport, we had an hour and a half before our next flight, the one that would take us back home. We used the time to get what I needed to cover my skin, just in case. At Aaron's age, he didn't need as much coverage. As time passed, a vampire's skin grew somehow…thicker…not allowing light to reflect. Mine hadn't reached that point yet. He didn't need to take any precautions and he could be outdoors in any condition. I envied that. I missed lying out on the warm sand of the beach on a sunny day.

Walking around the airport with Christian and Aaron, I felt somehow like I was in a dream. For the longest time, I had been alone. Now, suddenly, I had more love than I ever imagined. If I was dreaming, I did not want to wake up.

"You look happy, Lily," Aaron said to me while we were standing in a hallway, waiting for Christian to come out of the men's room. "It's good to finally see you like this. You'll see, everything will work out."

I wished I could be as sure of that. I felt safe now, while we were in transit. I wasn't sure I would feel the same once we were back in Oregon. It would only be a matter of time before he found us. That thought terrified me and panic rose like bile in my throat. I had never been as afraid of anyone as I was of Ian and I knew when he came for me again, he would not be coming alone.

"I am happy. I'm happy I have you all in my life and I'm happy Christian is *alive*. It's just that, well…how do I keep him that way?" I asked. I was leaning against the wall, feeling like I was waking up to reality again, my knees going weak at the thought of anything happening to him. I needed the wall for support.

"You will not be alone in this. I promise. Kalia is making preparations, like I said." He paused and looked at the bathroom door, hearing the hand dryer whirring. "The first thing you need to do when we get there is feed. You look thirsty." He stopped as Christian walked out to the hall.

"Ready," he said, taking my hand. I nodded to Aaron, acknowledging what he said.

We walked to the terminal and, finding our gate, we sat on the seats nearest the window, waiting for our next flight to begin boarding. I watched the plane being loaded with the luggage of the awaiting passengers. I tried to clear my mind of all the conflict that was still to come. I *had* to be strong…for Christian.

THE REST OF our trip was uneventful. Christian slept on and off, with his head against my shoulder or against the window. Not once during the time he slept did he let go of my hand. When he was awake, we looked at magazines together, me flipping the pages, him reading over my shoulder and commenting, making me laugh. When we got tired of that, we talked.

"Why didn't we just fly to Oregon...I mean, no planes?" he asked. I thought he was joking, until I saw by his eyes that he was serious.

"I don't know if you remember me telling you but that was only my third time flying. It was the first time I flew with a *human* on my back," I emphasized the word "human" just to tease him.

"You're kidding me?" he asked, raising his eyebrows.

"Dead serious. I only discovered recently, by accident, that I could do it at all."

"You mean you spent ninety years not knowing?"

"Yup! Why do you think I'm so bad at landing? I need to practice that," I explained, laughing at myself and my tuck-and-roll landings. Not a very convenient thing to do when you had someone on your back. "And besides...I'm afraid of heights," I shamefully admitted.

The shock in his eyes was evident as he stared at me wide-eyed. I couldn't imagine what exactly he was shocked at, my fear of heights or the fact I could fly.

"I can't imagine you, afraid of anything. You seem so fearless!"

I needed a minute to let that sink in. Me? Fearless? I certainly didn't feel that way, not when it came to Ian. I couldn't imagine anyone seeing me as fearless. "I don't understand."

"I cannot see you as fearful of anything," Christian explained. "With the exception of our...intimacy, that is. You seem so sure of yourself when it comes to everything else. I feel...safe...with you. I feel like nothing can hurt me if I have you to protect me. It's strange though, because, it should be the other way around. I should be the one protecting you. Isn't that what men are supposed to do? Protect the women they love?"

"That's just a gender role, dreamed up by society. It has nothing to do with us. I'm the vampire, remember? I'm the immortal one with superhuman strength." I buckled my seatbelt, preparing for take-off. Not that I thought a seatbelt would make much difference, especially to me, but I knew the flight attendants would be walking down the aisle to make sure all passengers followed instructions.

"So...what can destroy you? What do I need to watch out for? You already told me sunlight can't," he asked.

"The most dangerous thing to us is fire. Decapitation isn't good either. Other than that, I don't know. You've seen how I heal," I said.

"You mean...your head?" he asked with a look of terror in his eyes.

"Yes, exactly. Don't worry. He'd have to catch me first and that's... nearly impossible," I said trying to keep it as light as possible. "It won't come to that."

Conversation stayed light when he was awake, and I did my best to keep up the appearance of fearlessness. As soon as we landed in Portland, and made our way off the plane, we headed straight for the car rental booths. I was happy to see the darkness outside. Christian and I waited in the background while Aaron made arrangements for a car. He was able to get an SUV with tinted windows and planned to leave it with us once we arrived at the cabin.

The drive to the cabin was about two hours, though Aaron drove the way Fiore did, so I couldn't tell how far it truly was. We were on very dark, winding roads through most of the drive and it was hard to figure out our location. I sat back in my seat, the feeling of panic hitting me again. Christian was in the backseat, though Aaron had suggested I sit back there with him. I felt he should not sit alone in the front, like he was our taxi driver.

Aaron kept his eyes straight ahead, on the road. *Kalia and I will have to leave once you're settled...for a little while...* He thought. He looked at me briefly. I nodded, understanding he was trying not to alarm Christian.

We need to gather the others make plans to move you if necessary... I nodded. The others? I wondered. I kept it to myself.

I will stay with Christian while you feed. Kalia will go with you...plenty of animals around...need to find out where Maia is... I nodded again. I knew Maia knew the location of the cabin. I wanted to say we should keep our whereabouts secret from her, just in case, but I didn't know how Aaron would react. I had a bad feeling about Maia but I wasn't quite sure what it was. How loyal was she to Ian? I had no way of knowing.

The drive up to the cabin was dark and tree lined. The dirt road that took us there was almost completely hidden. I would have never found it without Aaron. The opening we turned into didn't look wide enough for a vehicle. Tree branches scraped along the windows of the SUV as we drove through. After several minutes, I saw a dim light in the distance. As we got closer, I saw Aaron's car parked on the side of the cabin, the trunk open. Another light went on as we approached. The door opened and

Kalia stood on the porch, a wide smile on her beautiful face.

As the vehicle came to a stop, she ran down the steps and was opening my door before I could even grasp the handle. She pulled me out of my seat and grabbed me in a bear hug.

"Oh thank God!" she exclaimed. "You're safe! You have no idea what we've been through!"

I hugged her back, feeling the love emanating from both of us. It felt so good to be in her arms again, her loving, motherly embrace. The back door of the SUV opened and Christian stepped out, stretching. He stood there a moment, not wanting to interrupt our reunion. Kalia saw him and let go. She stepped over to Christian and I saw he had his hand out, ready to shake hers. Instead, Kalia wrapped her arms around him, squeezing. I saw Christian's eyes widen with surprise. I couldn't help but smile.

"Welcome," she said as she stepped back, getting a better look at him. "So you're Lily's Christian?" His face turned red.

"I guess I am," he said and shot a look at me. I smiled and nodded.

"Aaron," Kalia said hugging him now. She kissed his lips before pulling away. "There's wood in the trunk. Could you get it please?" Aaron nodded.

Kalia led us into the cabin. It was small and cozy. A fire was already glowing in the stone fireplace. I was surprised I had not seen the smoke rising from the chimney but the cabin was surrounded by a thick and lush forest. We followed her into the kitchen area as she opened cabinets to show us she had stocked them with canned and boxed food for Christian.

"I wasn't sure what you'd like so I bought a variety. There are drinks in the refrigerator: soda, iced tea, white wine, beer. There's red wine on top of the refrigerator. There should be everything you need in the bathroom. If there's anything I forgot, just tell me. I'll get it to you," she explained excitedly. I could see her motherly instincts hard at work.

She led us toward a closed door, a bedroom. There was a sofa bed against the wall, in front of a large window. There were also two chairs in the corner, a table and lamp in the middle. She walked over and turned on the lamp, shedding more light on the room. She had already pulled out the sofa bed and dressed it in white sheets and two soft-looking blankets, one over the bed and one neatly folded on the bottom, four pillows propped against the back. She smiled as she looked from the bed to me and I dropped my eyes to the floor.

Sorry…only one bed since…we don't sleep…

*Umm…thanks…*I thought, my eyes still on the floor. I knew Kalia didn't feel as uneasy about our relationship as Aaron did and her views on making an immortal were also not the same.

"I brought some of your clothes. They're in the closet. We also brought some for Christian, some of Aaron's. We didn't know what size, or if he would be with you but I'm glad we took the precaution. I can see they'll be a bit…long," she said, referring to the height difference between Aaron and Christian.

"Thank you," Christian said. "For everything. You've really gone out of your way. I'm sorry to be such trouble."

"Christian!" I said firmly. "It's not your fault. Don't ever think that. It's me."

"It's neither of you," Kalia interjected. "If it's anyone's fault, it's Ian. Remember that."

I nodded, to please her.

Aaron returned from stacking the wood by the fireplace and stood in the doorway of the bedroom. "Lily?" he said. "Why don't you go with Kalia? I'll stay with Christian a while."

Christian turned to face me.

"Umm…yeah…okay," I said, not wanting to part with him. How would I have been able to watch him get on a plane without me? I had no idea. "We'll be back shortly…there's something I have to do before they leave."

He looked at me, sudden understanding clicking into his terrified eyes. He kissed me and stepped back. I walked out of the room with Kalia as he and Aaron followed, into the living room. I was glad Christian hadn't asked for specifics, though I knew his mind was wondering.

TWENTY-TWO

Aaron and Kalia left after giving us instructions and making sure we were settled. We were to stay put until they returned. We could, however, wander the surrounding area, as they owned the fifteen acres surrounding the cabin and no one lived in its proximity. They had brought my cell phone with them. If there were any change in plans, they would call and alert us. Otherwise, they suggested I answer my phone for no one else. It was unlikely Ian would call but just in case…

They provided enough wood and matches to last a year, though the wood would need to be cut down. They advised me to keep the fire, in both living room and bedroom, burning at all times. I nodded though Christian looked confused. He thought it was warm enough in the cabin without the fire. I knew better.

They parted reluctantly, especially Aaron, wondering if he would find Christian the same way he left him when they returned. I assured him that, yes, Christian would be the same. I knew exactly what Aaron was thinking. I felt instant guilt.

We stood on the porch and watched them drive away, waving to them until the car disappeared from view. Kalia sent me a message as the car bounced down the dirt drive. *In the kitchen utility closet by the water heater…look when Christian is not close…no need to scare him more than he already is…*

"Now what?" Christian asked as we walked back into the cabin, arm in arm.

"Now we wait…" I said.

He sighed. "No better place to pass the time than this cozy cabin in the woods, alone with the love of my life."

I couldn't help but smile widely at that comment…the love of my life.

"Are you tired?" I asked as soon as I was able to speak again, still glowing from what he said.

"Are you kidding me? I feel wide awake. I slept a lot on the plane. I feel good," he said. To me, he still looked much too pale though the circles under his eyes were starting to fade. I guessed some of that had been from exhaustion after all. He still walked a little unsteadily, too, though he tried to hide it.

Kalia had stocked the freezer with red meat. That would help replenish some of the iron his body had lost. If he didn't want to eat, my only other option was…No! That wasn't an option at all. I dismissed it from my mind as we settled ourselves on the sofa in front of the roaring fire.

"Your color looks…I don't know…different," he said looking at my face. I could feel my cheeks were still a little flushed from feeding.

"Yeah. That's normal after…" I hesitated.

He nodded and stayed silent. I knew he didn't want to discuss the subject any further so I said nothing else about it. "Are you hungry?"

"No. Not yet. I am thirsty though. You want a drink?" he said as he stood. I could see the look in his eyes as he realized what he had said. "Oops! Sorry."

"Nope. I'm all set," I said trying to help him relax.

He walked into the kitchen and opened the refrigerator. After a few moments, he closed the door and reached for a bottle of red wine instead. He found a glass and looked through the drawers for a corkscrew. He poured himself a glass and joined me on the sofa. I watched his every move with amazement. It was so different the way a human moved, so slow and calculated. I watched him put the glass to his lips, inhaling the aroma before taking a gulp. He sighed.

"Good stuff," he said. He took another sip before setting the glass down on the coffee table and leaning back against the sofa, his legs stretched out in front of him, his arm across my shoulders. "What will we do with ourselves here?" he asked with a mischievous look in his eyes.

"I'm sure we'll think of something." I played along, making him smile. I could look at that smile all day.

"Okay…" he started while his gaze was on the fire. "I can't help it. I'm curious."

"About what?"

"You and Kalia. What did you eat? I am assuming that's what you were doing and…your color," he said.

"We found a mountain lion," I said. His eyes widened. "They're not easy to catch but, with Kalia's help…then on the way back, we stumbled upon a herd of mule deer, probably what the mountain lion was tracking."

"That's a pretty hearty meal," he said. "You weren't even gone that long."

"We're pretty fast. I try to move at a human speed most of the time, around humans. Alone, or with others of my kind, there's no need to pretend."

"You purposely move slower around me?"

"Yes. I saw no need to alarm you. Isn't it enough that you know what I am and…how I feed…sometimes?" I said, knowing he only knew about my most recent feeding.

He considered what I said for a moment, taking another gulp of his wine. "I want you to be yourself around me."

"Okay…" I said laughing and shaking my head. "You asked for it." The next thing he saw was me kneeling in front of the fireplace, a poker in my hand, adding another log to the fire. The expression on his face was comical. "What's wrong?"

"How? When?" He shook his head in confusion. "I didn't even feel you slip out from under my arm…"

"What can I say? I'm fast," I said slipping his arm back onto my shoulders as I nestled my head on his shoulder.

"Wow…" His voice was pure amazement. He sat still for a few moments. I tried my hardest to repress the laugh that was trying to erupt from me. "I have to use the bathroom. I will be a bit longer," he said, standing and setting his empty glass on the table.

"Okay. I'll be right here," I assured him.

As soon as he left the room, I grabbed his glass and went to the kitchen to refill it. I was anxious to see what Kalia meant about whatever was hidden in the closet. I pulled door open. There was a mop, a broom and a dust pan. Cleaning supplies? Confused, I started to move things aside when I saw something shining in the back, against the wall. I reached my hand back to where I could touch it and felt the cold metal under my fingertips. I grazed my hand along the length of it, trying to surmise what it was without actually pulling it out. A sword! My hand was touching a sword and by the feel of it, a damned long one! I realized they had left the weapon here in case we were found before they could return. What hadn't she thought of?

By the time Christian returned from the bathroom, I was sitting on the sofa, my socked feet resting on the coffee table, a full glass of wine in my hand.

"Thank you," he said, taking the glass from me. "You don't mind, do you?"

"Mind what?" I asked, not knowing if he referred to having to go to the bathroom or drinking wine.

"That I'm drinking wine?" he asked, holding the glass close to his lips but not daring to take a sip until I assured him it was okay with me.

"Not at all."

The more he drank, the more flushed his face became. It was actually kind of…cute. He talked more, too, which was nice. I loved hearing the sound of his voice and didn't mind one bit when he went on and on with stories of some of the digs he had been on. They were fascinating and I found myself relaxed and full of questions as I listened. When he went into the kitchen to get another glass, I suddenly remembered my cell phone. I went into the bedroom to retrieve it, seeing his head turn as he felt me walk past but not catching a glimpse. I returned to the living room, this time moving the coffee table aside so I could sit on the floor, leaning against the sofa.

Seeing what was in my hand, his eyes grew wide. He sank down beside me. I powered the phone on and waited.

"What's wrong?" I asked.

"Um…is this the first time you're turning that on, since we got here, I mean?" he asked, his voice cautious.

"Yeah. Kalia left it charging in the bedroom. Why?"

"You're going to have a lot of messages from me. Some of them might not make any sense."

I looked down at my phone, which was ready to go and had full signal, which was shocking considering we were deep in the mountains. Twelve new messages!

He looked at the screen too. "They're all from me. I'm sorry. I couldn't stop myself. I was miserable when you left," he defended himself. "I needed to hear your voice, even if it was just on your voicemail."

I put my hand on his, trying to reassure him. "It's okay, really." I held the phone to my ear, preparing to listen to the messages. He grabbed it from my grip moving faster than I had ever seen him move.

"No! Don't listen to them please. Delete them!" he said franticly.

"Why?" I asked, still shocked he had been able to get the phone out of my hand.

"Because I don't want you to hear," he started, tossing the phone on the sofa behind his head. "At first, I was just sad, crying and pleading with you to come back or call me at least. Later, I was angry. I said some things I wish I hadn't said."

"Like what?" I asked, curious. I couldn't imagine anything mean coming out of his mouth.

"Well…like that I thought you were using me, playing with my head, that you had someone else. Then I was telling you things you didn't need to know like…someone maybe watching me, just being paranoid. My last message was…" He picked up his glass again and took a long swig before speaking. "Just the beginning. I heard someone breaking in and the phone was grabbed from my hand before I could finish."

"Didn't you call the police?" I asked bewildered.

"No. I had to call you first."

My breath stopped in my throat. He had been trying to call me when he was taken. Me! Not the police. "Who was it? What happened? Did you get a good look…?"

He shook his head. "Whoever it was came up behind me. All I felt were cold hands, something against my nose that…stank…and then everything went black," he said with a shaky voice. His whole body trembled so I decided not to push the issue further, not yet.

"It's okay," I said. "You don't have to talk about it now."

His eyes filled with sadness and were starting to well up with moisture. I took the glass out of his hand and set it on the floor, next to him. I climbed up on his lap and took his face in my hands. "Everything will be fine. I promise you!" His heart beat faster and at a deafening volume in my ears as I put my lips on his. I wanted to erase all those memories from his mind…somehow.

I don't know exactly what happened, or how, but we were lying on the floor, a blanket draped across us, desperately trying to catch our breath. Sweat glistened off his hair and skin, making his scent all the sweeter. I wasn't hungry at all, having feasted on the blood of three animals, enough to hold me for about a month, so I wasn't worried about that. I was, however, worried about any harm I might have caused while I was…out of control. I turned on my side to get a better look at him, propping myself on my elbow, when I noticed the pile of clothing on the floor behind us.

The room was starting to fill with light from the rising sun. The sound of his heartbeat, trying to slow itself to a more reasonable pace was enough to confirm what had just happened.

He turned to look at me, a bead of sweat hanging off his nose, a wide smile on his face. I felt panic course through my body.

"I told you there was nothing to be afraid of," he said, his voice gentle, dreamy-like.

"I didn't? Please tell me I didn't…"

"Not at all. Don't you remember?" he asked, looking a little hurt. I thought about it. I felt his lips on mine, hungry and wet. His warm hands all over my skin, caressing every inch, his face above mine. I struggled against him, trying to pull him closer…closer to my lips…but…

"I didn't let you," he said.

"Thank God! I'm sorry," I said, still trying to catch my breath.

"It was the most amazing thing ever! You have nothing to be sorry about," he said looking into my eyes. His lips were just inches away from mine. "I love you," he whispered before he kissed me.

I remembered. I saw it as he kissed me, the images flooding my mind again. Our bodies as one, finally.

"Are you hungry now?" I asked, raising my head. I heard the soft grumble of his stomach as we lied there, basking in the glow.

"Yeah…I guess I am," he said, stroking my arm. "I can get it though." He started sitting up, trying to get the motivation to move.

"That's a good idea. It's been years since I cooked. Who knows what you'd end up with if you let me," I teased. "I can at least make you coffee."

"Sounds good!" He laughed as he walked away, taking the blanket with him and grabbing my pile of clothes as he strode into the kitchen. "Are you coming?" He dropped the blanket on the kitchen floor.

"Ugh! That's really mean," I huffed as I stood, wrapping my arms around myself, trying to conceal everything he had not only touched, but kissed just moments ago. I walked into the kitchen, feeling completely exposed, and embarrassed.

"You are breathtaking," he said, kissing my lips, taking my arms and placing them around his neck. I felt the butterflies in my stomach, instantly.

As soon as he let me go, I walked over to the window and pulled down the blind. I could see that today the sun decided to shine. Even though he knew what happened to me in the sun, I was not yet ready for him to actually *see* it. It was enough he was seeing all of me, standing at the kitchen sink, filling the coffee pot. I saw his smile as he peeked at me from behind the refrigerator door.

"I should probably make an omelet. Kalia put green and red bell peppers in here. They'll go bad if I don't use them. Plenty of eggs too, and cheese…" he spoke as he gathered ingredients in his arms.

"Are you going to cook naked?" I asked. The coffee pot was already brewing, making gurgling noises, steam escaping from the top. I let my hand hover above the steam, enjoying the warm moisture against my cold skin.

"Sure. Why not?" He laughed. He pulled a frying pan out of the cabinet next to the stove and grabbed a knife from the drawer. He looked around, opening cabinets and drawers. He pulled the drawer out under the stove. *Where would a cutting board be?*

"Don't worry about it. If there isn't one, use a plate. I'll wash it after…"

"What?" His shocked look told me he didn't say that aloud. Oops!

"Well…naturally…" I tried to explain. He cut me off.

"I didn't say that. I only thought it. I'm almost positive," he said doubting himself.

"Well, I figured that's what you'd need next. I do remember some things. I was human once," I said, hoping he would buy it. He didn't.

"You heard my thoughts! You heard me, Lily," he said looking a little worried. "How long have you been doing that? How much have you heard?"

I had no choice. It was pointless to lie to him now. I grabbed the blanket from the floor and wrapped it around myself. There was something about confessing to him when I didn't have any clothes on that made me feel more exposed.

"I've barely done it. Maybe once or twice. I've respected your privacy," I admitted.

I saw his eyes change from confusion to amazement to realization. "That's how you guessed my age. You didn't guess at all! You just picked it out of my head!"

"Sorry. I know that wasn't fair," I said, trying to smile, hoping he wasn't angry with me. He didn't miss a trick. He hadn't figured it out then but now he put the pieces together, with just one slip from me. He laughed as he started slicing a wet bell pepper on a plate.

"What else can you do?" he asked. He was slicing the peppers with a butcher knife, the only one he found in the drawer. Could I tell him everything? Would he still look at me the same if he knew? I decided I would give it a try. After all, he knew I was a vampire and still loved me.

"You already know I can fly," I started as he cut. "I have incredible strength. My senses are enhanced. I can hear your heartbeat, constantly, always. I can, of course, read minds but many vampires can do that. I've just recently been learning how to block my thoughts from others. I can also jump from really high places, if I am ever in really high places, that is. Oh yeah, and, I can put images in people's minds, have them see what I want them to see." I thought a minute, his hand still chopping while he listened to me, not interrupting. "And, I heal very fast. I think that's it."

"That's it? Are you sure? You didn't..." He stopped. The knife clanked to the floor. He leaned over the counter, holding his left hand. As soon as I realized what he had done, the scent filled my nostrils, making my mouth water. My fangs brushed against my tongue. The room started spinning.

"Please turn the water on." His voice sounded weak, like he was going to faint.

I ran to the sink and turned the water on, making sure it wasn't hot. I took his arm, as gently as I could, and guided his hand toward the flow, my head still spinning. I didn't feel thirsty but the natural instinct of my body took over. I tried to calm myself, repeating over and over that this was Christian. And...Christian was hurt!

"Let me see," I said, finally gaining more control. "Let me see how bad it is. I don't know if we have a first aid kit."

His face scrunched up in pain. He uncurled his fingers, letting out a moan. The cut was long, a perfect diagonal line across his palm. It looked deep too, something that might need stitches.

"Hold this on there tightly. I'll see what we have." I handed him the towel from the refrigerator door and ran to the bathroom to check the medicine cabinet. Empty! I ran back out to the kitchen. He leaned against the counter, holding a soaked red towel over his hand, looking even paler than he already was. The scent of his blood was stronger, making me feel dizzy all over again. STOP IT! I told myself.

I flung all the cabinets open and pulled things out, letting cans and utensils hit the floor around him, making him jump. There was nothing. After all, vampires didn't have much need for a first aid kit! I grabbed the knife from the floor and turned to him.

"Hold out your hand!" I demanded. "Close your eyes if you need to!"

He didn't close his eyes. In fact, he stared with his eyes wide, his face turning whiter by the minute, as I took the knife and sliced my own hand, flinching from the sting. He didn't blink as shock and terror filled his face. I held my bleeding hand above his, just inches from the cut. My blood poured over the open wound and he finally flinched, as the combination of our blood began to bubble. As soon as the gash was covered, I pulled my hand away, holding it over the sink to catch any blood that still flowed. I watched as my skin began to close itself then caught him in my arms just before he hit the floor.

"How ARE YOU doing?" I asked as his eyes tried to focus on my face. I had carried him to the bedroom and laid him on the bed. The bedside lamp was on since the curtains were drawn to keep the sunlight out.

"What..." he mumbled, looking around him. He tried to sit up so I propped the pillows and helped him pull his body up.

"I think you fainted," I said.

Just then, he remembered his injured hand. He flexed his fingers for a moment before raising his hand to look. He pulled it closer to his face and, very slowly, opened it. His eyes grew wide at the sight.

"It'll be fine. Back to normal in no time. See?" I held his hand and lightly ran my fingers across it. His eyes focused and he stared at the raised skin of the closed cut with bewilderment. "How does it feel?"

"A little stiff." He moved his eyes from his hand to my face.

"How do *you* feel now?" I asked. The color in his face returned. The circles under his eyes were fading.

"I feel like I've slept for hours, rested..." he mused. "Like I have more energy somehow. How long was I out?"

"I'd say about a minute." I studied his face. His heart beat stronger than when he was in the basement, when I first found him.

"Why do I feel so good? And I thought I cut myself..." He shook his head.

"You did. The green pepper was wet and it must have slipped out of your hand. It was a big cut. Don't you remember what I did?" I held his hand on my lap, cradling it in my own.

"Not really. I remember a lot of blood...the room spinning...the coppery smell...then, nothing."

"I couldn't find a first aid kit so I took care of it my way. I sliced my

241

own hand and…" I swallowed hard before I spoke again, unsure of how he would react. "I used my blood to close your cut." His face was serious, thinking, remembering.

"Is that why it looks like it's an old cut? Why I feel so strong?" he asked.

He didn't miss a thing! His scientific mind caught every little detail, every little thing I did.

"At the moment, you have my blood coursing through your veins," I explained, giving it a moment to sink in. His mouth gaped. It sank in. "It wasn't much. It'll wear off, little by little throughout the day."

"So your blood is in my veins right now?" he asked, snapping his mouth shut afterward.

"Yes. But like I said, it was a small amount, only enough to heal your cut."

"And that's why I feel so much stronger?" he asked, trying to put all the pieces together. He pulled his hand out from mine, holding my hand palm up now so he could examine it. "There's nothing on yours. Mine is a little discolored and raised but yours is perfect."

"I told you I heal *very* fast. That's why I'm the immortal." I laughed, trying not to make a big thing out of it.

"So, I'm still mortal, right?"

"Absolutely! I would have to…" I closed my mouth. "How about that omelet? And the coffee's ready. Feel well enough to stand yet?"

"I love how you change the subject. Yeah, I can get up. Actually, I feel like I could run a marathon." He turned so his feet could touch the floor. I jumped out of the way so he could stand, waiting with my arms out in case he felt lightheaded again, though I doubted he would.

He stood still for a moment, making sure the room didn't spin. "I'm okay. No dizziness for once," he turned to look at me. "Thank you."

"You're very welcome," I said, lowering my arms. "I would do anything for you."

"Anything?" His eyes looked a little fearful but the smile was still on his lips. I nodded, not knowing where he was going with that but not sure I wanted to know either. "I'll meet you in the kitchen." He signaled toward the bathroom with his head.

He was in the bathroom in a second, his speed suddenly matching mine. I laughed, wondering if that's how I looked to him when I moved, like a blur.

Moments later, I sat with him as he sat on the living room floor, his plate on the coffee table. He ate everything: the omelet, which was made with no more mishaps, toast, and bacon. He finished one cup of coffee and I poured him another. When I returned, I held the cup in my hands for a while as I watched him push his empty plate aside. He looked at me with amusement in his eyes.

"What is it about coffee that you like so much?" he asked. I quickly handed him the cup.

A bit embarrassed, I answered. "I think it's the warmth and the aroma. It reminds me of my parents, I guess. Of a simpler time."

"Makes sense," He looked past me, toward the window. It was glowing yellow even through the drawn blind. "Can we go outside today? I could use the fresh air. I've been in darkness for so long."

"But the sun," I said, my voice cracking a bit. "Just let me…"

"No! No makeup please. I want you to just be…you." He said it with a gentle, coaxing voice but to my panicked mind it sounded more like a command.

"But, you'll think I'm hideous! I can't," I pleaded.

"I love *all* of you. Remember that."

I gulped. I knew he loved me. I felt it every moment I was with him but this was too much, even for me.

"Please Lily. I promise. It'll be fine," he assured. "Just you. No cover-ups. Not anymore."

I hesitated, thinking it was a big mistake but I couldn't deny him anything, not now, not when we had gotten so *close*, so much closer than I ever dared to dream.

"Ugh! If you insist," I whined. "Let's at least get dressed."

∽ TWENTY-THREE ∾

After washing the breakfast dishes and getting dressed, we were ready to go out. I hesitated at the open door, sunglasses on, keeping my face as low as possible. He put his hand on my shoulder.

"I'll go first." He stepped out into the sunlight looking more energized than usual. The birds were singing in the trees and the air was crisp and clean. The sweatshirts we had chosen would be enough for the warmth radiating from the sun. He stood about ten feet away from me, facing in the opposite direction. He said nothing. I knew he was trying not to rush me.

I told myself he wouldn't judge me. I counted to three in my head, trying to coax myself. One…two…three. I stepped out from under the shelter of the cabin, onto the porch. Okay, I made it this far. Now the porch. I walked down the steps on shaky, unsteady legs. Still, he didn't turn. With both feet planted on the bottom step, I took a deep breath and held it.

I stood behind him, close enough to touch him, though I didn't dare. I felt the warmth of the sun on my face, my hands. I bent my neck to feel the heat on my face, closing my eyes. It wasn't often I was able to enjoy it. Images of trips to the beach with my parents flooded my mind. Children running through the sand, splashing in the water, the scent of suntan oil, fresh and fruity, the feel of grainy sand stuck to my skin, the salty, briny smell of the ocean. I kept my eyes closed for a while, enjoying the memory, my father sitting on the sand reading his newspaper, his wide rim straw hat shielding his eyes from the intense sun. My mother reading her novels, holding the book with one hand and a paper fan in the other. It made me smile. I heard his deep intake of breath. My eyes snapped open. He was facing me, staring wide-eyed. I swallowed hard, suddenly conscious of what he was seeing.

"I told you…" I said and hung my head in horror. His hand went to my chin, lifting my face. My eyes met his.

"Absolutely amazing!" he said, his eyes still wide with either horror or fascination, I couldn't tell which. "You *are* the sun. I may need sunglasses to look at you."

"Are you horrified?" I asked. "I told you it wasn't a good idea."

"Lily, I love you. I can't say it enough. This just makes you more beautiful. You glow, like an angel's halo."

"Okay. It's all out in the open now. There's nothing more to see." I realized, again, he was calmer than me. "Let's go explore."

He took my hand, examining it for a few moments under the bright light, his eyes squinted. I watched his face without saying a word. I could see honest fascination in his eyes, not fear. I relaxed a bit.

We hiked through the mountains and forest for hours. I could tell him when I heard an animal and what animal it was, catching its scent and knowing from the sounds it made. He named trees and rock formations, explaining them to me.

We rested every so often, sitting on a rock or on the ground, taking in the views, the sounds, and the smells around us. He always sat close, our bodies touching. Every time he looked at my face, I saw awe in his eyes. He never said anything to make me feel self-conscious.

He was getting thirsty and we hadn't thought to bring water with us. "Can we fly back?" he asked.

I gasped. "Are you serious? You want to go through that again?"

"Sure. You said you needed practice so why not practice with me?" He said this so calmly.

"We need a high place to take off from. I don't know how to do it from level ground yet. I haven't tried." He looked up into the tree above us but the first branch wasn't low enough for either of us to grab and hoist ourselves up.

"That's a little high."

"You said you can jump."

"I guess I could try…" I felt a strange sense of confidence. He believed I was fearless, that I could do anything. I was starting to feel it too.

I rose and looked above me. I held my arms above my head, making sure I was directly below the branch. Once we were on that it should be no problem climbing higher. I looked at him. He still sat on the ground, waiting for my assessment.

"Okay. Let's do this," I said. He rose, his face filled with excitement, his heart racing.

He stood behind me, and, after grazing my neck with his lips, clasped his hands around my neck. I bent my knees and lifted my arms. "Ready?"

"Ready!"

He let out an excited yell as we reached the branch I'd aimed for, my hands tightly grasping the branch above which, I was glad, was at just the right level. I climbed higher, with him on my back.

"See? I told you you could do it!" His speech was fast, from excitement or my blood, I couldn't tell. "It's gorgeous up here."

He stood by my side, arms wrapped around the trunk. He looked around, sighing. The view *was* breathtaking. The air was cleaner, the birds louder. Everything looked brighter. The green looked greener and the blue sky, bluer. We could see the snow capped mountains in the distance. After a several minutes, he broke the silence.

"Now…about the landing," he started. I interrupted with a nervous laugh but his face was all business. "What if you change your body position when we're about, say…ten feet or so from the ground? Then, when you're ready to touch down, we count to three and I let go. We land separately. You go right and I go left. That way…"

"How high is too high for you to make it without getting hurt? That's the last thing I want to do," I said, interrupting him. I pictured what he was saying and it seemed logical.

"I don't know, maybe…" he thought a moment. "Let's see, I'm six feet tall so, I'd say a little more than that, but not much. There's also grass surrounding the cabin so that should work. I can let you know when I'm ready," he explained. His mind made the calculations. His breathing sped up in anticipation.

"You really liked flying with me?" I asked surprised. I couldn't imagine anyone liking that experience. I also couldn't believe he trusted me so completely.

"You have no idea," he said, still looking around. "I have one question first, though…" His head continued to turn slowly in all directions. "Am I seeing everything so much clearer because of your blood in my veins?"

I thought about it for a moment. It should be out of his system by now, considering the small amount of blood I used. Maybe I had shed more than I thought; regardless, there was no need to worry about it. The process had been purely one-sided…this time. I shook that thought out of my head, angry with myself. I assured him it was the reason. That for the moment, he was seeing things the way I saw them. A smile lit up his face.

We climbed about four more branches, separately, him almost but not quite keeping up with me. Once we were firmly planted there, I turned so he could get behind me. He wrapped his arms around me and kissed the back of my neck, again with the chills!

"Ready?" I asked, mirroring his excitement, shocked at my own reaction and anticipation. Not very long ago, I hated heights, feared them more than I feared even Ian. Now, I was ready to do this with Christian's life in my hands!

"Ready!" he yelled. I heard him inhale and hold it.

"Here we go…" I said as I sprung off my bent knees.

We soared through the air in the direction of the cabin, the ground whizzing by below us, causing a blur of movement, like in a photograph taken from a moving vehicle. It was so different this time, no cold rain pelting our faces, no wind except for the slight breeze from our speed. His arms were wrapped tightly around me, as were his warm legs. I couldn't quite tell where his body ended and mine began.

I searched for the cabin. Once I saw the smoke coming from the chimney, I told him I was ready to change my position, just to prepare him.

"Okay!" he yelled, his voice still filled with excitement. "I'm ready!" I felt his grip tighten around my neck but his legs slightly loosened at the same time.

As soon as we were vertical with the soft, green ground, I yelled. "ONE…TWO…THREE…" He hesitated for just a second but I heard him take a deep breath and his hands unclasped. The heat of his body disappeared. I shifted my position again, aiming to the right. Had it not been a slight hill, my landing may have been perfect. As it was, I ran about fifteen paces, trying to slow myself down when I finally lost my balance and rolled to the ground. I lay on my back trying to catch my breath, my arms draped over my eyes to shield them from the sun that was now lower in the sky. I heard his laughter.

He was on the ground, about five feet to my left, laughing out of control.

"What's so funny?" I yelled.

"You…you should've…" he tried to stop his laughter. "Should've seen your arms flailing. You looked like a wild goose!" He laughed again.

"UGH! I'm glad you got such enjoyment out of that!" I stood and stomped away, as best I could on the soft grass. He still lay on his back, his face turned toward me, laughing. I sat on the bottom step of the porch, pouting.

"Aww! It was so cute," he sang. "I'm sorry. I didn't mean to laugh. I'll stop now."

I pictured what he must have seen. A giggle escaped my lips before I could stop myself. He sat next to me, his body as usual touching mine.

"You landed on your feet, though," he reassured me. "So did I, by the way. If we would've been on level ground it would've been perfect."

"Are you okay? Was that too high?" I asked, suddenly realizing I didn't know if he had been hurt.

"I'm perfect! I've never been better. I've never felt more alive than I do with you, right now," he said. Suddenly his hands were on my face, turning it toward his. He closed his eyes and slowly, very slowly, his lips met mine. My stomach did a wild flip as soon as I felt the heat of his lips, the burning moisture of his tongue. My body stiffened, along with my lips. He noticed and pulled away.

"Lily, what…"

"Shh!" I whispered. "Listen…" I sat totally still. I heard his heartbeat speed, his breathing uneven, nervous. His pulse was quicker than when he'd been kissing me. He stared at me, eyes full of questions.

"Something's wrong," I whispered again, leaning closer to him so he could hear me. "Something's wrong."

His body stiffened. He sat up straight, concentrating on his hearing, his eyes wide with fear. The color drained out of his face again and I could tell the side effects of my blood were wearing off. Bad timing!

"Hide," I whispered to him. "You have to run and hide…now!"

"No! I'm not leaving you. I refuse…" he pled, shaking his head.

"I will handle this. I refuse to risk your life. DO AS I SAY…NOW!" I demanded through clenched teeth. The shock and hurt on his face told me he would do as I said but he didn't have to like it. He rose and after kissing the top of my head, walked away, backward, his eyes pleading with me to change my mind and let him stay. I shook my head before I stood. He turned and ran toward the wooded area. I watched him disappear before I turned to climb the steps.

Turning the knob slowly, I listened. I heard the slight rustling of clothing, a body moving around inside. I saw no cars outside so I was sure it was not someone I wanted here, not Kalia or Aaron. They would have warned me. My eyes scanned the living room from where I stood and beyond that, the kitchen. The clothes that were lying in the kitchen doorway had been moved, only slightly, but they had been touched. I tried to remember if either of us did that before we went out but I was sure the only thing we had cleaned up were the dishes.

I heard a door open and close in the direction of the bedroom…the closet. My breathing came faster, audible. I tried to control it as I walked to the fireplace. I grabbed the poker and headed, as quietly as I could manage, toward the sound. There was no heartbeat, that much I was sure of. Whoever was in here was a vampire. Ian!

At the first sign of movement, I sprang, swinging the poker with all my might. I felt it make contact with something at the same instant a growl escaped my throat and a body went flying across the room, falling to the floor on the other side of the bed, where I couldn't see! Damn it!

I heard a groan. I waited. The poker still grasped in both hands, ready to strike again. A black mass with hair flying wildly flew at me, growling angrily. I ducked just in time but cold hands grasped my ankle. I turned and swung the poker again, this time aiming down toward the body at my feet. I hit hard! The hand released its grasp. I jumped away, trying to get a better look at the body now writhing in pain on the floor. Jet-black hair was spread on the floor, the chest area rising and dropping with strain. Slowly, very slowly, the body rolled over, grunting in pain. I gripped the poker tighter, my knees bent, ready to strike again.

"DAMN IT, LILY!" A female voice groaned. "WHAT THE HELL?"

My mind reeled. That voice…I knew that voice…

"Fiore?" I asked, my voice shaking.

She pushed her hair away from her face. Her green eyes wide, still writhing in pain on the floor. There was blood on her face, probably from the first time I struck her.

"What are you doing here? Is Ian here? What do you want? How did you find me?" My questions flew. She sat up, hunched over her knees. I still held the poker in the air, ready. She held one hand in the air, signaling surrender. I stood in a fight stance.

"I tracked you…that's what I'm best at and…no. Ian is not here. I left him. Did I miss anything?" she asked, obviously trying to remember my questions, as she wiped blood from her face. The gash the poker made on her skin was already closing. I didn't dare drop the poker, not yet.

"Damn you can fight!" she said with obvious surprise. "I had no idea how protective you could be." She looked around the room. "Where is he?"

"Why should I tell you?" I demanded, my tone harsher than I had ever used with her.

"I am not here to hurt you or take you back. Ian doesn't know where I am. I told you, I left him." She was trying to get to her feet. I readied the poker to strike again. She dropped back to the ground. She looked at me with pleading yet…amused eyes. "Please, Lily. Put that down. I'm here to help you." Her eyes looked sincere yet, I couldn't let my guard down. Not when it came to Christian.

I raised my arms higher above my head just as I heard a sound behind me. I spun, with the poker in front of me, ready to swing, when I saw Christian's terrified eyes in front of me, his face totally white. He caught the poker in his hands.

"What are you doing here? I thought I told you…"

"I couldn't help it. I was worried. I thought maybe I could…" he started before I cut him off.

"Help? You thought you could help? What, pray tell, could you do against a vampire? Go ahead, I'm waiting." My tone and sarcasm hurt him. It showed in his eyes. I felt it in my gut.

Instead of answering me, his eyes searched the room until they found a disheveled and wild looking Fiore sitting on the floor. His head tilted a little to the side, reminding me of a curious dog. I laughed. His eyes turned back to me. Shock at my reaction registered on his face. I snapped out of it, releasing the poker into his still grasping hands.

"Christian…Fiore. Fiore…Christian," I said.

"Hi," Fiore said, her voice gentle. She looked at me. I nodded and walked to her, my hands stretched out in front of her. I pulled her up. The cut on her face was almost completely nonexistent now but the dried blood that remained was not a pretty sight. I walked her over to the bed and motioned for her to sit down.

Christian made his way to one of the chairs, the poker still in his hands, and sat down, resting it across his lap. His fingers wrapped around it. If Fiore did anything that could be considered a threat, Christian was ready to defend me. I smiled at that thought, though it terrified me.

"How did you find me so fast? My God! We just got here." I didn't conceal my amazement. Her eyes were still on Christian. I stiffened protectively, this time for different reasons.

"You were never out of my sight," she stated. I started pacing. She looked at me finally. "I had a feeling...knew what you were going to do. That's why I sent the others away. If Ian is not around, they have to listen to me. I guess you could say I am, or was, the second in command. Anyway, I was just going to let you do it, disappear. But then, as soon as you left the theater, a feeling of emptiness hit me and I knew I couldn't."

"Couldn't what? Let me escape? You came to take me back, didn't you?" I asked, horrified again.

"No! I swear. That's not my intention at all. I didn't want to be without you. I realized that," she lowered her eyes, looking embarrassed. "I realized I loved you and I wanted to go with you so I stayed right behind you, most of the way. I lost you in Portland, when you got in the car and I couldn't get a cab fast enough to stay on your trail but I had your gloves in my pocket so, I followed your scent." She looked up at me again, waiting for my reaction.

I said nothing for several minutes, trying to make sense of what she was saying. Christian sat still and quiet, unusually still for a human. He also waited for my reaction. My legs felt weak and I wavered, Fiore rushed to my side before Christian could react. He had the poker shaking above his head. I looked at him and shook my head so he reluctantly lowered it.

"What about Ian? And the others?" I asked, still in her hard, cold arms. It felt so strange now after being surrounded by Christian's warmth lately.

"Who cares about them?" she spat as she led me to sit on the bed. "Ian was only using me, just as much as I was using him. I felt no loyalty to him. They were just something to pass the time."

"How? How was he using you?" I asked confused. I couldn't imagine what she meant. The land was his, the cottages were his, Fergus and Ryanne were...his.

"He was using me for my blood," she stated, waiting a moment to let me digest that before continuing. I saw her turn her eyes toward Christian. He quickly sat, dropping the poker at his side with a thud. He dropped his gaze. "I'm what is considered an *elder* in our world. My blood is ancient, more powerful. To drink from me is like drinking from the fountain of youth or something. Maybe that's not a good analogy but...my blood gives more strength, power, more control. It enhances any of the special *gifts* we end up with when we become immortals. That's what he wanted me for. That's all, nothing more." She sounded sad suddenly. I wondered why but didn't ask.

"So that's what gave him the ability to talk to me even when he wasn't close," I said aloud, trying to make sense of it all. "That's how he got so strong, so much stronger than I remember him being." She nodded. "What did you just do to Christian…just now?" I asked, remembering how he looked like he was silently obeying her commands.

"I told him to put the poker down and relax. That's all." She looked at me, trying to gauge my anger. She relaxed when she saw nothing but my search for understanding.

I couldn't stop my next question. I blurted it out before I could think about what I was saying.

"Why did you let him do that to you?"

She turned her face away from Christian, her eyes focusing on mine. Her expression was blank. "Because…I was in love with him."

My breath caught in my throat. I saw Christian's eyes widen. His jaw dropped just as I was sure mine had. I snapped it shut. Christian noticed and did the same. I didn't know what to say but, suddenly, I felt like I understood Fiore. I completely understood the insanity loving Ian could cause. I worried about Maia. How far gone was she?

I stood in front of Fiore and threw my arms around her, squeezing her. I saw Christian's shoulders drop, relaxing. I heard him breathe a sigh of relief. Fiore held me just as tightly as I held her, burying her face in my shoulder.

"I love you," she sighed.

"I love you, too," I replied. I saw a smile spread over Christian's face but worry filled his blue eyes. I thought I saw a touch of jealousy

IN THE DAYS that followed Fiore's unexpected arrival, things remained eerily quiet.

Christian and Fiore got along…sort of. They seemed extra polite toward each other and a bit…wary. They watched each other out of the corner of their eyes, especially when the other was close to me. I watched them with amusement, wondering what was going through their minds but still respecting their privacy, not prying, though I was often tempted.

I had spoken to Aaron first thing that morning. The phone vibrated in my pocket as Christian and I stepped out of the bedroom, Fiore glaring at him from the living room. I ignored that look as she soon changed it to a greeting smile. Aaron said everyone was assembled at the Astoria house, except for Riley. She had a business problem and was taking care of that before meeting the others. As soon as she arrived, they would head to the cabin.

"Are we going after him?" I asked in confusion. We did not have any indication that he knew our whereabouts. Nothing pointed toward the possibility of his coming here. Except for…

Fiore assured me he had not seen her or spoken to her since he left. She assured me he had gotten no information from her. There was one possibility that frightened her. That possibility was that he was already aware we had fled. She explained to me that, in the airport in London, she had, only briefly, caught his scent. She had run around the airport looking for him but had not found him. However, she was concerned that if she was correct, and it was his scent she had caught, it was very possible he had also caught ours. I shivered at the thought. I explained that to Aaron and that's why the decision was made. We would gather and await his arrival.

"How do you play games?" Christian suddenly asked. I followed his gaze to the pile of board games Kalia had left for us to pass the time.

"What do you mean?" Fiore asked, an amused look on her face.

"I mean…how do a bunch of vampires who can read each other's minds play games? How does anyone ever win?" he asked, his voice filled with the sincere curiosity of a child.

"We don't win. It's fun anyway," she said with a laugh.

"I guess…" he said sliding closer to me, putting his arm around my shoulders. Fiore straightened in her seat, a chair she had brought from the bedroom.

The fire was still roaring in the fireplace. We sat still, all our gazes fixed on it.

"It won't be much longer now," she stated with a calm, even voice. "He'll be tracking you just like I did. I found you easily; so will he. We need to figure out what we're going to do with him." She nodded toward Christian. His back stiffened.

"I know…" I started and then looked at him, knowing that hiding was not an option he was even considering. "Aaron will have a plan."

"What if he gets here before them? You know he won't be alone."

I nodded. I knew Ian would be coming with his own army.

"Have they heard from Maia yet?" she asked.

"No. Not a peep and they're worried. That makes one less for us," I said. "We have no idea how many will be with Ian. I imagine at least two." I pictured Fergus and Ryanne. My face scrunched with disgust.

"We need to find a safe place for Christian," she explained. "And that makes one less for us. Someone will have to stay with him."

"No! I'll be with the rest of you!" Christian said firmly. "I can help… somehow."

Fiore laughed, making Christian turn bright red. He glared at her. She smiled. Moments later, his eyes softened. He smiled. I wasn't sure I liked the way Fiore was controlling his mind but I didn't say anything. As long as it kept him calm, I had no reason to complain. He relaxed again and sat back, his legs stretched out in front of him.

"It's hot in here! Why do we have to keep the fire going?" He fanned himself with his free hand. Fiore and I exchanged looks.

"In case we have to throw someone into it," I said. He nodded but his eyes showed terror. The arm he had draped across my shoulders suddenly squeezed me. I could sense what had him worried. What if it was one of us? I shuddered to think it.

THE NEXT EVENING, Fiore and I cleaned up and tended the fires. Christian had fallen asleep on the sofa. She suddenly pulled me into the kitchen, her face serious.

"We'll need to feed before Ian gets here. We'll need the extra strength." Suddenly, her eyes grew wider and a smile flashed across her face, exposing her glowing white fangs. She grabbed my arm and this time pulled me into the bedroom. I heard Christian groan, his breath still even from sleep.

"What are you doing?" I asked in alarm.

"Something I should've done long ago," she said as she brought her wrist to her mouth. I shuddered when I heard the unmistakable sound of tearing flesh.

"What are you doing?" I gasped. I tried to step back, out of her reach, but I wasn't fast enough, especially since I was now against the wall.

"Drink!" She commanded. I shook my head, my hand covering my mouth. "Come on…before it clots."

I smelled her blood and my head spun, the room turning around me. I steadied myself against the wall. She locked her eyes with mine. I tried to look away but couldn't move.

Please, Lily. Do this. Do this for me…for him. I'm trying to make you… stronger…invincible…

Without thinking, my hand dropped and I found myself grasping her wrist, hungrily bringing it to my open, eager mouth. I closed my eyes as

I let her boiling blood spill in and fill my mouth before I swallowed. I sucked harder, wanting more, my head spinning, my throat on fire. She sighed, from pain or pleasure I couldn't say. The only thing I know is the more I tasted, the more I wanted. I drank and drank, inhaling her scent, listening to her muffled moans, my head spinning out of control until… her hand pushed my head. I fought against it, wanting more. She pushed harder, though her strength was faltering.

"Enough!" she said. "Enough, Lily." She cupped her hand under my chin and pushed my head up, my grasp on her arm breaking. I licked the blood off my lips, savoring the taste, savoring the last drop. The room spun even more. I felt like I was going to faint. She knew it and carried me to the bed, setting me down gently, still clinging to me as I clung to her. It felt like fire coursed through my veins. I stifled my cries, burying my face in her neck, my nose taking in her smell, my fangs ready to break the skin, wanting more.

"Shh…it's okay. It'll pass," she whispered. I closed my mouth, my face still buried in her neck, shielded by her thick, sweet smelling hair. I stayed like that for several more minutes, feeling the fire, enduring the pain, breathing faster with every fiery moment. My mind suddenly flashed to Ian. To the night he'd made me what I was…a vampire. This was how it felt! This was what my physical death had felt like!

"It's almost over," she whispered in a soothing tone. "You'll be so much stronger because of it. You'll see."

She stayed with me, holding me until, finally, I calmed. My breathing slowed and the burning through my veins subsided. She sat up, looking at me.

"How do you feel?" she asked.

"Okay, I think," I said, trying to sit up. She assisted me. I looked around the room. "The spinning stopped and the burning is almost gone. My eyes…I can see every little detail in the blanket, every thread," I stared at it. She laughed. It wasn't a mocking laugh. "I can hear Christian's breathing, from here, even with the door closed."

"Yes." She nodded. "Everything will be so much more enhanced… everything. The only thing is…" She hesitated.

"What? Is there a problem?" I questioned, nervous once more.

"I wouldn't call it a problem…exactly. It's just that you'll be more connected to me now. Just like Ian is connected to you, and me for that matter. Just like he is connected to Christian, after tasting his blood. He'll find us because of that. He's physically and mentally connected to the three of us."

I nodded. I always knew the connection was powerful between maker and newborn and it made sense that we would always be connected. It made sense though I had never really experienced it myself, except with Ian, having never tasted anyone else's blood that I hadn't killed. Unknown, nameless, strangers. That's all most of my prey was. This was different. I shivered. Fiore sat, silently on the edge of the bed waiting, watching me absorb this information. I thought about what this meant, having Fiore's ancient blood in my veins, what it could mean for me, for Christian, for our future.

"So, my eyesight and my hearing are already noticeably enhanced. What else do I need to know?" I saw the smile in her eyes though her mouth was not turned up in the corners.

"Basically, all your own talents, or gifts, will be much stronger, plus… you may acquire some of mine," she explained. "You may discover new ones. It's always a possibility."

It took a minute for her words to sink in, *plus you may acquire some of mine*. Did I hear that correctly? Her gifts on top of mine?! "That thing that you do with your mind…the thing you did to Christian…when you told him what to do, in your head. Is that what you mean? Could I, maybe, do that?" I was excited now. I watched her face eagerly, waiting for her answer.

"It's possible. Some of us are immune to it. You have to keep that in mind. Like Ryanne, it doesn't work on her for some reason. No idea why. But I can tell you who it does work on…" Her voice trailed off, a mischievous look in her eyes. I could tell she was teasing now.

"Yeah, I know. You already showed me," I said, a little annoyed.

She shook her head. "No. Not Christian. He's a human. It's easy with a human. Mind control is a piece of cake with them. So easy it's almost boring. I'm talking about Ian." She looked at my eyes, waiting for a reaction.

I couldn't sit still any longer. I started pacing the room as soon as my feet hit the floor.

"So I could do that to him? I could tell him what to do and he would *do it*? Just like that?" I asked, my speech coming at an extremely rapid speed, from my excitement.

"It's possible. You'll have to try on someone first, make sure it works. Unfortunately, it doesn't work on me anymore. And you know, of course, it's only Christian and I here."

"Oh yeah." The thought of experimenting on him seemed, I don't know…cruel.

She put her hand on my shoulder to stop me from pacing. I stopped, annoyed. "What's with the pacing? You're making me dizzy," she said, her tone a bit sarcastic. "If you are going to use it, and perfect it, you will need practice. I know how you feel about Christian but it's for his own good, right? You're trying to protect him. I doubt he would mind. I somehow think he would do *anything* for you."

I nodded, a smile spreading across my face at the mention of his name. She was saying the same thing Aaron had said. "I'll talk to him…"

"NO!" she said firmly. "He can't know you're doing it. It has to be spontaneous. If he knows, he'll be on guard, expecting it. His subconscious will block it. And the other thing is, the thing that makes it most difficult to use when fighting is, you need to maintain eye contact. That's not an easy thing to do when you're fighting for your life."

I stared straight ahead now, at the wall. Eye contact? Hmm…

"Christian's waking up," I muttered, turning my face toward the door. "His breathing's changing. Let's go before he wonders what we're doing."

"Hey sleepyhead," I said as I sat on the edge of the sofa. He turned onto his back, yawning. I smiled at him. His eyes lit up, which was the reaction I was looking for. Fiore plopped herself onto the chair, a magazine in her hands.

"How long did I sleep? I'm sorry I fell asleep like that…" He looked disoriented.

"I'd say about two hours."

"I'm going for a run," Fiore said, tossing the unopened magazine on the coffee table. "Maybe I'll hunt. I need to get out for a while, expend some energy. Is there any civilization around here?" she asked. Christian's eyes grew wide.

"Um…not for miles. There are a lot of wild animals though. I had a mountain lion recently. Deer too," I quickly suggested, trying to set Christian's mind at ease. He never brought up the subject of my feeding on humans, and I didn't think it was something he was comfortable with. Fiore shot a knowing look at me and winked.

"Gotcha! Okay…I'll be back. You guys can have some *alone* time," she said as she closed the door behind her.

"Now that we're alone," he started, taking my cold hand in his. The temperature difference in our bodies never ceased to amaze me. "Hmm…

you feel colder. Your skin feels somehow harder…"

"Oh? Don't be silly!" I replied. I hadn't realized Fiore's blood would make me feel different to him. But, of course, if anyone would notice, it was he. I smiled, trying to take his mind off it. It worked. He smiled back and shook his head, dismissing the thought. "Now that we're alone…"

He chimed in. "Oh yeah, now that we're alone, I want to talk to you."

"What about?"

"About us." His face was serious again. I bit my lip and nodded, encouraging him to continue.

"You know how much I love you, right?" he asked. I nodded. "Well, I was wondering what's going to happen to us now. What are we going to do once this is all over?"

"What do you mean?" I asked, not sure where this was going.

He sat up and put his feet on the floor, never letting go of my hand. "What are your plans for me?"

I shook my head. "I still don't understand…"

"I don't know how to say this but I'll try." He paused a moment, taking a deep breath. He turned his body to face me. "I told you I'll love you forever. It's just that…well…there's forever for you." His eyes grew more intense. "But for me, there's no forever. There's only now, and tomorrow, and the day after that, if I'm lucky."

My stomach started turning as I watched him reach for his warm glass of iced tea with his free hand and take a sip before continuing.

"With every day that passes…hell…with every second that passes, I get closer to death. Do you realize that?" I nodded. "What do we do about that?"

"What are you asking me?" I said, stalling, though I knew exactly what he was trying to say.

"I'm asking you if you want me forever." His eyes locked with mine. There was no escaping this moment.

"Of course I do. You know I love you. I love you with all my being. It's just that, well…" I couldn't find the words. I couldn't figure out what to say to him when I had tried so hard to keep those thoughts out of my head. Now he was confronting me with the one thing I knew I wanted but had been trying to deny myself, mostly out of respect for Aaron, but also out of fear. "Are you asking what I think you're asking?"

He nodded, never taking his eyes from mine. "I want to be like you. I want to know that I have forever with you. I can't leave you alone. I won't!"

"You want *me* to make you a vampire?" I was speaking too loud, mostly out of frustration. I regretted my tone as soon as he dropped my hand. He stood and walked over to the fireplace. He picked up the poker and moved the wood around, facing away from me. His heart was beating fast, nervous.

"That's exactly what I want!" He turned to face me.

My jaw dropped. I hesitated and then spoke, trying to be gentle this time. "Didn't you tell me you're afraid of death? Just recently, on the plane?"

"Well, yeah but…"

"What do you think this is?"

"I don't understand…" He was still kneeling in front of the fire, ashamed to look at me.

"Making you what I am *is* death. It's eternal death. The only difference is you're conscious of it. You know you're dead. Walking death. It never ends. And…it's a very painful process."

He gasped. He looked like he had just been slapped in the face as he turned to look at me. He hung his head and walked to me. I knew he was trying to hide his eyes, which, by the way he was breathing, I was sure were full of tears about to spill over. I had stung him with words…again!

"I'm sorry. I didn't mean for that to come out as harshly as it did. It's just that the thought of you being this…this thing…is confusing to me. Believe me, I've thought of it. I've wanted it. But for one thing…Aaron doesn't condone it and he's like a father to me. Another is that it's…very painful. But the most important thing is that it's you." He sat again. I took his hand in mine. "I can't kill you."

He turned to look at me. His eyes were moist and all I wanted to do at that moment was kiss the tears waiting to spill and make all his hurt go away but I didn't move. My mind was full of possibilities. He and I together. Forever.

"If I could do it all over again, I would not be here. I would have been long gone, in the ground," I explained. "This isn't the kind of *life* you should have, as much as I do want it."

"I thought you were happy with who you are…what you are," he said.

"I didn't think I was that great an actress," I said, surprised he had been fooled. "It's a very lonely existence. I've been alone for so many years, I've lost track of how many. Usually, vampires are very territorial. They are loners. It's unusual for groups, or covens, to live together. Especially for long periods of time. I got lucky when Kalia found me on the beach."

His expression changed. I could see he had questions and I realized he knew nothing of my past. The only thing he knew was Ian was my maker. He knew nothing of the pain.

"Do you want to learn about my past?" I asked.

"Absolutely! I want to know as much as possible about you. Please…"

"I can show you."

"What do you mean…show me?"

"Lie down," I said and moved to the floor so he could lie on the sofa and I could kneel on the floor by his head. "I will show you if you promise that you'll trust me."

"I trust you. Completely."

"Keep your eyes on mine."

I took a deep breath and looked at his lips, his nose, his hair, before locking my stare on his beautiful blue eyes. My life started flashing before my eyes: my parents, the store, Elizabeth and I in my room with paper spread out around us, the failed blind dates, the teasing about my crazy stories, college, ice cream in the park, the mysterious man by the light post, the dinners, the flowers, the front porch, the wedding plans, the trip to Ireland…

I watched his face as I thought of all this, as I pictured every detail I could and saw him reacting as if he was there, living it.

Suspicions of what Ian was, loneliness, more suspicions, confrontation, one night of passion, his teeth clamping on my neck, weakening, in and out of consciousness, the burning, screaming, alone, always alone…

As I relived it, in my mind, I realized Christian was reliving it physically. His screams mixed with my own, his body arching on the sofa, his hands in fists. Sweat poured down his reddened face. His heart sounded like it was going to explode, it was beating so fast. I reached a hand out to touch him, calm him. I hadn't expected him to *feel* what I was seeing. I just wanted him to see. Somehow I had transferred my pain on to him. I had to stop it!

My mind flashed to another time, another city. Hunting innocents, loneliness again, terrified eyes, uncontrollable thirst burning through my body, hunting criminals, jumbled thoughts of other minds, flashes of other minds' memories…

I showed him all of it, the years I spent alone, after my desperation of losing Ian. I showed him how and where I lived, always alone. I showed him the events leading up to my meeting him, my date with Jack, Ian's reappearance, my knowledge of Jack's death, my falling in love with him, my needing to leave him, the panic I felt when I thought he would be disgusted by what I was. I showed him everything up until the point before he fell asleep on the couch today.

His heartbeat slowed down but his breaths were still coming fast with every image. I stopped imagining my past. I simply knelt next to him, looking. His eyes blinked, once, twice, trying to focus on the room, then on me, his stare blank. I felt exhausted.

I continued to sit on the floor, my head leaning against his arm, when I felt his hand on my head, his fingers entangled in my hair.

"My God, Lily! I had no idea," he said, his voice shaky. "How long does that horrible pain continue?"

I wasn't sure which pain he was referring to but I assumed it was the physical pain. "About twenty-four hours. It takes that long for your body to die physically. The mental and emotional pain is a whole different story."

"Don't you see?" he asked, sitting up. "You don't have to go through any of that again! You don't have to go through the emotional pain, the loneliness. I'll be with you!"

It hadn't worked. Not one bit. Everything I showed him and made him feel and he still wanted to join me. My head jerked up and I stared at him wide-eyed, my mouth gaping. I couldn't believe it!

"Didn't any of that bother you?" He stared at the fire, thinking.

"Only the parts with you hurting and with...Ian. But I understand why you did what you did with him recently. I know why."

I bit my lip. I hadn't wanted him to see me and Ian together by the brook. I had meant to leave that out but got carried away. But maybe it would help him see how trapped I felt in this life. Maybe it would help him see the true horrors of it.

Just then, Fiore came through the door, her face whiter than white.

"We have a problem!" she announced.

⤜∾ TWENTY-FOUR ∾⤛

Christian and I exchanged confused looks. Fiore's frantic look told us our talk would have to wait. I got up from the floor and sat on the sofa next to Christian. Fiore was pacing in front of the window, pulling the blind aside to look out into the darkness. I saw the concentration in her face as she tried to focus her eyes, forcing them to see in the blackness.

"What's wrong?" I asked. I had a tight grasp of Christian's hand.

"I went hunting, as you know. Apparently, I wasn't the only one. Someone's out there," she said as her eyes still scanned outside. "Turn the light off. I can't see."

Christian jumped up to turn off the lamps. The soft orange glow of the fire was the only light in the room.

"What do you mean? Other hunters? But this is private property. There are signs posted." She shook her head.

"That's not what I mean." She moved away from the window and stood in front of the fireplace. Christian squeezed my fingers, never taking his eyes off Fiore. It must have been surprising for him to witness fear in her. She always looked so calm and relaxed, even when I had attacked her with the poker, thinking she was one of *them*. "There were animals...dead. Their bodies just lay there..."

"It was probably hunters or another animal, a bear or something. It's normal out here. Hunters don't always follow rules," I explained. Christian looked at me, trying to gauge my fear.

"No! That wasn't another animal. They weren't ripped apart. There were no bullet holes. They were just...drained. Completely drained of blood."

My jaw dropped. I realized I was holding my breath when I felt Christian nudge me and I let out a puff of air. I looked at him, thanking him with my eyes.

"So, what was it?" I wanted to ask what kind of animals they were, what size, but, what did it matter? They were dead animals. No bullets. No torn flesh. No blood.

"Someone's out there," she said in hushed voice. I turned to Christian to see if he caught that but he didn't move. His eyes bulged. He heard.

"Did you see or hear anything?" I asked.

"No. That's the thing. I'm good at tracking…really good. I heard nothing but the expected sounds of nature, a coyote even. I saw nothing but the carcasses. I didn't catch a scent that wasn't animal. There was no human scent, except his." She nodded toward Christian. "I know Ian's scent. I know Fergus and Ryanne. I smelled none of them."

"Could it be Aaron or Kalia?" Christian asked. I shook my head.

"They wouldn't go around draining animals and just leaving their carcasses. They would clean up after themselves," I said. I couldn't help but notice the look of disgust in Christian's face. He wiped it off as soon as he realized I was watching.

"Well, I don't know. We're okay in here for now. I checked around the cabin. Everything looks the same. I caught no familiar scent out there we need to worry about yet. You better get on the phone with Aaron though, see what's keeping them." She went to retrieve my cell phone from the kitchen.

"Lily, what can I do?" Christian asked. I smiled at him, trying to comfort him.

"Just keep doing what you're doing," I said, my hand on his cheek. "Just keep loving me."

Out of the corner of my eye I saw a small object flying toward me. Without taking my eyes off Christian's worried, yet smiling, face, I raised my hand and caught the cell phone. His eyes widened. Fiore was checking the locks on the kitchen windows, not that a simple little lever would stop a vampire from entering a building where he was not welcome. It was more a gesture than anything, probably for Christian's sake.

"That was pretty impressive," His eyes lit up as he tried to lighten the mood. "Remind me if we ever play baseball, I want you on my team." He laughed. I forced myself to smile at his comment though my mind was elsewhere.

If Ian were on our trail, it wouldn't be long before he would act. How far would he take this? How far would he dare to take his obsession with me and his vendetta with Christian? But why hadn't he done something already? If there were that many dead animals, as Fiore described, he would have to have been here for at least a couple of days. But Ian didn't need to feed that often. He wasn't much older than me and I could go a long time without feeding, unless…

"Aaron," I said into the phone. Fiore was back in the room, after checking the windows in the bedroom, and sat on a chair in front of the window. I walked back and forth in front of the fireplace.

I explained what was happening to him, described what Fiore had seen, that she hadn't caught any scents. I told him about my suspicions. But mostly, I listened. I nodded and tried to remember everything he told me so I could relay it to Christian and Fiore. When I closed the phone, I stopped walking, their eyes on me, waiting.

"We are to stay here," I said. Christian nodded, waiting for more. "They will be leaving within the hour. Riley is not with them." I swallowed.

"So who's coming?" Fiore asked. "Aaron, Kalia, Pierce, Beth, and Maia? Am I missing anybody?" I explained to Fiore who everybody was the day I called Aaron to tell him she arrived and she was not a danger to us.

I shook my head. My eyes focused on Christian's face, trying to work up the courage to form the question on my lips. He saw the struggle in my eyes and moved to stand at my side.

"What is it, Lily?" he asked, his voice warm and tender.

"How did you get to Ireland? After you came to…that night…how did you get there? Who?" I had been so afraid to ask the question. I had put it off for as long as I could, afraid of what I might hear, though in the back of my mind I think I always knew the answer.

He shook his head with panic, remembering. "I, I don't…"

Fiore stood and tip-toed over to sit on the coffee table. Christian's eyes settled on her for a second. She nodded encouragement. He turned back to me.

"It, she kept me unconscious most of the time. I had horrible headaches, awful, that made me dizzy and she gave me pills, to help, she said. They made me really sleepy. I woke up in a hotel room once. That's the day we went to the airport. She said if I didn't go with her, you would die! What else could I do?" He shook his head, looking past me. I stood still, not touching him, though I wanted to comfort him. "She said they would let me go soon if I co-operated with *them*. I didn't know who she meant, she kept saying *them*. I asked but it just infuriated her more and then the headaches would start again and more pills. Once we landed in Ireland, I was out again somehow, woke up in that basement. You know what happened after that. You know how you found me."

Fiore and I exchanged a quick glance. Christian didn't notice. He was still staring straight ahead.

"Did you get her name?" I asked.

"She wouldn't tell me. But at the airport, at the counter, I looked over her shoulder when she was talking to the ticket agent. I saw her passport. It said, Samantha Maureen Fitzgerald. That's all I got to see before she closed it and showed them mine, which I was shocked she had."

"Samantha Maureen Fitzgerald?" I thought aloud. Christian finally looked at me.

"That's all you saw?" I asked though I had heard him say so.

"Yeah…sorry. My mind was so foggy from the pills, I guess."

"I have no idea who that is?" I turned to Fiore. "You?"

She shook her head. "I don't know but, then again, who knows who Ian is acquainted with. He's always so secretive."

"That's very true." I turned back to Christian. "Do you remember anything else about her? Like, what did she look like?"

He thought about it a moment, his eyes staring off into space again. I waited, knowing this was a painful memory for him.

"A little taller than you. She had a small build, like you. I remember her hair was very red, fiery red." He looked pained to be thinking about that day, trying to recall details. "There was something strange about her eyes. It's the first time I've ever seen eyes like that, so big and pale gold."

I froze, not able to close the mouth I knew was now hanging open… her name trying to shove itself into my subconscious. Fiore stood, looking at me, confusion on her face. "What is it? Do you know who it is?" she said.

I heard her voice. I felt Christian's warm hand as he took mine, pulling it to his chest, trying to snap me out of it. It couldn't be! The eyes matched the face I was picturing but not the hair. The hair didn't match, though the body build did but many were built like me. I didn't think of myself as unique.

"I thought maybe…" I shook my head. "I thought maybe Maia but, no. It doesn't all fit. And, why would she? What would she have to gain from it?" I shook my head as if that would dismiss the thought.

Fiore leaned in closer, trying to understand what I was saying. Christian's arms were wrapped around me, my face buried in his chest. I listened to the sound of his heartbeat, counting each drum as I heard it. He held me tighter. Fiore's stone cold hand was on my back, a noticeable contrast to Christian's skin, snapping me out. No one spoke until I did. "Maia?" I asked myself, only I said it aloud.

Fiore sat on the edge of the coffee table. She grimaced a moment. "Well, let's consider what we know so far. You said Maia and Ian are somehow *together* now..."

"Yes. She had been away, supposedly visiting friends in England. When she came back, shortly after I started living with the Kalia and Aaron, Ian was with her," I explained. My face was still buried in Christian's warm chest, his arms around me.

"Okay," Fiore replied. "What did she introduce him as?"

I thought about it, trying to remember if she had used any kind of a label for him. "I think just...Ian..."

"So, she didn't use boyfriend or anything like that," she said, still trying to put all the pieces together. "Did he act like there was something special between them, like he was attached?"

I pulled my face away from Christian's chest finally and looked at her. "I don't think so." I could picture the exact moment. He was standing near her but, separate. He wasn't touching her, not holding her hand, no arm around her. She was the one looking at him possessively. He was looking at me. That angered her, so much that she didn't stop herself from hurting me, even in front of Aaron and Kalia. "She was looking at him the way I used to look at him. He didn't pay attention to that."

"Okay," she said. "He was leading her on, the way he does. I think we both know what that's like." I nodded. I knew full well how manipulative he could be when he wanted something. He would unleash his charm and make you believe anything, including that he loved you.

"That makes sense! He planned meeting her. It wasn't a coincidence at all. That's not even a possibility anymore. He's not even from this area." A light bulb went off in my head. "He just used her. He planned this very carefully."

"Exactly," Fiore said with a knowing look. "He did the same thing to us. He used us for a while and then, when he had no more need for us he...discarded us the best way he knew. He simply stopped any and all feelings he had shown. Only, you were smart enough to move on after..." Her eyes looked sad, staring straight ahead. "Me on the other hand, I stayed and tried to make the best of it. I even went as far to help him when it came to you, though it hurt me to know he wanted you. I was willing to do anything he wanted in order to hurt you, to get back at you, until… until I got to know you." She smiled at me, a tender, warm smile that lit up her eyes.

I nodded, trying to ease her mind, trying to assure her I had forgiven her for following his ridiculous orders.

"Do you think Maia is involved in this?" Christian's voice surprised me. He had been quiet until that moment. "Do you think she could be helping him?"

Fiore looked at me with widened eyes. She was thinking the same thing but had not yet voiced it. I stared at her. I shook my head, more out of confusion than denial. The thought had crossed my mind also but…

"I really don't know what to think. I always knew she didn't like me, since the day she met me. I figured it was just jealousy, a sibling rivalry of sorts. She was the center of Kalia and Aaron's attention until I came along. It was worse when she brought Ian into the picture but, as far as I saw, he didn't tell her about me." I was remembering that day again. "Ian was introduced to me as if I'd never met him before, even in front of her. I saw no indication as to her knowing otherwise. I was too distraught over the fact that he was standing in front of me though to even think of listening to anyone's thoughts.

"She glared at me. She caused me physical pain, a stabbing pain in my stomach, which Aaron stopped. I figured it was because of the way he was looking at me."

Christian stiffened now. Anger filled his eyes. I took his hand in mine to comfort him and he immediately relaxed.

"Aaron told me she's not answering her cell. They haven't heard from her since she left. They don't know where she went. They were waiting for her to return, so she could join them in coming here. Kalia checked her room, to see if there were any clues to her whereabouts but…" I tried to remember Aaron's words. "They found nothing. They don't see anything missing. Her suitcases are still in the closet, like she left in a hurry and didn't bother to pack. That's strange."

"I agree," Fiore said. "Unfortunately, we really have no evidence to support suspecting her. For all we know, she may be in trouble too. I mean, how do we know he didn't do something to her?"

"Yeah, I guess you're right. He could've done something to her," I said, suddenly feeling sad for Maia, not knowing whether or not she was hurt, or worse. "Ian knows many others. He could've gotten anyone to help him. He takes what he wants no matter who he hurts in the process." I thought of Maia and what she must have been feeling. I remembered what it was like for me, the love and wanting I felt for him. The desolation I felt trying to keep him happy, by my side. I felt pity for her.

Fiore's expression changed, with another realization. "If it is one of them out there, Ian possibly, we need to be careful. We can no longer discuss anything. We can no longer think about anything. Do you understand what I'm saying?" She asked looking from my face to Christian's. We both nodded. We both understood they, or he, could be listening to us at this very moment.

"So now what?" Christian asked impatiently. "We just sit here and wait?"

"Basically, yes," Fiore stated. "The others should be here soon. As far as we know, there are three, possibly four, of *them* coming. We should have six…plus you, Christian," she amended herself, knowing how Christian felt.

"Our odds are much better than theirs," I assured Christian. "You have nothing to worry about."

He looked at me with a furrowed brow. I could tell that as much as I wanted him to be assured, he wasn't. "What can I do?" he asked.

"Nothing!" Fiore and I said at the same time. She looked at me to continue. "We will keep you safe. We will come up with a plan, together… somehow," I said knowing we couldn't actually discuss it. We wouldn't be able to talk, or even think, about our strategy without someone hearing what we meant to do, knowing every move we made before we made it. This would complicate things. "I won't risk anything happening to you."

He started to open his mouth to protest. I looked him in the eyes and told him, in my mind, to stop. *Don't argue with me,* I thought. *I won't let anything happen to you.* He snapped his mouth shut. Fiore smiled. She nodded her head in approval at my successful first attempt at mind control. I smiled back, though I couldn't help but feel a little guilty. It felt like more of an invasion of privacy than listening to his thoughts, though the look on Christian's face told me he suspected nothing. The way he saw it, he'd changed his own mind about voicing his protest. Though he still looked worried, he had a slight smile on his face. I looked back at Fiore but she was already pulling the curtain aside to look out the window.

"How much longer do you think it will be before they get here?" she asked, her concentration mostly on the outside.

"It shouldn't be much longer if they left right away."

"Do you even know where we are? I don't remember anyone saying where we were going. We just drove, in darkness. I don't recall seeing any signs. You?" Christian started pacing. His hands were tightly balled up into fists at his sides. I couldn't help but laugh at him, wondering if that's how I looked to him. He was already picking up my bad habits.

"Stop right there! Change the subject." Fiore stood against the window, her dark hair a clear contrast to the light colored curtain.

"Oh – right." Christian nodded.

"Christian, are you hungry? I could make you something. Who knows when you'll get another chance to eat." I looked at him and winked. He smiled.

"Yeah, I could go for something. Some coffee too..." He turned and walked toward the kitchen. I looked to see if Fiore was going to follow too but she still stood at the window. She looked thoughtful.

"Are you coming? You could keep us company," I said.

"No. I think I'm going to take a look around while we wait for your family." It was strange to hear them referred to as my *family* but I realized family was exactly what they were. "I suggest you go after me and feed. You'll need all the strength you can get. I don't want to take any chances. What if what I gave you wasn't enough?"

"No. I can't leave him. I'll be fine. I've gone for days without feeding."

"Christian will be with me. He'll be safe. I promise," Fiore vowed.

"It's not that. Who's going to keep you safe?" I asked.

"Trust me," she said walking over to me and putting her arm around my shoulder. "I can certainly take care of myself. How else do you think I've survived three hundred years?" She laughed as she squeezed me to her side.

"I guess..." I said. I couldn't help but feel nervous. As strong as I knew her to be, I still knew Ian. Ian would stop at nothing to get what he wanted and right now I knew he wanted all three of us. I wasn't sure who he wanted more, me for not loving him, Fiore for defying him, or Christian for surviving. Somehow, I had the feeling I was number one on his list.

⤳ TWENTY FIVE ⤳

As I waited for the water in the pot to start boiling, I looked through the refrigerator to see what I could throw into boxed macaroni and cheese to make it more appetizing. Christian looked at me with amusement on his face but said nothing. He leaned against the counter, ankles crossed, arms folded. I went back to moving things aside until I spotted two overly ripe tomatoes in the back corner.

"Do you think these are still good?" I asked holding them up to the light.

"You can't tell if the tomatoes are good and…you're gonna cook?" He smiled. "How long has it been since you've cooked? Considering you eat…"

"Ha! Ha!" I glared at him in a playful way. "I do have a good memory. Give me credit for that."

He laughed as he took the tomatoes from my hands to inspect them. He squeezed them gently with his fingertips. "They're fine."

"Thank you. That's all I needed to know." I reached for them. He pulled them away and went to open the drawer. He pulled out the knife and set it on the counter, turning on the faucet.

"Oh no! I'll handle that. I am not letting you do anything that requires a knife!" My hands were already grasping the soft tomatoes, juice running between my fingers. "Oops!"

He laughed in spite of the fact that he was embarrassed. A soft pink washed over his face. "I cut myself once and now I'm not trusted!" He shook his head.

"I just don't want you bleeding all over the clean floor," I joked. "Besides, I would love to make you dinner for once. I can handle macaroni and cheese…I think." I set the plate of cut tomatoes aside and went back to the pot on the stove. The water bubbled softly. I ripped open the box and started pouring in the contents when his hand caught my wrist.

"It's supposed to be a roaring boil," he said.

I set the box back on the counter, dejected. "I saw that."

"Of course you did." His eyes smiled though his mouth didn't show it. He slid his arms around my waist, pulling me away from the stove, my body against his as his eyes searched my face.

"Lily?" he whispered. I raised my eyebrows. "Can you make me one promise?"

"Anything."

"Please promise me you won't leave me here…"

"What do you mean? I wouldn't do…" I started.

"I mean if something happens to me, if…I don't make it out of this. Please don't leave my body here."

My face slammed against his chest as I squeezed him harder, letting his heat engulf me. "Why would you even think that? How could you think I would let anything happen to you?"

I felt him shake his head. His arms tightened around me. I pulled my face away from his chest and looked up at him. His lips found mine and he kissed me with such urgency it felt like a goodbye. I kissed him back, though I refused to entertain the thought that it would be our last kiss. I couldn't believe that. When he pulled away, to look into my eyes, I saw the fear.

"We will get out of this. Do you hear me?" I said a little harshly but I needed him to believe, as I did. "We will have our happily-ever-after…one way or another." The water on the stove started gurgling, steam fogging the window over the sink. He noticed the pot at the same time and his arms relaxed, dropping to his sides.

The noodles were boiling, the tomatoes were ready, and I sat on the counter, waiting. He put the butter on the counter and opened the powdered cheese sauce. "Uh…" He looked toward the refrigerator. "Is there any milk?"

"For what? Your coffee?"

He laughed. "You're so cute!"

"I don't get it. What are you…?"

"How do you think we're supposed to mix the cheese?" He watched my face. I shrugged. "Macaroni and cheese is made with milk."

"Oh." I hopped off the counter prepared to look in the refrigerator, though I already knew there was very little milk left. "I didn't know. I guess it has been a while."

Lily...Lily...hurry! I need you! Come alone...

My head snapped toward the window. Fiore's thoughts were coming from that direction. Christian followed my eyes.

"What is it? Do you hear something?" he asked, not taking his eyes from the darkness.

"I think Fiore's in trouble. She's calling me," I said taking my eyes from the stillness of the outside and looking at him.

"Let's go!" He moved the pot to another burner and turned the stove off.

"No. You're staying here. She told me..."

He shook his head. "No way! I'm not letting you go alone."

Despite the fact that I loved the way he felt he could protect me, I didn't have time to argue with him. My hand reached up, palm flattened against his chest, stopping any advance. "Listen to me Christian," I explained. "She said to leave you here. There has to be good reason for that. I won't be gone long. I promise." I opened the closet door and reached in the back, next to the water heater. "Here. Take this."

His eyes widened in terror. His jaw dropped as he tried to speak but couldn't.

"It's just a precaution. You won't need it. She wouldn't tell me to leave you alone if there was immediate danger," I tried to put his mind at ease though I was having a hard time convincing myself. "Please, Christian. Take it."

His arms slowly extended, his fingers recoiling as soon as they touched the sword. "Are you saying this is what we have to use...to..."

"It's the easiest and fastest way. You don't need to be as close. Just take it! I have to go," I insisted. My voice softened. "I don't want to leave you either but I have to, just for a few minutes. I would feel better if I knew you had this."

He took it from me but held it away from his body, as if it burned him. "Thank you," I said. I stood on my tip-toes to kiss his lips. "I'll be right back. If you need me, say so. I'll stay tuned in." He nodded.

The darkness swallowed my surroundings as I ran toward Fiore. I felt the coolness of the rain, my hair sticking to my face as it blew wet in the wind. I reached a steep hill and jumped, soaring in the air, without thinking twice about it. The further I ran, the more a coppery scent filled my nostrils. As it got stronger, I slowed, searching for the source in the blackness. A dark shape moved to my right, next to a copse of trees. I crouched, ready to leap.

"Lily! Over here!" It was Fiore. She leaned over something I couldn't see.

"What is it?" I asked, trying to move past her so I could see what was on the ground. The smell of blood was overpowering. My eyes scanned the area, noticing every detail in the trees, the grass, and the raindrops. She moved a few inches to the side, still not rising. I focused my eyes on the ground. I saw an arm, a dark sleeve, a small wrinkled hand. I let my eyes search the shape. I could see thin legs, one lay twisted in an unnatural position, small stocking feet.

"I don't know what this means," Fiore said as she rose, breaking the shield of her body. My eyes moved to the top again. My jaw dropped and I stumbled backward, her arms catching me before I fell. My breath caught in my throat. Where the head should be there was nothing! Nothing but a bloody collar! I gasped.

She pulled me to the side and pointed to the ground, her arm firmly across my back for support. There, in front of a moss-covered boulder, was Clara's head. I felt weak and dizzy; my knees no longer supported my weight. I didn't hit the ground. Instead, I was wrapped in Fiore's arms. I pounded my fists against her chest, pushing her back. "WHY?" I screamed. "WHY IS HE DOING THIS?

"Shh…calm down…shh…"

"NO!" I pushed her away. She stood, shocked. I threw my head back, raindrops hitting my face with anger. "IAN! YOU COWARD! WHERE ARE YOU?"

Fiore stood, frozen in shock at my anger.

"COME AND GET ME! I'M HERE. IT'S ME YOU WANT! ME! ONLY ME!" I spun around and faced the opposite direction, in case he didn't hear. "I'M WAITING FOR YOU! I'M READY FOR YOU!" I dropped to the muddy ground. My fists pounded the ground. "Please… enough already. I give up…I want you…" My head felt like it was spinning. I jumped at the feel of her hand on my back.

"Did you know her?" she asked as she squatted next to me, her hand still trying to comfort me. I stopped pounding the ground. I rose to my knees and looked toward the lifeless body. Emptiness crept through my veins.

"She was my neighbor, in Olympia. Clara Warren is…was her name. I had one conversation with her the whole time I lived there. He's going to pick off anyone I came in contact with, one by one, isn't he?" I stared at what was left of the sweet old woman. I hung my head, my hair falling around me like a veil. Fiore noticed what I was doing and did the same, bowing her head in a moment of silence for a woman she never knew.

I stayed that way for about four or five minutes, grieving. Fiore waited until I raised my head before she spoke again. "I'm sorry. I don't know what to say. I'm not very good at this sort of thing." She raised herself to her feet, pulling me along. "I don't know what he's trying to prove with this."

"I know. I don't expect you to understand him any better than I do. So much time spent with him and I know nothing." I thought about the little I had learned about him in the time I spent with him. Most of the things I thought were true about him turned out to be lies anyway so it didn't matter. "We can't leave her here." The thought of both of us carrying her, separately, made me feel sick to my stomach. Fiore made her way to the rock where her head had fallen as if she knew that would be more difficult for me, to be able to see her eyes. I bent down and slid one arm under her torso and one arm under her knees. I tried to focus on the ground as I walked, refusing to remind myself of what I was cradling in my trembling arms.

"I don't want to take her into the cabin, you know, Christian…" I said still walking straight ahead.

"I understand, of course. We can find a safe place for her until we can give her a proper burial."

"They're here!" My steps sped with excitement.

"Who?" Fiore was crouching with Clara's head still in her hands, ready to attack.

"No! It's my family," I exclaimed feeling an ounce of relief at last.

We rushed along the wooded path until we came to the cars parked alongside cabin. There were only two of them. I recognized one immediately. *Kalia…I need your keys…don't say anything…come out…*

Kalia and Aaron made it down the front steps in one bound and rushed to us. Shock mixed with a bit of relief filled their eyes. Reading my thoughts, Kalia unlocked her trunk while Aaron took the body out of my arms. He set it down as if it was a sleeping baby. Fiore followed and did the same with her burden. I ran into Kalia's arms as soon as the trunk was closed.

"You're safe now. We're here." She stroked my hair while I had my arms wrapped around her waist. "Unfortunately, they're right behind us. We need to get inside."

Aaron led us to the steps with a gentle hand on my back. Fiore followed, her eyes searching Kalia's calm expression.

"Did you see them? How many are there?" she asked.

"We saw one, a figure running through the woods as we drove along. It was about ten miles from here but I know it wasn't human," Aaron explained to Fiore. He seemed to be sizing her up as well.

"Have you heard from Maia yet?" I asked, not waiting to see for myself.

Kalia's expression changed from calm to the deep worry of a mother, lines forming on her otherwise ageless face. "No, not yet. We keep hoping."

"Oh my God! Are you alright?" Christian asked as he ran to the door just as we stepped in. He wrapped his arms around me not caring that the others were waiting to get through.

"Um…fine. False alarm. Fiore thought she saw something," I lied.

"I did see something," Fiore interjected. "Turns out, it was just their cars driving up." She motioned toward the others. Christian seemed to accept this.

"I'm so glad you're all here," I said as I looked at the others for the first time. I was shocked to see Riley, her red hair glowing around her face, made it after all. The three of them smiled at me but only Beth stood to greet me. She wrapped her arms around me and kissed my cheek.

"You've got a gem here," she whispered in my ear. I knew she was speaking of Christian. I felt the usual flutter in my stomach at the thought of his name. "He's worth protecting. He's a powerful one."

Before I could ask what she meant by that, Aaron was calling the room to order. Someone had already pulled chairs in from the bedroom and there was a place for everyone to sit and join in the meeting. Pierce kept his eyes on me as I took my place next to Christian. There was a slight grin on his face. I wondered what they'd talked about in my absence. My hand went up to touch the charm he had given me and I felt warmth emanating from it. I searched under my shirt collar for the dragonfly and wrapped my fingers around that. It was cold, just like the skin beneath it. *That's odd!* I thought. My fingers found the Raidho again…warm. The dragonfly… cold. Hmm…

"Okay, now that we are all here," Aaron announced. "We have much to discuss."

"Um, excuse me, Aaron but…" I glanced at Fiore. "We were talking earlier and we thought maybe it wasn't a good idea to discuss anything. We don't want to let them know what we're planning since they might be listening." Fiore nodded.

"You're right. They might be listening, actually, I'm sure they are but, it doesn't matter. Does it?" He looked around the room. All eyes were still on him. "The inevitable is happening. We can't stop it. Do we agree?" Everyone nodded, except Kalia. Her laptop bag sat on the floor next to her and she took something out of it. I watched as she pulled out what looked like sheets of white cardboard. Aaron's eyes were also on her but he continued talking to the rest of the assembled party.

"Good! Now that we agree, we can continue. I need everyone to pay close attention to what I am about to tell you." He pointed to the card Kalia was holding up. Then he pointed to his lips and then to his ears. I nodded, though I wasn't sure what I was agreeing to. I looked at what Kalia held. I focused my eyes on the words but tried to listen to Aaron at the same time. The words on the card were printed neatly in black marker. The first one she held read: Focus your eyes on the writing and your ears on Aaron's words, Lily. Trust yourself!

"We need to stay together," Aaron's voice said but the card read: We need to split up. Kalia nodded and smiled at me as she switched cards. I waited for the next card, holding my breath. I heard Aaron clearly, his detailed plan unfolded before us. I kept reading. Christian tried to read along with me but Kalia motioned with one hand for him to keep his eyes on Aaron's face. I squeezed his hand, assuring him. I would explain it to him later. Kalia, I realized, didn't know I had already discovered how to keep Ian from my thoughts and had been practicing that new skill.

Pierce gave you a charm to wear around your neck, the next card read. Take it off and place it around Christian's neck. He needs it more than you do right now. She held the cards face down on her lap while I did this. I put my hand in my shirt and held the warm charm, closing my fingers around its heat for a moment, before pulling it over my head. I looked at Pierce, his eyes soft and warm. He nodded for me to proceed. I placed it around Christian's neck. His eyes questioned but his lips stayed closed. He closed his fingers around it, his hand twitching slightly as he felt the heat. He tucked it into his shirt. My eyes focused on Kalia again. Aaron continued.

The way his plan was drawn out, we were to stay together and wait for them. Once they were here, we were to fight them until there was no one left but us. It was a bit more detailed than that but I wasn't following every little detail. I had other plans to worry about. At least, if he was listening and if I was letting him hear the real plans, he would get a jumbled mess. That's what I hoped for, that he would be confused.

"Does anyone have any questions?" Aaron looked around the room. Everyone was looking at me. I bit my lip and shook my head.

"Now we wait," Beth said as she stood and stretched. "Lily, don't you have something to show Pierce?" she asked. I followed her gaze to the kitchen.

"Um…I don't…" I looked at Pierce who was also staring at me. He made hand gestures. "Oh…"

Reaching into the closet, where Christian had replaced the sword, I gripped the handle and pulled it out, knocking the mop and broom out. I replaced them with shaky hands. My stomach knotted up, thinking about what I held and its purpose. I couldn't help but feel panic. I feared Ian, hated him, maybe even loathed him sometimes, but I didn't know if I could destroy him. I didn't know if I could carry it out with my own hands. Yet, that's what they were expecting of me. Kalia made it clear, through Pierce's coaxing, that it had to be destruction by my hand that would keep him dead. I had no idea why. I wanted to ask though I knew I couldn't say anything. At the moment, I wished that someone besides me spoke Spanish. It was the only way to have a conversation that Ian would not understand. But wait…

Kalia led Pierce to the bedroom, holding the sword I handed him. Beth followed, after taking the charm from Christian, closing the door behind them.

"Aaron," I said. "¿Hablas español, no?" All eyes were on me now. Christian stopped on his way to the kitchen and stood frozen on the spot.

"Sí. ¿Por qué?" Aaron looked surprised.

I breathed a sigh of relief. Finally, a conversation I could have that wouldn't give anything away. "¿Quiero saber por qué tiene qué ser yo quien lo destruye?"

"Ah, mi hija…" He smiled. He explained what Pierce had explained to him. Pierce believed in magic. He believed in the spell he was putting on the sword, the one that, wielded by my hand, would destroy my creator.

For that reason, it had to be me. He was my creator and only my hand could keep him buried for all eternity. So, not only did I have to destroy him and burn the head, but I also had to be the one to put him in the ground. Aaron was able to explain only what he was told by Pierce. Any other questions I had would have to wait until…after.

I walked back to the sofa and let my body go limp. Christian rushed to my side. His arms wrapped tightly around me. Riley's green eyes looked at me with compassion. "It's never easy…to do the right thing. You'll find the strength when the time comes." She walked out the door.

☞ TWENTY-SIX ☜

The sun shone through the thin bedroom curtains. I heard hushed voices in the living room. Christian's even breathing told me he was asleep, finally. He stayed awake with me most of the night. I hummed to him quietly, rubbed his back, stroked his hair, and still, he did not relax enough to sleep. It was when the first light of morning broke through the horizon that he finally closed his eyes.

Judging by the amount of light coming through the window, I knew it was still quite early. I tried hard not to move, afraid to disturb him. Somehow, I had a feeling today was the day and he needed all the rest he could get.

His face looked worry-free and peaceful. His lips twitched from time to time and I hoped he was having a pleasant dream. I looked at him as he lay on his side, one hand limp against my waist, and sighed. My Christian. How could you love me? How could you love a monster, a killer? How could I love a *human*? I regretted the day he walked into that coffee shop…into my life. Not for me but for him. I couldn't regret loving him, as hard as I tried. He had saved me from myself and my loneliness. He had somehow managed to tear down the wall I had built around my heart so many years ago. I learned it was possible to love again. Now, I would have to let him go. It was either that or…

"Oh…what are you doing awake already?" I was so into my thoughts I had not noticed his eyes open. He was searching my face, no doubt wondering what I was thinking.

"Don't you think he's dragging it out a bit?" He moved up to rest his head on my chest. I put my arm around him, enjoying his warmth.

"I know. I was thinking that too," I said.

"But let's not think about that right now." He moved to rest his chin on my ribs, eyes looking into mine.

"Sounds good to me," I smiled at him, hoping my fear didn't show. This waiting game was torture.

"I love you," he whispered. My stomach did its usual flip. I touched his cheek with my finger tips. He closed his eyes and sighed, pushing his face against my hand. "I was thinking…"

"What?" I asked. His skin felt like fire under my fingers. I was surprised his face wasn't red.

"Well, I love you and you love me. Right?"

"Right." I bit my lip. My stomach felt like it was doing somersaults.

"I know I won't live forever, at least, that's what you tell me." He sat up and turned to face me, his expression serious. "Anyway, after all of this is over, there's something I want you to do."

I hugged my legs to my chest, clasping my hands around my knees. I nodded, encouraging him to go on, though terrified to hear another word.

"Lily, I want you to marry me. I want to know you're truly mine until I die." He held his breath but his heart raced. I sat frozen, dumbstruck. Did he just say what I think he said? How? Was that possible? Thoughts flashed through my mind like a stampede. I couldn't make myself swallow. I didn't remember how! Images of myself, walking down a long aisle, toward his smiling face, Kalia beaming at me, Aaron walking proudly next to me, his arm entwined with mine, rushed before me. I looked at him, his eyes innocent and loving.

"Lily?" he whispered, worry wrinkling his forehead. "What's wrong? I didn't mean to upset you, honest, I didn't."

"I'm not upset. It's just that…" I didn't know what to say. The thought of being his wife, of being Lily Rexer, was beyond anything I could've imagined. But, it was also beyond anything that was possible. "I don't see how that's possible."

"Why? What makes our love so different?"

"Have you forgotten what I am?" I asked, my tone a little harsh. His expression didn't change.

"Of course not. How could I? That makes you more beautiful."

"Have you really thought about it? I mean *really* thought about it? What it means to have a vampire for a wife?"

He took a deep breath and swallowed hard. He stared at the rumpled sheets for a moment before he spoke. "All I need to know is I love you more than I have ever loved anyone in my life. I want you, all of you, for as long as I can have you."

"Christian…I wish it were that easy. I wish things were black and white between us, but they're not. Think about all the gray."

"What are you talking about?" He looked into my eyes with disappointment.

"There are too many downsides. For one thing, making love like a regular couple is not easy for you and me," I explained.

"We managed once. We can work on it. Think about how much fun it will be, practicing." A smile formed on his lips but the disappointment in his eyes did not diminish. I knew the disappointment was because I did not accept right away, as he had anticipated. I hated hurting him.

"I can never give you children. Did you know that?"

"I don't care about that. It's you I want."

Okay. So far, my reasons were not working. "What about the fact that you will continue to get older every day? Your hair will gray, your skin will wrinkle, you will change physically and I will not. I will stay forever nineteen, with black hair and smooth skin. Did you think about how that will impact you? Or the people around us, for that matter?"

"I don't care about any of that. I just want you. Or…are you worried about me being gray and wrinkled?"

"Of course not!" I fired. "I'm not that shallow. I love you the way you are. I would love you when you're eighty, just as much!" A smile so big spread over his face his eyes glowed, wiping all previous worry off his face.

"Then there's nothing to stop you from saying yes. Is there?" he asked, still smiling.

I buried my face into my knees, hiding my eyes. Yes. I could picture myself walking down the aisle to him. I could picture us as husband and wife, Mr. and Mrs. Christian Rexer. I couldn't, however, picture myself losing him when his time came. I would rather lose him now, leave him, knowing he is still alive, than lose him later. To have to stand by his casket, to have to bury him, after years of happiness, would destroy me.

"Lily, my love?" he whispered, barely audible. I raised my head. My eyes felt moist. For the first time in almost a century I felt like I could really cry. I wiped my eyes with my sleeve and saw it was stained with red. I was crying! I was crying blood tears! Now he would see, truly see, what a monster I really was.

He wrapped his arms around me and pulled my huddled body close to him, holding me tightly. "Shh…please don't cry. I didn't mean to upset you. I shouldn't have pushed. I'm sorry. Let's forget about it. Okay?"

"How can I forget about it? How can I forget about something that's hurting you?" I asked. He wasn't concerned about the fact that I was staining his shirt. He didn't seem to care. Nothing about me bothered him. The problem was all me.

"We don't need to talk about it right now, I mean. There's plenty of time later." His hand stroked my hair, soothing me. I wanted what he was offering more than anything. He didn't care what I was or what I did. He loved me unconditionally and I was the one thinking of all the obstacles. Why was I such a chicken? And, suddenly, the answer to that question was very clear in my mind. I knew exactly why I stopped myself from doing anything that made me happy. Why I stopped myself from opening my heart to anyone who wanted a piece of it, no matter how small. I raised my head, pulling away from his chest to look into his eyes.

"Okay. I'll marry you," my shaky voice whispered. "Let's get out of here in one piece first."

"No," My stomach knotted. "I don't want you to do anything you're not sure of. Let's get out of here first. Then, I'll ask you again." His eyes looked glassy, like he was about to cry but was forbidding himself the luxury.

"I'm serious. I do want to marry you," I argued.

"Not like this, Lily. I want you to take the time to really think about it. We are under too much pressure. It was wrong of me to ask now. I'm sorry about that. Take all the time you need. I'm not going anywhere." He kissed my forehead, brushing my hair out of the way with his fingertips. His touch put a different feeling in my stomach, the fluttering of wings.

"If that's the way you want it," I said. "We should get dressed. We have a lot to do."

"I love you. Never forget that," he said.

"I love you too, Christian. More than you'll ever know." I leaned over and brushed his lips with mine, lingering with my forehead against his, my eyes closed, inhaling his scent.

"I do know."

In the living room, five smiles greeted us as we stepped out of the bedroom, dressed and ready for anything the day might bring. Aaron, however, had a look of dread on his face. They heard us. I avoided Aaron's eyes as I passed him. I couldn't look at him without feeling guilt. He was worried and I knew why. Yet, I couldn't come right out and assure him that I wouldn't do what he feared. I couldn't even assure myself anymore.

Kalia put her arm around me and squeezed me to her side. Her eyes told me she heard every word and that, somehow, she was happy for me. I wished I had the same easygoing spirit as her. Things would be so much easier.

The whole room had stopped talking when we walked in and I felt the uncomfortable silence. Riley sat on the sofa, paging through a magazine, a pile of fabric next to her. Fiore, Beth, and Pierce were standing by the fireplace. Their conversation was momentarily paused, Fiore's hands still in the air as if she were frozen.

"So, what now?" I asked breaking the silence. Christian moved to the kitchen, pulling a can of soda out of the refrigerator but waiting to pull the tab, trying not to make noise.

"We are ready," Aaron said, still not taking his eyes off my face. I felt my body stiffen. The last thing I wanted right now was to feel defensive toward Aaron. We had much bigger problems to worry about. "But first, Lily, are these yours?" He walked over to the sofa and held up the pile of fabric next to Riley. It looked like fabric but upon closer inspection, I realized it was clothing. My clothing!

"Where did you get these?" I asked, taking the two muddy shirts from Aaron. I spread them out on the back of the sofa to examine them. One was the shirt I had worn that day, by the brook, when I had given in to Ian's desires, and the other was just an old, battered t-shirt I wore often when I wasn't going anywhere. I had left both when I fled Ireland.

"Riley found them outside last night. She caught a scent and went out to investigate," Aaron explained. Riley turned to look at me, confirming what he said with a nod. "They were on the hood of Kalia's car. Whoever put them there was already gone."

"So, what does this mean?" I asked. What could two of my shirts being thrown on the hood of a car have to do with anything?

"I think this means Ian may not be here at all," Riley explained. "Whoever is here is someone who doesn't know you."

"I think what she means is he sent a tracker. Someone is following your scent. Some unknown," Aaron said, his expression softening. He wasn't thinking about what happened in the bedroom at the moment. That was a momentary relief.

"Are you saying it might not even be him?" Christian asked from the kitchen. His soda was still in his hand, unopened.

"No. I don't think that's a possibility," Aaron answered. "I don't have a doubt in my mind that it's Ian. I just think he sent someone else. For all we know now, he's sitting comfortably in his cottage in Ireland, waiting."

"Could that be why he hasn't tried to get into my head?" I asked. It was strange that he had not sent any messages to me, any threats. I figured he was staying silent just to drive me crazy with anticipation. Now it made more sense. He wasn't close enough, physically, to communicate with me.

"It's very possible. He needs to be much closer. If he's in Ireland, or even in another state, waiting for someone else to do his dirty work, it would seem logical that he has to keep silent," Riley said. The others nodded.

This new possibility put more questions in my mind. Who knew where this cabin was besides Maia? But if Maia were involved, and I still refused to believe she could be that evil, why use a tracker? She could just tell him the exact location. And if it were an unknown, a tracker, it had to be a damn good one! Had he followed me through Ireland? Had he been on my tail all along, maybe even on the same flight with us? But what about Clara? How had a tracker found the time to do that? Ian did know where I lived before Oregon. He could easily have given someone the address and that's why we were just sitting here waiting, still. And what about the dead animals in the woods? One vampire couldn't have made that mess. There still had to be more than one. Unless it was just one, a newborn. But could a newborn be that skilled in tracking?

"Lily, honey," Kalia said. "We need to get started."

"Oh…yeah. Sorry. I was just thinking." I said, looking around the room. I hadn't noticed everyone had moved. Fiore laced up her boots. Riley closed the zipper on her backpack. Beth and Pierce already stood by the door, ready to walk out into the morning sun.

"You have Fiore's blood in your veins. Trust yourself and your instincts," Aaron said, kissing my forehead. Kalia squeezed me to her side again, only this time she whispered in my ear. "Take care of him. He's unique. He's more powerful than you think." She dropped her arm and went to join the others who now waited on the porch. Why does everybody keep saying that?

Panic filled my overflowing mind. The snap of Christian's soda can made me jump. The room filled with darkness. The sunlight, gone from the window, was replaced by shadows on the floor. The sword lay sparkling on the coffee table, calling me to it. I heard it in my ears. Lily…

I picked it up. It felt like it weighed a ton. I sank to the floor against the sofa and cradled it to my chest, like a fragile newborn. It felt like an extension of my body, breathing as I breathed.

Alone at last...My head jerked toward Christian. He entered the living room, his soda can sweating all over the wooden floor, his lips closed. He hadn't said anything. The sword had a strange glow to it. I could see the same glow coming from under Christian's shirt. The metal against my chest suddenly burned me. I let the sword fall out of my hands, a clang echoing through the room.

ᘓ TWENTY-SEVEN ᘓ

"He's out there," I said keeping my eyes on the door. The sword lay at my side, glowing, and untouched.

"I figured," Christian said, his voice strong and sure. He crossed the small space separating us and held out his hand. I took it and he pulled me up. His chest still had that faint glow. He ignored it. He wrapped his arms around me and kissed me, with more passion than usual. The sensation made me dizzy and light headed. When our lips parted, I saw resolve in his blue eyes. He was determined. That was supposed to be my job, to protect *him*.

"Get in the bedroom," I whispered, afraid to take my eyes from his. "You have to hide."

"I want to stay with you."

"No. Go! I don't want you here. Please!" I demanded. He squeezed me again before loosening his grasp. I watched him walk away, his eyes never leaving mine until the door closed behind him.

Where were the others? Would they hear if I called for them? They were expecting to catch Ian's hounds and destroy them, then come back for us. They expected Ian to be far away. He wasn't. He was right outside. Knowing I would likely be left alone if we thought he weren't close, he had kept out of sight and out of mind. He had tried to confuse us and succeeded. I jumped back, falling over the sofa and landing on my feet on the other side when the door burst open with a crash.

"Hello," Ian's voice sang. "It's good to see you again." He looked smug, familiar. My hands were fists at my sides. My muscles tensed. My ears rang. I could feel the heat from the sword reaching me where I stood but it was too far to grab. I had been repulsed by it but now I longed for its protection.

"Why would you leave me after telling me you love me?" His voice was bitter. "You showed me you love me. Or have you forgotten? What about the passion you showed me? You were made to love me!"

I found my voice though it was shaky. "That was all fake!" Why lie now?

He tilted his head to the side. "Passion like that cannot be faked, Lily. Why can't you get it through your thick skull? You love me. You'll always love me."

"I don't love you. It was an act! I wanted you to trust me so you would leave me again. Isn't that what you're best at? Leaving?" I fired at him.

"Why don't you take a closer look at yourself?" he said, taking a step toward me. I took a step backward, my hand using the sofa for support. "You're pretty good at leaving yourself. I'd like to take credit for that. I like to think I taught you *something*."

My eyes widened in disbelief. "You taught me nothing at all! I fell for your lies. My parents fell for your charade and now you fell for mine. I don't love you!"

He laughed, throwing his head back for emphasis. "That is such a lie! I can see it in your eyes when you look at me."

I gulped. Is that what he saw? Love instead of fear and loathing? "I am madly and totally in love with Christian and you know it! Why else would you be here?" I stepped back a few more paces. He mirrored my movements.

"You don't think it's possible to love more than one?" he asked, his tone calm. Memories of the whispered promises he had made to my human ears flooded my mind. He watched with curiosity. "I can love more than one."

"Like Fiore? Like Maia?" I asked, my voice full of accusation.

"I told you it was possible. Anything is possible." He looked around the room. "Where is your little pet, anyway? I can hear his pathetic heart."

My grip on the soft back of the sofa tightened. I glanced toward the bedroom, giving him away. "YOU STAY AWAY FROM HIM!"

"Temper, temper," he mocked. "I don't really want him. You know that. He's just an annoying obstacle, easily disposed of, unless…"

"Unless what?" I backed up another step. My hand was still gripping the sofa though I no longer needed the support, strength fueled by anger.

"Unless he's willing to share," he said, a mocking smile on his lips.

"You are sick!" I darted around the front of the sofa and picked up the sword in one swift swoop. He was on me within seconds, knocking it out of my hands. It landed on the floor under the window. My head bounced off the coffee table, which was now split in two right down the middle. I lay on my back, trying to catch my breath. He straddled me, pinning down my shoulders.

"You never could control your temper," he said looking into my eyes with amusement. "I always loved that about you. You're like a Chihuahua who thinks she's a Great Dane. It's quite adorable."

"GET OFF ME!" I screamed. He didn't move. I tried to squirm under him, tried to turn my hips to no avail. The more I tried, the more he smiled, relishing in my struggle.

"I have one question, though," he said. "How did you manage to get Fiore away from me?"

He didn't know. "I didn't. She came to me."

His face knotted. He didn't like rejection. He had to have his own way. He looked down at me, rage filling his eyes. He stared at me for a moment without a word. I broke the silence. "Where is my family?"

"They're being entertained, don't worry. They won't be bored," he answered. "They're busy chasing useless newborns. It's pretty funny actually."

"Where are the rest of your Irish goons?" My words didn't cause the reaction I expected. His eyes continued to bore into mine. I realized I had stopped struggling under him. His face was closer, icy breath blowing loose strands of my hair, tickling my forehead.

"They're all busy. Don't worry your pretty little head about them. It's all about you and me now." He lowered his face to mine, his lips cold and hard, and his tongue prying my lips apart. I felt my body arch instinctively toward his, wanting. I closed my eyes and allowed his tongue into my mouth, losing myself in his kiss for just a moment before my teeth clamped. I tasted blood before I heard his scream. The bitterness made my stomach turn. He fell to the side.

I scrambled away, landing on my stomach in front of the window, my head slamming against the wall. My hands felt the sweltering heat, the flash of light momentarily blinding me. Before I could get to my feet, I felt a hand tugging at my shirt. I swung my free arm to strike before I realized the sneakers in front of my face belonged to Christian.

"NO, CHRISTIAN!" I was yanked to my feet anyway. The sword dangling from my finger tips, the weight of it too much to keep a hold of. "Get out of here," I pleaded. His eyes looked fierce, crazed. He looked from me to Ian. Ian stood in front of the fireplace, frozen to the floor, the front of his shirt drenched with his blood. His eyes looked like the eyes of a madman, wide and unblinking. His lips, however, had a sinister smile. The blood oozing out of his mouth made it look like a scene from a low budget horror film.

"Christian," he gurgled. "Good to see you. I've missed our daily chats."

Christian let go of the back of my shirt and darted toward him before I could react. He lunged himself into Ian's soaked chest but Ian caught him without faltering, spinning him to face me. His forearm across Christian's neck, he held him in front of him, like a shield.

"Lily doesn't seem to think you are willing to share her." His tongue, though torn apart from my bite, lapped at the remaining blood on his bottom lip. The damage I caused was already healing. I got a better grip on the sword, steadying it with both hands. I held it over my head. It was all show. I knew I couldn't hit him without hurting Christian.

"Let him go, Ian. I know you want me." I tried to keep my voice from shaking. Christian's eyes looked dazed. His feet slid around on the floor.

"We could be such a happy little family, the five of us," he said.

Five of us? My mind went through the names...Fiore, Christian, Ian, Maia, me.

"No. Let him go and I'll go with you," I pleaded. He considered for a moment and then shook his head.

"Oh, no! I'm not falling for that again," he said. He looked at Christian. "Just say the word and he can go with us."

What? What word? Oh...

"Don't you dare!"

"Why are you so determined to guard his humanity? What is he to you, really?"

"I LOVE HIM! I LOVE HIM WITH EVERY FIBER OF MY BE-ING!" I stepped closer, not close enough to cause any damage yet, but still...

"Then you should be more than willing to have him forever!" Baring his fangs in an exaggerated smile, his free hand reached up to grab Christian's hair. He yanked his head back, pulling his feet off the floor completely. Ian looked at me as his teeth sank into the soft flesh of his neck. I shuddered. Christian's legs flailed out of control before his body went limp, submitting to the bite as his eyes locked on mine. The heat of the sword was almost too much to bear, burning my skin like a hot iron.

I sprang. A scream left my lips as I flew over the remains of what was once a coffee table. I knocked Christian out of his arms, his body sliding across the floor to the kitchen doorway. He lay limp and lifeless. Ian jumped, avoiding the sword held high over my head.

He wiped at his mouth with exaggerated motions. Christian's blood now mixed with his all over his chin. He opened his mouth and stuck his fingers in, wiping at his tongue in a grotesque manner. I watched with disgust, ready to swing but distracted by his absurd actions. He staggered backward, his legs wobbling, his eyes wide with…fear?

"What did you do?" he asked, his fingers still wiping blood off his tongue. I stood frozen. The sword burned my skin. I felt the searing pain, light glowing from it casting shadows on the floor. "What did you do?" he repeated. He pulled at the collar of his bloody shirt. He brought the cotton to his opened mouth and wiped his tongue. My stomach tightened.

He tried to step toward me but swayed, grabbing the mantle to steady himself. His face looked whiter than usual.

"What are you talking about?" I asked, finding my voice. I still heard Christian's faint heartbeats in my ears. I wanted to go to him but didn't dare take my eyes off Ian.

"Poisoned blood…you let me drink poisoned blood?" he asked. I heard a moan escape his lips. What was he talking about?

He staggered toward me, his body swaying like a drunk. His eyes looked like they were ready to roll back in his head. I steadied my grip on the sword, bringing it to the side, ready to swing.

"Please, Lily…don't let me die," his voice was a whisper. I felt a pang of guilt. "I love you. I'll always love you." He stumbled again, reaching out to steady himself with the back of the sofa. I readied my body, parting my legs slightly and bending my knees. His eyes, struggling to stay open, searched my face.

I took a step back. I needed more room to swing.

"You loved me once, remember? I made you. I gave you eternity," he whispered.

How could I forget? I felt sudden pity for him. I wanted to drop the sword and take him in my arms, comfort him. My arms started to lower, the heat in my hands growing stronger.

"Yes, Ian. I do remember. I remember how I loved you. I remember how you killed me, twice…when you took my life and again when you left me."

His eyes widened. He was having a hard time focusing on my face. "You love me still. I know you do. Why can't you accept that?"

My head was spinning. The urge to reach out and hold him, comfort him, was fighting to take control. My arms lowered even more, making the sword feel like it was too much weight to bear. I took a step toward him, my legs shaking. He looked at me, trying to release his grip on the sofa, trying to meet me half way. His lips turned up at the corners. Happiness shone in his crazed eyes. I took another step. He held his hands out to me, his body swaying.

Taking a couple steps, I closed the distance between us and wrapped my free arm around him. I felt him sway in my grasp. I heard him sigh as my stomach knotted. He kissed my ear as my knees went weak. My head tilted and I invited his lips to taste my neck.

His lips parted. He drew his head back to look at me. Christian's blood stained the corners. "You would be nothing without me." My grip around him tightened as my body stiffened. That did it!

"I'm done loving you. I am nothing *because* of you! Good bye, Ian," I whispered in his ear.

In one swift movement, I pushed him back with one hand as I swung the sword with the other. I heard the thud on the wooden floor. His body dropped to his knees before it fell to the side. His head rolled off the sofa and under the coffee table. I let my fingers open and the sword hit the floor with a loud clang, the burn marks visible on my hands. I grabbed his head by his shining hair and tossed it into the fireplace. I watched as his eyes stared at me from within the orange flames, as the acrid odor of his burning hair assaulted me.

I ran to Christian and dropped to my knees. Searching for his pulse, I held his limp arm in my hand. I pumped his chest, like I had seen on TV. I laid my head on his chest. Silence. I beat his chest again. I listened. Nothing. I moved to his head and tilted it back, pinching his nose shut. I took a deep breath and released it in his mouth. I pumped his chest again...one...two...three...please...Over and over I did this without thinking, just letting my instincts take control.

"Please, Christian. Don't leave me," I cried as I pumped his chest in a frenzy. "Please come back." I kept working. After what seemed like an eternity, I stopped. I felt the wetness running down my face. Blood tears poured out of my eyes and I couldn't stop them. I didn't want to stop them. My body shook with my sobs. I tasted my own blood in my mouth.

I looked at his face with blurred vision. It couldn't be! He couldn't be gone!

I felt an agony worse than anything, worse than my human death. I crawled to lean over him, kissing his parted lips. I closed his eyelids over the blue sky of his eyes forever. I sobbed harder, my body shaking out of control. I lay my face against his as I sobbed, never wanting to let go. I felt the warmth escaping his body, my fingers in his hair for the last time.

"What is that smell?" A voice asked. It was a voice I knew. I lifted my head and turned, my eyes blurred with tears.

"Maia?" She looked down and saw Ian's headless body on the floor. Her eyes darted to the fireplace, wide with realization. Like a robot, I managed to get to my feet.

She stared at me, her mouth hanging open. She backed slowly to the door, turning to run when I started to move. Arms wrapped around me. My knees gave out and I let myself drop.

"Shh…" Aaron's voice soothed.

"But…but…" I couldn't get the words out. I gulped. "Maia…"

"I know…I know. Pierce is after her," he said.

"But Christian," I said as the tears started again.

"Oh…" he said, his lips in my hair. "I'm so sorry, Lily."

"No! It can't be. This can't be it!" I said, trying to push him away. I wanted to run back to him. I could slice my wrist and make him drink. I could…This couldn't be. It couldn't be!

"Lily, please," Kalia was the one speaking now. I felt her hand on my back, saw her mud splattered face. "I'm sorry…"

They both held me, Aaron and Kalia. My mouth opened to scream, but no sound came out. I could hear their words, filled with love. My head was spinning. I could see their faces, filled with sadness. The ground was tilting. Then I saw their eyes, filled with hope. I went limp. I felt cold arms tighten around me.

I saw Christian's beautiful smile before everything went black.

 END

After nearly a century of wandering the globe alone, Lily finally has everything she never knew she wanted, family, friends, and most of all, their love. As Lily attempts to start her new life, in the lively streets of Lima, Peru, she feels she is constantly being followed. With Ian, her first love and maker, now gone, who is left to destroy the happiness she has finally found? Someone still longs for Lily's destruction. Vengeance or jealousy threaten to destroy her, and Lily must summon all the strength she can find to protect everything she cherishes against vampires, hunters, and witches.

ACKNOWLEDGMENTS

I would like to thank my husband, Neil, and my sons, Jason, Ryan, and Collin, and my mom, Carla, for their patience and support. I couldn't have done this without you. I would also like to thank my English editor, Amy Schuster McKenzie, and my Spanish editors, Betsy Ramirez Lloyd and Oscar Ramirez Barcelli and my first fans, who read Lily while it was full of mistakes and typos, Melinda Meyers Miller, Patty Nichols, Donna McLaughlin, and Janet Chan. Thank you also to my critique partner, Diane Nelson, for pointing out what I didn't catch and to Meghan Tobin-O'Drowsky and Carol Hansson for finding those little things. Michelle Halket, what can I say, thank you for believing in me. A special thank you to all of my family and friends for their continued support and encouragement.

ABOUT THE AUTHOR

LM DeWalt is a Peruvian American who has been living in the US for 30 years. She works as a teacher of ESL, Spanish, French, and accent reduction and is also an interpreter and translator. She has written for several Spanish language newspapers but her passion was always to write novels. Her love of vampires, and all things paranormal, started when she was seven years old and saw Bela Lugosi's Dracula.

She currently resides in Northeastern Pennsylvania, where it's way too cold, with her husband, three teenage sons and two cats.

Printed in the United States
by Baker & Taylor Publisher Services